CM DOPORTO

THE WINNING SIDE

UNIVERSITY PARK SERIES BOOK 3

The Winning Side
Book 3
from
The University Park Series
By CM Doporto

The Winning Side
Book 3 from
The University Park Series
Version 3

Published by:

http://www.cmdoporto.com
Cover design by Cora Graphics
Edited by Monica Black and Jessa Markert
Copyright 2014 by CM Doporto

eBook ISBN: 978-1-502208-50-7
Paperback ISBN: 978-1505756821

Acknowledgements

I'd like to thank my husband, son, and mom for their continued support. Lord knows I couldn't do this without each of you.

A huge shout out to my critique partner, Sam. Your help has been wonderful and I'm glad we work well together. Many thanks to my street team, CM Doporto's Heroes and Heroines. I appreciate your dedication and time with supporting my books and getting the word out. A big thank you to Smexy Fab Four for managing my street team and Wickedly Innocent Promotions for all the support. Thanks to Cora Graphics for creating another beautiful cover! Many, many thanks to Monica for the edits on this book. You're awesome! And Jessa for stepping in and helping with edits, too.

I would be remiss if I didn't mention the bloggers and reviewers who take the time to read and post reviews. Your support of indie authors helps get the attention of readers we work hard to obtain.

A huge thank you to you, the reader. Without you there would be no one to read my story. I appreciate you taking the time to read it. I hope you enjoy it as much as I did writing it.

Most of all I want to thank our Heavenly Father for providing me with the opportunity to do what I love, write.

Dedication

To anyone who's had to fight for the one they love,
this book is dedicated to you.
And now three remain: faith, hope, and love.
But the greatest of these is love. 1 Corinthians 13

Chapter 1

I wasn't the only one caught in The Raven's trap. He was too, except his trap was deadly. He'd been clean for nine months, sixteen days, and thirteen hours before the temptations of the world trapped him once more. It would be hard as hell to pull him away from it for good, but I was determined to help him do it. No matter the cost.

"Relax. Everything is going to be okay." I flipped the back of his collar, tucking it over his tie.

"I can't relax, Lexi. I really eff'd up." Raven stared into the mirror, working his tie into a perfect knot. Worry etched deep into his temples and his entire body looked frail, like he'd been hit by a train. Then again, he'd almost died from alcohol poisoning mixed with hydrocodone. He was lucky to be alive.

"I know, but you're going to march into the coach's office and plead your case to him." I encouraged him the best way I knew how, even though I wanted to punch him in the face. I had to put my feelings aside and support the man I loved. He needed me and I feared that if I didn't give him what he needed, he might never recover from the blow. Maybe a part of me felt guilty about the stunt my parents pulled — even though Raven was responsible for his choices and needed to be held accountable for them.

He turned to me, resting his hands on my waist. "But, what if he refuses to give me another chance?"

"Don't think that way. You have to keep a positive mind about this, Raven." I lifted his chin, aligning our eyes. "I know it's not easy, but you have to believe in yourself and know that you can turn things around for good."

"You believe me, don't you?" His lips twitched to the side.

"As long as you're telling me the truth." I held my gaze steady to his, watching for any signs of dishonesty. I saw regret, pain, and anguish all circling around in the centers of his eyes. The strong, well-built quarterback that could topple a two hundred and fifty pound guy looked so vulnerable. So fragile. The weakest I'd ever seen him. I had to trust my instincts and believe he was telling me the truth.

"I promise you, I didn't take those pills. Someone must have slipped them in my drink. When I woke up in the hospital, I didn't know what the hell had happened." His shoulders slumped and his chest crumpled inward like all life had been sucked from him. "All I wanted to do was drink away the pain... drink away the memories of you and me."

Tears welled in my eyes and I quickly blinked them away. I had to be strong, strong when Raven was at his weakest, even when all I wanted to do was sob with him in the misery we both experienced. "We'll talk about it later. Now isn't the right time. You have to get your head together and tell Coach what happened."

"What if he doesn't believe me?"

"Hopefully he will."

"What if he tells me I have to play?" He shifted his weight. "To be honest, I don't think I can. I've never felt so weak." He sat on the edge of the bed, looking feeble. He was in no condition to play football. He ran his hands over his head repeatedly, but it did nothing to tame his messy hair.

I zipped up his duffle bag. "Maybe he'll allow you stay here instead of going to the hotel. I think you need to rest all day and see how you feel."

"No doubt that's what I need. But when the media gets word that I'm not available for the press conference, they're going to wonder what the hell happened."

I sucked in a deep breath. He had a point and I had no idea how he was going to get around what happened thirty-six hours ago. "Maybe he'll say you have the flu and its unknown whether you'll play."

"I've played with the flu, this is worse." Raven fell against the mattress and I couldn't help but feel sorry for him. He had a lot riding on him. That stress, coupled with a near death experience, was enough to put any man down.

I crawled across the bed and hovered over him. His mesmerizing eyes had lost some of their luster and his smooth tan skin looked gray and pale. But regardless of not being one-hundred percent, he was still damn hot.

"This wasn't how things were supposed to be," he sighed.

"I know, but we're going to make the best of it, regardless of what happens."

"You promise?" A hint of sadness crept through his voice.

I cupped his cheek. "I told you I would stay by your side because I love you. All I ask is that you're honest with me."

He placed a soft kiss on my lips and I prayed, yet again, he was being honest with me. Because feeling his touch made me want to forget about everything that had happened and allow him to make love to me as we shut the world out, but reality reminded me that we had more pressing issues at the moment. We were facing a new reality — Raven being kicked off the team and losing any chance of being drafted.

"Raven, let's go." A strum of knocks sounded at his door and then it flung open.

I rolled to the side and saw Josh standing in the doorway. "Make out later, we have a bus to catch."

Josh was dressed similar to Raven, wearing a starched, white, button-down shirt with a tie and dress slacks.

"I have your jacket," Shelby yelled from the living room.

"I don't know, man." Raven rose slowly. "I don't think I can make it."

Josh adjusted the bag in his hand. His brows knitted tightly together as he appraised Raven from head to toe. "You feel that bad?"

"Yeah, I really do." Raven leaned to the side and nearly tipped over when he reached for his duffle bag.

"Whoa." Josh extended a hand, keeping him from toppling. "What are you going to tell Coach?"

"I'm going to have to tell him what happened. I can't hide it." Raven looked at him with sleepy eyes. I wasn't even sure he could make it to the training facility at this point.

"You're fucked." Josh shook his head, his nostrils flaring. "But I don't think you have much of a choice."

Raven shuffled past Josh. "Thanks for the support." He patted him on the shoulder and then walked down the hall.

Josh looked at me for a moment and I shrugged. "It is what it is."

"Damn it!" Josh stomped his foot and then spun on his heels, trekking out of the room.

I grabbed my purse and coat and then went to the living room. Raven pulled on his jacket and I picked up his bag. "I'll carry this for you."

He placed a kiss on my forehead. "Thanks, baby."

"I'll drive." Shelby took the keys from Josh's hand. He hesitated for a moment, but allowed her to take them. His face was beet red and scrunched with fury. I think he knew what was about to happen and he was pissed about it. The star quarterback wouldn't be playing in the bowl and the team might lose without him. Raven remained silent. He knew it, too. I followed them out of the apartment, locking the door behind us.

After we all piled into Josh's truck, Shelby drove toward the training facilities. The sun shined brightly and the sky was crystal clear, a stark contrast from the somber mood looming inside the vehicle. Banners hung from the light poles, waving in the crisp January wind, reminding the city to support the university's bowl game.

Luckily for Raven, it was in Arlington, just a twenty minute drive from Fort Worth and not out of town. Then again, if the game would've been out of town, Raven wouldn't have been at Jared's. Typically, the team would leave several days before the game, but since it was local, they were only leaving two days ahead instead.

A large purple and black bus waited in front of the stadium along with family, friends, and fans — everyone faring goodbye to their favorite college football team, wishing them good luck, and cheering for them to bring home the trophy. Many of them were probably waiting to see their number one quarterback. Would Raven be able to hold that title?

"Did you call Coach?" Josh asked.

Raven stared out the window with his head pressed against the glass. "Yeah, I told him I needed to talk to him before we left."

"You should've come up here first thing this morning," Josh huffed. "Avoid all this unneeded attention." He shook his head, eyeing the crowd and the people running up to see who was inside the truck.

"I know, man. But I literally couldn't get out of bed." Raven voice sounded weak. A part of me kind of hoped the coach wouldn't allow him to play — not because I didn't what him to partake in the biggest game of the year, but because I feared for his safety. He could really get hurt.

Josh took a deep breath and flung open the door the second Shelby put the truck into park. He grabbed his bag and slammed the door shut, shouldering past the groves of people.

"Josh, wait!" Shelby scurried after him, trying to balance herself in stacked heels and the huge handbag hanging off her arm. Her wavy blonde hair whipped around her as she followed Josh inside the facility.

We got out of the truck and Raven shut the door. A few people called for his attention while snapping pictures of him. He gave a slight wave as he leaned against the door, unable to hold up his own weight. I stood in front of him, adjusting the collar of his jacket. "You look handsome."

"No I don't. I look like shit." He ran his hand over his face.

"Well, you might feel like shit, but you still look good." I winked.

"Thanks for being here for me, even though I don't deserve it." His eyes wandered off toward the crowd behind us and it seemed like he was having a hard time concentrating.

"I'll be here, waiting. I'm not leaving until I know what the coach tells you. And your mom will be waiting for your call." I gripped my waist with my hands and looked around at all the smiling faces. I couldn't deny that I was slightly peeved that I wasn't among the elated crowds. Instead, I was the one with a knotted stomach and baited breath.

If they only knew.

"You can wait inside." Raven took my hand and we walked toward the double doors.

While the fans waved, Raven put on his game face, smiling back and giving a big sweep of his hand. I smiled at everyone, playing the perfect part of the girlfriend, even though we hadn't discussed why he had left me in the first place. My first priority was getting the story straight regarding what had happened at Jared's place, and then helping him pull himself together for his discussion with the coach.

I was relieved when the doctor showed Raven's medical report to Trish and me. Armed with the facts of what he had taken gave me a basis to go from — he had drank way too much alcohol, but hadn't been doing cocaine like I'd thought. The doctor said he had the equivalent of three hydrocodone pills in his system, which wasn't that high of a dose, but coupled with large amounts of alcohol was nearly enough to kill him. I had honestly feared that he had been snorting cocaine, popping pills, and slugging down bottles of liquor.

I still had to find out why he'd sent that text to me. Though, deep down, I knew my mother had something to do with it. One step at a time. I had to take everything in strides and stay calm, but most of all, supportive. The talk about us would have to wait.

I sat outside the coach's office with Shelby at my side. Josh was too pissed to wait with us and went to the bus instead. He told Shelby that he couldn't be around when Raven got out of his meeting, claiming he needed to decompress before he beat Raven with his fist. I agreed that he should distance himself because Raven couldn't take an ass kicking right now. He could barely stand on his own.

"Lexi?" a voice called from down the hall.

I turned to see Shawn sprinting toward us.

"What's up with him?" Shelby asked.

"I don't know." I perched on the edge of my chair, contemplating whether to meet him halfway or just wait. I stood up slowly and took a few steps in his direction. "What's wrong?"

Shawn took several deep breaths. "Where's Raven?"

"Talking to the coach." I shot Shelby a questioning gaze.

"Shit!" He slammed his fist in the palm of his hand. "I really need to talk him. I've been texting and calling him since early this morning. I even went to the hospital."

"He got released yesterday evening. He came home and went straight to bed."

Shawn took another deep breath and gripped his waist. "I have to interrupt their meeting."

"Wait," I held out my arm, "can you tell me what's going on?"

Shawn looked at me and then at Shelby before motioning for us to come closer toward him. "I saw Jared slip some pills into Raven's drink."

The air in my lungs stalled and the room spun around me. I sucked in a deep breath, trying to steady myself. "You saw him?"

"Well, sort of."

I grabbed a fistful of his shirt. "And you didn't stop him?" I seethed.

Shawn held up his hands. "Hold on, let me explain." He whipped out his phone from his pocket and I released his shirt. I smoothed out the wrinkles with the palm of my hand, deciding that I should give him the benefit of the doubt. He swiped his screen and then hesitated for a moment. "Promise me you're not going to get pissed when you see this picture."

I rolled my eyes, but braced myself. God only knew what I was about to see. "Okay, I promise."

He held up his phone, showing us the picture. I stared at it for a moment. Macy had her lips firmly planted on Raven's while he squeezed her butt with one of his hands. "I don't want to see this skank making out with my boyfriend." I pushed his hand away from me.

"Wait." Shawn shoved the phone into my hand. "Look at what's going on in the background."

Hesitantly, I took the phone from his hand and expanded the picture. In Raven's other hand was a glass, and Jared was dropping something in it. "Holy shit. Did Jared drug Raven?" I looked at the picture closely, zooming in to get a better view. It wasn't completely clear, but something small, like a pill, had fallen from Jared's fingers into Raven's drink.

"Let me see that," Shelby said, trying to catch a better glimpse.

I handed her the phone. "Where did you get this picture?"

"From a girl I know. She was taking pictures of everyone that night and apparently snapped this one. She sent it to me last night. I have to show it to Raven."

I grabbed the phone from Shelby's hand and shoved it into Shawn's chest. "What are you waiting for? Get in there! You need to show him and Coach." I pointed toward the coach's office.

Shawn knocked on the door and it opened. "Coach, I'm sorry, but you have to see this picture. It's about Raven and it's urgent."

Shawn was in the office for about fifteen minutes before he stepped out. I darted out of my seat, eager to know what happened. "What did he say? What happened? Is he going to let Raven play? What did Raven say?" I fired off several questions.

"Take it easy, Lexi." He motioned for me to calm down, but there was only one thing that would release the chords tightly wrapped around my stomach. Shawn ran his hand over his short hair. Based on the disappointment he was visibly wearing, I knew it wasn't good.

"Coach wasn't happy. Pissed about the whole thing. It's all over Facebook, Twitter, and Instagram, so there's no making up any stories about this. Raven has to come clean about what happened, but the good news is this picture," he held up his phone, "might just save his ass."

I exhaled and then took a step back, realizing I was totally in Shawn's space. "Thanks for speaking up, Shawn. Raven needs all the help he can get."

Shawn sat with us as we waited for the verdict. I bounced my leg to an offbeat rhythm and tried to keep my mind focused on positive thoughts. But no matter how hard I tried, visuals of the articles I'd read on the internet about Raven's past incidents inundated me and my sister's words rang loud in my ear. *Raven will end up in jail.*

I hated that I couldn't be there to save him — to keep him away from Jared and the hoes that were dying for a piece of him. I had promised I'd be there for him and I wasn't. Now, he was paying for the mistakes he'd made. With every decision, there are consequences — good or bad. I could only hope that Raven's consequences would tilt to the favorable side. The walls around me closed in, but I pushed them back, willing myself to stay strong. Raven needed me and I had to believe that there was hope for him. For us. This wasn't the end of his career.

It seemed like an eternity had passed before the door finally opened again. Raven walked out of the coach's office and closed the door behind him. I got up and rushed to his side. His face was blotched with red marks and his entire body slumped toward the floor. With each step he took, his frame shrunk until he was nearly my height. His eyes glazed over and it looked like he'd been crying. My heart immediately ached for him as I prepared for the worst.

"What did he say?" I placed my hands on his forearms, holding onto him for support, even though he was the one that needed it more than me.

Raven's eyes drifted to the floor and he sighed. "I've been dispelled from the game."

"Shit," Shawn muttered.

"Oh, no." Shelby covered her mouth. "Josh is going to be pissed."

"It's okay," I quickly assured him. "It's just one game."

"What about the team?" Shawn asked the question I had wanted to ask, but was too scared to.

Raven looked up slowly, devastation looming in his eyes. Everything seemed to stop as I waited for him to answer. I counted the seconds and said a silent prayer that he wouldn't say the words that would end it all for him.

"I-I'm on probation. For now," he said, as if the words ripped a hole in his chest.

"Damn it." Shawn slammed his hand on a table next to him and continued muttering a string of expletives. "It's alright, man." Shawn stood and hooked an arm around Raven. "You had a good year and you'll be back on that field in no time."

"That's right." I straightened and gave him an easy smile. "We're going to get through this little faux pas and get you back on track. Coach will see that you're worthy of playing and will reinstate you in no time."

Raven's face twisted in disbelief. "Easy for you to say. I was already on my last chance. Not sure if I get anymore." He shucked Shawn's arm off and shuffled past me.

"Raven, wait." I trekked behind him. "Don't get discouraged. You showed Coach the picture, right?"

He stopped and then turned to face me. "Yes, I did. I'm sorry you had to see all of that." He shook his head and squeezed his eyes shut, as if trying to wipe it away from memory. I wished I could do the same. I didn't want to think about what else happened outside that picture. But if I knew Macy, she got what she wanted, along with whoever else, no doubt.

"What's done is done," I said with a tight lip, wanting to say more but refraining myself. "But that picture might be your saving grace."

"Let's hope so. I have to go in front of the ethics committee and board of admissions to see if I'm allowed to say at the university."

"Oh." I pressed my lips together, unsure of what else to say. This was worse than I thought.

Σ

Chapter 2

As we exited the training facility, a school newspaper reporter immediately greeted us. Social media had done its job and now she wanted the scoop. It would be impossible to keep what happened under the radar for very long.

"What the heck?" Shelby scampered back, bumping into Shawn. "This isn't good."

"Aw, hell." Shawn shook his head in disgust. "I freakin' hate social media at times."

"Hang tight." Shelby darted across the parking lot, leaving us to deal with the hungry-for-information journalist.

"Is it true that you were in the hospital for alcohol poisoning and a drug overdose?" A thin, petite girl with short blonde hair and a big plastic badge marked 'PHU Media' shoved her phone in Raven's face, ready to record his response.

"No comment." Raven raised a hand, motioning for her not to ask any more questions. Her lips turned down but she retrieved her phone. She paused as though thinking of another way to get the details, but Raven didn't wait. He took me by the hand and pushed past her.

A string of flashes stopped us and I quickly turned my head, protecting my eyes from the blinding light. "Will you be playing in the bowl or have you been suspended from the game?" An older man with thick-rimmed glasses pressed his pen to his pad, ready to capture Raven's reply.

"Sorry, I'm not at liberty to say right now," Raven answered. This situation would get worse before it got better. I held on to

Raven's arm as he led us in the opposite direction. Unfortunately, that didn't stop the reporters from following us and firing question after question.

"The hospital report said you took hydrocodone. Is that correct?" A middle-aged man wearing a polo-style shirt from a local TV station shoved a microphone in Raven's face. A large, black camera lens focused on us, and suddenly, Raven's stardom didn't seem that exciting.

Raven shook his head. "Sorry, no comment." We stepped to the side, trying to escape the scrutiny from the heavy piece of equipment waiting to record Raven's reaction.

"Will you be entering into a drug rehab center?" the reporter asked, still thrusting the microphone under Raven's nose. Raven tilted his head to the side, trying to avoid the persistent man. Several students appeared, snapping pictures with their phones while others recorded the scene. This wasn't good. Raven didn't need any more social media exposure. A sharp grunt released from low in his throat and I prayed that he wouldn't do something stupid.

"C'mon. Give him some privacy." Shawn stepped in front of us, trying to ward off the onlookers, which was probably for the best seeing as Raven's face was flushed and his fingers were tightly clenched.

At that moment, the sound of tires screeching along the pavement turned our attention away from the media. It was Josh's truck — Shelby's timing was impeccable.

"Get in!" Josh sat in the driver's seat, his face in a state of panic.

"Let's go." Raven grabbed my hand and we pressed through the reporters, cameras, and microphones. Shawn blocked everyone from following us, allowing us to break free. Raven opened the door and we jumped in, leaving the reporters dumbfounded and empty-handed. The door slammed shut and

Josh took off, tires spinning as they struggled to grip the asphalt.

"Damn! They're like freakin' vultures," Shelby huffed. I turned around to see the crowd of parents and fans, along with some of the football players, rush toward the front of the building. Everyone was probably wondering what the hell just happened and where Raven was going — not to the hotel with all the other players, obviously.

"Hey, shouldn't you be on that bus?" Raven hooked a thumb, pointing behind us.

"I'll have Shelby bring me back. Coach said he'd wait for me. He asked me to make sure you got home."

"Really?" Raven's voice lifted in a clear indication of hope.

"Yeah, and when I saw the TV station van pull up, bypass the players, and head straight for the athletic offices, I knew they got word. But I guess that's no surprise since it's on every social media site."

"Damn." Raven leaned forward and covered his face with his hands. I rubbed his back, giving him a supportive and soothing touch, though I knew it would take more than my touch to ease his worries. It would take a miracle.

"Word is out, man. Everyone knows you were in the hospital." Josh gripped the steering wheel until the whites of his knuckles pressed through. He let out an audible sigh and shook his head. The expression held more pity than anger. It was obvious Josh had been down this beaten path before.

"I'm so screwed." Raven voice was thick with regret.

"Don't worry. I'll call my uncle and you can talk to him." Josh gave a quick glance over his shoulder.

Raven lifted his head. "It's okay. I'll deal with this. I don't think I need an attorney this time. Besides, your family has done enough for me."

Josh looked at Raven through the rearview mirror. "Don't be hardheaded. Just talk to him. Get some advice on how to handle this situation. He helped you last time and I know he'll be happy to talk to you. Don't be a fool about this."

Raven gave a slight nod, but by the way his hands clenched into fists and his body stiffened, it was evident that he didn't want to have a conversation with Josh's uncle. Regardless of whatever demon Raven was battling, Josh was right. Raven needed sound advice and since he didn't have a father to lean on, Josh's uncle was probably the best person to confide in, aside from his mother, Trish. Too bad my sister wasn't on Raven's team, she'd be damn good for a situation like this.

Silence filled the cabin of the truck once again and I thought about the best way to support Raven. I didn't have all the answers or the best advice; being there for him was the best I could offer, and I would do that.

We made it to the apartment in record time without media trucks or wannabe paparazzi following us. We got out, while Josh and Shelby stayed behind. Raven grabbed his bags and we headed toward the stairs.

"Hey, Raven," Josh called, leaning out the window.

Raven adjusted the strap of his bag and looked over his shoulder. "Yeah, man?"

"If you need to talk, call me." Josh gave a sympathetic, man-to-man offer — one you'd expect from a true friend. Josh was a good guy and I hope he could reason with Raven. "I'll give my uncle a heads up."

"Thanks, man."

Raven went straight to his room and closed the door. I hated that he shut me out, but I figured he needed to be left alone until he was ready to talk. He'd been through a lot today and the news was less than satisfying. The only positive was the picture that Shawn had shown Coach. It made my stomach turn and left a sour taste in my mouth, but if it saved his football career, I didn't care who saw it. I might have looked like the stupid girl that ran back for more abuse, but I didn't care. I loved Raven and I would stand by his side, no matter what.

I sat on the couch, flipping through the TV channels, when my phone buzzed.

Shelby: Is Raven okay?

Me: He's in his room.

Shelby: Just give him some space. He'll come around. I'm going to stay with Amber. Let me know if you need anything.

Me: Ok. Thanks.

Just as I was about to set my phone down, a picture of Delaney and me flashed on the screen. I answered it quickly, not wanting to wake Raven in case he was sleeping.

"Hello?"

"Hey, how's Raven?" Delaney's voice was soothing to hear. I hadn't talked to her in a few days — only sending her a text when we left the hospital last night.

I took a deep breath and relaxed against the pillows. It seemed like the past twenty-four hours had been one big blur. "He's doing okay medically, I guess. When it comes to football... not so good. He won't be able to play in the bowl game."

Delaney gasped. "Oh shit. That sucks."

"Yeah, I know, but it's probably for the best. He's really weak right now. He could get seriously hurt." I made sure to keep my voice low; I didn't want Raven to hear me talk about him.

Delaney muttered something about Raven in the background and I couldn't help my curiosity.

"Where are you?"

"Luke's apartment."

"Tell him not to say anything. I'm not sure it's been announced." Delaney loved to talk and I didn't want to contribute to the rumor mill.

"Okay. Hey, Luke, don't say anything...they haven't made an announcement yet," Delaney said.

Loud and clear through the line, Luke said, "Okay."

"So, are you going to stay there?" Delaney asked.

I looked at our Star Wars Christmas tree, wishing I'd never left. The present I had bought for Raven was missing. I silently wondered if he had opened it or threw it away. I couldn't even think about telling him what my mom did to the lingerie he had bought me. So much had happened in the last ten days. Nothing like I'd planned.

"Yeah, I guess. Until the dorms open next week." I tried to remember what day it was and when the halls would reopen for spring semester. My head wasn't cooperating and it was probably due to lack of sleep and food.

"That's good. Raven needs you."

"I'm going to be here for him. Do whatever I can to help him get on the right track. I-I love him, Delaney. There's nothing I wouldn't do for him." I wiped the tears that suddenly appeared.

"I know you do. I'll check on you tomorrow. If you need me, I'll be there."

"Thanks, Delaney. I appreciate it. Tell Luke I said thanks for everything."

"I will." She giggled at the incoherent words my brother muttered in the background. "I gotta go. You brother obviously wants something."

I shook my head, trying not to think about what that 'something' he wanted was. I was happy for them, and I hoped Luke would be able to tame her wild ass. She definitely needed him.

"Okay, call me later. Bye."

"Bye." Her voice lilted in elation and I hung up the phone quickly.

I lifted my legs onto the couch and pulled a blanket over me. I snuggled against the cold leather and closed my eyes, wishing I was in the next room with Raven, feeling his warmth instead of my own. Tonight I had a feeling I'd be all alone. But it didn't have to be that way. If only Raven would let me in and allow me to help him in his troubled world. If only he'd open his heart fully to me instead of keeping it guarded with defensive plays.

A faint sound woke me. I blinked a few times, trying to focus on where the noise originated. A blue screen with a rainbow border at the bottom illuminated the TV. 'Off the air' flashed across the screen in large type. It took me a second to process the message. Did TV stations actually turn off anymore? I grabbed my phone and glanced at the time. Five minutes after one in the morning.

I checked my messages, seeing that I'd missed a call from Raven's mom several hours ago. I wasn't sure if he'd called her, but I decided to give her a ring later. Part of me was relieved that my mom hadn't tried to call me, while another part wished my dad would've checked on me. Based on the way he looked at me when I left, I had a feeling he was gravitating toward accepting my decision to be with Raven. I set my phone on the coffee table and walked toward Raven's room.

I cracked the door open and peeked into the room. The street light filtered in through the window, casting a shadow on Raven. He sat in a chair located in the corner of his room, resting his head against his hand. He looked so weak, vulnerable, and ready to cave with just one touch.

"Raven?" I entered slowly, approaching him with caution. "Are you okay?"

He didn't answer, keeping his gaze focused on the ground. The hurt, the pain, the disappointment... he wore each of them visibly, even in the dark. Every part of me hurt for him. I only wished there was something I could do to make everything better.

I knelt in front of him, trying to connect my eyes with his. I hated seeing him like this. It created an agony inside shared only between us. Our connection existed on a deeper level, not just intimately or physically, but soulfully. Regardless of his refusal to acknowledge me, I wasn't giving up.

"Is there anything I can do for you?" I placed my hand on his leg and left it there for a minute. He didn't move, his body remaining stiff like a statue. When I felt it was safe, I rubbed his leg in a slow stroke, kneading it with a deep touch. "Tell me, babe. I can't stand seeing you this way. Tell me what I can do."

His eyes met mine and I saw the walls of defeat that were surrounding him.

Consuming him.

Piece by piece.

I wanted to tear them down, one by one.

Unfortunately, I knew I couldn't do it for him. He had to do it on his own. If he was going to get through this setback, he'd have stand tall and make the decision to press forward — leave the past behind and start making better choices.

"I'm here for you." I spoke each word whole-heartedly, hoping he sensed my sincerity.

"Are you?" He glanced at me, warily.

"Of course I am." Confusion laced my voice and I quickly retreated, knowing I had to tread carefully. Words were Raven's worst enemy and they knew how to take him down faster than a two-hundred and fifty-pound linebacker. "I said I'd be here for you, no matter what."

"I know, but do you really want be here for me? After everything I put you through, what I did..." He shook his head, the disgust evident. He wasn't proud of what he'd done but he had to forgive himself for it, just like I had.

I sighed as my body sunk deeper into the carpet. How could I make him see that I was willing to forgive him? "Raven, if I didn't want to be here, I wouldn't be. I'm here because I love you. I didn't have to go the hospital to see you, but I wanted to. I care for you, more than you realize."

"Yeah, well, that's only because you thought I was dead."

My heart dropped to my stomach, recalling the torment I'd experienced when Delaney rushed into my room — when I thought the unthinkable. I clutched a hand to my chest. Destroying himself was killing me in the process. "Raven, please. Yes, I rushed to the hospital to make sure you were okay, but when you told me everything was a lie and that you still loved me, I knew there wasn't a place I'd rather be than with you."

"But I'm so messed up." His voice shook and his eyes glistened in the dim light.

"No one's perfect. I'm certainly not. But together, we are stronger. You even said it yourself."

A meek smile spread across his lips and he let out a slight laugh. "Did you just steal my line?" My heart melted at his expression. Seeing him happy was all I wanted.

"Maybe. All I know is that when you're hurting, I'm hurting, too."

He sat up and leaned forward, clasping his hands together. "I never intended to hurt you. I'm sorry."

I hesitated to broach the subject, but I had to know. I had to glean the real reason why he left me. Was it something my mom said? Did he really want to be with me? If I was going to give him another chance, I had to know that he wouldn't disappointment me. My heart couldn't handle it. It was barely functioning as it was, still on the verge of breaking down. It was taking everything I had to keep it together.

"I know you didn't, but help me understand why you sent me that text."

He took a deep breath and pressed his lips together in a firm line. For several seconds, he didn't speak, only twiddling his thumbs against each other in a rough movement. It was as though each thought tormented him and he didn't want to relive them.

"If you don't want to talk about it right now, I understand." I got up and he grabbed my hand.

"Come here, baby." He pulled me onto his lap and held me tightly in his arms. It felt like it had been forever since I was in his strong arms. Warmth surrounded me and I reveled in the comfort of his embrace. Only he could impart that security I needed to ease my fears, even though he was the one causing them.

Trust.

I wanted to trust Raven so badly, yet he continued to do things that made me it hard for me to do so. I needed to trust that he cared enough about me. About us. That he wasn't going to run away from me every time someone told him he shouldn't be with me.

"I'm so sorry." He stroked my hair. "I'm sorry that I nearly drank myself to death. That I was with those girls. That I was at Jared's house when you asked me to never go there again. I'm sorry that I allowed your mom to get to me. That I let her convince me that I wasn't good enough for you. But you have to understand, it's not easy for me. When I look at you," he lifted my chin, aligning my eyes to his, "I see this innocent and perfect woman that deserves a man that's just as perfect. One that isn't broken and shattered. A man without a tarnished past and with a bright future. And when I look at myself, I know I'm not that man."

Tears fell from my eyes. Hearing him talk that way about himself crushed me on every level. "Don't say that." I pressed a finger to his lips, halting any response he may have had. "You're more than you realize. You just need to believe in yourself instead of letting your past dictate who you are. We all have faults, we all make mistakes. All I'm asking is that you stop making bad choices. Instead, choose me." My shoulders lifted in anticipation.

He wrapped his hand around mine, kissing my finger gingerly. His eyes closed and his chest caved inward as he kept his lips firmly pressed to the tip of my finger. Slowly, his eyes opened. "You haven't asked for a life like this and you're here, regardless. Why do you keep coming back, Lexi?" His voice cracked, making him sound like a man at the end of his rope. I'd use all my strength to pull him back in and keep him from falling off.

I cupped his cheek. "Because I care about you, Raven. I'm in love with you. Can't you see that?"

"Even though I'm not good for you?"

"Quit saying that. You know that I'm better with you."

"I think it's the other way around."

"Then stop leaving me and just let me love you." I pressed a soft kiss to his lips. He stared at me intently and in the depths of his eyes, I saw it. The love and remorse. It was all there. And once again, I was willing to do anything for him. As long as he wanted to be with me.

"You'll take me back?"

"I never gave you up."

Σ

Chapter 3

I woke up a few hours later in Raven's arms. Being held by him seemed to relinquish every worry and ebb the pain in the center of my heart. I just hoped that I did the same for him. More than anything, I hoped he was being honest with me. That he truly loved me enough to be with me. I lifted from his chest, trying not to wake him. His white dress shirt was unbuttoned, revealing his rippled torso. Damn, he was so sexy. It took everything in me not to rub my hands all over him.

His eyes opened slightly and he gave me sleepy, seductive smile. "Hey."

"Hey."

"What time is it?" He glanced at his bare wrist.

I turned and glanced at the clock on the night stand. "A little after five."

"I guess we feel asleep." He ran his fingers through my hair and all the familiar sensations that once consumed me reappeared. His eyes took me in fully, making me tingle in all the right spots. My heart rate picked up, thrashing against my rib cage. I took in a deep breath, trying to steady the flow of my blood.

"It's easy to do. Being next to you is so comforting." I traced a finger along the crease separating his pecs. His muscles twitched beneath my touch and heat consumed me. Raven's body was made for worshipping and I would make him my king. No questions asked.

"I missed sleeping next to you." His hand slid behind my neck and his fingers dug into my hair. He drew my face to his and kissed me in a way that made every bad memory evaporate and begged for me to believe him. I wanted to — more than anything. I loved him too much and couldn't be without him.

Our kiss grew deeper, filled with intent and need. And I found myself lost within his addictive trap once more. A trap that I would willingly lock myself in and refuse to be released from, as long he allowed me.

His kiss told me that he loved me.

That he needed me.

That he couldn't be without me.

And I soaked in every part of it.

Our tongues slid against each other in a perfect melody that wrapped around my heart and soul. I couldn't get enough of him. And it was obvious he couldn't get enough of me. His hands dropped to my waist and he picked me up as he stood. I hooked my legs around him, pressing my body against his. An electric hum reverberated off us and rippled through the room, intensifying our connection.

He laid me on the bed, his mouth never separating from mine. His body pressed against mine and I went limp, reduced to a heap of boneless flesh and skin. Flesh and skin that was acutely aware of every sensation flowing through it. Feeling the entire length of his body on mine was sheer pleasure. It not only comforted me, but made me feel secure and safe.

His lips dropped to my neck and I whimpered as his mouth took possession of my body. My hands dove into his hair as his lips suckled on the nape of my neck. I was ready for him to take me, over and over again. Until I had absolutely nothing left to give.

I eased his shirt over his shoulders, exposing his bare chest. He quickly shucked it off and I took advantage of his weakened state by rolling him on his back. Even though I'd seen this heavenly sight many times, I allowed my mouth and tongue the pleasure they'd been dying for and traced over every indention that wound to the one thing I wanted most. I unzipped his pants and slid them down, eager to satisfy the need in him. In a quick move, Raven took the upper hand by flipping me onto my back.

"Ah. So you want control." I ran my hands over his tight butt. It was firm and muscular, and I pressed him against me, showing him I wouldn't mind controlling him for one night.

"Whatever you want, baby. I'll give it to you."

I hooked my legs around his waist, positioning myself in perfectly alignment with him.

"Oh, God, Lexi," he moaned in pleasure as he rubbed his perfect, athletic body against mine.

Kill me now.

The friction was driving me insane. I felt his arousal between my legs and shuddered, unable to control myself. I needed him inside me — where he belonged.

Resting his weight on one arm, he used his other hand to trace the curves of my body. I writhed underneath the sheer pleasure of his touch. My back arched, unable to restrain the emotions that begged for release. With pro-like moves, he stripped off my clothes and tossed them to the floor.

"Ten days without you is too long," he breathed heavily in my ear. Goose bumps shot down to my toes and my body revved up with an animalistic desire for him.

"You have no idea," I whispered, praying this moment would never end. I needed Raven to show me how much he loved me.

Prove his love to me.

Make love to me.

My body wouldn't take no for an answer.

"I want you so damn bad." His eyes bore into me and the room seemed to fade away. All that existed was him and me.

Raven knew how to make me his world when he wanted to. I felt the trembling in his arms and knew he was in no condition for sex, despite his tantalizing words and physical need. I didn't want to deny him, but I didn't want to be selfish either. Fighting against my bodily needs, I knew the right thing to do.

"But you need to rest." I stroked the sides of his hair, trying to calm myself. But being naked with Raven, it was nearly impossible. It was pure bliss looking at him with his clothes on, but without anything was divine torture. "You're weak." My voice faltered and I knew I was the weaker one.

"Baby, I'm never too weak to make love to you."

Oh God. I want him.

Not disagreeing with him, I kissed him greedily. My mouth dragged along his skin and I quickly became the one drugged with his love. I indulged sinfully in his taste, his touch... my desire for him. Our bodies moved in a perfect rhythm that only we could make, each thrust and rub bringing me closer to Raven. To a place I never wanted to leave. What I experienced with him was pure ecstasy. I was completely and totally addicted to his love. The Raven's trap was more than an addiction; it was my way of life.

Raven and I slept, wrapped in each other's arms, until late the next morning, exhausted from the events that transpired over the last ten days. Looking back on everything, he was right about one thing. I never imagined I'd be dealing with issues like this. But I was willing to do whatever I needed to because it was the choice I'd made. No one else. Not my mother, not my father, or anyone else. It was mine alone. I wanted to be with Raven, as long as he wanted to be with me.

"Good morning, baby." Raven stroked my cheek with his index finger.

"Damn, it's awesome to hear those words." I smiled, burrowing myself against the warmth of his hand.

"I'll make sure to always say them." He pressed a tender kiss to my lips and then rested his forehead against mine. He took several deep breaths, as though allowing the stress to unravel from every fiber in his body.

"Are you okay?"

He nodded and gave me a boyish grin. "Being with you makes everything better."

"Good. Let's keep it that way."

He grabbed me and pulled me on top of him. Wrapping his arms tightly around me, he planted kiss after kiss all over my face. "I'm going to smother you with my love and affection until you're sick of it."

"I could never get sick of this." I giggled and laughed, loving every minute of it.

"Good, because I'm not letting you go anywhere."

"I don't have anywhere else to go, so I guess you're stuck with me."

He stopped for a moment and looked at me. "What do you mean?"

I pressed my lips together, not sure if now was the right time. I hated bringing it up because it was what started the whole mess. "My mother told me that if I left to never come back." A lump quickly formed in the center of my throat, causing tears to quickly appear. I tried to snub them away but they escaped and spilled into my hair. It made me furious that I was allowing my mom to get to me.

I squeezed my eyes shut and buried my face against his chest, continuing to fight the wretchedness of what happened. Of how she treated me. Of what she told Raven and the trouble she caused for us. Why did my mom have to be so hardcore? Couldn't she just accept my decisions and be happy for me? Why did she insist on running my life for me? "It just sucks."

"Don't cry, baby." Raven quickly blotted my tears with the pads of his thumbs. "You can stay here with me."

"Are you sure?" I sniffed.

His lips formed a perfect smile. "Of course I'm sure."

"Yeah, but it sucks the way they treat me and the way they treated you. It's not right, Raven. My entire life, my mother has controlled me. Told me what I can and can't do. Dictated how I would live my life and my dad has just let her do it. It's not right. I can't live like that anymore. If my parents don't accept you, then I'm done with them."

"I know, Lexi. It's not right." He held my gaze. "I wish they weren't that way. Because you need your parent's support, as do I."

"I'm sorry," I whispered across his lips.

"It's not your fault." He stroked my hair in slow movements as I wept silently. I hated my mom, even though I didn't want to. But she was leaving me with very little choice. I wouldn't allow her to take Raven away from me. My love for him was too strong. Stronger than the relationship I had with them.

"My only hope is that my dad stands up for me."

"Do you think he will?" He tried to look at me, but I kept my forehead pressed to his shoulder.

I shrugged. "Maybe."

"Did he say something to you? I want to know. That is... if you want to tell me." He sounded genuinely concerned and it reminded me of what he had told me about being there for me, too.

"Um, well, at first he wasn't happy about me being with you. Then when he heard you were in the hospital, he told me to be careful."

"So he was okay with you coming to see me?" Raven nudged me with his cheek, still trying to look at me.

I raised my chin, connecting our gazes. "I think so."

"That's good." He smiled and his eyes relaxed. It warmed a part of me because deep down, I knew he needed my dad's acceptance. It would make being with me so much easier. Raven had enough rejection in his life, my parents were just adding to that unwanted list and I hated it.

For several minutes, we didn't speak. But through the gentleness of his embrace and the comfort of his words, we exchanged a deeper level of our torment with each other. I hoped that by me being transparent and open with him, he would eventually do the same. If I was willing to tell him how I felt, share my pain and anguish, then maybe he'd open up to me. This intimate moment was exactly what we needed. What I needed. He was doing what I had promised I'd do for him — being there for me. Raven was all I ever needed.

"Hey, I have an idea." His voice shifted to an enticing lure and I quickly pushed away all the sadness, curious to know what he had in mind. "Why don't you put on the black teddy I bought you?"

"Oh, well, um, I don't think I can do that."

"Did you leave them at your house?"

I bit down on my lip, trying to decide whether I wanted to tell him what happened. "Not exactly."

"What happened?" The muscles in his arms tensed and I hesitated for a moment.

"Well..." I swallowed the huge lump in my throat, recalling that night. My mother was bat shit crazy. She deserved to have her stuff destroyed, just to know what it feels like. "She... she, um, burned it all."

"What?" In a swift move, his head jerked back. "What do you mean she burned it?"

"Yeah, she threw all of the bras and panties you bought me in the fireplace." I rolled onto my back, feeling horrible about the situation. I covered my face with my hands as the tears struck once again. "I'm sorry. I tried to stop her, but I couldn't."

"It's okay." Raven lowered my hands. "It's not your fault."

I quickly wiped the wetness from my cheeks with the back of my hand. "I hate her," I said through gritted teeth.

"Lexi." His voice deepened.

"I'm sorry, but she's a horrible person. I want nothing to do with her."

"I understand." He pulled me into his arms. "We'll buy you some more."

"No." I shook my head. "You already spent too much money on me."

"I like spending money on you. Unless you'd rather free-buff it."

"What's that?" I sniffed and looked at him, trying to figure out what he was talking about.

"You know, go without panties." He gave a playful slap to my rear. "Makes it easier for me." He arched a brow.

"Raven," I laughed and shoved him away. He sure knew how to lighten the mood. "I like wearing panties."

"Oh, come on, baby. Don't wear any for me." A low growl escaped from his throat as he nuzzled my neck with his lips. He definitely knew how to tease me in all the right ways. And I never wanted to go a day without it. Our flirtatious morning quickly came to an abrupt stop when his phone rang.

"It's Coach." Raven quickly sat up in bed and grabbed his boxers from the floor. He put them on before heading to the living room. "Hello? Yes, sir."

I crawled out of bed and slipped one of Raven's white T-shirts over my head. A new scent encompassed me and I inhaled deeply, holding the fabric close to my nose. Glancing at his dresser, I saw the bottle of cologne I'd bought him for Christmas. He had opened it, and I couldn't wait to smell it on him.

After washing my face and brushing my teeth, I went to the kitchen and poured myself a glass of OJ. Raven paced the living room as he spoke to the coach. I tried not to listen to his conversation, but curiosity got the best of me.

"Yes, sir. Of course," Raven responded, his brows knitted together tightly.

Instead of standing there watching him, I decided to make us breakfast. Returning to the fridge, I took out eggs, cheese, spinach, and bell peppers. Since I hadn't eaten much over the past week, an omelet sounded good. Hopefully I could make it without creating a huge mess like I had last time. With one eye on Raven and the other one on the knife and peppers, I began preparing the vegetables for sautéing.

"Not a problem. I can be there." Raven stood up straight, some of the weight seeming to lift from his shoulders.

Had the coach told him to play in the game? Was he giving him another chance? I slowed the knife as I tried to figure out what the coach was telling him based on his reactions.

"Tonight at seven. I'll be there. Thanks, Coach." Raven hit the end button and let out a heavy breath. He started to dial a number but stopped, placing the phone on the coffee table instead.

I turned to Raven, placing the knife on the counter. "What did he say? What's tonight?"

He walked into the dining area and leaned against the kitchen bar. His fingers gripped the edge of the counter as he pressed his weight against it. The muscles under his pecs pulsed and I found myself enticed by his heavenly body once again. One thing was certain, I'd never tire of appraising him from head to toe. I blinked a few times and forced myself to focus on the more important issue at hand.

He pressed his lips together in a thin line and then said, "He wants me to attend a press conference tonight at the stadium."

"That's good, right?" I bit my bottom lip, anticipating his answer. He really needed a break and some positive encouragement.

Silence filled the air and his eyes glossed over. His jaw jutted outward and he took a hard swallow, as though fighting back the tears. I didn't want him to cry, but at the same time, I welcomed it if it brought us closer and gave him a level of healing.

"I still can't play, but the coach feels like I should make a statement about what happened." His grip relaxed as another layer of defeat coated his face. I hated watching him go through all these mixed emotions, but I had to remind myself that I was there to help him, to guide him in the right direction. I felt somewhat responsible for the mess my mother started, so it was the least I could do.

"What do you want to do?"

He glanced at the floor and his shoulders sunk. "I don't think I have much of a choice."

"Everyone has a choice. It's just a matter of making the right ones."

He let out a muffled *humph*, but didn't look at me. Defeat was beating him deeper into his own trap. The deadly trap I had to steer him away from — for good.

Fearing I might have said the wrong thing, I quickly walked out of the kitchen to the other side of the bar. Placing my hands on his arms, I turned him to face me. "Raven?"

"Yeah?"

"Look at me for a moment."

He placed his hands at my waist and pulled me close. His gaze met mine and I searched his eyes, wanting to unravel his deep, dark secrets; uncover the demons that haunted his mind and consistently tormented him. Why couldn't he let them go? Why did he allow them to tell him to stop trying? To stop believing in himself?

"It sounds like it's the right thing to do. I know it might embarrass you, but I think if you want to show the coach and the school that you're serious about straightening up and what happened wasn't entirely your fault, you need to do it."

Raven leaned forward, resting his forehead against mine. He took slow, deep breaths, drawing me in with every inhalation.

God, I love this man.

I was willing to do anything to help him, but would he allow me to get close to him? Really let me in?

The muscles in his arms tightened and his chest froze into a solid block, as though trying to hold it inside. He kept that invisible wall up and refused to release whatever it was that forbade him from moving forward, storing it deep within the grooves of his soul and protecting me from it. Why was he so afraid to share his problems with me?

"Raven?" I spoke softly, trying to wedge myself inside that wall. "It's okay, babe. You can trust me. Tell me."

"Not right now, Lexi." He gave a slight shake of his head. "But, you're right. I should do it. Besides, I have to meet with admissions board on Wednesday. It will show a good act of faith."

"Don't worry, babe." I ran my fingers through his hair, wishing I had the power to diminish his pain. "Everything is going to be all right."

"I hope so. If the school kicks me out, then I can't play." Defeat weakened his voice and it slapped me with his reality. "I mean... is all this really worth it?"

I stalled momentarily. He had a point. If all the love in the world couldn't heal his pain, then I didn't know what would. In all honesty, it was beyond me. Was I crazy for thinking I'd be able to pull him out of this pit? No. I shook the crippling thoughts from my mind. I wouldn't allow Raven's demons to defeat me, too. I at least had to try; otherwise, I'd never forgive myself.

My love for Raven was worth the battle.

I refused to give up and I wouldn't allow him to give up either.

Dreams and goals were worth fighting for — until your last, dying breath.

"Don't ever doubt that your dreams are worth the fight. It's worth every struggle, every let down, and every victory until you get where you want to be."

A half-smile formed at the corner of his lips. "And where is it that I want to be?" His gaze bored into me, but no matter how hard I looked, I had no idea what he was thinking. His vision seemed to travel past me, and I wanted to know what he saw in his future. Was I included in that not-so-far-off picture?

Because I wanted to be.

More than anything.

Being with Raven was all I ever wanted and I could only hope he wanted the same.

"On that field playing for a pro team," I reminded him. "Doing what you're good at and what you love doing."

His face lifted and a huge smile stretched across his lips. My heart lifted and I was relieved my pep talk gave him what he needed to believe in himself once more. The question was, had I convinced him that I wanted to by his side?

"So, I guess until that happens, baby, it's just you and me against the world."

Σ

.

Chapter 4

"Are you sure it's all right if I go?" I slipped on a pair of black heels and then picked up a black blazer I'd borrowed from Delaney.

"Yes. Mr. Marshall assured me it was fine. Besides, he said he wants to talk to you."

"To me?" I put one arm through the boyfriend jacket and stopped. "Why does he want to talk with me?" Several potential reasons ran through my mind.

Raven eased into his suit jacket and adjusted his sleeves, making sure his cufflinks showed. The black material had an eye-catching sheen, and the purple dress shirt with matching tie made him look even more irresistible. Caught up in his model-perfect attire, I had to look away before I started drooling.

"Relax." Raven embraced my shoulders with his big, strong hands and my knees weakened. "He just wants to go over a few things with you."

"What if he asks me questions?" For whatever reason, I felt like I was the one in the hot seat.

"Answer them." Raven slid his hands underneath my hair and adjusted the collar of my jacket. Tiny sparks shot through me as he paid special attention to the way I looked, though he should've been more concerned about himself. The length of his neck brushed my lips and the scent of his new cologne infiltrated my airways. I backed up against the dresser, unable to stand upright, reminding myself that now was not the time to get excited. Raven had a press conference to attend and William Marshall, Josh's uncle, was on his way to pick us up.

After the coach insisted that he make a statement about what had happened, he'd decided it would be in his best interest to speak to Mr. Marshall. If Raven wanted to prove that the incident wasn't entirely intentional, then he might have a chance to save his football career. Mr. Marshall served as Raven's attorney last year when he was suspended for recreational drug use. After breakfast, they talked on the phone for over an hour. Mr. Marshall offered to be there while Raven gave his statement to the media, fans, and alumni. They would all be anxiously waiting for him to confirm whether the rumors were true.

"What do I say? I mean... is there anything I shouldn't say?" I buttoned the next-to-top button on my blouse and made sure my shirttail was tucked into my pants. Thankfully, Delaney had some nice clothes for me to borrow since the majority of mine were still at my parent's house.

His fingers dropped to my chest and he undid the button I'd just fastened. "I told him everything I told you."

I shot him a confused stare and started to button my shirt again when he stopped me. "You look good like this."

Glancing down, I noted the slight cleavage that peeked from my shirt. With a raised brow, I said, "Are you sure? I don't want to flash everyone."

"Lexi. Lexi." Raven laughed, planting a kiss on my forehead. "You're not showing too much cleavage. Trust me. You look gorgeous."

"Okay, if you say so."

I turned and looked in the mirror, giving myself a once over. Delaney's clothes were a little loose on me and it looked like I'd lost some weight over the past ten days. My face appeared thinner and my cheeks a little sunken, but at least the black circles around my eyes were fading. It felt good to wear makeup and fix my hair. By the widening of Raven's eyes, I could tell he liked it, too. He embraced me from behind and I folded my arms over his.

"You have no idea how much I've missed you." He stared at me through the mirror.

"I'm sorry it took something like this to bring us back together."

"Me, too," he sighed.

I smiled at him, trying to easy his worries. "Everything is going to turn out fine."

"I hope you're right, baby." Raven pressed his cheek to mine and I reached behind me, cupping his face with my palm.

"Have some faith, Raven."

His phone buzzed, vibrating against the dresser. We glanced over and saw that it was a message from Marshall Law Firm. Raven picked up his phone and swiped the screen.

"They're downstairs. You ready?"

"Yes, let's go."

We walked out of the apartment and descended the stairs. The sun was setting and the warm, winter day was turning into a brisk, cool evening. A shiny, black Cadillac SUV was parked curbside, waiting for us. A short guy, probably in his early to mid-thirties, wearing navy-striped dress pants and a white, button-down shirt with the sleeves rolled up to his elbows, greeted us.

"Raven," he stuck his hand out, "good to see you again."

"Steve." Raven shook his hand.

Steve turned to me. "You must be Lexi."

I shook his cold hand. "Yes, Lexi Thompson."

"I'm Mr. Marshall's assistant, Steve Langevin. Nice to meet you."

"Likewise."

Steve opened the door and we got into the SUV. A husky, balding man immediately turned and greeted us. "Raven." He stretched his long arm across the backseat.

"Mr. Marshall." Raven gave him a hefty handshake and then turned to me. "This is my girlfriend, Lexi Thompson."

Mr. Marshall craned his neck, trying to get a better glimpse of me. His forehead tightened and his nose wrinkled as he struggled to turn his stocky body in my direction. "It's a pleasure to meet you." His strong Texas twang fit him perfectly.

I leaned forward, meeting his gaze. "Nice to meet you, too."

Steve got into the driver's seat and shut the door.

Mr. Marshall huffed and then grabbed the overhead handlebar, adjusting himself in his seat. "I had Steve prepare your statement. When you sit down with Coach Anderson, don't be afraid to refer to it if you need to. It's better to read it than to say something incorrectly."

Steve handed Raven a brown folder. "Thank you." Raven took the folder and opened it, glancing at the professional typed-out statement on blanch-white paper with the Marshall Law Firm logo at the top.

"Do you have any questions?"

"I think I'm good." Raven closed the folder and set it between us. "You've prepared me and I remember to say *no comment* when I'm not sure how to respond."

"You learn quickly, son." Mr. Marshall let out a deep, throaty laugh. "You'll do just fine. And if things start to get out of control, I'll step in as your advisor and attorney while Steve escorts you out of the room."

"Sounds good." Raven clicked his seatbelt and motioned for me to do the same. After I fastened my belt, Steve pulled out of the apartment complex and headed toward the freeway. As we passed the university, a sad, empty feeling overcame me and I wasn't sure why.

"Now, as for you, Miss Thompson, I'd like to cover a few important rules."

Rules? What type of rules?

"Yes, of course, sir."

"I've already advised Raven of what I'm about to tell you, but let it serve as a reminder to him as well. Watch what you post on any and all social media sites. It will come back to bite you in the ass and then we're all screwed. When you're three sheets to the wind with beer bottles in your hand, smiling half-naked for the camera, it makes my job ten times harder. I don't want to have to figure out how the hell we're going to get out of that situation."

I shot Raven a confused look. *Who the hell was naked on Facebook?* I picked up my phone, ready to access my Facebook page, but decided it wasn't worth it. If Raven had been half-naked, I'm sure he was smart enough to remove that picture.

"Do you understand?"

"Um, yes, sir. I understand." I held up my hands in surrender, making sure to keep them hidden from Mr. Marshall. Raven shrugged his shoulders, just as confused. Maybe he hadn't posted a naked picture of himself on Facebook after all. "We'll stay off social media sites."

Mr. Marshall cleared his throat a few times. "I don't want you to disappear from them, especially Raven. He needs his fan support. So continue life as normal, just post pictures that show Raven on his best behavior."

Best behavior? Are you kidding me?

"Oh, okay."

"Raven, what do you think would be acceptable things to post?"

Raven shot me a look that said, "Help!"

"Maybe Raven working out at the gym?" I suggested.

"Excellent. Show that he's not giving up on his dream."

I'll gladly take that shot.

"True." Raven shot me a quick wink. "How about me with my family at dinner?"

"Good choice." Mr. Marshall nodded his head. "Anything else you can think of?"

"Um, Lexi and me studying?"

Thinking about how some of our study sessions had turned out, I wasn't sure if that would be a good idea. Then again, it did sound enticing.

"Perfect." Mr. Marshall's voice lilted in joy. "Go to church with your family, take pictures with them. Go to some fundraisers. Hell, I'm invited to several every month. In fact, I'll have Steve respond that you and Lexi will attend in my honor. Show that you're cleaning up your act."

"Got it, Mr. Marshall." Raven nodded while running the palms of his hands over his knees. At the apartment, I was the one who was nervous. It seemed like I had transferred that emotion to him. I reached for his hand and he wrapped his fingers tightly around mine. With light, feathery strokes, I rubbed my thumb across the top of his hand, trying to calm his wound-up nerves.

"And by God, stay away from the damn parties. Especially Jared Harrington's place." Mr. Marshall struggled to turn around. "If I get word that you've stepped one foot in that shithead's place, I'll rip your legs off myself."

Raven's eyes widened. "Yes, sir. I'm staying far away from him."

"Good."

"Rule number two," Mr. Marshall took a deep breath before continuing, "no talking to the media."

"Understood," I replied, making a mental note.

"Now, there's no need to be ugly or a bitch if they confront you. But you just tell them *no comment*," Mr. Marshall and Raven said in unison.

Mr. Marshall hooked a thumb, pointing it at Raven. "See, he knows." A deep, belly laugh belted from his mouth followed by a hacking cough. I hoped the guy wasn't going to die from a heart attack anytime soon.

"Rule number three, don't get caught doing something with Raven that will get him in trouble. Or you, for that matter."

"Got it." I smiled at Raven, assuring him that I was one-hundred percent on board with helping him. "Behave ourselves in public."

"Basically, or don't get caught with your panties around your ankles or his jon hanging out of his pants."

My jaw hit the floorboard. Was he serious? Did he take me for one of Raven's hoes? I shot Raven a look that told him he better set Mr. Marshall straight.

"That won't be happening, Mr. Marshall." Raven placed his hand on the back of Mr. Marshall's seat, giving it a slight pull until the attorney made eye contact with him. "Lexi is a well-respected woman. I would never do anything like that to disgrace her and she would never do anything to dishonor me."

My heart lifted at Raven's words, as if given a pair of wings. I pressed a hand to my chest, completely overcome by the sentiment.

"I'm glad you got a good girl and dumped those cock-sucking hoes. They were all trouble for you, son." Mr. Marshall patted Raven's hand, giving his approval.

My hand dropped from my chest, the happy-good-feeling completely gone. I didn't know whether to be happy that Raven had finally left his tramps or worried over what his attorney thought of me. It really didn't matter. This was about Raven, and I reminded myself that Raven had shared everything with this man. He was here to help him, or at least, I hoped so. I shook my head, stunned at his colloquialisms. The man was no better than my sister. I reasoned with myself to give him a reprieve, otherwise I'd tell the man to shut the hell up because he didn't know me.

"Final rule..." Mr. Marshall adjusted his seatbelt, pivoting in my direction, "keep what's going on with Raven between the two of you. Don't go telling your family and friends. We don't need any more gossip spreading. Got it?"

"Of course." I nodded and smiled at him. One thing I didn't like to do was gossip. But if I knew Delaney, she'd be begging to know the scoop on Raven's situation.

"You've got the parking pass and our badges?" Mr. Marshall asked as Steve pulled into the parking lot in front of the pro-football stadium.

"Right here." Steve picked up a gray envelop and laid it on the console. "Raven, not sure if Mr. Marshall told you, but I called and talked to the assistant at the athletic's office and arranged for us to have a parking pass and media badges."

"Yes, he informed me. Thank you for picking them up for us."

The parking lot was filled with media vans from local TV stations and different vendors, all supporting PHU and the opposing team. Fans were already arriving from out of town in their bright blue and yellow decorated vehicles, including small and large RVs. Tailgaters claimed their favorite spots, setting up their barbecue grills and large, flat screen TVs sporting PHU's purple and white flag and the stately dragon. As cars passed by, a group of men with painted torsos were yelling and chanting, "Go Eagles!" These fans were serious when it came to college bowl games.

"Good afternoon," a security guard in full tactical gear greeted us as the dark tinted window slid down.

"Hello. We are here for Park Hill University's press conference." He handed the guard the passes.

The guard studied them for a second before handing them back to him. "Drive to where that man is standing and he'll direct you where to park."

"Thank you." Steve closed the window and drove forward.

"Sweet." Raven's eyes lit up as we were directed to the front row where all of the VIP and pro-football players parked. His smile quickly turned sour when we passed a group of fans displaying a sign with *The Raven — MVP* written in big, bold letters.

Raven wouldn't be the MVP. At least, not for this game. I unfastened my seatbelt and scooted next to him. "Your time will come," I whispered in his ear as I rubbed his arm in a soothing manner.

"But now is my time and I screwed it up." His jaw tensed and his face hardened. I couldn't argue against that fact, but I had to believe he would get another chance.

"It's not over until it's over," I reminded him.

A half smile escaped his lips. "Where did you hear that from?" He inclined his head in my direction.

"A really great football player." I winked.

He smiled and gave me a quick kiss. Steve opened the door and we got out. Mr. Marshall adjusted his suspenders over his round belly and then Steve helped him into his dark gray suit jacket.

"Don't forget this." Steve handed him a bowtie.

"Oh yeah, hate those damn neck chokers." The attorney buttoned his white dress shirt and then gripped the black, white, and gray striped tie with his thick, chubby hands and clipped it on his collar. He pulled out a handkerchief and wiped the sweat from his face and then ran a small black comb through the thin strands covering his partially bald head. Steve handed him two small bottles. One he sprayed all over him, and the other he poured in his mouth and then spat. He had a Rico Sauvé primping going on, but it seemed to work for him.

He grabbed a worn leather briefcase from the front seat and shut the door. "Alright, let's go."

Steve handed us our media badges and we followed him and Mr. Marshall into the stadium.

A journalist with a cameraman approached us and Mr. Marshall immediately held up his hand. "Save your questions for inside, folks."

"Are you representing Raven Davenport?" The journalist bypassed his request, but the stout attorney held his position and ignored her. Refusing to give up, she turned to Raven. "Is it true that you won't be playing in the bowl?" Her short, red bob bounced as she trekked after us.

Raven smiled at her politely. "No comment."

"Hospital reports indicate you were hospitalized for alcohol poisoning and drug usage." She extended her hand, holding her phone close to Raven, ready to record his response, but he remained quiet. His jaw worked from side to side and his brows furrowed while his hand tightened around mine. Hearing those statements must have struck a sensitive spot within him. I prayed he'd be able to make it through the press conference.

Steve stopped in his tracks and stepped in front of the reporter and her cameraman. "You heard Mr. Marshall, save it for inside."

"Just trying to do my job." She brushed her hair away from her face and flashed him a flirtatious smile, as if hoping to convince him for that exclusive story.

"And I'm just doing mine," Steve replied with a bit of gusto. The journalist dropped her hands in defeat and then walked off with her cameraman in tow.

We entered the facility and were directed down a hallway to a private waiting area. Sleek fixtures and shiny railings guided us down a long corridor. We passed through a set of double doors and entered what looked like the *behind the scenes* passageway for players and coaches. Being in a pro-football stadium was incredible and a little exciting, but I reminded myself that we weren't here for a joyous occasion. Heaviness settled over me and my body caved inward. Raven was right — it should've been his time. Instead of getting ready to explain why he wouldn't be playing, he should've been preparing to explain how they were going to sweep their opponent. This totally sucked.

We walked past a door marked *Press Room*, stopping at a door marked *Private Offices*. Steve opened the door, obviously familiar with where we were going, and presented a lady at a desk with his access badge.

"Hello. I'm from Marshall Law Firm, representing Raven Davenport. I requested a private office."

The young lady fluttered her faux eyelashes at us. "Yes, of course. Let me verify that we have a room reserved for you." Her long blue and white painted fingernails with blinged out silver stars on the tips danced across the keyboard.

"Okay. I have the *Porter* room reserved for you."

"Will we be notified when it's time for the press conference to start?"

"Yes," she squinted at the computer screen, "a message will be sent via text to 682-439-0856."

"Great. Is Coach Anderson nearby?"

"Yes, he's in the *Washington* room, which connects to the locker rooms and the media room. You will enter the Press Room through those doors," she said, pointing to a set of doubled doors behind us.

"Thank you."

"Your room is down the hall on the left."

Steve retrieved his badge. "Thank you for your assistance."

"Let me know if you need anything." She clasped her hands together and gave us all a big smile.

We entered a room the size of a small bedroom, equipped with a couch, table and chairs, and a bathroom. I took a seat on the couch facing a large, flat screen TV affixed to the wall and Raven sat next to me. Over the next hour, Mr. Marshall prepared Raven for his press conference, reviewing the statements that Steve put together. He briefly touched on the option of Raven pressing charges against Jared and Raven quickly informed him they would talk later about his decision. I hoped that he would. To my surprise, I found out that Jared was kicked out of school and off the team last year for misconduct. I made a mental note to find out what he had done. Shortly after that, Coach Anderson entered the room.

Raven stood up and shook his hand. "Coach."

"Raven. You're looking better today."

"I'm feeling better."

"Good." Coach Anderson wrapped an arm around him. "Are you ready?"

"Yes, sir. Mr. Marshall has prepped me on what to say."

"Perfect." The coach turned to Mr. Marshall and Steve and shook their hands. "I wish we were meeting again under different circumstances, but it is what it is."

"I can't disagree with that." Mr. Marshall pursed his lips.

Coach Anderson opened the door. "Let's go, son. We've got a room full of people."

Raven stood up and put his jacket on. "Wish me luck."

I lifted onto the balls of my feet and gave him a kiss on the cheek. "Always."

Σ

Chapter 5

The entire drive home from the press conference was painfully quiet. Raven sat far away from me, staring out the window. I only hoped he wouldn't have a change of heart — again — when we got home. It seemed like every time Raven slipped or took a fall, he distanced himself from me — as if he felt he didn't deserve to be with me. All I could do was assure him that everything would be okay and he'd get past this with me by his side.

The press conference seemed to go as well as expected. Coach Anderson spoke first, announcing that Raven would not be playing in the bowl game. That had spurred the media into a thirsting-for-answers frenzy, making it the hottest ticket in college football. Raven joined in the discussion once the crowd calmed. The media had shown him no mercy, bombarding him with the touchy and difficult-to-answer questions. Poignancy laced through me as I watched the man I love bare all his shame and disappointment for the world to see. Raven did exceedingly well, though — holding his ground and responding as Mr. Marshall and Steve had advised.

As soon as Raven opened the door to the apartment, I headed straight to the bathroom. My lower stomach had started cramping during the press conference and I pleaded with my body to wait until I got back to Raven's place. Although I was hoping my period would start, I had forgotten to grab a tampon before we left. I sighed in relief at the tell-tale sign of Aunt Flo making her appearance.

"Everything okay?" Raven asked as I exited the bathroom.

"Oh, yeah. Everything is great." I smiled and then stopped when our eyes connected. The sparkle in Raven's beautiful hazel eyes was gone, replaced by a heart-wrenching sadness. I had to be careful with what I said and how I said it. Every emotion I displayed could be interpreted in the wrong manner and I didn't want him to walk out on me again. I stalled for a moment, not sure what to tell him. Talking about my menstrual cycle wasn't something I was used to doing, especially with a guy.

A visceral feeling took over, helping staunch the uncomfortableness when it came to this subject. "I, um... I got my period," I said in a hushed voice. I had to get past the embarrassment. It wasn't something that ever came up when I was Collin. Probably because we weren't having sex and he never planned on it. Discussing it with Raven seemed a little odd, but since we were having sex, I felt compelled to tell him.

"Oh." Raven frowned and his shoulders dropped. "That doesn't sound like fun." His arms formed a circle around my waist and he pulled me close. "How long does your period usually last?"

My eyebrows shot up. Raven definitely didn't have a problem with talking about my menstrual cycle. In fact, he was making it easier for me. "Um, usually four to five days."

"That sucks." His hands slid down my back, resting on my butt. "I'm not sure I can wait that long." I felt a change in the air. The solemn Raven had vanished, replaced by a predatory calling that told me it wouldn't stop him from getting what he wanted.

Breaking eye contact with him, I traced the circumference of the button on his shirt, contemplating whether I should tell him I had been late. Our relationship had reached a different level, especially after spending a week with him, and since I was planning on staying with him for another week before the dorms opened, I thought he should know. I just hoped it wouldn't scare him off. That was the last thing I needed. "It's a good thing I did... I was late."

Raven leaned back, trying to catch my line of sight. "How late?"

So much for that thought.

"Almost a week." I finally looked at him, searching for any sign that he wasn't going to freak out. My heart pounded and my legs went limp. "And I'm never late."

His hands retreated from my waist and he took a step back. Darkness circled around his pupils as the inner demons released. I leaned against the wall, unable to support my weight. Folding his arms across his body, he remained silent for a moment. What was he thinking? Maybe I shouldn't have told him. Would he leave me again?

Dumb ass!

He'd just left one disappointment, the last thing he needed to hear was that I had been late. I had the worst timing — for everything. I told my mind not to go there, but it did, and horrible thoughts ravaged my head, taking those intimate moments with him that I cherished and discounting them as foolish.

"Lexi, I would never tell you what to do when it comes to your body, but have you considered getting on the pill? I mean... it wouldn't be good if you got pregnant."

A tiny part of me, deep within my soul, cracked like a mirror that had been dropped. Instead of it shattering into a million pieces, it caused a bad nick, leaving a permanent mark. Hearing those words hit me harder than I had thought. Even though having a baby right now was the last thing I wanted, it still hurt. I pressed my lips together as my throat tightened and my eyes watered. "Yes, I was just thinking that I should probably go to the health center when school starts again."

"I think that's a good idea."

"Then I'll do it. Because the last thing I want—"

Raven quickly scooped me into his arms, stopping me mid-sentence. My head jutted back like I had whiplash. One moment, he didn't want to get me pregnant, and the next, he was literally sweeping me off my feet and carrying me toward the bedroom. The tears of pain quickly turned into tears of joy. Hearing that didn't scare him off after all. Had he successfully battled those demons?

"Is for me to worry about knocking you up. If you're on the pill, we don't have to be cautious." A devious expression formed on his face and I knew what he wanted.

Me.

The Raven was back.

He laid me on the bed and I kicked off my shoes. I quickly took off Delaney's jacket and threw it on the chair behind him.

"Good toss." He looked over his shoulder, noticing how the jacket caught the edge of the chair.

"This really sexy football player showed me how to throw."

"Did he?" Raven undid his tie and unbuttoned his shirt and I felt the rush of adrenaline from my head to my toes. "I know a few other things he can show you." He unfastened his pants at lightning speed and whipped off his belt, dropping it to the floor.

"Sounds fun." I ogled him and his eyes bored into me, revving my desire for him.

"Oh, baby, you have no idea." His pants hit the floor and my stomach did a somersault. He was more than ready for me and God knew I was ready for him. "I plan on making up for lost time."

I grabbed his tie and pulled him on top of me. I eased his shirt off and my eyes widened in delight as I took in each section of his body for my viewing pleasure. Every ridge of his chest was well defined and it caused every nerve ending in my body to tingle. My lips dropped to his chest and I traced every line with my tongue. His fingers tangled through my hair as I covered every inch of his torso. If I weren't careful, I would end up pregnant, because I honestly couldn't get enough of Raven Davenport.

Before I knew it, he had me stripped down to my bra and panties. Raven's lips devoured my flesh as he kissed and sucked on my neck. My fingers splayed across his broad chest as I kneaded his smooth, tanned skin, unable to get enough of him. His fingers danced across my stomach and my body quivered in excitement. That was when it occurred to me. I was on my period. And he knew it.

"Um, Raven." I squirmed underneath his body, unsure whether I wanted to have sex while I was bleeding. "Did you forget that I'm on my period?"

Slowly, his lips stopped and he took in a long breath. "No. I just thought we could mess around. Unless that makes you uncomfortable." His hand glided up the inside of my thigh and my back arched into him. The teasing was killing me.

I wanted him.

All of him.

Not tomorrow.

Not in five days.

Now.

"We can do that," I whimpered in a low voice.

"I promise I won't touch you there, unless you want me to." His hardness pressed against me and I lost all self-control. Raven knew how to supercharge my body and I decided it was time I explore the unknown side of me.

"How about I pleasure you? Ya know... take some of that stress away that's been beating you down all week?" I stroked the side of his head, gliding my nails through his hair. With deliberate intent, I licked my lips and prepared myself to do what I had read in my romance books, even though I had no idea how to do it.

"Only if you want to, baby." Raven studied my face carefully, as if searching for the true answer.

"Let me show you how much I want to." I flipped him on his back and willingly threw myself into The Raven's trap, diving in headfirst.

Raven and I slept for what seemed like eternity, trying to rejuvenate our bodies and minds. Being wrapped in his arms restored everything, eroding the doubt, fear, and pain that taunted my mind. I gave him everything he needed and more, even though he asked for nothing. I love him and I wanted to him know it.

Feel it.

Never doubt it.

Slowly, I began to open my heart, exposing myself to him and praying that he wouldn't break my heart again. I had been through so much, I wasn't sure my heart would mend the next time. I had to take that leap of faith. Even though I had no idea how it would turn out, I knew Raven Davenport was worth it.

I didn't push him to watch the bowl game, but, to my surprise, he wanted to. I think he did it mainly to support Josh and Shawn. We even invited Luke and Delaney to come over. At first, I wasn't sure it was a good idea, but we had a good time. Raven and Luke seemed to be fine, and I was excited to hear that my brother agreed to train with him later that week. It reaffirmed that he was on his way to recovery — not only physically, but mentally. Having a good attitude and owning up to your mistakes are part of the battle and Raven faced them head on with determination.

PHU beat their opponent by a Hail Mary pass thrown by the second string quarterback, Kyle Reeves, in the last fifteen seconds of the game. Josh caught the ball and ran it in for the winning touchdown after Shawn hurt his ankle in the third quarter. We were all relieved to hear it was just a bad sprain. The game was so exciting. I never realized how much I enjoyed football over baseball. It made me happy that he supported his teammates, even though he didn't get to play. It was hard for him, but he did it. And I was so proud of him.

Wednesday arrived quicker than we expected and Raven was faced with his next challenge — meeting with the academic dean and the ethics committee. The fate of his career was in the hands of these people. Coach Anderson informed him that he would be present and not only would they decide if Raven would remain on the football team, but also if he would be allowed to remain enrolled at PHU. If they kicked him out of school, then he couldn't play. The situation was more serious than I had thought.

Raven had met with Mr. Marshall on Monday for advice on the situation. I was slightly disappointed when I found out that he refused to press charges against Jared. When I asked him why, he told me that he had done some things in the past for Jared that he wasn't proud of and if he brought him down, he'd go down, too. He said Mr. Marshall advised him to leave Jared out of it and move forward. It bothered me, but I did press him further for details. I just did everything to keep him in good spirits. We had to stay positive and believe that they would give him one more chance.

"Everything is going to be all right, man. Trust me." Josh hooked an arm around Raven's neck. "Just be honest with them. They'll see that it was a slip and that you're going to keep on the right track."

Raven stared at the floor, his face tense and body stiff. "I know. Your uncle feels that they will believe me and I'll get another chance."

Josh patted Raven on the chest and squeezed him in a tight hug. "That's right. You're going to be back on the field for spring training. Mark my words."

Shelby flashed me a wide-eyed look and I shot her a meek smile. I hoped Josh was right. Rumors were flying sky-high, but we did our best to ignore them. Some were in favor of PHU keeping Raven while others felt he'd had his chance. It was fifty-fifty and only God knew what would be decided.

I handed Raven his suit jacket. "We better go. You don't want to be late."

He glanced at his watch. "Yeah, that wouldn't be good."

Josh grabbed his keys from the coffee table.

"What are you doing?" Raven asked as he put his jacket on.

"I'm driving you up there. We're going to wait with Lexi and your mom. Is that's okay?"

"I think that's a good idea." Trish adjusted Raven's tie and then straightened his collar, making sure her son looked acceptable.

"Sure. I guess I need all the support I can get."

"It never hurts." Trish leaned forward and pressed a kiss to Raven's cheek. He embraced her and we all stood in silence. The love they shared was obvious. A part of me was a little envious that he had that type of relationship with his mother. It was something I longed for, but doubted I would ever have.

Josh dropped us off at the Wilson building where the admission's offices were located. We entered the renovated building and took the stairs to the second floor. Raven held on to my hand the entire way, gripping it tightly for support. I felt the nervous vibe through the tiny tremors of his hand and the sweat that lined his palm, but I didn't care. He needed me and I wasn't letting go. I wanted to hold him in my arms, stroke his hair, and tell him not to worry about anything.

Our heels hit the granite-tiled floor, slicing through the dead silence. It sent shivers down my spine, and I imagined what Raven felt like walking to the chamber of doom. I shook my head, not allowing my own demons to take over.

Mr. Marshall and Steve were waiting in the hallway along with Shaw, Luke, and Delaney.

Shawn hooked an arm around Raven and patted him on the chest. "Don't worry, man. I've got a good feeling about this."

"I hope you're right." Raven cracked a half-smile.

"Good morning," Mr. Marshall said in his deep, southern accent.

"Hello." Trish extended her hand. "Thank you so much for helping my son. It means a lot to me... to us." Her voice squeaked and she quickly wiped the area under her eyes.

"No worries." Mr. Marshall gave her a hefty shake. "I care about your son. He's a good kid and I want to see him succeed. He has a bright future ahead of him."

"We will pay you back. It might take me a while to do it, but I promise I will pay you for every penny of your time."

"Nonsense." The attorney waved off her comment. "You owe me nothing. I believe in giving back to the community and those in need. God always seems to reward me more when I do that. Besides, this is my Alma Mater. We need this guy." He patted Raven on the back.

Ahh... so the attorney did have an agenda. Lucky for us, he was on Raven's side.

"Well, I don't know what to say...thank you." She hugged the big man and he hugged her back. Turning to Steve, she shook his hand. "Thank you so much. I appreciate it."

"You're welcome." Steve adjusted his glasses and his eyes glazed over. "Raven's a good guy."

"Well, son, you ready to get this show on the road?" Mr. Marshall adjusted his purple and white bow tie, sporting the school colors.

Turning toward Raven, I said, "Good luck, babe. I know everything is going to work out for the best." I placed a soft kiss on his lips.

"Thanks, baby. Thank you for everything." He hugged me and then gave me a long kiss. Every emotion rolled from that kiss to me, and I took it all in. This guy really loved me. And he needed me more than he knew. My heart swelled, overfilled with my emotions and his. I swallowed hard, determined not to cry in front of him.

He released me and then faced his mom. "Thanks, Mom, for being here. I love you."

"Love you, too."

They hugged for a moment and Raven kissed her forehead.

Trish patted his chest and pulled away. "Stay strong, son."

"I will."

"Good luck." Luke shook Raven's hand.

"Thanks for being here," Raven replied in a sincere tone. It brought a smile to my face. Having my brother's support meant a lot to me. Maybe because he was the only family I had that was truly on my side.

With a deep breath, Raven rolled his shoulders. "Let's do this."

Steve opened the door and they walked into the boardroom.

The heavy oak door shut and I backed against the wall, plopping into a chair. I closed my eyes and prayed for the best.

Σ

Chapter 6

The door opened and a bellow of chattering resonated from inside the stately room. My heart thundered with a vengeance as I stood, my shaky legs threatening to plant me back in the chair. Trish grabbed my arm as she pulled herself up from the bench next to me, nearly pulling me down. Delaney stepped beside me, with one hand supporting my back as Luke, Josh, Shelby, and Shawn gathered in the hallway. We waited for the verdict.

Mr. Marshall and Steve exited the room first, there expression seeming positive. It gave my heart a bit of relief. I stood on the tips of my toes, looking past the gentleman for Raven. Slowly, he descended from the meeting. He met my gaze and I immediately knew the outcome — the expression on his face said it all. I ran to him and he lifted me in his arms.

"They're giving me another chance." The words echoed in my ears as he spun me around.

"Oh, babe, that's wonderful!" I squealed as I planted kisses all over his face. "What about the team?"

He steadied himself and then placed me back on my feet. "I can still play."

"You can?" Excitement bubbled inside of me.

"Yep!"

"Oh, Raven, I'm so happy for you!" I kissed him again and then our family and friends bombarded us with hugs and cheers. It was definitely the news we needed to hear and the third chance he needed. Despite all of Raven's faults, he did deserve another chance.

"Thank you, Mr. Marshall." Raven shook the attorney's hand. "For everything."

Mr. Marshall patted Raven on the back with his other hand. "Don't worry about it, son. Just stay clean, follow the rules I told you and Lexi about, and use your common sense for Pete's sake."

"Yes, sir." Raven nodded. "Got them embedded right here," he said, tapping the side of his head.

"We appreciate your help." I smiled, giving the attorney my heartfelt gratitude. Even though I didn't care for his rawness, I couldn't detest his genuine care for Raven's wellbeing.

Mr. Marshall's eyes softened. "My pleasure. Just keep this boy in line. I need his ass on that field come fall."

I pressed my hand to Raven's chest while looking him in the eyes. "Don't worry, I will."

"I know you will." Raven kissed my forehead. "Hey, I think this calls for a celebration!"

"It better be food and sodas." The attorney eyed Raven with a cocked brow. "I just got you out of this mess, I don't need you in another one."

"Speaking of the mess, is it true? Will Raven remain on the team?" The same school reporter that demanded answers outside of the athletics office last week was stalking us again.

Raven looked at Mr. Marshall and then Steve, as if waiting for their advice. Steve turned to the attorney with raised brows and a knowing stare. The attorney gave a slight nod.

The reporter inched her phone closer to Raven, obviously not giving up. "What were the results from the meeting?"

"If we give you an exclusive press release with some detailed information, privy only to you, will you leave Mr. Davenport alone?" Mr. Marshall lowered the girl's hand.

"Will it be different than what is sent to the general media?" The cute blonde retrieved her hand and rested it on her hip. For a small, petite girl, she was ballsy.

"Yes."

"How soon can I get it?" She kept a straight face, not faltering from her request.

Mr. Marshall cast a glance at Steve. "What do you think?"

Steve stuffed some brown folders into his briefcase and then rolled the sleeves of his shirt back. "Is two hours sufficient?"

"Yes. That will work." The journalist's hard expression turned into a smile and her blue eyes sparkled with content. "Here's my card with my email address." She handed it to Steve.

"Thank you, Miss Presley." He tucked the card in the pocket of his shirt. "I'll make sure to send it to you."

"Thank you." She gave us a quick onceover and then turned on her heels and walked down the hall.

"Lunch anyone?" Raven asked, apparently keeping Mr. Marshall's rules in mind.

"Yeah, I'm starving." Shawn rubbed his stomach in a circle for emphasis while keeping an eye on the journalist as she descended the stairs. By the hunger in his eyes, I was willing to bet he wanted more than just food. I waited for him to sprint after her, but he didn't.

"You kids go ahead." Mr. Marshall pulled off his bowtie, followed by his suit jacket. "Steve and I have some catching up to do at the office." He folded his coat over his forearm and handed Steve his tie. "Raven, I'll touch base with you later in the week."

"Okay." Raven laced his fingers through mine and guided us toward the stairs.

"Thank you again, Mr. Marshall." Trish shook his hand as they walked beside us. "I don't know how I'll ever repay you for all that you've done."

"Like I said, no need to." Mr. Marshall chuckled. "Just take care of your son and keep him on that field. That's the best way to pay me back."

"I'm more than happy to do that," Trish said in a high-pitched voice that indicated signs of happy tears. She latched on to Raven's other arm and we descended the stairs.

We walked out of the building and into the bright sunlight and chilly air.

"Where do you guys want to eat?" Raven shielded his eyes with his hand.

"It doesn't matter to me." Luke pulled his keys from his pocket and turned to Delaney. "What about you?"

"Whatever y'all decide is fine with me."

"There's an Italian restaurant over by the soccer fields." Josh hooked his arm around Shelby. "We ate there a few weeks ago and it was good."

Raven looked at me and then at his mom. "How does that sound?"

Trish nodded, giving her approval, while I said, "Works for me."

"We'll go get the car and pick you guys up," Josh said.

"We can walk." Trish took a step forward.

"Are you sure? I had to park several buildings away," Josh said, motioning with his hand. "It's a little chilly."

Trish wrapped her jacket around her thin frame. "I guess we can wait here."

"It won't take long." Josh started to jog off when Shelby said, "Wait up, I'm coming with you."

"We'll meet you guys there." Luke tossed his keys in the air and caught them singlehandedly. "Come on, let's go." He grabbed Delaney by the hand and she waved bye. The mischief in her eyes told me they might be arriving late.

Trish sat on a bench and motioned for us to join her. Raven slid next to her and I sat next to him. "I couldn't have asked for a better turnout." Raven extended his arms behind us and squeezed us simultaneously.

"Me either." I pressed my lips to his for a quick kiss.

"Son, I'm really happy for you." Trish placed her hand on his leg and gave him a soothing pat. "But, I'd like to know what they said. I'm sure they laid down some stipulations."

Raven pulled his arms back and dropped his hands in his lap. He exhaled and his shoulders curved inward, making his head align in height with his mom's and mine. "Yeah, they did."

Trish leaned closer to her son. "Well, what did they say?"

Raven twiddled his thumbs and his right leg shook, tapping against my thigh. I'd never seen Raven react in this manner. Either he didn't want to tell his mom what had been decided or he was having some serious reservations about it.

"Is everything okay?" I placed my hand on his arm. "You don't have to be afraid or embarrassed to tell us."

"Please don't shut us out, Raven." Trish patted his leg repeatedly. "We're here to support you."

"I know that," he responded in a curt tone.

Trish raised her head and motioned for me to stay calm behind his back. We had to be careful about what we said and how we said it. The last thing we wanted was for him to close down and wind up right back where he used to be. We had to keep those inner demons on a leash until he could get rid of them for good.

I moved my hand to his back and rubbed up and down gently, showing my support in a small gesture.

He covered his face with his hands and slid them down slowly. He straightened his body and took a deep breath. "Sorry. I didn't mean to bite your heads off. It's not easy admitting to your mom and your girlfriend that you can't get your shit together without a shrink helping you."

It made sense and I completely understood why he was embarrassed to tell us. Not everyone likes to seek professional advice to overcome a problem or addiction. But Raven honestly needed it; his demons were too much for him to handle on his own. I moved my hand to his arm. "It's okay, Raven, many people—"

"Oh, that's great, honey." Trish sounded enthusiastically ecstatic about his revelation, cutting me off mid-sentence. "Do you have to pay for it?"

"What?" Raven turned toward her, not sounding as happy.

"Seeing a therapist is very expensive." She clutched her purse close to her body. "I know."

Raven's head jutted back. "What do you mean you know? Have you seen a therapist?"

She nodded, not making eye contact with him. "Several times."

"And did it help?"

She pursed her lips together, as though withholding information. Based on what I knew about her, I knew why she had seen a therapist. I felt for her and Raven. My life was not perfect and I definitely had my own issues, but when you think you have it bad, someone else always has it worse.

Turning toward him, she said, "It did and it still does. When I have a little extra money, I go see my therapist. She's helped me deal with my problems."

Raven leaned against the bench and rolled his shoulders a few times, as if trying to shake off his mother's confession. "You never told me."

"It's not something you want to tell your kids, especially when you're their sole provider and the head of the house."

His head snapped in her direction. "Then you know how I feel. Being a guy, I should be able to deal with my problems and learn how to overcome them, not have someone solve them for me."

"But I had to learn that it isn't a sign of weakness." Trish cupped Raven's face with her palm. "Raven, whether you're a man or a woman, sometimes we aren't equipped to deal with what life throws at us. It has nothing to do with our determination, but how we learn to deal with those issues."

"Is that why you've tried to get me to seek help before?"

"Yes," she admitted, tears filling her eyes. "Not because I think you're weak or a failure... because I knew you weren't able to do it on your own." She shook her head. "Time and time again, you refused to listen to me, and I knew if you wouldn't do it on your own terms, it'd be a waste of time."

Raven remained silent for a moment, his upper body rising and falling in long strides. I wanted to see the expression on his face. Know what he was thinking. What demons he was fighting. Let him know that I'd be there to support and cheer for him as he worked on resolving those issues. That he didn't have to be embarrassed and I thought no less of him.

"That explains why the rehab didn't work," he muttered in a low voice.

My heart ached and my body slumped against his. I wrapped my arms around him and silently cried for him on the inside. Raven had been too proud, too determined, to do it on his own, and that caused him to fail. If only he hadn't been so hardheaded, maybe he wouldn't be where he was today.

Ugh. Men.

She wiped his face with a tissue. "Please don't get mad about what I'm going to say."

He nodded, remaining silent. "If you don't come to terms with the fact that you need help from a professional, you will continue to battle this for the rest of your life. You're getting another chance, Raven, to finish your education, to play football — something you love dearly — and you've worked too hard not to see that dream come true. If you can just face the fact that you can't do it on your own, I know the counselor will be able to help."

Raven sniffed. "I know, Mom. I'm trying."

"Don't try. Just do it." She gave his face a little shake. "Focus all that determination on whatever that therapist recommends, whether it's advice, recommendations, tactics, or prayers. Because I know you can do it."

"I know I can." Raven turned around and took my hand, holding it tightly.

"Because if you don't, everything you've worked for will be for nothing. There won't be another chance, Raven."

"I know. They told me this was it. No more chances. I have to see a counselor weekly and submit to a drug test." He wiped his eyes with the back of his hand.

"That's not so bad," I reassured him.

"I don't know about you, but I don't like someone watching me piss in a cup."

I bit my lip. I hadn't thought about the humiliation associated with the testing. "At least it's just one time."

He cast me dubious stare. "It's weekly. And I'll also have random breathalyzer tests."

"But you're not an alcoholic."

"Tell them that." He rolled his eyes. "All they see are the medical reports and assume if I'm drinking, then I'm doing drugs."

I brushed away a few pieces of lint that had fallen onto his shoulder from the tissue. "Then you'll just have to prove them wrong." I hoped to God that I was right and he was willing to follow through with their requests. He was at their mercy.

"I know. And don't worry." He tucked my hair behind my ear. "I'm not going to let either of you down. I want to do this. I'll see that therapist and allow them to help me this time."

Hearing those words were like hitting every right chord on the piano. I suddenly had a dying urge to take Raven and play every happy song for him as we sang at the top of our lungs.

He turned toward me, eyes red and glossy from crying. I wanted to kiss every tear that he'd ever shed. Kiss him until he felt nothing and had no remembrance of whatever had pulled him to the ground. My heart swelled, overcome by the problems he had faced, and the pain he'd endured. I knew with the help of his therapist he would win.

We would win.

I smiled as tears dripped from eyes. "I love you and I'm going to be right here, by your side, every step of the way."

"You promise?"

"With all my heart."

"Good. Because I want you with me. It's all or nothing, baby."

"Then you have all of me."

Σ

Chapter 7

We had a great lunch, celebrating the success of Raven's news. I could tell Raven was well on his way to accepting what he had to do. The way he talked to his friends, it was obvious football was in his blood. It was his life. And if he wanted it, then he was going to have to swallow his pride and allow a therapist to help him. The part that made me the happiest was that he wanted me by his side, and I knew that I was equally as important to him. It was all I ever wanted and asked for from any guy.

The question was — would it last?

I was relieved that his mom had asked him those tough questions. I wasn't sure if he would've completely opened up and told me everything. Something inside of me hinted that there was a little more to the story.

"I'll call you later, Mom." Raven opened the car door for Trish.

"You better," she warned, using her index finger for emphasis. "Lexi, make sure he's on time for his first appointment."

"I will," I assured her.

Raven closed the car door and we waved to her as she drove off. Josh darted past us as he chased Shelby in the parking lot. She giggled, playing hard to get before he scooped her into his arms. Seeing the way they interacted with each other was cute, but sometimes it was a little much. Were they always that happy? In the time I'd spent at Raven's, I never saw them fight or get angry with one another. I wanted to know what their recipe to success was because Raven and I needed it.

Just as Trish exited the apartment complex, a silver car that looked like my dad's entered the parking lot. I started to turn when I did a double take.

"Come on." Raven pulled on my hand, but I didn't budge.

"Just a sec." I stared at the car, trying to get a better glimpse of the driver.

"What's wrong?" Raven looked at me and then followed my line of sight. "Who's that?"

"My dad." I shuffled my feet, unsure of whether to run inside and lock the door or run toward him. I hated getting pulled in two directions at once. Not only was it confusing but also heart wrenching.

"Shit. What's he doing here?" Raven squared his shoulders and puffed out his chest. His jaw tightened and his nostrils flared. He eased me behind him, clearly trying to protect me.

The car stopped a few feet in front of us. My dad rested his hands on top of the steering wheel and leaned forward, looking at us through the front windshield. His face looked sad and my heart ached, wishing things had been different between us. If only they would have handled the situation like adults, none of this would have happened.

"I don't know."

"Do you want me to tell him to leave?"

I shook my head. Was he here to tell me he was sorry? Did he want us to have a father-daughter relationship? I had to find out. Not only did I owe it to myself, but to him as well. "No, let me see what he wants."

"Are you sure?"

"Yes." I eased from behind him. "But if he tries to pull me in the car, you better save me. I'm not going back home."

Raven took my hand and pulled me next to him. "Don't worry," he traced his finger down my cheek, "I won't let him take you. Not this time."

"You promise?" I stared into his eyes, searching for the answer I wanted to hear most. "Because you didn't come for me last time."

"Lexi, I promise I'll never let you out of my life." Raven closed his eyes and pulled me close. Enveloped tightly in his arms, he pressed his lips to my forehead. Through that one kiss, he transferred every care, all his concern, and most of all, the love he had for me. I knew he would never let me go again.

"Let me see what he wants," I muttered against his chest. "I'll be right back."

Raven released me, but kept a firm grip on my hand. I moved forward, keeping ahold of his hand until his fingers slipped from my reach. I straightened as I approached my dad's car, but with each step I took, my feet seemed to get heavier. I broke out in a cold sweat despite the cold air that blew across my face and swept through my hair. I told myself I had nothing to be afraid of, but the images of how he pulled me into the house when Raven took me home were all too recent.

"Hey, Josh!" Raven yelled as I walked toward my dad's car. I assumed Raven was preparing in case he had to swoop in and rescue me.

My dad remained in his car and it made me feel a little more at ease. He rolled down the window and rested his arm along the door. "Hey, princess."

At those words, my heart did a double beat and my eyes instantly watered. I blinked rapidly, trying to keep the tears at bay. I cleared my throat, hoping my emotions weren't going to give me away. "You haven't called me that in a long time."

"Maybe I should've never stopped." He smiled at me and then winked with his left eye; his signature expression that got me every time.

Instead of stopping at a safe distance, I found myself right at his door, wanting to feel his hugs — the only kind a daddy can give.

"Why did you?" I crossed my arms over my body, trying to hold myself together.

He stared at the ground for a moment before looking back at me. "I guess I thought you were too big for me to call you that."

Tears formed and I quickly sniffed them away. "I'll never be too big for that name."

"Good, because I'd really like to call you that more often." He inclined his head toward me and I felt horrible about everything. I knew my dad all too well. He did whatever it took to appease my mom, but I couldn't help but wonder why he never stood his ground. Her ways weren't always right, regardless of whether she thought it was to protect us. "Do you think we could go somewhere and talk for a while?"

I nodded and smiled at him. "Sure. Give me just a minute." I dried my tear-streaked face with my palms and walked back toward Raven.

Raven hadn't moved from his position, keeping a keen eye on my dad and me. Josh stood next to him with Shelby behind him. "Is everything okay?"

"Yeah. I'm going to go with him so we can talk. I'll be back later."

Raven eyed me suspiciously. "Are you sure?"

"Yes." I let out a long breath I hadn't realized I'd been holding. "I'll be fine. I really do want to talk to him."

Uncrossing his arms, Raven relaxed his shoulders. "Do you want me follow you in my car?"

A low laugh escaped my lips. Raven really was trying to protect me and it was so sweet. "No, it's okay. I've got my phone and some money." I held up my wristlet. "I'm good."

Raven turned to Josh and he shrugged. Then he stepped up to me. "Okay. Let me know if I need to come get you."

"I will."

We exchanged a kiss and then I walked back to my dad's car and got in, noticing a huge stack of clothes in the back seat.

"Ready?" Dad smiled at me as I clicked my seatbelt.

"Yes." I smiled at him, feeling the dryness of the tears that had stained my face. "What's with all the clothes?" I turned around and noticed they were my clothes along with a couple of bags.

"You didn't take much with you, so I had Luke help me gather a few of your things."

"More like my whole closet." I reached over and shuffled through them. "Thanks." In all honesty, a part of me was glad that I wouldn't have to go home to get my belongings, but another part kind of felt sad. Like my dad was confirming the fact that my mom disowned me.

"You're welcome. So, where to? Do you want to get something to eat?"

I adjusted the strap across my chest. "Well, I already ate."

"Okay. We can go to the mall, or —"

"Dad, you hate shopping," I reminded him.

He waved off my comment. "I know, but this is about you. Not me."

I reached for his hand and he took my hand in his. "No, it's about us."

His eyes glistened and the wrinkles around his eyes appeared. At that moment, I hadn't realized how much my dad had aged. Silver framed his face, his dark hair quickly turning a salt and pepper color. He and Luke looked so much alike, but his bright blue eyes they shared were now a paler blue.

"You're right, it is." He squeezed my hand. "I don't care where we go, I'd just like to spend some time with my baby girl."

The threat of tears inundated me once more. I took a deep breath, pushing the emotion back. "How about we go to the duck pond down the road?"

"Like the one I used to take you and Luke to when you were little?"

"Yes."

"Sounds perfect." Dad shifted the car into drive and we circled around the parking lot. I gave a small wave to Raven to let him know that everything was okay. I watched him for a moment, waiting to see if he was going to follow us, but we turned onto the street and Raven disappeared from my view. I knew I had nothing to worry about; my dad was trying to mend things between us. And for that, I was grateful.

We stopped at the corner store and bought a loaf of bread before going to the park. Luckily, there were some Mallard ducks floating in the water, catching the afternoon sunrays. We sat on a nearby bench and opened the bread.

"I saw the press conference last week. How is Raven taking everything?" Dad handed me a few slices.

Wow.

My dad had actually been following PHU football? That was a first for him, since he was a huge baseball fan — living and breathing baseball while encouraging Luke to do the same.

"As good as he can, I guess." I tossed a few pieces into the water. "I mean... he was disappointed that he didn't get to play in the bowl, but he did meet with the academic board today."

Dad popped his head in my direction. "He did? What happened?"

I hesitated for a second, wondering how much information I should divulge. Remembering the media would be featuring his story by the end of the day, I figured my dad would find out regardless. "It was good. They're going to allow him to play."

"That's great news." An appeasing smile appeared across his lips. "I'm happy for him."

I froze, holding a piece of bread midair. Had I heard my dad correctly? Something had definitely changed. He sounded like he was rooting for *Team Raven*, taking an opposing side to my mom's quest for *Team Collin*.

"Seriously?" I lowered my arm.

A low chuckle filtered through my dad's smile. "Look, Lexi, I've come to realize that you're going to see Raven whether we approve of him or not." His smile turned serious and he inched closer toward me. "I just want the best for you and if being with him makes you happy, then I guess I have to accept it."

"What about mom?" I took a tough swallow, feeling the tightness in my throat. "Does she agree with you?"

Dad looked away, keeping a steady eye on the ducks pooling around the edge of the pond. He tossed a few more pieces of bread into the water. "No. Unfortunately not."

"She doesn't know you're here with me, does she?"

He shook his head. "Just because your mother is being hardheaded doesn't mean we can't talk."

My throat relaxed. He was right. And I was glad that he was finally doing what he knew was right, despite what my mom was probably telling him. "Thanks, Dad. That means a lot to me."

"I'm sorry, Lexi. I'm sorry that I didn't stand up for you and that I allowed your mom to take over. It's just that... well, it's a long story. One you don't need to worry about. You have to understand that you're my daughter and I want what's best for you, in any form that may be. I know we're not perfect and we all have our faults, but I applaud for you being there for Raven. Sticking by his side through his tough times shows me how selfless you really are and what you must feel for this guy. So, if you choose to be with him, I accept that."

"Oh, Dad, thank you!"

My dad's eyes watered and he hesitated for a moment before leaning forward and gathering me in his arms. I embraced him, holding on to him like never before. His arms comforted me, just like when I was little. It was an affection I could never forget. I needed my dad's support. Being with Raven was tough at times and I knew it would take a lot of perseverance as I walked with him down his winding path. Having a parent by my side would make it easier for me.

"I love you, princess. Don't you ever forget it."

"I love you, too, Dad." Tears flooded my eyes and it felt so good to finally let go of all that negative energy.

"Looking back, I understand why you didn't approve of me being with him. From the outside, Raven doesn't appear to be the right one for me. He has a past, as you know, and still struggles with walking the right path, but he cares for me and shows me how it feels to be loved. Collin never did that. I couldn't be with a guy that was afraid to show me how he felt about me, much less marry him. With Raven, there's no question. I don't doubt his love for me."

"Then why did he break up with you and go and get drunk and drugged up?"

"He only got wasted because Mom convinced him that he wasn't right for me. He drank to forget about the pain of leaving me and while he was drunk, someone slipped a pill in his drink."

Dad narrowed his eyes. "Are you sure he's —"

"I know. At first, I thought it was a lie. But when his friend showed me a picture, that someone happened to take, of a guy dropping a few pills in his drink, I knew Raven was telling me the truth. Someone drugged him, purposefully. He did consume too much alcohol, but he didn't take those pills intentionally. He's been trying really hard to stay clean and... well, I want to help him do that."

"You've chosen a difficult task, Lexi." Dad kept my hands in his and the warmth made me feel so safe, as if he truly understood everything I was facing and wouldn't make me face it alone.

"I know."

"Just answer one thing. Do you love him that much?"

I looked my dad straight in the eye. Knowing what was written on my heart and embedded deep within my soul, I wasn't afraid to admit the truth. "I do, Dad. I love every part of him."

"Then I'll be here to support you." He pulled out his handkerchief and handed it to me. "I swear, you nor your mom ever have a tissue when you need one."

"Thank you, Dad." I blotted my face and wiped my nose.

"So, will you introduce me to him?"

"I guess." I started to pull my phone out of my wristlet when my dad stopped me.

"How about we just cross the street?" He cast an all-knowing look.

"What?" I glanced at my dad and then to the opposite side of the street. At the restaurant that faced the duck pond, was Raven's car. He had followed us after all.

"Either he really cares about you or he doesn't trust me with you."

I laughed. "He didn't want to lose me, that's all."

"Well, he hasn't." Dad grabbed my hand and pulled me to my feet. "Let's go assure him that you're not going anywhere but home with him."

Σ

Chapter 8

Introducing Raven to my dad went better than expected. At first, I didn't know if Raven was going to be amiable toward him, especially after everything that happened, but he seemed excited to finally meet him. And my dad seemed to approve of him. They chatted about Star Wars and The Walking Dead, both excited for the next season to launch in February. I figured Raven would eventually pull me in. Even though I didn't care to watch a show about the end of times with the revived on a man-eating quest for intestines and brains, if sharing my life with Raven included that, I'd happily oblige.

Raven held the door open as we entered the Baxter Building, where the financial aid offices and counselors were located. I had to apply for graduation and I also wanted to discuss my options regarding my degree. I wanted to discuss changing my minor and I hoped it wasn't too late. Purposefully, I had scheduled my appointment fifteen minutes after Raven had to be at his first session with the appointed school therapist. I reasoned with myself that it wasn't about trust; it was about doing my part. It was about being there for him; being his accountability partner and making sure he made it to his meeting on time.

We walked up the flight of stairs and Raven stopped. "Aren't the degree counselor's on this floor?"

"Yes, but my appointment isn't until ten forty-five." I grabbed the railing and placed my foot on the next step, leading up to the third floor. "I'll walk with you to your appointment."

He eyed me for a moment and his face turned hard. He pursed his lips together while gripping the strap of his backpack until the calluses on his knuckles smoothed. Passing me, he said, "I don't need an escort." Taking the steps two at a time, he darted to the top.

"Raven." I stomped after him, calling his name repeatedly, but he ignored me. "Don't be mad."

He paused when he reached the top of the stairs. A few students were behind us and we stepped aside, allowing them to pass. In a gentle fashion, I placed my hand on his arm. "The last thing I want is for you to think I'm watching you like a parent or a policeman. I'm not. I'm just here to support you. That's all."

He slumped against the wall and tilted his head back. Clenching his hands into fists, he closed his eyes. He took several deep breaths and I could tell he was battling something inside.

A past hurt.

A torment.

Something that I had to allow him to deal with because I couldn't do it for him. I took a few steps back, keeping a safe distance. The last thing I wanted was to come between him and his demons.

"I'll leave if that's what you want," I said in a low voice. "I was only trying to help." I turned to go down the stairs when his hand pulled me back.

"Don't go. I'm sorry," he whispered, his eyes pleading for my forgiveness.

It took a second for me to shove past his hurtful comment, but I did. Raven needed me and I would keep my promise, no matter what he said or did. "Why is it so hard to let me in? I only want to help you."

The green in his eyes turned a darker shade and his face stone hard. "You don't want in, believe me. My mind can be a cold, dark place. Not a place for someone innocent like you."

I swallowed — hard. It hurt hearing how tormented his mind was and I couldn't even fathom what it was like for him; how much pain and despair he encountered on a daily basis.

What he thought.

What he experienced.

What he fought.

What made him give in, time and time again.

"The only place I want in is right here." I placed my hand on his heart. "If we can get your heart healed, then I know it can heal whatever torments your mind. His body shifted and then relaxed under my touch. He released an audible breath as though pushing past the vice that kept his heart guarded and protected. "I'm not asking you to tell me those horrid thoughts, just open your heart to allow me in and love me."

"I do love you." He smiled and his eyes flickered a lighter shade.

"Then let me stand by your side. All I want is for you to get better."

He latched onto my hand and raised it to his lips, pressing a soft kiss to my palm. Slowly, his eyes met mine.

"This isn't going to be easy for me, Lexi. The last thing I want is to disappoint you or hurt you again."

"That's the last thing I want, too. But I'm going to keep my promise."

"At what point will you see that I'm not worth that promise?"

My nose stung and the muscles around my vocal cords tightened, but I refused to cry. It pained me to hear him talk about his life that way. That he wasn't worth much. Just like that day at the restaurant when he tossed that paper napkin to the side. Raven had treated his life with a nonchalant and carefree attitude that scared me. But I had to be strong — strong for Raven.

"Never. You're worth it, no matter what you put us through."

I couldn't deny that there was another side of his comment that made me weary.

The trust factor.

As much as I refused to think negatively, he'd laid it out for me in vivid colors — I might end up getting hurt in the end. Despite how much he wanted to do this, he couldn't hold to his promises. I appreciated the honesty, but it was working in the opposite direction of trust.

"But you don't deserve to be hurt anymore," he said, his eyes boring into mine, as if trying to gauge my honesty. I held my gaze steady to his, not flinching and definitely not blinking. I was being one-hundred-percent honest and I wanted him to see it. Even though I knew my heart couldn't handle another break, I was willing to stick through it. I only hoped that it resulted with me being by his side forever.

"And neither do you. So, you do your part and I promise I'll do mine."

"How did I get so lucky?" He pulled me closer, embracing me tightly, like he never wanted to let me go. I prayed that he didn't.

I shrugged. "You must be on God's special list. I'll tell you that."

He chuckled and a full smile brightened his eyes. This was definitely the Raven I loved to see. "I guess."

"C'mon." He latched on to my hand. "I don't want to be late."

We walked down the hall until we arrived at a door marked *The Center for Behavioral Counseling*. A list of names, followed by credentials, indicated who occupied the clinic. Raven's eyes traveled past the wording and then landed on me. I knew what he was thinking.

"Give it a chance."

He nodded, took a deep breath, and then opened the door. We entered the quaint office decorated in cool colors of light blue, green, and purple, which created an emotionally appealing atmosphere. Pictures of beach houses lined the walls and fresh flowers created a burst of sunshine. A student wearing glasses and a button up peach cardigan, greeted us. She was the poster child for a typical wanna-be therapist with subtle makeup and her hair in a tight bun. "Hello. Can I help you?"

Raven stalled for a moment and I gave him a gentle nudge. "Yes, I'm here to meet with Dr. Galen."

The dark headed girl gave a friendly smile that made her eyes narrow. "Your name, please?"

"Raven," he cleared his throat, "Davenport."

She stalled for a second and then adjusted her glasses, taking a few seconds before she continued with her tasks. Her finger looked like it had a mind of its own as it did several rapid clicks with the mouse. "Please, have a seat. I'll let him know you're here," she said with a little too much enthusiasm — vibrancy I wished Raven had and not her. The last thing he needed was another girl after him, especially at his therapist office.

"Thanks." Raven seemed oblivious to his hormone-inducing-scent and walked over to a row of chairs. I followed him, placing a hand on his lower back, just below the band of his jeans, letting the girl know that only my hands were allowed on him. Instead of sitting, Raven shoved his hands in his pockets. "If you need to go, I understand." He kept a tight lip as his gaze darted between the door, the receptionist, and me. I wasn't sure if he was considering walking out but I wasn't leaving until he went in the back to see the therapist.

I glanced at the time on my phone. "I'm good." In a bold action, I took a step toward the door. "Unless you want me to leave?"

"No." He shook his head. "I just didn't want you to be late." His face contorted in a nervous smile and fear loomed in the blacks of his eyes. Hidden behind his alluring eyes was a strife that he refused to reveal, and it was winning. He was allowing it to slowly destroy him. I just hoped that this counselor knew how to pull it out before it was too late.

Before I could reassure him that he'd be okay, the student stood up and said, "Dr. Galen is ready to see you." She leaned on her desk, shifting her weight to the side as she tried to show her curvy figure and painted on pencil skirt. I shot her a disapproving gaze that made her sit down.

Raven froze for a moment and then blinked. An unfamiliar expression appeared across his face, almost like a prophetic word gave him the reassurance he needed. He leaned forward, until the tips of our noses touched. "Wait for me, in case I get done before you do." He pressed his lips to mine. "Okay?"

"Okay. I'll wait on the second floor." I puckered my lips to his, wanting to show the girl that his lips belonged on me — only me — but he pulled away too quickly, only allowing me a peck.

Raven walked toward the small corridor with a confident and determined stride that I hadn't seen in quite some time. "It's the second door on the left," the student said, pointing him in the right direction.

I immediately noticed the quick sweep of her gaze and the flush on her cheeks as she appraised Raven from head to toe, despite my efforts to show he was taken. My boyfriend might have been broken on the inside, but he wasn't broken on the outside. It reminded me that I was the luckiest girl in the world.

As I walked out of the therapist's office, I hoped the girl wouldn't cause any trouble for us. Seeing as Raven hadn't even seemed to notice her flirtatious attempts to capture his attention, I had to take that leap of faith and try to trust that he would do the right thing if she made any sexual propositions. It was obvious that I would never be able to control the way women looked at him, and I definitely didn't want to be the jealous type, so I'd have to learn to deal with it and appreciate that women wanted what was mine.

As I walked down the stairs and toward the academic counseling area, I thought about what I wanted. I'd reviewed a few of my options last night after I got home from meeting my dad. Part of me wished I would've talked about my decision not to pursue a teaching certification with him, but I figured I needed to take things slowly. He was just coming around. I didn't need any additional shock to change his mind.

The area swarmed with students — most of them probably trying to make last minute changes to their schedules or hoping to enroll. I was glad that I had scheduled my appointment online because it looked like the wait was an hour or longer. I stepped in the line for *Appointments Only.*

"Can I help you?" A guy behind the counter asked, rolling his eyes. The tension and chaos in the room made it obvious that he was overworked and tired of hearing complaints from students. The majority of the clerical positions were held by students working part-time as they attended school full-time. Kind of like what I had done in the Writing Lab. Thinking about that reminded me to call Dr. Phillips to see if I could start tutoring again.

"Yes, I have an appointment at ten forty-five with Mrs. Sheffield."

The guy sighed. "Name and student ID."

I wanted to tell him if he didn't wear such tight T-shirts with the words *Suck It* on the front then maybe he could breathe better, but I refrained. "Lexi Thompson." I pulled out my ID from my wristlet and handed it to him. He reviewed my information quickly and then swiped it through a card reader.

"They will call you when she's ready." He handed me my ID. "Next," he said, looking over my shoulder. The guy seemed miserable working his part-time job and it reaffirmed my decision not to be a teacher. Life was too short to be that unhappy. While I knew the job was probably a temporary one for him, it still sucked if he hated what he did. Which explained the message on his shirt.

I took a seat and waited for the counselor. I thumbed through my school paperwork, making sure I had everything in place, just in case I needed it. Seeing all the classes I'd already taken made me feel a little sad. This was my last semester at PHU. I would be graduating after four years of hard work. Never in a million years would I have thought things would've turned out like they did, but I was glad that I had made the decision to start living my life for me. More than anything, I was glad I wasn't getting married to someone I didn't love.

"Lexi Thompson," a short, heavyset woman called.

"Right here." I raised my hand and then scurried toward her. Thirty minutes had passed and I wanted to make sure I was done when Raven's session with his therapist ended. Not knowing what to expect from his appointment concerned me, especially after seeing how much he hesitated going into the session.

"Hi. I'm Susan Sheffield." She stuck out her short, chubby arm and I shook it.

"Nice to meet you." I shifted my folder to my left hand.

"Likewise. You're here to apply for graduation?" She glanced at a clipboard as she started down the hallway. I promptly followed her, placing my folder in my backpack.

"Yes and I want to discuss my minor."

"Oh, okay." She blew a few strands of straggling hair away from her face and cast me a doubtful look. I followed her into a small office and she shut the door. "Have a seat, please."

I sat on the cold, hard plastic chair and waited as she rounded her desk. Her chair creaked as she took the load off her feet and pulled closer to the desk. She unfolded the reading glasses hanging around her neck and perched them on the tip of her nose.

"May I see your ID?"

"Yes, of course." I fished the card from my pocket and handed it to her.

Positioned in front of her computer, she said, "Let's see if you qualify for graduation." Her fingers typed a string of characters along the keyboard in a slow and decisive manner. For half a minute, she scrolled through the screen, humming to herself in a low tone. I tried to pick out the tune, but it wasn't familiar.

As I waited for her to review my information, I retrieved my folder, ready to answer any questions or produce any documents necessary. "According to my records, I should already have thirty-three hours in English."

"Just a moment." She studied the computer screen before finally saying, "Yes. You are correct. To graduate, you just need to complete the two courses in Education and the one in Creative Writing. Has the professor for your student teaching class contacted you?"

"Um, yes, he has." I recalled seeing the email over Christmas break, but with everything that had happened, I hadn't given it much attention.

"Then you should be all set." She took off her glasses and plucked a tissue from a decorative box on the corner of her desk. Using her index finger and thumb, she cleaned the lenses. "So, I'll go ahead and approve you for graduation and you can pay the fee and be done."

"Thanks, but I wanted to discuss dropping my minor." My stomach tied into a tight knot and my palms moistened. Why was I so nervous? I was one-hundred percent certain I didn't want to teach.

She stopped cleaning her glasses. "But you're so close to being done. Why change now?" She stared at me and for a quick second, I swore it was my mother's eyes drilling into me.

Don't freak out. Don't freak out.

The lady couldn't possible understand my decision and she definitely didn't need to know what I had gone through. The muscles tightened around my vocal chords, but I managed to speak. "It's not really what I want to do."

Her eyes remained fixed on me and my entire body broke out in a cold sweat. I watched her mouth move, but all I heard was my mom's voice. Scolding me. Chastising me. Telling me that I would get that education degree so I could homeschool my kids — Collin's babies. I glanced around the room, wondering if she knew my family or Collin. Had Collin come to speak to her? Tell her that I had made a terrible mistake and that he was going to fight to get me back?

"Lexi?"

I snapped out of the horrid reverie and blinked several times. I was definitely freaked out.

"Darling, are you okay?" Mrs. Sheffield extended her arm, offering her hand for support. I kept my hands to myself, not wanting to disgust her with my sweaty palms. A wave of nausea rushed over me. I had to swallow several times before I lost my breakfast in her trashcan. "Do you need some water?" She rolled away from her desk and pulled a plastic water bottle from a stash sitting on the floor. With a concerned expression, she handed me the water.

"Thank you." I extended a shaky hand and took the water. My moist hands made it difficult to grip the small lid so I used the edge of my sweater to crack the seal. After several small sips, my racing heart calmed.

Mrs. Sheffield hesitated for a moment, as if trying to gauge the needle on my freak-o-meter before finally speaking. "I'm sorry if I said something that alarmed you. I know there are a lot of people that took the shooting at Pine Elementary really hard. If you knew anyone there, I'm terribly sorry for your loss."

At first, I had no idea what the lady was talking about. Then I recalled the incident. Right before Thanksgiving break, a shooting had occurred at a local elementary school. One of the teachers killed had graduated from PHU two years prior. I didn't know her, but it had left a somber mood over the campus. Since I was in my own world during that time, I hadn't joined in any candlelight vigils or prayer sessions. My tears over Collin were enough for me at the time, but my heart did cry for all the children and teachers who lost their lives in the shooting.

"Oh, um, well I didn't know anyone and my decision not to be a teacher has nothing to do with the shooting. It's something personal."

"I understand. If you want to drop your minor in education, that's perfectly fine." She turned to her computer. Her fingers typed at a much quicker speed than before and she clicked her mouse repeatedly. "We can drop you from those two classes and you will still have enough credit hours to graduate. In fact, you'll have enough hours for a minor in creative writing with the class you're registered for currently." She smiled, continuing to type and click away.

"Perfect. I'd prefer that." Relief settled my wacked-out nerves. "Can you make that change?"

"Yes. I'm doing that now. You'll be enrolled in fifteen hours, which will keep you at full-time student status."

Her printer started and it startled me. "Great."

"This should be an easy semester for you." She grabbed the paper from the printer and placed it in front of me. "Please review your degree plan with the hours earned and sign at the bottom."

I definitely need easy.

I reviewed the information and then signed the paper. "Thank you, Mrs. Sheffield."

"You're welcome, Lexi. If you need anything, call me." She handed me her business card and opened the door for me.

"I appreciate that." I thanked her and then walked out of her office.

My phone chimed and I retrieved it from my pocket as I hurried to the main area. I wondered if Raven was waiting for me. Before checking my messages, I saw that it was almost noon and I knew his appointment was only an hour long.

Raven: I'm headed to the gym. Need some time to myself.

Darn. I thought he would wait for me.

Me: Is everything okay?

I flew down the stairs and out the front door wondering if I could still catch him. While I respected his request for some space, I wanted to make sure he was mentally in check. I scanned the area, but he was nowhere in sight. I headed toward the parking lot behind the building, hoping I could meet up with him. As I cornered the building, I had full view of the parked cars, but the Charger wasn't there.

Damn.

Raven: I'll be fine. I just need some time to process a few things.

Me: Okay.

I hated to point out that I didn't have a car and while I didn't mind walking, the weather was quickly turning into a drizzly day with temperatures dropping. The cold air slapped me in the face and I zipped up my coat. Raven's apartment was a good mile away and having forgotten my hat and gloves, I wasn't prepared to walk. I thought about calling Delaney when I remembered there was something I had to do. I hooked my backpack on my shoulder and headed to the one place I kind of dreaded going, but knew I had to — the University Health Center.

Σ

Chapter 9

"Is he okay with you coming back to the dorm?" Delaney asked after Raven shut the door behind him.

"No, not really." I trudged to my room and looked at my duffle bags on the bed. I didn't feel like unpacking; mainly because a part of me wanted to stay with Raven, but the other part wanted a little space. Raven's counseling sessions wore not only on him, but me as well. His dramatic shifts in attitude gave me whiplash and to keep to my promise, I knew I had to do something. "He didn't want me to leave, but I told him it's just easier if I stay here on Monday and Wednesday nights since I have class at eight in the morning."

Delaney sat on my desk chair and swiveled around. "You might as well just move in with him."

"I can't do that." I unzipped one of my bags and pulled out a pile of folded clothes.

"Why not?" She popped her gum and then sucked it back into her mouth. "You've been staying there the past three weeks."

I looked over my shoulder. "It's too soon."

"But you said it yourself, he needs you. And I'm not just talking sexually, but for moral support."

Sighing, I said, "I know, but I realized he needs some space to himself. It's been kind of tough on both of us after he's had an intense counseling session. Knowing that I can come here, gives me back my sanity."

"It's been that rough?"

"It hasn't been a walk in the park." I stacked some shirts in my dresser and shut the drawer.

"Well, I'm glad you'll be staying here a few times a week. I've been totally binge watching Pretty Little Liars on Netflix since Luke has been at baseball practice around the clock. You'll have to catch up so you can watch the next season with me." Delaney continued turning around and around in the chair.

"If I have time. I've been tutoring again."

Delaney grabbed the desk, stopping her make-shift Spinnaker ride. "You have?"

"Yeah. I needed the experience and the extra money." I removed another pile of clothes from my bag and then placed them in another drawer.

"I thought your dad was depositing money into your account."

I had told Delaney about Dad and me making up and she was really happy for me. She didn't blame me for not calling my mom as my dad had wanted. I told him that she was the one that needed to apologize first, and until she did, I wasn't going to budge.

"He is, but editing papers is preparing me for an editing job. Besides, it's not fair that Raven pays for everything." I flipped through a mile-high pile of clothes on hangers and folded them over my arm.

"Wait a minute. You're not actually going to wear those are you?" She pointed to the clothes and darted toward me.

"Some of them are a couple of years old, but they're still in style."

"Uh, no. Maybe for Suzy Homemaker, but not for the new Lexi Thompson." Delaney gathered the stack of clothes from my arms and tossed them on the bed. She immediately rummaged through them while giving her diva-stamp-of-approval. "So, you really think you want to be an editor?"

"Yeah." I shrugged. "I really enjoy reading papers and correcting them. And you know how much I enjoy reading."

"Better you than me." She held up a plaid dress with ruffles around the neck. "Oh. My. God. Please tell me you didn't wear this!"

I snatched the dress from her hands. "It's really old. Like... ancient eighth grade old."

She laughed. "I bet you wore it for your pictures."

Pressing my lips together, I shoved it in a bag to return to my parent's house. I had worn it, but she didn't need to know that.

"Shit, you did." Delaney covered her mouth and shook her head.

"So what if I did. It was in style back then."

"Why the hell did you bring it here?"

"I didn't. I told you my dad brought me my entire closet, which apparently included all of my old stuff."

"Obviously." Delaney huffed. "Hey, did ya know that Raven has been working out with Luke?"

"Yes, they both told me." I smiled. It was a relief to see that Luke didn't have anything against Raven. I wasn't positive if Raven was doing it for approval or to get in shape, but I was glad they were spending time together. "He has to get ready for that scouting camp in a few weeks. Aside from that, he really needs the stress release."

"Aren't you supposed to be helping him with that?" Delaney arched a brow as she used her tongue to form a bubble in a sexual manner.

I threw a pair of socks at her. "Stop it!"

She blew air in the bubble until it popped and then cast me a wicked grin. "What? Just sayin'. I know you've been having mind blowing sex with him."

"Laney! What the hell? Are you reading my text messages or snooping through the trash at his apartment?"

"Gross." Her face twisted in disgust. "No. I just see it in the way you two act around each other. It's obvious. That's all."

My eyes went wide. "It's that obvious that we're having sex?"

"Yes and lots of it," Delaney deadpanned.

"What?" I leaned forward and tugged at the pants in her hand. "How do you know that?" Were Raven and I showing too much PDA? I always hated when couples sucked face in front of everyone. Or worse, had she heard something?

"Relax." She laughed. "I swear, you can be too serious at times."

I shrugged. "Sorry. I just don't want to be the talk of the school." Her lips twitched to the side and the look in her eyes told me she knew something that I didn't. "Laney, is there something you're not telling me?"

"No." She continued on her task of freeing me from my *good girl* clothes. "This really isn't any of my business, but..."

"But what?"

She hesitated for a few seconds. "I care about you, Lexi, so don't get mad when I say this."

"Just say it." I crossed my arms, feeling the tightness through my muscles. I braced myself for the worst. Delaney, unlike me, always seemed to be in the know. "Laney?"

"Are you using any protection?"

"Are you serious?" I dropped my arms to my side. "That's what you want to know?"

She cringed and her body pulled inward. "Sorry. I just don't want you to end up pregnant."

"Um, that won't happen." I hung a stack of Delaney-approved-clothes in my closet. "I went to the health center and got an IUD."

"Good, but why didn't you just get on the pill?"

"I thought about it, but since I'm not used to taking pills on a regular basis, I didn't want to forget and then screw myself." I grabbed a stack of clothes from her. "Do you ever forget to take them?"

"Every once in a while, so I just double up the next day." Her eyes wandered off and I sensed there was a story behind that faux pas. "But I try not to let that happen, because it's risky."

"And that's my point. With the IUD, I don't have to worry about it and the best thing is that it was immediately effective and will last for five years."

"Really? Damn. I should have done that."

"Look into it." I shoved more clothes into my closet, unsure how I'd ever fit everything into the tiny space.

"Maybe I will." She handed me another stack of clothes. "Because you know I can't resist that hot, sexy brother of yours."

I rolled my eyes and smiled. "I know. You remind me all the time."

"Do you think the counseling is helping Raven?"

"I've seen a little progress, but I think it's too soon to tell. After his first session, I didn't know if I'd be able to handle it. He pretty much ignored me the entire night and the next day, which is understandable, but it did make me feel out of place."

"How so?" She unzipped one of my bags and dumped everything onto my bed.

I sighed, but didn't have the heart to tell her that I wasn't planning on going through all my bags. "I mean that it's not my apartment."

"Oh, yeah. I see what you mean. Why don't you just hang out with Josh and Shelby when he's going through his issues?"

"I do, when they're there. But most of the time, they're locked in Josh's bedroom."

"Ha-ha. I bet." Delaney held up a light pink sweater to her chest. "This is hideous. You have to trash this thing." She flung it behind her.

"Hey, I like that sweater." I dashed after it and then gave it a once over. She was right. It was ugly. I shoved it in the return-home bag. "I think coming back to the dorm will be good for both of us. When Raven is having a bad day, I'll come back here so he can have some time to himself. Time to process whatever he's going through."

And time to fight his demons.

"And you trust that he'll be okay?" She threw one of my skirts over her head. "He won't plunge off the edge and go back to where he was, will he?"

"I'll check on him. It's not like I won't see him. And, if needed, you can take me to his apartment, right?"

"Yeah, of course."

"Who's apartment?" Raven stood in the doorway, carrying my bags.

"Your apartment, silly." I smiled at him, trying to displace any unnecessary fear or jealously. Although Raven hadn't shown any jealousy, I wanted to keep it that way. That was one less thing I didn't have to worry about in our relationship.

"Hey, what's this?" Delaney held up a pink and silver Victoria Secret's gift card.

"Where did you get that?" I asked, taking it from her hand.

"It was buried in your clothes." She pointed to the mound on my bed.

Raven looked over my shoulder as I opened the flap.

Have fun shopping with Raven. Love, Dad.

"Holy shit. Is he serious?" I looked at Raven and a huge grin spread across his face. Was my dad trying to make up for my mom going bat shit crazy and burning all the lingerie Raven had bought me?

Sweet!

"Damn!" Raven covered his mouth with his fist. "Five hundred bucks. We can buy you a lot of sexy stuff." Raven cocked a brow. "When are we going?"

"Whenever you want." I eyed him with a hungry stare. No matter how hard I tried, I couldn't seem to get enough of him.

His taste.

His touch.

His scent.

I was permanently caught in The Raven's trap. I shook my head, trying to calm my raging hormones.

"Is that it?" I looked at the two bags by the door.

"What do you mean is that it?" he huffed, gripping his waist. "I brought up like five bags. And there's still more at my apartment."

"I'm sorry." I walked past him and headed for the closet. "I didn't ask my dad to bring all of my clothes."

"I know." He grabbed my hand and spun me around. I slammed against his body and rested my hands against his broad chest. "If you'd just stay with me, we wouldn't have to haul all of your stuff back and forth."

His scent laced around me, making it difficult to stand my ground. "I am going to stay with you."

"Yeah, but not every night." He pressed his lips to the sensitive part of my neck and my mind quickly forgot why I'd talked myself into coming back to the dorm. "I need a little bit of this every night." He popped me on the butt and I squealed.

"Okay, I'm outta of here." Delaney dropped the clothes in her hand.

"No. I need your advice." I tried to wiggle out of Raven's arms, but he only held me tighter. "I need you to help me pick out clothes that will make me look sexy." I glanced up at Raven and he let out a low growl as he continued to nibble on my neck, not paying any attention to Delaney. I leaned to the side, trying to break free, even though I really didn't want to. "Raven, stop," I pleaded, but my tone betrayed any actual conviction.

"Looks like you're about to get undressed, so I'll help you later." Delaney headed for the door.

"Thanks, Delaney," Raven said as he kicked off his shoes and started to pull his shirt off. His stomach tensed and I caught a nice view of his chiseled abs.

"Shit, I almost forgot." Delaney turned around before pulling the door shut. "Whoa! Can you wait until I get out? I don't need a glimpse of the freak show."

"Hurry." Raven tossed his shirt on the chair. "I don't have all day."

Delaney's eyes landed directly on Raven's midsection for a full count of three before she finally tore them away and looked at me. "Do y'all want to grab a pizza with Luke and me later?"

Raven looked at me, waiting for a response. "I'm game if you are," I said, feeling the hunger pains bubble up in my stomach.

His lips spread into a full smile. "Sure, but I'm game for something else first." Raven encircled his arms around me and pressed his lips against my ear as his hands wandered up and down my backside.

"What time, Delaney?" I grabbed his arms, trying to stop him from feeling me up in front of my roommate. He stretched his neck, trying to kiss me. I laughed, unable to resist his tempting offer. After all, I was already in his trap and I was there to stay.

"Is an hour long enough?" Delaney appraised Raven from head to toe and then gave me a wide-eyed warning.

"No, but we'll make it work," he said, undressing me with his eyes.

I giggled as Raven picked me up and tossed me on the bed, landing on top of my clothes.

"I warned you, Lexi," Delaney said in a sing-song voice as she shut the door.

"I know. But I can't resist The Raven's trap."

There was definitely a change in the air and it wasn't just the signs of spring. Raven was acting like a different person, shifting his entire demeanor from a cup half-empty to a cup half-full. He was slowly releasing his demons that were determined to destroy him — destroy us — and I couldn't be happier.

It was evident that counseling was helping him, but it was also the excitement around Pro Day. Over the past few weeks, Josh had been literally bouncing off the apartment walls, keeping Raven pumped up for the big day. The day where scouts come to the university to see the football players on the field and assess their talent for the pros. They watched recorded games, studying their weaknesses, and practicing every day as they honed in on their strengths. Josh was a positive influence on Raven and I was glad he had him in his life.

"Oh my god. I'm so freakin' nervous." Shelby sat next to me on the bleachers inside the indoor practice field. "And this weather isn't helping."

"I know. It definitely makes everything feel more intense." The white canopy protected us from the treacherous rain and hail that beat down on the dome-covered facility. Mother Nature Texas decided that March fifth marked the beginning of spring. But inside, the vibe was much different. An electric buzz floated through the air as ten seniors took turns proving their skills for America's top pro football teams. The media lined up and down the sideline with their cameras, capturing all of the player's moves.

The practice field was setup with bright orange cones and other equipment ready to test the agility of the players. Coach Anderson stood on the sideline with his tablet in hand, proudly showing off his top-trained talent. The assistant coaches scrambled around, shuffling players on and off the field and being attentive to the scouts and pro coaches as needed.

"I hate when I get this nervous." Shelby shook her right leg, causing her blonde curls to bounce up and down. She leaned forward, clutching her knees for support. "That's why I had to sit over here. Josh's mom isn't any better and between the two of us, we drive Josh's dad crazy. We're like two hyped-up cheerleaders."

I glanced at the can of Red Bull in her hand. "I'm sure that's not helping."

She took a huge gulp. "Yeah, but I need it." She looked around the complex, trying to spot Josh. "What's taking so long? Why haven't they started yet?"

The adrenaline-junkie's vibes were passing over me, revving up my blood. I had nothing to be overly anxious about since Raven wasn't actively working for a spot on a national football team — he still had one more year left to play. It was great exposure for him, though. I was thankful that Coach Anderson had invited him to throw the ball for Josh and a few other teammates. No doubt, Raven had already caught the attention of several pro teams, despite his off the field issues. Since PHU had recently been named one of the top five universities for developing talent, this was an opportune time for Raven to show off his talent as well. "Relax. Josh has this. He's going to get drafted. I just know it," I reminded Shelby as I chewed on the inside of my cheek.

"He has to nail this." She looked at me with an intensity that made me scoot a little to the right. Even though she was a small girl, I didn't want to get in the way when her arms went flaying about as she cheered on Josh. "Ya know, since he didn't get to go to the Combine." Shelby glanced over her shoulder to where Josh's parents were standing. "I know his family is worried, too. If he doesn't land with a team, they'll be devastated."

Josh had a different take when it came to football. Where Raven's attitude was playing for the fun and love of it, Josh took it dead seriously. He lived and breathed football — making his ultimate goal to go pro. And, obviously, so did Shelby. That must have been why he was so mad when Raven was expelled from the bowl game.

"I don't think you have anything to worry about. His stats are good and several teams are talking about him."

"Yeah, but if he doesn't get picked up, then all of this was for shit." Her high-pitched voice quickly transformed into a deep, serious tone. "The training, the workouts..." she threw her hands up in the air, "don't mean a damn thing unless he lands a contract."

I nodded, knowing there was nothing I could say that would lessen the tension. Raven had recently given me another crash course because I knew very little when it came to pro football. My whole life had revolved around baseball because of Luke and Collin. But I was a quick study and with the help of Google, I was picking up on the particulars of the sport. The best part was that I liked football more than baseball. I don't know if it was seeing Raven suited up in tight spandex as he ran up and down the field, or the speed associated with the game as guys rammed into each other, but I loved it.

"Girl, I know what you mean. This mama's been preparing her boy since he was ten years old." Shawn Jackson's mother and father were sitting next to me since the exhibition started. "Betty Jackson," she leaned over me and I moved back to give her more room, "nice to meet you."

"Hi, I'm Shelby Scott, Josh Marshall's other half." She shook her hand.

"And this is my husband, Ron Jackson." Betty slapped her husband on the arm when he didn't acknowledge her. Ron tipped his Desert Storm Veteran ball cap and then turned his attention to the field. His perfect posture and quiet demeanor explained his ex-military training. It was even present in the way Shawn stood and responded to people.

"Shawn's a great player. I was watching him with Josh's parents. I heard that Tampa is really interested in him." Shelby kept one eye on the field.

"Yes, ma'am. We're excited about that, but I just want my boy to be happy. If none of this works out for him, then that's okay by us. It's all in the good Lord's hands." She pressed her hands together and then raised them to the ceiling. Shelby gave her a stiff smile and then turned her attention back to finding Josh. "I've been praying my heart out for Raven, too. That poor boy. I'm so glad he met a nice girl like you, Lexi. You're exactly what he needed to get his act cleaned up." She wrapped her arm around me and squeezed me tightly.

"Thank you." I smiled, happy to know that they supported Raven and were proud that he was working hard to make a change. "I really appreciate Shawn being there for him. He's a good friend, just like Josh." I shot Shelby a quick glance and she cracked a quick smile at me. Unsure of what Betty knew, I decided to end the conversation at that.

"I'm glad they're friends." She patted my leg, allowing her long, painted red nails to brush against my thigh. Thankfully, I didn't feel a thing through my jeans, but they still gave me the heebie-jeebies with the way they curled at the tips.

Since he'd been throwing the ball for several of his other teammates, Raven was already on the field when Josh made his appearance.

"There's Josh." Shelby grabbed my hand and perched on the edge of the bench. "I think I'm going to hurl."

"Relax, he's going to do fine." I gave her hand a tight squeeze and she released mine before I lost all feeling in my fingers.

"Come on, Josh. Show 'em what you got!" Shelby held up two crossed fingers at his mom and she showed Shelby hers as well. It must have been a little ritual they did for him. His mom was an average sized woman, with short, red hair that was teased all over, giving her that big-Texas-hair look. With all the makeup she had on, she fit the wife role of a big Texas oil and gas tycoon perfectly. Josh's dad resembled his brother, Will Marshall, with the exception of having a full head of hair. His belly was nearly the same size of the attorney's and they had the same stance that demanded authority and showed power.

The chatter settled to a low murmur as Josh got into place. Raven tossed the ball in his hands as he waited for the signal to start. The scouts waited eagerly as several assistant coaches raced to set up the field for a three-cone drill, placing markers at the twenty, forty, and sixty yard lines.

"Here we go." Shelby clapped her hands and rubbed them furiously together. Her bony shoulder blades protruded through her off-the-shoulder shirt and her eyes narrowed as she kept her gaze steadily on Josh. With that game face, she sent a clear message — nobody better mess with me or my guy.

"You can do it, Josh," I cheered as I waved to him and Raven. Afraid that if I didn't show Josh enough support, she might rip me in two.

"Come on, Josh. Come on." She ranted as he got prepared to catch the ball. The scouts, coaches, and spectators watched intently as Raven passed the ball to Josh in several different plays. For fifteen minutes, Josh displayed his skills, showing his sound hands, quick feet, and impressive balance while luring in the emissaries not only from Cleveland, but several other teams as well. Shelby clapped after each obstacle, managing not to yell her head off, as they instructed us. But I could tell it was killing her. The girl was definitely hardcore when it came to her man and football. Not that I wasn't, but I managed to keep myself a little more on the subtle side.

I kept a watchful eye to see if any of them took note of Raven's abilities. As I suspected, several scouts were evaluating his talent and commenting on Raven's prized possession — his throwing arm. It was no secret, with a top twenty ranking and throwing on average six touchdowns per game last season, and leading his team to the bowl even though he didn't get to play, Raven was one of the most talked about quarterbacks. He would be a top contender in next year's draft, as long as he continued on the right path. But, could he?

The whistle blew and Josh tossed the ball back to Raven. Every one gave him a round of applause and Shelby stood up and let a loud "whoop, whoop". Raven hi-fived Josh as he dashed off the field.

"Hell. That was so freakin' nerve racking." She exhaled a long breath, as if she'd been holding it in for the last fifteen minutes. "He screwed up on that twenty yard dash." She shook her head. "He's going to pay for that. I just know it."

"I know I don't know as much as you, but by the nods and smiles coming from the opposite side of the field, I think he did well."

"We'll see." Shelby jumped off the bleachers and pulled up on her skinny jeans. "I'll be back."

"Okay."

She walked toward Josh's parents and hi-fived them. For a few minutes, they spoke, their emotions clearly indicating they were reviewing how Josh did. Josh's father didn't show as much emotion, keeping somewhat of a straight face. His wife and Shelby clearly made up for it.

We stayed until the end and waited for Josh and Raven to come out of the locker room. The second Josh appeared, Shelby ran to him, yelling, "There's my guy!" She jumped into his arms, clamping her legs around his waist. They kissed like no one else was in the room and it made me feel a little awkward as I stood next to his parents. They clapped, nonetheless.

Raven walked out next and I waited patiently for him, although a part of me really wanted to barrel into him like

Shelby had Josh. His hair glistened, still wet from the shower. He brushed his hand through it, giving it a messy look. Damn he was sexy. He wore running pants and a tight, purple Under Armour shirt with a large dragon across the front. Every bulge and ripple showed through the fabric and I couldn't wait to land my hands on him tonight.

"You were great!" I threw my arms around him, locking my fingers tightly around his neck.

His hands rested on my waist. "I did well?" A huge smiled spread, like he already knew the answer. Seeing Raven happy warmed every part of me, in every right way.

"Hell yeah, baby. You had those scouts turning their heads even though they were supposed to be watching your teammates."

"Really?"

"Yep." I pressed my lips to his and he kissed me, unable to stop the grin from ear to ear.

"I just have to keep playing well and next year, I'll be here." Raven glanced over at Josh and Shawn who were being hailed by the media. "Better them than me." His eyes widened and he sighed in relief.

"Yeah, well, they just saw you." I winked.

He shot a quick glance at the familiar reporter making her way toward us. "Are you alright with all of this?" His eyes pleaded for forgiveness.

"Of course. I'm excited. You're going to have a kick ass year." I released my arms and took a step back. It was his time to shine, not mine.

He leaned his forehead to mine. "Baby, as long as I have you by my side, I know it will be."

Σ

Chapter 10

"Wow. This tastes really good." Delaney stuffed another sushi roll into her mouth.

The seaweed wrapped roll with shredded crabmeat and avocado slices neatly placed inside the tightly formed circle, stared at me. I felt for the person that spent so much time crafting the perfectly displayed piece of a food just so she could tear into it. Tiny sesame seeds speckled the white rice that looked like it was glued together. "Is it really that good?"

She moaned and closed her eyes, chewing slowly like it was the world's best aphrodisiac.

"Delaney." Luke nudged her and she finally stopped acting like the food was turning her on. "You're making a scene." He looked around the table, gauging the reaction from others close by. No one was paying any attention to her hideous love of Asian food.

"Sorry. I can't help it. It's just so damn delicious." She pointed to the little black tray in front of me. "If you're not going to eat them, I will."

"I guess I'll try one." I picked up my fork and stabbed it.

"Damn, it's not alive." She picked up another one and fed it to my brother. He took the entire roll in his mouth and I wondered why he'd been introduced to this so-called mouth-watering food and I hadn't. "I still can't believe you haven't tried Sushi before."

I shrugged. "My mom doesn't like fish, so we never ate it."

"How is it that Luke's eaten it and you haven't?"

Should I bring up the fact that Collin wasn't a fish eater either? I picked at it, unsure whether I should try it. The only fish I really ate was fried catfish because mom couldn't stand seeing it on our plates and the batter somehow masked the shape of it ever being a creature that swam in the water. "I don't know? Luke, care to tell us?"

Luke stopped chewing for a moment before swallowing. "Dad and I go out and eat it sometimes." He took a drink of his water and then picked up the chopsticks, carefully capturing the delicately formed roll between the two wooden sticks like a pro.

"That sucks." I watched as he dunked it in soy sauce. "Why hasn't dad taken me?"

"I don't know," Luke said, his mouth full of food. "Ask him next time."

I'd told Luke that Dad and I had made up and he was glad to hear that he'd accepted Raven. Even though he sounded supportive at the time, I picked up on the slight disappointment that flickered in his eyes. Did he still wish I were with his friend? For the most part, he didn't blame me for not calling mom, agreeing that she needed to be the first to apologize.

Stepping outside my comfort zone had become more common, so I took a bite of the roll. Half of it hit the plate as it fell apart. Using my fingers, I tore the seaweed with my teeth.

Delaney laughed. "You're supposed to put the whole thing in your mouth."

I covered my mouth with my hand. "I don't know how to eat these things." I chewed, surprised at the flavor. I continued to eat the rest of my rolls, liking each bite more and more. From now on, I was making it a point to try different kinds of fish and definitely more Sushi rolls. Raven would be happy to hear that I was onboard for eating seafood, since it was his favorite. Picking up my phone, I sent him a message:

Me: Hey, when you get out of class, stop by the new cafeteria. I'm here eating with Delaney and Luke.

Raven: Okay. Class just got out. On the way.

"Did you tell Raven to stop by?" Delaney asked.

"Yes." I tossed my phone in backpack. "He's on the way."

Delaney swiveled in Luke's direction. "So, what's the plan for Spring Break?"

Luke gazed at her through the corner of his eye as he continued to eat. "Practice and games."

"Are you serious?" Delaney pouted her lips and crossed her arms, clearly disappointed.

Luke wiped his mouth. "Yeah, I told you." He tossed the napkin on his tray.

"You did? Because I don't remember."

Luke lowered his head and shot her one of his *I already told you* looks. "But the good news is I'm free after Monday's game."

"You are?" Delaney jumped in her seat and clapped her hands. "So what are we doing?"

"My parents want me to join them in Breckenridge for the rest of Spring Break," Luke said, in a low tone. The breaking news seized her celebration and her body slumped forward.

"Oh, I thought we might do something together. Ya know, since it's our senior year." She looked at me. "Are you going, too?"

I shook my head.

"You're not going?" Luke whipped his head around, causing his hair to fall in his eyes.

"No. Didn't Dad tell you?"

"No." He ran his fingers through his hair and leaned forward. "How did you get out of this trip and I didn't?"

I shrugged. "Mom didn't buy me a flight."

"Shit. You suck."

"Think about it, Luke. It would be totally weird if I went." Our Spring Break skiing excursion had been a family outing for the past five years with the Norris'. This would be the first year that I wouldn't be joining my family. Since the dynamics had changed, it didn't make sense for me to go. I was relieved because going on the trip with my mom would be disastrous. I was certain she would still be on her get-back-with-Collin scheme.

"Yeah, I guess you're right." He turned to Delaney. "It's only for a few days."

Delaney faced dropped. "I guess I'll be hanging out with you." She looked at me with hopeful eyes and I felt sad for her. I was surprised that Luke didn't invite her to go with him.

"I guess. I don't have any plans for Spring Break."

"We do now," Raven whispered in my ear and a shiver shot through my body. His sexy voice never ceased to turn me on. His smell traveled over me as he wrapped his arms around me and kissed me on the cheek.

"We do?" I asked, totally surprised because we hadn't discussed going anywhere.

"The Raven's in the house." The backup quarterback, Kyle Reeves, along with Cage Rutherford and few other football players, chanted from the table behind us. The cafeteria soon joined in the sing-a-long and Raven bowed, eating up the attention. I couldn't help but sing and clap along, proud to see how everyone supported him.

After a few minutes of fame, Raven sat next to me. "What's up, man?" Raven reached across the table and exchanged a fist bump with Luke.

"Busy as shit." Luke shook his head.

"I understand. You're three for three, right?"

"Yeah. We are."

"Cool. By the way, that protein drink you told me try," he shot a thumbs up, "I like it. Better than the other stuff I was drinking."

"I told you," Luke said, matter of factly. "So where are y'all headed for Spring Break?"

"South Padre Island." Raven smiled brightly and pulled me close. "Like I promised you."

Split emotions filtered through my head. It sounded like fun, and I was excited that he was delivering on his promise, but the cautious part of my brain reminded me that it wouldn't be a good idea. "But, I—"

"Now that just sucks. What am I going to do?" Delaney crossed her arms and slammed her back into her chair.

"You can come with us. We have a big group going. Josh's parents have a huge condo on the beach. We're going to party it up and celebrate my baby's birthday." Raven planted a huge kiss on my lips.

"I can?" Delaney instantly perked up, like a dog thrown a bone full of meat. Any mention of a party and she was in — with or without my brother.

"Raven. I think—"

"The Marshall is in town!" Cage roared, over and over. Everyone in the cafeteria turned their attention to the front entrance and chanted, "The Marshall is in town!"

"Josh!" Raven stood up and yelled across the cafeteria. "Dude, get over here."

He shuffled through the cafeteria with his arm draped around Shelby. Shawn strutted behind him, talking with the stalker-reporter that always happened to be everywhere Raven and I were. *How convenient.* If that wasn't enough to worry about, the Silicone Triplets trolled their way toward Raven until they saw me.

"That's right, bitches. Turn your skank asses around." Delaney motioned with her finger.

I looked over my shoulder, watching them shoot me dirty looks. "They don't give up, do they?"

"Can you blame them?"

Appraising my hot and sexy man, I grabbed him by the face and thrust my tongue in his mouth. Raven responded willingly, diving his hands into my hair as he kissed me fervently. Heat swamped my face, but I didn't pull away. Never had I made a bold move like that before, but I sort of liked it.

Raven pulled away slowly, looking slightly dazed. He rolled his tongue across his lip, as if savoring my taste. "Damn, you should do that more often."

I ran a hand through my hair while holding on to my lower lip. Having a taste of him like that spurred a plethora of ideas. "Don't worry, I will." I winked.

"You go, girl!" Delaney lifted her hand in the air. "Show them who he comes home to at night."

I laughed and slapped my hand against hers. "You've got that right."

Raven shook his head, wearing a devious grin. "Trust me, you have nothing to worry about, baby."

I smiled at him, and then glanced back at them, showing them I had no fear. But I couldn't help but wonder if he was really done with setting out his bait and happy with the catch he'd caught. Only time would tell. They quickly averted their mission, stopping at a table near the front. And that's when I saw him. Collin. He was sitting at a table with Forbes, Jordan, and a few other baseball players.

For the past three months, I'd managed to steer clear of his path, but I knew that I'd eventually run into him. With a population of under ten-thousand students, it was apt to happen sooner rather than later. And since this was the grand opening of the mega cafeteria, with food to satisfy every craving, or so that's what they claimed, half of the school was packed in the overly large dining room.

Crap.

I turned my back, hoping he hadn't seen me. Delaney shot me a knowing look, telling me she saw him, too. Then again, I didn't care. I'd moved on and things were definitely over between us. But had he accepted that? Surely, he'd moved on after all this time. I couldn't deny that a tiny part of me wanted to ask Luke. I just wanted to make sure he was happy and that he was dating someone that was perfect for him. Despite our non-connection, Collin really was a great guy.

"Luke, my man." Josh high fived my brother. "I'm ready for another workout session. When are you free?"

"It wasn't enough for you?" Luke smiled, hinting at something else, but we all knew he was joking.

"Shit, you kicked my ass, but I want more."

"What? You were crying like a baby." Shelby nudged his arm. "Complaining how much you were in pain."

"Shel." Josh shot her a discerning look. She rolled her eyes and sat next to Delaney.

"Damn, I'm that good?" Luke rubbed the scruff on his chin. "Maybe I should open up my own gym."

"Sign me up, man. I'm there." Raven slapped the table and Josh did the same.

Delaney leaned against him. "I told you you're awesome."

He cocked a brow. "Yeah, but I thought you were talking about something else."

"Ha-ha. You can show me later." Delaney ran the tip of her finger across his lower lip and then licked her finger. "You had some wasabi."

"I wouldn't want that getting on you." Luke raised a brow and Delaney slapped his arm in a playful manner. Turning to Raven and Josh, he said, "You're ready for some more torture?"

"Bring it on, man," Josh said with a big grin.

It was obvious he took a keen interest in helping people reach their potential in the gym and enjoyed it. Based on the talk, my brother was a great trainer and I was glad because according to the latest baseball news, it didn't look like he would be signing with a major league team. Deep down, he really didn't want that anyway. It's what my parents wanted.

"Yeah. Stevens just isn't doing it for me. I mean he's good, but I get so much more out of my workouts with you," Josh said.

"Coach just needs to can Stevens. I mean, he needs to get with the times. His workouts are so old school," Raven added.

"No kidding." Kyle leaned back in his chair, catching some of the conversation.

"Guys, I'd like to help you, but my schedule is pretty tight with baseball in full swing."

"And don't forget me." Delaney reached under the table and Luke jumped. He shot her a *what the hell* gaze and she laughed before turning to us.

"Uh, I got first dibs, bro," Raven reminded Josh.

"Yeah, yeah, I hear ya." Josh dismissed Raven's comment. "Let's talk." Josh pulled out a chair, swung it around, and then straddled it. They continued talking about working out and I joined in the conversation between Shelby and Delaney.

"What's the plan?" Shelby removed her Chick-fil-a sandwich and fries from a bag. "When are we leaving?" She tore open the ketchup packet with her teeth and squirted it all over her fries.

"Um, I just found out that Raven wants to go, so I haven't had chance to talk to him." I glanced over at Raven, still unsure if we should go. He shot me a quick smile, and I hated to be the lame one to tell him we shouldn't go. I hadn't seen him this happy in a long time. Spring Break was all about partying and with Raven on his last string, it just didn't sound like a good idea.

"Josh said that Raven's therapist canceled his session for next week."

I bit my lip. How was it that she knew more than I did? "Oh. I hadn't heard." I turned to Raven, pulling him away from his conversation with the guys. "Hey, you're not seeing Dr. Galen next week."

"No. He's going out of town for Spring Break."

"Why didn't you tell me?"

"Yeah, man. Whatever!" Raven slapped the table and it shook, completely ignoring my question.

"You said it, bro. Not me." Josh pushed Raven and he bumped against me.

For a moment, I began to feel like I wasn't all that important to him. It reminded me of how Collin used to treat me. Now that Raven and I were settling into our relationship, I hoped the same thing wasn't going to happen. I shook my head, ignoring the lying voice in my head, but I was still peeved that I was just now finding out. "Raven."

"Yes? Sorry, baby." He turned to me, giving me his full attention. "What did you say?"

My heart did an extra beat and I wanted to punch myself for even thinking that stupid lie. "Why didn't you tell me about this trip sooner?"

"I'm sorry." He latched on to my hands. "Josh found out this morning that we could get the condo for the week. Josh, Shelby, and me, were talking about it this morning before class." He reached behind him, grabbing Josh by the shirt. "Isn't that right, dude?"

"He's telling you the truth, Lexi." Josh gave me a reassuring expression. "My parents were having some work done on the place and they weren't sure everything would be finished by next week. My dad called me this morning and said we could use it if we wanted to."

"You were already in class so I couldn't call to tell you." His hands traveled along my arms until they reached my waist. He pulled me close to him, until our knees touched. "And that's why it was the first thing I said when I saw you." His eyes rounded into perfect puppy dog eyes, pleading for me not to be mad. There was no way I could stay mad at him.

"And since you didn't stay with me last night, like I wanted you to, you weren't there for the conversation." He pulled me into his lap and cradled me like a baby. His baby.

"Raven." I felt myself slipping into his trap that I so willingly lost myself in time after time. I pawed at his chest, but that didn't stop his PDA for me. He planted kisses all over my face, not caring if the entire cafeteria saw him. Especially the Silicone Triplets. "Stop," I squealed, laughing uncontrollably, but it was only a half-hearted protested.

"Stop? That's not what you said the other night," he teased. My entire body flushed with hot and cold chills and I felt all eyes drift to us. "I kind of remember you begging for more."

I clamped my hand over his mouth. He was definitely embarrassing me. Although I wanted every girl who had been consumed by The Raven's trap to know that I was his, I really didn't want him to share our intimate moments with them.

"What? You don't want everyone to know that we're officially a couple?" he mumbled through my small hand, his voice carrying over my palm. "You weren't afraid to suck face with me just a minute ago."

"No, it's not that. It's just that... well, you know." I eyed him, hoping he caught on.

He pulled my hand away. "I'm not afraid to tell everyone how I feel about you."

"Neither am I." I cupped his face. "But I'd rather you just show me instead."

"Alright. I can do that." He rose to his feet, still holding me tightly in his arms. "I was going to wait until your birthday next week, but what the hell. I'll do it right now."

"Right now?" I swallowed hard, wondering what he had in mind. The familiar tingles began to inch their way through my body and I squirmed in his arms. Raven never ceased to surprise me.

"Yes, right here."

"Wh—at?" Before I could ask anything else, he stood me on top of the table. "Raven...what are you doing?" My blood pumped faster, causing my heart to thrash against my chest. He held on to my hands, making sure I was steady before letting go.

"Woo hoo!" Josh jumped up, giving us some distance. Luke vacated his chair and watched intently at the show Raven was about to put on for everyone.

Raven cleared his throat a few times before saying, "Excuse me. Can I have everyone's attention?"

The chattering dwindled to a hush and all eyes landed on him and me. My entire body froze and a cold sweat broke out over my skin. The muscles in my legs weakened and my knees shook. A heaviness settled over my stomach and it tensed into a tight knot.

Don't throw up. Don't throw up.

Suddenly, the sushi didn't seem to settle well with me. I prayed Raven wasn't going to do anything overly embarrassing. If so, I'd kill him. After I had my way with him first. I tried to smile, but I was certain that I looked like a girl with stage fright. I just hoped that my picture with hashtag #LexiThompsonScaredShitless wouldn't be the next popular post on every social media site.

Raven grabbed my left hand and a few guys whistled.

Oh, shit.

My body caved forward and I took a long, hard swallow. Surely, he wasn't about to do what I thought he was going to do. I mean, what would I say? What would I do? I loved him. I wanted to be with him. Forever. But it was too soon. Or was it?

Oh my God. Oh my God.

"Lexi Thompson," he smiled, stopping momentarily. He bowed his head, staring at the floor for a few moments, trying to compose the bright, neon light beaming from his entire body. Without so much as a word or note, his body sung a melody that said he loved me. All of me. More people clapped and whistled, causing my pulse to kick up to top speed. The blood rushed through me, stealing the air in my lungs, and making my head dizzy. I inhaled, but only managed to take a few shallow breaths. Out of the corner of my eye, I saw Delaney snapping pics of us with her camera and Shelby recording us with her phone.

Was this really happening?

I waited with baited breath until he finally looked up, his eyes capturing all of me, appraising me with such intensity that it shook me to my core.

"Since the day I met you in the writing lab..." he trailed off to turn and face the crowd momentarily. "Yes, she was my tutor." A few people laughed and my nervousness transpired into an unexplainable level of excitement laced with a reassuring calmness. He turned his attention back to me. "I knew that you were someone very special. Little did I know that you would be that special someone for me. I know that the past few months have been a little rough, but there's no one I'd rather have by my side than you. You are truly an angel sent from heaven, and I don't want to let another day pass by without you knowing how much I love you. Lexi, not only have you helped me find a new and better life, but you have also showed me it is possible with you. You are my new beginning and I want you to be my ending." His voice softened and his eyes glistened with tears. "I love you, Lexi."

My heart skyrocketed and my lips spread into the biggest smile ever. My nose burned with the threat of tears, but I didn't care. Raven was professing his love for me, in front of everyone. "Oh, Raven, I love you, too."

"Lexi Thompson, I guess what I'm saying is..." he knelt to one knee and the tears started free falling. I sniffed and wiped the streaks from my cheeks. I leaned forward, refusing to let go of his hand. Several of the football players whistled and I prepared myself for what was coming next. "Will you do me the honor of being Mrs. Raven Davenport for the rest of your life?" He reached into his jacket and pulled out a small, burgundy box. He popped open the lid and held up a shiny ring, sparkling with diamonds.

I gasped, covering my mouth with my hand. It was the most beautiful ring I'd ever seen. Flashy, big, and most of all, picked out by Raven. My throat tightened, still shocked at hearing the words coming from his mouth.

Raven asked me to marry him! Say something, you idiot!

At that moment, all sense of fear vanished, replaced in its entirety by love, hope, and faith. The only thing missing was trust. I had to know if I could trust him. But I was willing to take that chance. Deep down, I knew I loved him with my entire soul. I wanted to know what the future held for us.

I nodded. Repeatedly.

"Yes. Yes, I'll marry you."

I leapt into his arms, and he caught me, twirling us around and around. Wrapping my arms around his neck, I kissed him, over and over again. Showing him just how much I loved him and how much I wanted to be his wife. I just hoped he wouldn't let me down.

Σ

Chapter 11

Traffic was backed up for miles on State Highway 100. What was supposed to be a nine hour drive had turned into an eleven hour drive and we weren't even on the island yet. We'd left at five in morning, hoping to avoid traffic, only to hit rush hour in Austin and two-lane construction all the way through San Antonio. But no amount of traffic could stifle my excitement. I was finally going to see the ocean and the best part would be seeing it with my fiancée, Raven.

Raven had convinced me that he would be on his best behavior, because the last thing he wanted was to mess up a good thing. And he was right; things were going well and life was definitely good, which was precisely what worried me. But Josh promised that he wouldn't allow things to get out of hand and since it was his parent's house, he was calling the shots — no wild parties, no all-night drinking binges, and definitely no drugs. Despite my better judgment, I decided we should go.

"Damn. Come on people," Josh huffed and wiped the sweat from his brow. "Quit looking around and just go." We were bumper-to-bumper, inching through the small town of Laguna Heights. Box shaped, stucco buildings lined the highway, and townspeople shuffled in and out of the quaint family-owned businesses. It was life for them as usual, but not for the thousands flocking south in the middle of March.

Young people packed every small corner store, filling up their tanks and loading up their ice chest with beer and groceries. It was as if every college student on Spring Break in

Texas had the same plan — party on South Padre Island. And we were no exception.

"I can drive the rest of the way," Raven offered.

Josh didn't say anything, just looked around as he sighed. Shelby leaned over and stroked his hair. "Maybe you should let Raven drive for a while. You've been behind the wheel since we left. I know you're tired."

"Oh my God! I see the ocean!" I squealed as I got a glimpse of the blue water behind a few houses. Rolling down the window, I allowed the warm ocean breeze to sweep through the truck. The sun bounced off the water, giving it a golden glow. It was truly amazing and beautiful. I couldn't wait to sink my toes into the sand and allow the waves to wash over my feet.

I could definitely get used to this.

"That's actually the bay. Once we cross the bridge, you'll get a nice view of the ocean," Josh said, letting out a long, heavy breath.

"Lexi, you want to sit up front?" Shelby asked as she unfastened her seat belt.

I nodded enthusiastically, like a little kid dying to see something for the first time. "Yes, please."

Josh put the truck in park since we were barley moving. "Go head and drive, Raven. Shel and I will get in the back."

"Alright, bro."

We switched places and a few cars honked at us as we stalled everyone from moving two car spaces forward. I shook my head. It wasn't like the thirty seconds they lost would get them there any faster. Sitting in front, I had a great view, not only of the traffic, but of the water that followed the highway for miles.

"Are you excited?" Raven took my hand in his.

"Yeah." I brushed my finger across the top of his hand. "Is it that obvious?"

"You've been smiling since you found out we were going." Raven inched the truck forward.

"That's because I'm so happy. Happy we're engaged and happy we're here." My cheeks ached from the constant smiling, but I didn't care. I'd never been so happy in my entire life. I glanced at my hand, unable to stop looking at my ring. Part of me wondered how he could afford to buy me a diamond the size of Texas, but I'd wait to ask him at the right time.

"Are you really that happy?" He held my gaze for a few seconds, searching the depths of my eyes. Not only was I willing to tell him exactly how I felt, I'd show him, repeatedly.

"Yes, I really am." I held my eyes wide open so he could see the sincerity in my reply. Then I squeezed my eyes tightly together, feeling the rise of butterflies that continued to carry my heart away, giving it to Raven. "And I can't wait to hit the beach with you."

"We're going to have a great time." He raised my hand and kissed my ring finger. "Just like I promised you."

It just didn't seem real — I was going to be Mrs. Raven Davenport. When? I had no idea. Once I graduated and Raven finished school we could figure it all out, but for now, I wanted to enjoy every minute with him. I pressed my lips together, speechless. Not only had he totally surprised me by asking me to marry him, but he was taking me to the beach. I had the best of both worlds and by the look on Raven's face, he felt the same way.

"We probably won't hit the island for another hour. If you want, we'll go straight to the house so you can see the ocean before the sun sets. Then we can grab a bite to eat and head to the store afterwards," Josh said, reclining in the back seat as he covered his face with his ball cap.

"Works for me." I winked at Raven and he smiled. Being with him made everything ten times better.

"That's fine," Raven told Josh.

Finally, after thirty minutes, we made it to Port Isabel, the town on the other side of the island. It had your typical chain restaurants and stores, with Wal-Mart being the hot spot for not only islanders, but also visitors. Straight ahead, I spied the longest and tallest bridge.

"Are we going over that?" I turned around and asked Josh.

"Yeah," he muttered underneath his cap. "That's the only way to get to the island, unless you want us to catch a ferry."

"No. It's fine," I giggle, feeling like a total idiot. "I've never been on a bridge that crossed that much water."

"We'll be fine." Raven patted my leg.

The light turned green and we entered the massive bridge. The sight was unbelievable. My stomach tightened and my heart pumped faster, but I wasn't scared, just overly excited. I had finally made it to the beach after twenty years and three-hundred and sixty-two days.

Better late than never.

The ocean rocked gently, creating tiny waves as we crossed it. I leaned out the window and yelled, "Woohoo!" Everyone laughed and Josh soon joined in, yelling at the top of his lungs. I couldn't believe what I'd been missing all these years. I knew now that I was going to be a beach girl — snow was a thing of the past.

Palm trees swaying in the spring breeze and the smell of the salty air mixed with sweet blossoms told me we were definitely on an island. As the sun lowered, the island woke in a buzz of college students as they cruised up and down the strip. Bright neon lights in a variety of colors lit up the t-shirt and souvenir shops. The island had a small town feel, nothing like a commercialized resort, and it was evident the locals wanted to keep it that way.

"Make a right, just before the Holiday Inn," Josh instructed as we approached the south end of the island.

"Yeah, I remember," Raven said.

"You've been here before?"

"Yeah. The past two years."

A tiny piece of the excitement dwindled away, but I wasn't going to let that ruin my time with Raven. I had no control over what Raven did in the past. And it was just that — in the past.

We entered a private drive and Raven stopped at the gate. "What's the code?"

"Thirty-five fourteen," Josh said, checking his phone. We crossed the pebbled drive and entered into the gated community.

We turned onto the street and pulled up to the Marshall's house. It was no condo; it was a freakin' mansion, standing three stories tall and overlooking the ocean. Not the bay, but the blue Gulf Coast. Nestled in a small community with million dollar homes surrounding it, it was one of the largest structures. And we were staying there for the entire week! It was like we were on our own sweet escape. I was glad I had decided to come. This was going to be fun.

Raven pulled into the three-car garage and I was surprised to see a Jeep already parked. I thought we were the only ones staying at the house. "Whose car is that?"

"It's an extra car we keep here," Josh said as Raven turned off the ignition. We piled out of the car and stretched for a second. "If we fly down, we have it here to get around the island."

Must be nice.

"Oh, yeah, that makes sense." I didn't know what else to say. Raven had introduced me to Josh's parents at Pro Day and I was surprised to see how down to earth they were. I never pegged them for being this rich.

Raven tossed Josh the keys and he opened the door. We entered the house through the kitchen and I did a double take. It was a chef's dream. White cabinets and a large island spanned across the massive kitchen. Black granite and stainless steel appliances with dark mahogany, wood floors gave it a sleek modern flair. Josh flipped on the lights and a rainbow of colors danced across the room. Diamond drop crystals hanging from strings over the island lit up the kitchen like a fine dining establishment.

"What the hell?" Josh walked into the living area. "Dad let mom do all this?"

"Man, she went all out this time." Shelby slipped off her flip-flops and dug her feet into the shaggy, light grey carpet. "We're going to have a hard time keeping this place clean."

"No shit." He shook his head. "Why the hell would she get wood floors? If there's a hurricane, this wood is gone."

"It's not wood," Shelby knelt and touched it with her hand, "it's ceramic."

Raven tapped his foot on the floor. "Never seen tile floor that looks like wood."

"Shit," Josh huffed. "If they make it, my mom knows about it. Trust me."

"Sounds like my mom," I laughed.

My mom would die for a place like this.

The house looked like it belonged in Architectural Digest, the magazine my mom fantasized over, clipping pictures and floor plans for my dad to see. She wanted him to build her a huge, three-story house — as if the thirty-five hundred square foot house wasn't large enough for her. But since her goal was to keep up with the Norris', she had to have everything bigger and better. Poor dad.

"My mom needs to meet your mom."

No, I don't think so.

I didn't respond, just looked around as Josh continued turning on lights throughout the house. White leather couches and large ottomans gave the untouchable room a slight feeling of hominess. The Marshall's place was a true vacation getaway.

I just wasn't sure if it belonged by the ocean, maybe Las Vegas or New York. You almost didn't want to touch anything, for fear of leaving smudge prints. If something was ruined or broken, I definitely didn't want to be the guilty party.

Just past the living area, near the front entrance, a shiny, black, baby grand piano caught my eye. "Oh wow. A piano." I headed straight for it. I hadn't played since Christmas and even though the memory had been painful, things had changed. I was with Raven. I ran my fingers across the sleek curves of the instrument. It called to me. Notes sounded in my head as I hit a few keys.

"Sit down and play." Raven rubbed his hands up and down my back.

"I'll play later." I relaxed against his chest. "As long as you'll sing with me."

"Have you heard this guy sing?" Josh placed a hand on Raven's shoulder.

"Yeah, and he's not bad."

Raven shook his head. "I'm not that good."

"Whatever." Josh leaned against the piano. "So you play?"

"Does she play?" Raven huffed. "She plays like John Legend."

"What?" I gasped. "I do not."

"Relax," Raven laughed while gathering me in his arms. "She's really good, man," he said, trying to stroke my ego.

"I'm glad I brought my guitar." Josh did a drum roll on the top of the piano. "We can jam out later."

"I didn't know you played the guitar."

"Yep. Been playing since I was in junior high." Josh walked out of the front room and back into the living room. He hit a button with a remote and the outside coverings on the windows retreated, slowly revealing a gorgeous horizon with a motionless ocean.

"Wow." I dashed over to the windows to enjoy the spectacular site.

"I know. It's badass." Shelby pressed her hands against the glass. "I want to live here so badly."

"We will, baby. Just give it some time." Josh wrapped his arms around her. "But I'll get you a better place than this."

Shelby's eyes widened. "How about the Caribbean?"

Josh laughed, tilting his head back. "Whatever you want, Shel."

Raven embraced me from behind. "It's beautiful. Just like you." He nuzzled my neck and I reached up behind me, pulling him closer. The past week had been magical. I glanced at my ring, still not believing I was going to be Mrs. Raven Davenport. One thing was certain, I was glad I said yes. Spending the rest of my life with Raven was all I wanted. Nothing more.

"Do you want to go check out the beach first or head out to get some dinner?" Josh asked.

I looked at Raven. "I'm really hungry, so I'm okay with grabbing some food."

"Thank God." Shelby shot me a look of pity. "I didn't want to be rude, since you hadn't seen the ocean, but I wanted to stop on the way in. I'm dying of starvation."

"Shelby, if you were that hungry, you should've said something. The beach will always be here. It's not going anywhere," I assured her.

"Believe me, next time, I will." She winked.

We unloaded the truck so we'd have room for the groceries and then headed to a local restaurant that Josh claimed had the best fish tacos. I was eager to try them, since I had discovered my newest food fetish — fish.

Josh pulled into the small parking lot and we filed out of the vehicle. "This looks like an old Taco Bell."

"Yeah, it might have been, but trust me, the food is delicious."

"I was just reading some of the reviews." Raven glanced at his phone. "Says that Captain Roy was ranked top three for shrimp four years in a row."

"I believe it." Josh opened the door to the small restaurant. "He makes the best bacon-wrapped, jalapeño-stuffed shrimp. Ever."

And Josh was right. The food was incredible and the tacos were equally as tasty. "If we ate here every night, I'd be perfectly fine with that," I said, licking the barbecue sauce from my fingers.

"Hey, save some for me." Raven grabbed my hand and tried to lick my fingers.

"Babe, stop." I struggled to reclaim my arm, laughing the entire time.

Josh shook his head and Shelby smiled. "If you want, we can buy you guys some sauce at the grocery store for later."

Raven kissed the top of my hand and then let it go. "Not a bad idea." He reached over and pinched me on the butt and I yelped. I quickly covered my mouth, but it was too late. The entire restaurant heard and all eyes were on me once again.

"Will you stop?" I eyed him with a huge smile that I couldn't seem to control.

A devilish grin played on the edge of his lips. "I can't help it." He waved his hand around his head. "Must be something in the air, because I just can't wait to see you in a bikini."

My smile vanished. "Oh, well, we're going to have stop at one of those t-shirt shops because I don't own one."

"What?" Shelby whipped her head in my direction. "What do you swim in?"

"A one-piece."

She gave me a quirky expression. "Seriously?"

I wiped my fingers on a napkin so that I wouldn't further entice Raven until we got back to the house. "Yeah. I've never had a bikini." For a second, the memories of the old Lexi Thompson filtered through my head, reminding me that I was living in a dream. A dream that would soon burst and be over with when Mom found out I was engaged.

"Lexi grew up in a really strict house," Raven informed Shelby.

"And my parents tried to control my life up until a few months ago," I openly admitted.

Shelby's eyes softened and she tilted her head to the side. "That must have been terrible, growing up like that. I had no idea."

I glanced away, trying not to allow the memories to ruin my Spring Break or anyone else's. "Yeah, but it's in the past."

"That means one thing." Shelby straightened and smiled brightly, her blue eyes sparkling like the waters of the Gulf.

"What's that?" I asked, even though I knew what she had in mind.

"We're going shopping." She held out her hand in Josh's direction and moved her fingers for him to hand her something.

"Aw, shit." Josh shook his head as he pulled out his wallet and removed a credit card.

"No, that's okay." I motioned for Josh to take it back. "I have my own money."

"Relax." Shelby laughed. "The credit card belongs to his dad. He won't notice a couple hundred bucks."

Raven looked at me and gave a slight shrug. Was she serious? A couple hundred dollars was my monthly allowance, not my one-trip shopping spree for the day. Immediately, I knew that Shelby loved to blow money. It was obvious in the clothes she wore, the hand bag she carried, and the tons of shoes she packed. One bag carried her shoe collection for the week. I didn't even want to know what her closet looked like. No wonder she got along with Mrs. Marshall so well.

"Are y'all done?" A waitress appeared with the bill.

I nodded and Raven relaxed against his chair. "Yeah, I think so."

"Sweetie?" Shelby looked at Josh and he rolled his eyes before burying his face in his hands. "Put it on this." Shelby handed her Mr. Marshall's credit card.

We hit a few stores and Shelby helped me pick two bikinis — one, turquoise with white polka dots, and the other one, solid black. She was just as bad as Delaney, wanting me to buy more, but I refused to allow Josh's parents to buy me clothes, especially when they didn't know. Part of me felt sad that Delaney didn't come with us, claiming she didn't want to be the third wheel. Or fifth wheel, in this case. I was kind of peeved at Luke for not taking her with him to Breckenridge. I just hoped she didn't do anything stupid.

After we stocked up on food for the week, we headed back to the house. The strip was buzzing with excitement, people cruising up and down in convertibles, on bikes, or on their Segways. It was like the town never slept; it didn't matter that it was a Monday night. We were a little tired from the drive and getting up at the crack of dawn, so we decided to head down to the beach for the night.

Shelby and I spread out a few blankets while Josh and Raven made a fire. The night air was a little chilly. Though I didn't care, I wondered whether the water would be warm enough for us to swim. I was willing to dive in just to see what the salt water felt like against my skin. And if Raven was willing to go in with me, I would definitely do it.

"I didn't think it would be this cool." I pulled a sweatshirt over my tank top

"I know." Shelby put on a hoodie. "Normally it's a little warmer than this."

"I'm sure it's too cold for a night swim." I stared at the water, wanting to see what it felt like.

"Yeah, baby." Raven placed another log on the fire pit. "We should probably wait until the middle of the day tomorrow."

"Hey, it's perfect for the hot tub." Shelby nudged Josh.

Josh raised a brow. "You want to get in?"

Shelby nodded and tossed her hair over her shoulder. After they ogled each other for a few seconds, she turned to us and asked, "Hey, you guys want to join?"

Raven looked at me. "Go ahead. Maybe we'll join you after a while. I want to relax here by the fire and water," I answered, settling against Raven.

"Okay." Shelby pulled off her hoodie and threw it at Josh. "Last one in has to get the towels." Giggling, she took off running toward the house.

"Shel, wait!" Josh chased after her.

Raven held me closely as we listened to the soft roll of the tide. The fire crackled softly, creating a nice lull, and I rocked gently in his arms. It was like the ocean water had brought him back to me after it had carried him out, threatening to never return him. But it did, and I would be forever grateful.

"Are you happy?" He picked up my left hand and stared at my fingers.

"More than you'll ever know." I wiggled my fingers, allowing the golden light of the fire to catch the facets of my ring, cascading a shimmer against us.

"What about you?" I turned my head slightly and glanced at him.

He smiled. "You have no idea."

"Were you planning to ask me in the cafeteria?" I was dying to know.

"No, not at all." He ducked his head and I felt a surge of warmth on the back of my neck. "I had just picked up your ring and talked to your dad."

"You talked to my dad?" I shifted my body and looked directly at him.

"Well, yeah. I had to do the respectable thing and ask him for your hand."

Raven never ceased to surprise me. "I can't believe you asked him."

"Is that a bad thing?"

"No." I smiled. "You did good." I couldn't wait to give Dad a call and tell him I was engaged. I had no idea that he knew, but I was dying to know if my mother knew. I'd have to ask Luke later. We had told Raven's mom, stopping by there for dinner after he proposed to me. She was ecstatic and couldn't wait for us to get married. It was a great feeling.

"Good." He nodded and I relaxed against him. "I was actually planning on proposing here."

"Here?"

"Yeah, right here on the beach for your birthday. But I couldn't wait." He shrugged. "So I figured, 'what the hell? I'm going to do this right now.' And so I did."

My eyes watered and I covered my face. Every part of my body tingled with excitement. Just hearing what he had planned made my heart swell and my body rise to a new height. Raven had to be the most thoughtful guy I'd ever met. I sighed, letting a tiny whimper escape.

"Are you crying?" He pulled my hands away from my face. "Why are you crying?"

"I...I'm just so happy." Tiny sobs escaped my lips. "And I'm..."

"You're what?" He used his thumb to wipe the tears from my yes. "Tell me. What's wrong?"

I shook my head. "It's nothing."

"No. I can tell something is up." A look of concern formed in the crevices of his eyes as they searched mine for the truth.

Hesitating, I glanced away. He deserved to know what I was thinking, feeling, but I was afraid to tell him. What if it scared him and he decided that he didn't want to marry me? What if all of this was a mistake? The destructible thoughts continued to plague my mind.

"Lexi. Please." He lifted my chin. "Please don't shut me out."

Funny you should say that.

I sighed and pulled at the fear looming inside, gathering it, determined to take control. If I was going to marry him, I had to be honest with him. I didn't want to enter into a marriage with any reservations. "It's just that sometimes I feel like you shut me out."

His head jutted back and a look of surprise hit him. "Really?"

"Yeah," I quietly admitted.

"Can you give me an example?"

I pressed my lips together, garnering the courage to say it. "Every time you've told me that you don't want to be with me."

"Oh, Lexi." He pulled me close, wrapping me tightly in his arms. "I never meant to shut you out. It had nothing to do with you. It was all the shit — all my baggage — I've been learning to deal with."

Wiping my nose on my sleeve, I sniffed. "I understand. I'm just really scared it will happen again."

He pulled away, looking me directly in the eye. "I promise I'll never shut you out again."

I wanted to believe him; to let go of all the fear telling me he would hurt me again. Even though I had said yes to his proposal, and was willing to give us a shot, because all I wanted was to be with him, I still worried. "How can I be sure?"

"Lexi." His chest rose and fell in long strides. "Because things are different now."

"Different how?"

"It's hard to explain." His eyes narrowed and his lips parted. I waited for him to speak, but he remained silent.

I closed my eyes, knowing he wasn't ready to let me in completely. Why wouldn't he open his heart fully to me? Why didn't he trust me?

"Lexi. Please, just believe me." He tucked a few stray stands of my hair behind my ear.

I connected my gaze to his. "Raven, if we're going to get married, we have to trust each other. Even with our deepest secrets. That's the only way we're going to get through the tough times. I promise to be here for you, no matter what. That's what a relationship is all about. It's the foundation a marriage is built on. Don't you want that for us?"

"I do."

"Then just tell me."

He stalled for a moment, shifting to the right. I eased out of his hands even though he didn't want to let me go. I knelt in front of him and took his hands in mine. "With me, Raven, you don't have to be afraid."

"I'm not afraid, Lexi."

"Then what is it?"

"I..." he looked behind me, staring into the ocean. It seemed as if he was lost in the movement of the waves, allowing them to lure him away. Further away from me. After a long minute, he reconnected his gaze with mine. "I just don't want you to reject me."

"Oh, God. Raven, why would you think that?"

"Because my entire life I've been nothing but a big *reject*. I don't need you rejecting me, too." He jerked his hands from my grip.

"Babe, you're not a reject."

My heart sank, pulling me deeper into the sand. I pressed a hand to my chest, trying to steady my breathing. All of this had to do with him being the product of a gang rape. No one deserved to go through that torment. Not him. Not his mom. Why did life have to be so hard? "I would never reject you. I love you, Raven. Can't you see that? Your mom loves you, and so does your family."

"I know you do and that's what Dr. Galen has been helping me to see. Don't get me wrong, my mom's been great and so has my family. It's just...when you know you were created by someone taking advantage of your mother and the pregnancy wasn't wanted, it's a tough pill to swallow. Not to mention, her initially not wanting to raise me."

"I'm sorry. I wish there was something I could do to change all of that." There was no way I'd ever fully be able to understand what he experienced daily. Thank God Dr. Galen was helping him process through his tough issues, because I had no idea how to help him stop believing that lie.

"Yeah, me too," he whispered, his voice heavy.

"Have I ever done anything to make you feel rejected?"

"You didn't want to tutor me." His eyes glazed over and I swallowed hard.

Jab me one, why don't you?

"Okay." If I was demanding him to be honest with me, then I had to do the same. "I'm not going to lie to you. I was basing everything on rumors, but once I got to know you, I wanted to help you. The only thing I was afraid of was falling for you. And once I realized that I couldn't stop the inevitable from happening, nothing about your past mattered to me." I pressed a hand to his face. "None of your mistakes matter to me. All that matters is that I have your love. All I want is to trust you and know that you're never going to hide things from me."

He shook his head and I retrieved my hand. "Lexi, I've done things I'm not proud of."

"I know and you don't have to tell me if you don't want to, but when they affect our relationship and our future, I think I have a right to know. Otherwise, how can I help you and how can we stay strong?"

He twisted his mouth to the side and his eyes wandered off. "I guess you're right."

"Just... please don't shut me out. That's all I ask." I placed my hand on his and he laced his fingers through mine.

"Shutting you out is the last thing I want. And I'm working on it. Just give me a little time."

"Okay. But how can I be sure you're not going to run away from me or back to the life that wants to destroy you?"

"Because I'm releasing the demons that have been tormenting me all these years. Dr. Galen has shown me things." His expression turned lighter and his eyes brightened. "He's helped me identify why I...why I used women," he shook his head, the disappointed returning, "why I turned to drinking and drugs when I felt abandoned and rejected. It was all because I was seeking attention — a need to feel wanted." He let out a slow, audible breath. "But I'm a different man now. I've changed for the better." He smiled as he revealed his inner most secrets to me. It was as though the burden had been lifted from his chest and he could finally breathe. The air felt lighter, fresher.

I glanced up at the midnight sky, thanking God.

"Raven, it's wonderful that he's helped you understand what has caused you to do the things you're not proud of and how to finally get rid of these demons." I smiled and wrapped my arms around him. There was no question about it; I had seen a change in Raven. The way he acted, carried himself, and his outlook on life. He had changed.

He pressed a tender kiss to my lips. "You still want to be with me?"

Tears flowed down my cheeks. "Always."

"Good, because we're not done with that list of yours."

"List?" I wiped the tears away once more.

"Yeah, that list we've been working on since we fell for each other."

I rested my arms around his neck. "Oh, that list."

"Yeah. That list." Sexiness laced his voice and my body tensed.

"What did you want to mark off?" I bit my lip, hoping he knew what was on my mind.

"I figured we could mark something off my list, too."

"You have a list?" Was there something Raven hadn't done? This was news to me.

He cocked a brow. "I may have done a lot of things, but that doesn't mean I've done everything."

I rolled my tongue across my bottom lip, eager to feel his lips all over me. "What's the first thing you want to mark off?"

"Sex on the beach."

Ha! "Seriously?" I looked around for Josh and Shelby. Some of the lights were still on in the house and I wondered if they were still in the hot tub. Maybe they were having sex, too. "We won't get caught?"

"If anyone walks by, just lay still, like we're asleep."

"I don't think we've ever had motionless sex before." I giggled.

"Then I guess I haven't made passionate love to you." His eyes darkened and a hunger circled the center — a hunger for me.

"Then I guess you need to show me."

"I will." He slipped his fingers through my hair and drew my face to his. His lips lingered on mine and my eyes fluttered closed. I was ready to sink into The Raven's trap; allow him to carry me off to the sea and never return.

Slowly, he laid me against the blanket and covered us with the throw Josh and Shelby had left behind. I melted into the warmth of his caress. Hot and cold shivers struck me and I knew I was sick with his love, but it was a sickness I wanted for the rest of my life.

"Damn, Lexi, I could never stop loving you." His hands roamed freely over my body and I closed my eyes, relishing in every stroke of his touch. I was forever caught in The Raven's trap, soaking up every bit of him.

His lips on me.

Feeling me.

Connecting with me.

Touching me softly.

And I let him go on and on, touching me like I needed to be touched. And I gladly returned the favor, skimming my hands over his body in slow, deliberate strokes. I took in every part of him, showing him all the love I had for him. I was sure the passion we were creating was lighting up the beach for miles and miles, but I didn't care.

His love was good.

His love was genuine.

And I was glad that his love came back to me. And the best part — it wanted only me.

Σ

Chapter 12

"Get up! There's a beach that's calling us!"

My eyes darted open just in time to see Shawn dive onto our bed. He'd burst into the room Raven and I were staying in without even a warning.

"What the hell, dude?" Raven pulled the covers over me. "Can you knock next time?"

I hoped I hadn't flashed him. After last night on the beach, it seemed Raven and I couldn't get enough of each other. We hung out with Shelby and Josh for a while in the hot tub and then finished our night with endless lovemaking. I was a little spent, to say the least.

And totally nude.

I blinked a few times, looking for my phone. "What time is it?"

Shawn propped himself on his elbows, not getting up from our bed. "Almost noon."

"When did you get here?" Raven sat up in the bed, keeping the covers over his hip area. I caught a glimpse of his butt and my cheeks heated. He was totally nude, too. And Shawn was in here like it was no big deal.

Awkward.

"I left Houston around five this morning." He ran a hand over his face, like he was tired. "We were ready to get the hell out of my aunt's house."

"Why were you at your aunt's house?" I asked, keeping the covers pulled to my neck.

"I had to drop my mom off. That was the deal. If they were going to fund my way down here, then I had to take my mom to her sister's house in Houston."

"Dude, you should've come with us."

"Nah, it's alright. Kyle came with me, so it wasn't that bad. It's just that my aunt is nuts. She was preaching the whole time about us going to hell for coming out here. Kyle and I were ready to leave last night." He sighed and took a few deep breaths.

"Where is he?" Raven reached toward the floor, picked up his boxers, and then slid them on, not giving one thought over exposing his butt to Shawn and me.

Embarrassing. I inched further into the covers. I guess they were used to seeing each other naked in the locker rooms, but I was right there. Shawn had to have known what we were doing last night.

"He's in the kitchen, eating with Josh and Shelby." Shawn nodded with his head. "I thought we could hit the beach today. Cook out. Drink a little beer."

"Beer?" I eyed Shawn. Although I didn't want to be a party pooper, Raven was skating on thin ice. They'd most definitely do a drug or alcohol test at his next appointment.

"Just a few, Lexi." Shawn got up from the bed. "Don't worry, your boy knows his limits." He patted Raven on the back.

"That's right." Raven puffed his chest in the mirror, flexing his muscles. Shawn joined in, showing off his biceps. I had to admit, the scene was divine. Raven's fine carved torso made me want to trace every indention with my tongue and squeeze every muscle with my fingers. I could never get enough of his body, especially when it was on mine.

I cleared my throat and looked away. He was doing a good job of distracting me. Even though I didn't mind Raven drinking, I was concerned over what could result from it. What if they found out? I knew he wasn't an alcoholic or a druggy, but his actions had the school on high alert. It was his own fault, but he was under their scrutiny if he wanted to play football and stay at the university.

"I brought a canopy and thought we could set it up." Shawn relaxed his arm. "Kind of like we do when we tailgate."

"Yeah, that's cool." Raven stopped showing off his muscles. "We'll beach bum it and just chill."

"That's what I'm talking about." Shawn stepped up to Raven. They both made a deep whooping sound and then slammed their chests against each other, like they did when they were on the field, proving their manhood and testing their strength.

Men.

"Alright, see you on the beach." Shawn darted out the room, shutting the door behind him.

"Raven?"

"I know what you're going to say." He held up his hands in surrender.

"You promised." I eyed him, trying to keep calm. The condition I set was that he wouldn't get drunk and definitely wouldn't do any drugs. He promised me, claiming that he just wanted to get away and show me a good time.

"I'll be good." He jumped on the bed, pinning me between his arms. He whimpered and his eyes drooped, like a puppy dog. He knew how to hit the soft part of my heart. I decided to go easy on him. After all, we were there to celebrate my birthday and my senior year.

"Don't get me wrong. I want you to have a good time." I stroked his messy hair with one hand. Even with bed head, Raven was damn hot. "To have a week here to remember."

"And that's all I want, too." He tucked my messy hair behind my ear. "Lexi, the last thing I want is to get kicked off the team."

"I know. I just think you need to be extra cautious." He traced the dove on my neck, the one he gave me for Christmas. Goosebumps covered my skin and I shivered from the warmth of his touch.

"I thought we didn't have to be cautious anymore." He pressed soft kisses just above my breasts and a whimper escaped my throat.

"If you're talking about sex, then no." I dropped the covers, wanting to feel more of him. His eyes widened and a snarly expression crossed his lips. "But if we're talking about you being on your best behavior, that's another story."

"When it comes to you, Lexi, I'm not sure I can be on my best behavior." He rose up, supporting himself with his arms, and rubbed his body against mine. His muscles flexed against me and I hooked my legs around him, pressing him into me. "Then again, I don't think I want to." His intent for me was obvious and so was mine.

I wrapped my arms around him and pulled him close to me. "Good, because I don't want you to."

"Damn, this IUD rocks," Raven said with a huge grin.

"Ha-ha. I know something else you can rock."

"You want me to rock your world, baby?"

I nodded, unable to speak.

His eyes turned darker and he lowered his head, pressing his lips to mine. He kissed me deeply, our tongues swirling together. I was ready to make sweet music with him again. With a driven purpose, his mouth left mine as he traced a path down my neck. My back arched as his lips and tongue traced over my breasts. Raven knew how to tease every part of me in a way that made my body scream for his. But he didn't stop there. Raven's mouth was on a mission. My stomach tensed as his lips seared my skin to a nice one-hundred and ten degrees. My fingers dove into his hair and I squirmed, anxious to experience his love for me. Every muscle fell limp as I relaxed into him. And boy, did he rock my world! Not just once, but a few times.

Once we made it out of the bedroom, everyone was already on the beach, relaxing under the purple and white canopy that donned 'PHU' in big letters. The sun was shining bright and there was a slight breeze coming off the Gulf Coast. The temperature was much warmer than last night and the water sparkled invitingly. Salt lingered in the air and I inhaled it. The beach was definitely one of God's awesome creations.

"Damn, it's about time." Josh threw a football to Raven.

Raven caught it, one-handed. "Oh, whatever. Like you two didn't screw all night in the hot tub."

Shelby blushed. "Josh, why did you tell them?"

Josh shot her a look. "I didn't. But you just did."

Shelby's jaw dropped and a look of terror washed over her normally cheerful face.

"Don't worry. Your secret's safe with me." I winked as I set my beach bag next to hers.

"Celebrating the honeymoon early?" Shawn nudged Raven as his brows arched in a telltale sign.

Raven tipped his chin and shook his head. Then he looked up and said, "I don't kiss and tell. Not anymore." He tossed the ball to Shawn.

"I got ya." Shawn snickered. Raven gave him a friendly push and Shawn struggled to keep his footing in the sand. "You done whipped my boy," Shawn said, looking directly at me as he laughed.

"Sorry." I smiled and gave a slight shrug. "What can I say?"

"It's all good," Shawn assured us as he cradled the ball to his bare chest. The ball seemed so small next to his huge pecs. I tried not to notice, but Shawn had a great body, almost as hot as Raven's. Tattoos covered both his arms and a tribal mark covered the area between his shoulder blades. "Kyle, let's play for a while." Shawn motioned for him to get up.

"Alright." Kyle put his beer down and jogged to an open spot on the beach.

Since we were further down the island, and on private property, it wasn't as crowded. I stepped from under the canopy and hooded my eyes from the sun, peering down the shoreline. For miles on end, beach umbrellas and canopies in a rainbow of colors covered the brown sand along with thousands of people. The island was packed with spring breakers.

"What do you think?" Raven wrapped his arms around me as I stared at the waves rolling in along the shore. Small seashells tumbled in the water and then disappeared as the tide retracted.

"I think I'm ready to get in." Giddiness bubbled up inside of me. I couldn't wait to dive in with Raven. There was something about getting in the ocean for the first time with him. Maybe he just made it that much more special.

Two girls wearing bikinis walked toward us, and I immediately caught Raven staring at them. Kyle threw the ball to Shawn without even looking as they drew his full attention. "Hey." He shot them a big grin, showing his pearly whites.

"Hi." A girl with long, blonde hair and a spray-on tan waved at him as she slowed her pace. The girl next to her wasn't hard to miss. With wavy dark hair and boobs the size of cantaloupes, she had me gawking, too. Her bikini top barely covered them and they were too perfect and perky to be real. Raven shot Shawn a wide-eyed look.

"Now that's what I'm talking about." Shawn tossed the ball behind him as he made a direct path to the girls, strutting along the wet sand. The girl with the big boobs twirled her long waves around her fingers as a flirtatious grin played on the edge of her red lips. "What are you ladies up to?"

"We were just checking out the beach," the blonde said, keeping her eyes firmly on Kyle.

"Glad y'all made your way down here. I'm Kyle." He placed his hands on his waist and puffed out his chest.

"I'm Megan and this is my friend Christine." She gave a slight nod with her head, still keeping her eyes firmly on Kyle.

"Hi, Christine. I'm Shawn Jackson." He held out his hand.

"Nice to meet you guys," Christine said with a hi-pitched voice that kind of sounded like Minnie Mouse as she shook his hand. I wasn't sure if she was doing it on purpose or if that was just the way she talked. Maybe her boobs were squeezing all of the air out of her lungs. Who knew? "You guys like to play football?" She eyed the ball lying in the sand.

Kyle and Shawn looked at one another and laughed. "Do we like to play football?"

"Why? You girls want to play with us?" Shawn walked backwards and retrieved the ball. He tossed it in the air a few times, squeezing his arms and chest so they got a full view of his muscles.

Megan and Christine looked at each other and nodded. "Sure. We'll play with you."

Shawn and Kyle winked at each other and made a few hand gestures in their own secret language. I wondered if the girls realized they were about to play with college football players. It didn't matter to me either way. I had my football player and he loved to play with me.

"Come on, let's get in." I took off my swimsuit cover and threw it on the dry sand. I did a sexy pose, hoping he liked the black bikini Shelby helped me pick. Raven had begged for me to try it on, but I told him he couldn't see it until we got on the beach. Raven's eyes traveled up and down my body, a smile of delight spreading across his lips. "You like it?"

"Like it? I love it." He gathered me in his arms. "Damn, Lexi, you're one hot woman." A smoldering look funneled from his eyes and his lips zeroed in on mine. We kissed for a while, almost forgetting where we were. His hands traveled down my back and I pulled away when he squeezed my butt.

"Raven." I slapped his arm. "We're in public." Out of the corner of my eye, I saw Shelby shoot me a thumbs up. I nodded, telling her she had done well.

"Sorry. It's just that..." He pulled away and eyed me one more time. "You're tight, baby." He shook his head, as if he couldn't get enough of me.

I laughed, throwing my head back. Raven was a charmer. He knew how to make me feel like the most beautiful woman on earth. "Okay, now it's your turn." I motioned for him to take his shorts off.

"No. I told you I'm not wearing that damn thing out here."

"Why not?" I pouted. "I think it's sexy. That's why I bought it for you."

"Underwear models wear that shit." He peeked down his shorts and I inched forward, trying to catch a glimpse. "Not football players."

"Oh, come on. For me?" I gathered his shirt in my hands and pulled it off, determined to see him in the hot boy swim trunks I bought. Shelby told me if Josh wouldn't wear them, then Raven surely wouldn't. Maybe she was right, but I at least had to try to convince him.

He leaned forward and whispered, "Lexi, my friends are going to make fun of me."

"So? They're just jealous because you have a better body than they do." I reached for the string holding up his swim trunks and he swatted my hand. "Ouch!"

"Sorry." He picked up my hand and kissed it.

I gave him the same puppy dog eyes he had convinced me with earlier in the bedroom. He sighed and his shoulders curved inward. "Okay." Slowly, he untied the laces and ran his thumbs under the band of his long swim trunks.

"I'm waiting." With my two fingers, I motioned for him to drop them.

"Alright. Alright." He rolled his head around as if I was torturing him. It was kind of fun. Not that I liked tormenting him, but it was exciting to see him out of his comfort zone. Raven was so laid back, acting like nothing ever fazed him, so it was kind of thrilling to watch him squirm a little. With a quick movement, he pulled down his shorts and stepped out of them. "Happy?"

I took my time, eyeing him from head to toe. The black and purple tight swim trunks clung to his well-defined body, showing off his tight rump and the bulge in front. Raven's body was made for sin. "Hell yeah. You look damn hot." I licked my finger and touched his chest, making the sound of something burning. "Sizzling hot."

"Woo hoo!" Shelby yelled as she clapped her hands.

"Sexy!" Josh whistled as he held up his phone, snapping a picture of us. Shawn and Kyle quickly turned around to see what all the commotion was about. When they saw Raven in his boy shorts, they started hollering and waving their arms in the air, just like they did when they made a touchdown on the field.

"Great." Raven narrowed his eyes at me. "See what you've done. He's going to show that picture to the whole team. They'll never let me live this down."

"I'm sorry. I just—"

"That's it. You're going to pay for it." Raven smiled and waggled his brows at me. He then picked me up in one quick sweep and hoisted me over his shoulder.

"Raven! Wait!" I squealed as he ran toward the water. My body bounced against his as he barreled through the waves and into the depths of the Gulf Coast. Water splashed against his legs and onto my face and arms, awakening my skin with millions of chill bumps.

"Shit!" I yelled. "This water if freakin' cold."

"Too bad. You want me to wear these damn shorts... we're staying in the water."

"What?" My teeth chattered and I felt his upper body shiver. "You can't be serious."

"I am." He walked into the ocean and stopped when the water was at his waist. He lowered me into the ocean and my feet touched the soft sand, tickling my toes. I had to admit, even though it was cold, it really was amazing. He held me close as we rocked back and forth with the movement of the waves. "See, it's not that bad."

"Easy for you to say. You're used to s-sitting in tubs of ice for y-your muscles." I bit my lip, trying to keep my teeth from chattering. But it was no use; I was freezing. Releasing from his hold, I moved my arms back and forth in rapid strokes and started jogging in place, trying to get the blood flowing.

"Yeah, this is nothing." He rolled his shoulders a couple of times as he splashed water on his chest and arms. Then he took a deep breath and went under, springing up a few seconds later. "Wow! That feels great." Water dripped from his hair and he ran his hands through it, smoothing it back. Damn, Raven was one fine specimen. But it still didn't change the fact that I was slowly turning into a Popsicle. "Go under. It feels freakin' awesome."

"Hell no." I stared at him like he was crazy. There was no way in hell I was about to submerge my head in the frigid temperatures. This was absolute torture. I couldn't enjoy it with the way my body was convulsing. I rubbed my arms, trying to warm myself, but that didn't work either.

"You're freezing, aren't you?" A look of concern filled his eyes.

I shook my head, unable to speak.

"Let's go a little deeper. Sometimes the water is warmer."

I wrapped my arms tightly around his neck and clung to his body as he led us further into the ocean. Usually, his body heat warmed me up, but his skin was just as cold as mine. I looked around, noticing we were the only idiots in the water as far as I could see.

"Does this feel better?" He stopped when a warm pocket of water swept over us. It made it somewhat bearable until the chilly waves washed over us, soaking my hair. The salty water rushed up my nose and down my throat, burning it. I coughed and squeezed my eyes together, trying to flush the dousing of straight chlorine I'd just inhaled. "I guess not, huh?"

I wiped my nose and sneezed a few times. Nothing like getting a sinus rinse times ten. So much for trying to look sexy and hot for Raven. I was sure I looked like a wet mop. "I think I've had enough of the ocean," I admitted, trying to pull my hair away from my face.

"Let's just hang out on the beach instead." He took my hand and led us back to shore.

"Man, this sucks. I was really looking forward to being in the ocean. Why is it so cold?" We trudged through the sand and out of the icy water. The minute the sun's rays hit my skin, I sighed in relief.

"I guess it hasn't gotten warm enough yet." He wrapped an arm around my waist as we walked toward the canopy. "Tell you what, we can go to the Caribbean or somewhere tropical for our honeymoon."

I smiled. "I think I'll like that much better."

"How was the water?" Josh asked as he sipped his beer.

"Freakin' cold, man." Raven handed me a towel and I wrapped it around me. "I remember it being much warmer last year."

"Aww, that sucks." Josh looked at Shelby and she glanced up from her magazine. "I guess we'll just have to swim in the pool."

"That's fine with me. I really don't like the ocean anyways." She twisted her face and then shook her hands. "I can't stand the seaweed or the feeling of something brushing against my legs." She adjusted her sunglasses. "I'll just sit here and work on my tan."

"But you just got that spray on shit, didn't you?" Josh looked at her from head to toe. Shelby's skin was a nice tan color, nothing like Christine's.

"Yes, but it's already fading away." She reclined her chair and tossed her magazine to the side. "Besides, there's nothing better than a good dose of Vitamin D."

"I totally agree." I turned to Raven. "Will you pull that lounger over here so I can lie on it and dry off?"

"Anything for you, baby." He winked and went under the canopy to get the chair.

"Damn, you two already sound like an old married couple."

"Yeah, whatever," I laughed. "Actually, we sound like newlyweds. You and Shelby sound like an old married couple," I joked.

Shelby laughed. "You got that right." She leaned over and reached for Josh's hand. "But I love my old man."

He latched onto her hand and kissed the top of it. "And I love my old lady. She's smokin' hot."

Shelby winked at him. "You've got that right." We all laughed. Life was great. Not only for Raven and me, but also Josh and Shelby.

Raven set up our chairs just outside the canopy, directly in the path of the sun so we could warm up. We laid in the recliners for an hour or so, just relaxing and enjoying our time away from school. Most of all, we soaked up every minute with each other.

Raven and Shawn fired up the grill and we cooked burgers and hotdogs. Later that evening, we played a game of tag football, after Megan and Christine claimed that they couldn't take any more from Shawn and Kyle's so-called easy tackles. They weren't shocked to find out that the guys played football for PHU. They actually went to an opposing school, but Shawn and Kyle didn't seem to mind. It wasn't hard to figure out why. The girls were actually nice.

We laughed and talked with our friends long into the night, finally ending up in Josh's heated pool and hot tub. My senior Spring Break had definitely been one to remember. I just wished Delaney and Luke were here with us. Even though the water was cold, I still enjoyed the beach over the mountains. Spring Break with Raven was so much better.

Σ

Chapter 13

"Happy Birthday!" a familiar voice echoed in my ear and I slowly opened my eyes. "Get up, girl. It's your day!"

"Laney?" I blinked a few times. "You're here!" I threw my arms around her. "I can't believe you came."

"Did you think I was going to miss celebrating your birthday?" She hugged me tightly.

"Yes. I mean, no." I was confused and still half-asleep. "How did you get here? Did you drive by yourself?"

"Nope." She plopped on the bed. "I came with your brother." Her face glowed with radiance and it wasn't the highlighter or blush. It was a sparkle of happiness that emerged from deep within her. "So, now you two can celebrate your birthdays together."

"Luke came, too?" For the past twenty years, we had celebrated every birthday together. This would've been the first one apart. But he was here. "He didn't go to Breckenridge?" I sat up in bed and quickly checked to make sure I was dressed. Thankfully, I had put on a night shirt, one that Raven had picked out for me when we went shopping with the VS gift card.

"Nope. He told your parents he was coming here instead." She had a huge smile on her face. I was glad he had decided to bring her. "He changed his flight to Dallas and we left last night. We spent the night in San Antonio and got up this morning." She raised her brows at me and I immediately knew what she was hinting at.

"That's great! I'm so glad you guys came. Where are you staying?"

"Luke talked to Josh and he said there was plenty of room for us to stay here." She relaxed against the bed, allowing her long, dark hair to spread out. "Josh already showed us to our room and it's just a big as this one! This house is awesome."

"Tell me about it. His parents must be very well off." I did a quick sweep of the room, noting the white wood furniture with the exquisite furnishings. Each of the five bedrooms had its own theme and we were apparently staying in the nautical room.

"I guess so." She rolled onto her stomach and smoothed the wrinkles from the navy blue and white bed cover. "So, I guess that means no house party, but that's okay. We're going to have one helluva of night. You're twenty-one, girl!"

"Finally!" I did a little dance. "But I don't want to party too hard. I mean, I told Raven I didn't want him getting drunk, so it's not right for me to."

"Says who?" Raven stepped into the room, carrying a tray with food on it and a single red rose in a vase. "Happy birthday, baby." He set the tray on the nightstand and leaned over, giving me a sweet kiss. He had on a muscle shirt and shorts and his tanned skin made him look like he was a regular on the island. Sexy. I was one lucky girl.

"Thank you. You didn't have to bring me breakfast." A perfectly folded omelet with shredded hash browns on the side and sliced strawberries waited for me.

"I wanted to. It's your day. I want you to feel special. Why not start it with breakfast in bed?"

"Aww, babe. I don't know what to say. You're going to make me cry." Raven was the sweetest guy ever. I swallowed a few times, warding off the tears.

"It's just the start." Raven kissed my forehead and handed me a card.

I glanced at the front — *For my fiancée.* I opened it and removed the card. Lying flat inside was a hundred dollar bill. "But you already gave me my birthday present." I showed him my ring. "And something else." I gave my body a little shake.

"I know." He grinned from ear to ear. "But I still wanted to give you something. I figured you might want to go shopping with the girls."

"And we know just where to take her," Delaney said, taking the card from my hand.

"Yes, I'm sure you can show me how to spend it," I teased.

"Hell yeah." Delaney turned to Raven. "I'll make sure to pick out something sexy for her."

"Please do. I want my baby to look really hot for her twenty-first birthday. I'll make sure it's a birthday she'll never forget."

"Oh no, that sounds dangerous." I threw back the covers and got out of bed. I grabbed the fork on the tray and started eating. "Maybe we should just hang out here. Have a nice dinner and watch a movie." I covered my mouth, trying not to show my food. I desperately needed food to recharge.

Delaney started laughing hysterically. "Are you serious?" She sat up. "That sounds like my old roommate."

I set the fork on the plate and crossed my arms. She was right. I did sound like the old Lexi. I didn't want to, but things had changed. Raven was on probation; I didn't want to do anything to jeopardize his chance at going pro. We didn't have to celebrate my birthday at a bar or with a big party. "I know, I just…"

Raven put his arms around me and turned me to face him. Looking me directly in the eyes, he said, "I promise things won't get out of hand. It's your day. Not mine. Let's have some fun and celebrate, okay?"

I chewed on the inside of my cheek, contemplating whether I really wanted to give in. Why did I have to be the one to make the decision? It didn't seem fair. He should've been the one telling me he wanted us to take the safer route, the one less risky, but that wasn't Raven.

He lived.

Lived for the thrill.

For that once in a lifetime chance.

He didn't worry, not like I did. And that's why he needed me. I brought balance to him, helped him see the other side. But the more I told myself that I shouldn't agree, the more I realized I sounded like Collin. And that was the last thing I wanted.

I wanted to live.

Live like Raven.

If just for one night.

"Okay." I spread my lips into a huge smile. "I want to have a good time and go dancing somewhere." I did a little twerking action, showing Raven what the night had in store.

Raven arched his brows. "Oh yeah, baby." He raised his arms over his head and rocked his body against mine, doing an enticing dance that sent every one of my hormones on high alert.

I was in trouble.

Big trouble.

"We're going out!" Delaney chanted as she jumped up and down on the bed, dancing without any music.

"Where's the party?" Luke came into the room, looking at us like we were a bit crazy.

"Luke!" I ran up to him and gave him a hug. "Happy birthday, Brother."

He hugged me tightly. "Happy birthday to you."

"I can't believe you're here."

"It's our twenty-first birthday," he kept one arm around me, "did you think I'd be apart from my twin?"

Our relationship had definitely taken a turn. Ever since Raven started working out with him, he seemed more accepting of our relationship. Now that we were engaged to be married, I think he finally accepted the fact that things were officially over between Collin and I. "What do you want to do tonight?"

Shrugging his shoulders, he said, "I don't care. You decide. It really doesn't matter to me."

"I thought we could go dancing."

"That's fine. Just tell me where the party is and I'm there."

"It's right here, honey." Delaney crooked her finger for him to come to her.

He winked and then strutted his way toward her, doing a little gyrating action with his hips. Raven and I laughed as he teased her. Delaney acted like she was pulling on a piece of rope, reeling him in slowly. He stood at the edge of the bed, looking up at her. Delaney locked lips with him and he wrapped his hands around her waist. With swift movements, he lifted her in the air. Delaney squealed as he swung her around, holding onto her tightly. They looked so happy together.

All of sudden, music started blaring through the house. We looked around, trying to figure where it was coming from. Raven pointed up at the speakers mounted inside the ceiling. The house was wired with a kick ass sound system. It almost felt like we were at a club.

"Happy birthday!" Shelby screamed, piercing my ears as she rushed to join us. She threw her arms around Raven and me, dancing with us. "This is going to be one awesome party. You and Luke celebrating twenty-one years together!"

"I hear it's someone's birthday." Josh walked in next, his guitar around his neck. He strummed to the beat, doing a great job for a fast, top-forty song.

Luke shook his head and laughed as Josh leaned against him, serenading him. My brother was definitely the more serious one, but he was loosening up to Josh's playful antics.

Kyle danced his way into the room, wearing a large sombrero and carrying a bottle of Tequila. Megan shimmied behind him and Raven shot me a quick look. Apparently, they had hooked up last night.

"Oh no." I shook my head. "I'm not doing that. I want to remember my birthday, not pass out drunk."

"Just one shot." Shelby took the shot glass from the top and urged him to open the bottle. Kyle poured the clear liquid into the glass and Megan held out a lemon wedge and salt shaker.

Raven ran his hand down his face and looked at me. "They're determined to make you feel good."

"Uh. No. They want to get me drunk." I backed away, burrowing myself deep into Raven's arm as he protected me. "No, thanks."

"Please?" Shelby begged.

"I haven't finished my breakfast." I pointed to the tray of food behind me. "But I promise, I'll do a shot or two tonight."

"A shot or two? Sweetie, you're going to do a lot more than that," Shelby laughed, showcasing the rounds of her cheeks.

"Give it here. I'll do it," Luke said, setting Delaney to her feet.

"Woo hoo!" Josh yelled as he strummed his guitar faster.

"Hell yeah!" Kyle handed him the glass and everyone chanted Luke's name, over and over.

Luke downed the tequila in one quick gulp and then wiped his mouth with the back of his hand. Megan offered him the lemon and salt. "I don't need it." He held the glass up to the bottle. "Pour me another one."

"Oh, shit. He's going to be drunk before we even get to the bar." I peered from behind Raven's shoulder.

"No, I won't," Luke said in a very confident tone. So my brother knew his limit when it came to shots. He was full of surprises today.

"We're going to party, and party." Delaney sung at the top of her lungs as Luke slammed another shot.

"Yeah!" Luke grunted and shook off the sensation that had probably burned his throat, like it had mine when I tried it at the frat party. He handed Shelby the glass and then turned his attention back to Delaney. They danced to the beat of the music and Luke got down, really showing another side of him. I couldn't believe that was my brother. I had never seen him act or dance that way before. He was definitely ready to party.

"Where's the birthday girl?" Shawn marched in, maracas in hand, with Christine next to him. A Mexican serape covered her entire body and she looked a little hung over. She had spent the night with Shawn and it looked like they had started their morning off with their own private party.

"Right here!" I laughed and danced around the room. My friends took turns twirling me around and around until I became dizzy. I was having so much fun and I hadn't even had one shot. I couldn't even contemplate what tonight would be like. But if I knew Raven, he would deliver on his promise of making sure it was a night to remember.

Delaney and Shelby took me to get pampered while the guys stayed at the house. We invited Megan and Christine to go with us, but they said they had to get back to their hotel, promising to meet us tonight. Raven told me to get ready, because he had lined up something fun for us to do.

We started the afternoon by getting a full body massage, compliments of Shelby. Or Josh's parents, if I knew her, which I did. I kind of felt guilty, but Delaney said for me not to worry. Apparently, she was always blowing either Josh's money, or his parents'. It didn't seem right, but I decided that I might as well enjoy myself. After the massage, we stopped and got something to eat before heading to the nail salon.

We got our toes and fingers done in bright, neon colors. Shelby insisted we get gel nails so it would last longer. The sand was torture on regular nail polish. I honestly didn't know the difference, so I just got what they did. We stopped at a small boutique that Shelby claimed had the cutest clothes before heading back to the house. I thought the clothes looked a little outdated, like something my mom wore when she was in middle school, but I let them pick me out something and hoped Raven wouldn't be disappointed.

We pulled into the garage and went inside the house. Raven and the rest of the guys were sitting on the couch, watching a movie. "You girls back already?" Josh asked, looking up briefly. "Did you buy the whole store?"

"No, we didn't. Just got a few things." Shelby raised the bags in her hands and trotted off to her bedroom.

"Did you have a good time?" Raven reached up and pulled me onto his lap. My legs shot up in the air and everything turned upside down.

"Raven," I giggled as I toppled onto him. "Yes. I got my nails and toes done and had an awesome massage." I showed him fingers and toes.

"You look pretty." He sniffed me. "And smell great, too."

"I look pretty?" I ran a hand through my frizzy hair. The humid temperatures of the island were not kind. "I'm sure I look like a poodle after that massage therapist rubbed my head and scalp."

He swept my hair from face. "You're pretty no matter what. But go get ready." He popped me on the butt with his hand and I squealed. "We've got everything planned. We're going out to eat and then headed to a club to dance the night away."

I glanced over at Luke. "You okay with all of this?"

"Yeah. I told you, whatever you want to do."

I pivoted, sliding off Raven's lap. "It's your birthday, too. I just want to make sure you feel included."

"I'm good." He waved me off.

"You look good." Luke eyed Delaney from head to toe.

Delaney plopped in his lap and wrapped her arms around his neck. "I do?"

"Damn," she waved the space in front of Luke's mouth, "someone's been drinking."

"Does my breath stink?" Luke tested his breath against his hand. "I haven't had that much."

Delaney rolled her eyes. "Just don't pass out before we leave the house."

"If you don't hurry, I might." Luke kissed her on the forehead. "I know it takes you like two hours to get all fixed up."

"No it doesn't." Delaney ran her hand down his chest and Luke's eyes widened. "Only when you don't let me get ready." Their lips locked again and I turned away. I had never seen them kiss so much. It was kind of weird.

"Take it to the room." Shawn leaned forward, trying to see the TV.

"Sorry," Delaney said, breaking their kiss and getting up from Luke's lap. "Come on." She grabbed him by the hand and pulled.

"What?" Luke said, giving a slight shake of his head. "I'm watching the game." He pointed to the Ranger's game on the TV.

Josh made a comment that I didn't catch and Raven whistled a sexy tune.

"Yeah, I need your help." Delaney did a little shake, trying to entice my brother.

"I guess," Luke said, getting up from the couch, a smile dying to be revealed.

The guys whistled and made remarks, teasing and taunting them. Luke paid them no attention and followed Delaney. *Wow.* She really had a grip on my brother. I hoped she wouldn't break his heart, but it wasn't my business. I just wanted them to be happy and from what I could tell, they were.

It took hours before we finally made it to the restaurant. Thanks to Delaney and Luke, we were running late, but no one seemed to care. We were there to have a good time and celebrate our birthdays. We piled into Luke's car after Raven announced he'd be the designated driver for the night. It was kind of weird seeing him drive my brother's car, but Luke didn't seem to mind. He was either too *into* Delaney to care, or too drunk to make a fuss. I couldn't wait to give him a hard time later.

We devoured an incredible seafood buffet at a local restaurant. My pallet had definitely found something new to savor. From scallops, to lobster, to crab legs — it was all delicious and I couldn't get enough of it. Just as we were finishing our dinner, two waiters appeared. One had two slices of key lime pie with a candle on top and the other held two very large stuffed animal lobster heads.

"Hell no." Luke shook his head. "I'm not putting that thing on."

"Oh my God," I laughed. "That thing is going to swallow my whole body."

"Uh." Delaney crossed her arms and made perfect duck lips. "Why not?"

"Laney." Luke gave one of his stares that said, "Don't push me", but she batted her long lashes at him and his faced relaxed. "Oh, alright." He motioned for the waiter to give it to him. Everyone cheered as he put on the overstuffed sea creature. The other waiter helped me put on mine, and it covered half of my body, as I expected.

"Great. Now we really look like twins," Luke said.

"Is that a bad thing?" I asked, struggling to move.

"Smile!" Delaney said as she took our picture.

"Um, you can't see our faces," Luke reminded her.

"Whatever." She snapped several shots of us. Everyone laughed and I'm sure we looked ridiculous.

The waiters lit the candles and everyone sang happy birthday. The waiters helped us remove the lobster heads and we blew out the candles. After we finished our dessert, we headed to the bar. It was a few buildings over from the restaurant, so we walked. The line extended into the parking lot. It looked like every college student on the island was there.

"Damn, it's going to take us an hour to get in." Delaney checked her phone. "And it's almost ten."

"No it won't. Just follow me," Josh said, taking the lead. We followed him to the front of the line.

"If he thinks he can buy our way in, he's crazy," Delaney told Shelby.

Shelby gave a slight shrug. "Who knows?"

"Just wait," Luke said, lighting up a cigarette.

"I thought you said you were going to quit." Delaney pulled it from his mouth and took a drag.

"Hey."

"What?" She laughed and then put it back in his mouth.

Josh spoke with a huge guy standing at the front door. He had on a neon yellow muscle shirt and jeans. Sweat trickled down his bald head and he wiped his forehead with the back of his hand. It was definitely warmer tonight; the air was humid and sticky. I was now glad that Delaney had pulled half of my hair up. Otherwise, I would've really looked like a poodle.

"He's needs to see our IDs," Josh said, stuffing his wallet into his back pocket. "Come on." He took Shelby by the hand and waited for the guy to unhook the red rope that blocked the entrance. The bouncer released the latch and moved to the side, checking our IDs as he allowed us entry.

"No way." I smiled at Raven and he winked.

"Bullshit." Delaney shook her head and asked Josh, "What did you tell him?"

"That I had a section reserved for us."

"Sweet." Delaney turned to Luke. "Why didn't you tell us?"

"We wanted it to be a surprise," Raven said, pulling me close. "Happy birthday, baby."

I gave him quick kiss. "Thank you."

We entered the huge, two story nightclub. Colored lights flashed through the smoky air, giving the place a very seductive atmosphere. Eighties music blared through the speakers and everyone was dressed to match it. I looked at my outfit and it made sense. "So that's why you wanted us to dress like this?" I yelled to Delaney and Shelby.

"Yep. It's an eighties club." Delaney laughed as she danced her way to our reserved seating. She and Shelby had on neon off-the-shoulder shirts and short jean skirts paired with Chucks, which had most of the guys turning their heads. "I'm glad you trusted me." Delaney put her arm around me as we shuffled through the groves of people and entered the reserved area.

With a direct view of the dance floor, we had the best seats in the house. Our reserved area was the size of a large cabana, with plush couches, lighted palm trees, and curtains on the side, for a bit of privacy. It was sweet.

"Why didn't you just tell me? I probably would have picked out something different." I looked down at my see-through blouse that revealed my black bikini top underneath.

"What, you don't like what we picked out?" Delaney flagged the waitress in the cabana next to us.

"I kind of look like Madonna or something." I held up my hands, showing them my fishnet gloves and jelly bracelets coupled with a big leather band with spikes, which they had picked out.

"That's the whole point."

Raven laughed. "You do look like Madonna from the eighties."

"Great."

"It's good. I mean, I'm liking your get up, if you know what I mean." He pulled on my black tulle skirt and acted like he was trying to catch a glimpse of what was underneath. "And we can do it like a virgin, if you know what I mean."

"Ha-ha." I swatted his hand away in a playful manner. "I'll remember that for later."

"Not sure if I can wait until later." He pulled me close and my chest pressed to his. Even under his neon green polo shirt, I could feel every bulge waiting to be explored, inch by inch. My fingers traced a direct path to the button on his shorts and I gave it a little tug.

"Damn, can't you guys wait until we get home?" Josh shook his head as he motioned for us to get out of his line of sight.

"Whatever, man." Raven waved off his comment and we sat down.

"What can I get you to drink?" A waitress with brown crimped hair wearing a white T-shirt and shorts with paint-splattered suspenders appeared.

"Fireball shots for everyone," Josh informed her.

"Except for me, I'll take a Coke," Raven quickly interjected.

"One Coke and five Fireballs. Anything else?"

"Yeah, what do you have on draft?" Luke asked as I turned my attention to Raven.

He was keeping his promise and I couldn't be prouder. "Thank you." I smiled and rubbed his leg, feeling his huge quad under my fingertips. He looked damn hot in tan shorts and Sperry's. I retrieved my hand, keeping it under tight control. I could wait until later.

"Hey, I told you, I'm not screwing up this time." He crossed his leg over his knee and rested his arm behind me. "Besides,

I'm designated driver. The last thing I want to do is wreck your brother's car."

Luke quickly turned his head in our direction. "That's right," he pointed at him, "I'm trusting you."

Raven nodded. "I've got your back, dude. Don't worry."

Luke shot him a thumbs up and then wrapped his arm around Delaney. It was neat seeing them together after they hid their relationship for so long. They seemed more at ease and definitely *into* each other. The angst between them had definitely disappeared.

"Is that a pool?" I leaned forward, catching a glimpse of outside. There was a huge swimming pool jammed with tons of people in the center of the patio. Some were playing water volleyball while others were drinking at the swim-up bar. "That's so cool."

"Yeah, you didn't see that when we came in?" Raven asked.

I shook my head. "No, I must have missed it."

"That's why we told you to wear your bikini." Shelby winked. "I can't wait to get in there later." She leaned against Josh, stroking his short blond hair.

"Whatever you want, sweets. We'll do it." Josh snuggled up to her and kissed her on the neck. Shelby squealed and they exchanged a playful struggle for each other's affection.

"What the hell is this?" Raven held up his hand. "Why don't you two get a room?"

Josh shot Raven the finger and Raven shot him one back.

"Leave them alone, they're in love." I nuzzled him. "Like we are."

Raven took my hand and kissed my fingers. "Baby, I'm more than in love with you. I'm crazy for you." His lips claimed mine and my eyes fluttered closed. I drank in all of him — from the sweet taste of his lips, to his tantalizing tongue that did a divine dance with mine, to his scent that melted every part of my body. I devoured it all, shackling myself in his embrace.

"Shit, is this the make out booth or what?" Shawn asked as our lips parted.

Raven leaned forward. "Hey, man, glad you could make it." They exchanged fist bumps.

"Someone has to watch out for your ass," he joked, putting his arm around Christine. "Lexi will be drunk before the night is over."

"Hmm. Maybe." I shrugged. "Glad to know you have his back."

"I'll always have his back." Shawn gave a playful punch to Raven's arm.

Kyle and Megan joined us shortly after Shawn and Christine sat down with us. Later that night, we ran into Jordan and Forbes who were there with a few other guys from the baseball team. I knew Collin wasn't there, since he was in Breckenridge with my family. I was glad I didn't have to worry about that.

After two rounds of Fireball shots and two glasses of Malibu and Coke, I was ready to dance. The music had me bobbing my head side to side and I was eager to show Raven my moves.

"Oh. My. God. We have to dance. I love this song!" Delaney shouted, pulling Luke to his feet.

"Are you serious?" Luke rolled his eyes. "Michael Jackson?"

"Come on." Delaney waved for me to follow and I grabbed Raven's hand, pulling him with me. Josh and Shelby joined us. The dance floor filled up quickly as everyone rushed to partake in the zombie dance. We all moved like a pack of sardines, to the left and to the right, following the beat of the music in perfect sync.

A third of the way into the song, Shelby and Josh started yelling and whistling. I turned around to see Luke doing a perfect moonwalk, followed by some smooth Michael Jackson moves. My jaw hit the floor. Never in my life had I seen my brother dance like that. "What the hell? When did he learn those moves?" I asked Delaney.

Delaney shrugged as she clapped along. "When your brother is drunk, he really loosens up."

"Apparently so." Who knew? Luke apparently had an alter ego. Maybe it was suppressed like mine had been. Everyone cheered as he tore up the dance floor, and I couldn't help but praise his perfect performance.

The song ended and immediately transitioned into a top-forty hit. The crowd erupted into a frenzy and everyone flooded the dance floor. The Latin beat had Raven moving his hips, much to my body's delight. I took a step back, taking in every part of him in, from his head to toes.

Oh yeah.

"Come on, baby." He swayed from left to right, enticing me even more. I tried to follow his footsteps, but I had no idea what I was doing. "I don't know how to salsa," I cried, stumbling along.

Raven lowered his hand to the middle of my back and our bodies molded together; Raven's body fit perfectly with mine. "Don't worry, baby, I'll show you all the moves." His voice surrounded me and I fell victim to his words.

"Mmmm. You promise?"

His eyes answered me with full, sexual intent. I couldn't wait to get him home tonight. He laced my arms around his neck and I relaxed into him. "Just let the rhythm move you." I closed my eyes as his pelvis rocked against mine, showing my body what he wanted it to do. And, eventually, I got it. We danced for what seemed like hours, sweat trickling down our bodies and our breathing heavy with exhaustion. But neither of us wanted to stop. We were too *into* each other.

"We're going outside." Shelby pulled on my arm and I turned around. "Come with us."

"Want to get some air?" Raven asked, inhaling deeply.

"Yes, I need something to drink." I wiped the sweat from my forehead. "And, I'm hot."

"You're damn right you are," Raven whispered in my ear and I shivered in excitement.

With hands locked, we followed Shelby outside. Delaney screamed when we met up with the rest of our friends on the other side of the swim-up bar. Luke swayed back and forth with a cigarette hanging off his bottom lip, ready to either pass out or throw up. "Shit, your drunk." I flagged the bartender. "I need a water, please."

"No. I feel good." He smiled and the cigarette fell to the floor. "Besides, I'm not passing out. Not tonight." He grabbed Delaney's butt and she shrieked.

"Luke!" She threw herself on him and they started kissing, showing a little too much PDA.

"Oh God," I sighed, looking at Raven.

"What? Don't look at me. He's your brother."

"Yeah, but you're going to be the one taking care of him," I reminded him.

"I don't think so. That's what his woman is there for." He pointed at Delaney. "She can do it."

Delaney and Luke laughed, not paying attention to anyone as they continued kissing each other.

"Shots!" Shelby yelled as soon as the Fireball song started playing.

"Nine Fireball shots," Josh told the bartender.

"Put it on my tab." Shawn held up his finger as the bartender flipped over a bottle of vodka and shot a squirt of something into it with the soda nozzle. Josh shook his head, but Shawn said, "I've got this one." At lightning speed, the bartender poured our drinks and lined them up for us. We grabbed our glasses and Raven motioned for us to wait.

"Happy twenty-first birthday to my baby," Raven held up his soda as everyone raised their glasses, "and to my good buddy, Luke."

Luke gave a slow nod, holding up his glass with a wobbly hand. "Cheers!"

"Here's to twenty-one!" Shawn yelled and we downed our drinks together.

Shelby jumped up and down, screaming, "Fireball!" Then she slammed her empty glass on the bar, and said, "Another round. And this time, he's paying." She hooked a thumb to Josh.

The bartender poured us another round, except for Raven, and Luke, when he motioned he didn't want anymore.

Thank God.

I shimmied against Raven to the beat of the song, keeping my backside firmly pressed to his front.

Damn he felt incredible.

I could have rubbed on him all night long if he let me.

I never wanted the night to end.

Raven I continued to dance in our private circle as our friends danced nearby, with the exception of Delaney and Luke, who had disappeared after Delaney asked for the keys. They played the Fireball song what felt like ten more times and every time they did, Shelby ordered another round. We took a few more shots, until my throat was coated with the sweet and spicy taste of cinnamon. But I didn't care. It was my twenty-first birthday and I wanted to have a good time. As long as I didn't pass out or throw up.

"Let's take a walk." Raven pulled my Malibu and Coke from my hand and set it on the bar.

"Okay." He led me through the crowd and I held on tight as the floor tilted under me. People bumped into me, but I managed to make it to the back of the patio. Raven helped me down the stairs and onto the beach. My feet immediately sunk into the cool sand, but I managed to stay upright, using him to steady my steps. Tiki-torches lit the path and we followed it to the shore. Several people were on the beach, drinking and laughing under the bright moonlight and crystal clear sky. I couldn't have asked for a better birthday.

"How drunk are you?" He pulled me close and I struggled to stand straight.

"Just a little." I used my index finger and thumb to show him how much.

"Good, because I want you to remember your birthday."

"I will." I pawed at his chest, eager for him to help make it more memorable. "As long as I don't do any more shots."

"I think you're done for the night."

"Well, I don't know about that." I ran my fingers through his hair, eager to feel more of him. Between the liquor and dancing, I was more than turned on. I definitely had that drunk-sex feeling and right now seemed as good a time as any. I looked around the beach, but there were too many people. It wasn't like the spot near Josh's house. Someone would definitely see us.

"Lexi?" Raven called for my devout attention. I held my gaze to his with blurred vision, even though I wanted to close my eyes and let him take me right there. "I want you to know how happy I am that you're going to be my wife."

"Aww, Raven. I can't wait to be your wife." My smile enveloped me from the inside out. I loved Raven with all my heart.

"So, when do you think you want to say *I do*?"

His question took me by surprise. Between all of the Fireball shots and Malibu and Coke I had drank, I couldn't think of a date, so I said, "Whenever you want."

"Shit. Mexico is right over there." He pointed across the ocean.

I laughed. "I don't want to get married in Mexico." I gave him a slight push and he caught me before I lost my balance.

"No?" He held me tightly in his arms, keeping me from falling on my butt. "What about Vegas?"

I shrugged. "Maybe." Then the words registered. He was asking me when and where I wanted to get married. He was dead serious. I honestly hadn't given it much thought. Everything had happened so quickly, I just wanted to revel in the excitement and all-over-feel-good sensation that had consumed me night and day. "How about back home? I want my Dad to walk me down the aisle," I hiccupped and then giggled, covering my mouth.

"Okay, we can do that." Raven's perfect white teeth shone bright in the darkness. I'd never seen him so happy. It was as though nothing else in the world mattered. Only us. I found myself spinning with him and prayed I wouldn't pass out. I wasn't ready for the night to be over with. I had another agenda.

"Yeah, but I want something else first." I ran my hands down his chest, giving his pecs a hard squeeze. I may have been drunk, but I knew what I wanted.

He raised a brow. "Oh yeah, what's that?"

"How about birthday sex?"

His eyes widened in further delight. "I thought I already gave you that this morning," he replied, his words hinting that he'd be okay with another round.

"Oh, yeah, you did," I said in a seductive tone. "But the truth is... I can't get enough of you."

"Then, I'll give it to you." Raven picked up my hand and trailed kisses along my arm. "As much as you want." Chill bumps spread all over me and I shivered. He pressed a kiss to my neck and I leaned back, allowing him to devour me to his desire and mine as well.

"But you know what?" I pushed him back as the pangs of hunger struck me.

"What's that, baby?"

"I think I need a Whataburger first."

Raven laughed. "Lexi, you never cease to amaze me."

"What? Did I say something wrong?" I repeated the words in my mind. A greasy burger followed by sex. Was there anything better?

"Come on, baby. Let's go find everyone and get your burger." Raven picked me up and hauled me across the sand, as if he couldn't wait. And neither could I. This had been the best birthday ever.

Σ

Chapter 14

It was the best-worst birthday ever. My head pounded viciously and I felt like I'd been dragged up and down the street a few times. Since I couldn't remember much after we left the club, maybe I had been. I stood under the spray of the shower, allowing the warm water to beat down on me, hoping and praying I felt better once I got out.

After standing there for several more minutes, I finally shut the water off. I jumped when I saw Raven waiting outside with a towel. "Raven," I gasped.

"Sorry. I didn't mean to scare you." He handed me the towel and I wrapped it around my body, too worn out to dry myself.

"Were you watching me?" My words slurred together, making me sound half-drunk rather than sexy, as I had intended.

"Yeah." His eyes traveled up and down, taking me in slowly.

If I hadn't been so hung over, I would have pulled him into the shower with me. But sex was honestly the last thing on my mind, for fear of puking all over him. "Maybe I'll feel better later and we can get wet together." I ran a hand through my wet hair.

His face lit up, like I had I said the winning words. "I'd like that."

I dragged my heavy body to the bathroom counter and used it for support. Never had I felt this bad. This totally sucked. With the hand towel, I wiped the condensation from the mirror. Not only did I feel like shit, I looked like it. I managed to brush my teeth without throwing up, but didn't have the energy to brush my hair.

"Are you alright?"

I shook my head. "No. I feel like I've been hit by a train."

"I told you to slow down." He helped me to the bed and I sat down. "I knew you would hate today."

"Being hung over sucks." My body swayed back and forth as I tried to sit up straight. "Never again. What about Luke? How's he doing? He definitely had more to drink than me."

"Delaney said he threw up and then passed out in the car. Josh and I had to carry him to bed. You probably should have thrown up. Ya know, gotten it out of your system."

"I thought that burger would have helped." The thought of food made my stomach turn and threatened my throat with the pungent taste of vomit.

"What burger?"

"I thought we stopped to get something to eat." I tried to recall what happened after we left the nightclub, but it was all a blur. However, I did remember wanting a Whataburger, which sounded horrible right now.

"No. Delaney wanted to get Luke home. Besides, I don't think food was on your mind. You practically attacked me in the car." He laughed as he stepped into the bathroom and retrieved my clean clothes.

"Oh, please tell me I didn't."

"Yeah, you straddled me and said you were ready to take me downtown."

I laughed. "What the hell does that mean?"

"Hell if I know. I had to remind you that driving with you on my lap would definitely be hazardous." I covered my eyes with my hands, completely embarrassed. I could only hope everyone else was too drunk to be paying attention.

"I can't believe I mauled you while you were trying to drive."

Ugh!

Kneeling in front of me, he helped me slip on my panties and shorts. He even hooked my bra for me. What a man. "If it makes you feel better, I hadn't actually started the car yet. But you can show me what this 'downtown' is about later, if you want." His lips grazed the top of my shoulder and I collapsed into his arms, too weak to hold myself up. The offer sounded so enticing, but I couldn't even think of sex right now. "Do you want to dry your hair?"

"Nah, it's okay." I leaned against him, wishing I felt better. I didn't even have the energy to towel dry it.

He pulled my hair to the side and then slipped my shirt over my head. "It's really wet."

"Okay, I guess. But can you do it for me?"

"Of course." He kissed my forehead and returned to the bathroom.

"Grab the brush while you're in there." I tried to run my fingers through my hair, but it was all matted. "Damn, what did I do to my hair?"

Raven laughed again. "That must have been the chlorine."

"Chlorine?"

"Yeah, you stripped down to your bikini and jumped in the swimming pool."

"Oh, how embarrassing." I had become the thing I despised most — a drunken idiot.

"That's not all. When we came home, you rode my ass like never before." My head shot up just in time to see Raven adjust his shorts. "Damn, you wore me out before passing out cold."

"You're lying." Heat inundated my cheeks. I had never acted that wild.

"When you're drunk, a sexy vixen comes to life."

I guess there's a first time for everything.

He plugged in the hair dryer and flipped it on, combing the knots out of my hair. "I kind of like it." He winked.

I smiled. "I'll remember that." My head fell forward and I stared at my legs and toes. There was a big, purple bruise across my right knee and the nail polish on my right big toe was scraped. I wondered how that happened. The gel nail polish was supposed to be durable. Maybe not for clumsy drunks. That's when I finally recalled kicking off my shoes and stripping off my clothes before jumping in the pool. I had done exactly what he'd said. *What an idiot!*

After Raven dried my hair, I pulled it into a ponytail and got back into bed.

"Do you want me to bring you something to eat?"

I moaned. "No. I just want to sleep."

"Okay." He kissed me on the cheek and pulled the covers over me. "You picked a good day for it. It's raining outside."

I listened for a moment at the sound of the rain tapping on the window. The soothing sound immediately eased the throbbing in my head. "Good. It will help me sleep."

"I'll check on you in a little while." Raven flipped off the light and the room darkened. I slept for a few more hours, finally getting up around four in the afternoon feeling somewhat alive.

"Good afternoon, sunshine," Josh said with a rolling pin in his hand.

"Morning." I shuffled my feet against the cold tile, feeling the sluggishness in my legs. It felt like the blaze from the Fireball liquor had lost its fire, replacing my body with a heap of ashes instead. I sat at the bar and slumped over the cold marble. I hated this feeling.

"You had one hell of a birthday." Shawn snickered, but I didn't have the energy to say anything back.

"Leave her alone. She had a great time." Shelby wiped her hands on a towel and came to my side. She wrapped an arm around me and my body practically fell against her. "Didn't you?"

I gazed up her and smiled. She had flour on the tip of her nose. It reminded me of myself when I was in the kitchen. I glanced to see what they were cooking. Flour covered the island, along with garlic and tomatoes. The smell of Italian food drifted through the air and my stomach couldn't decide if it was hungry or gun shy, for fear of tossing it back up.

"Too much," I moaned.

She released me and I swayed to the side. I grab the counter and steadied myself. The room did a quick spin and I closed my eyes.

"All I know is that you need to show me how to swing on a pole." Shelby slapped her hand on the counter and my eyes shot open. "You worked that thing like a pro."

"Wh-what pole?"

"The pole that was by the pool. You were swinging on it before you jumped in the water."

"Oh. No. Please tell me I wasn't." I slumped further on the stool and shielded my face with my hands. That's when I noticed the bruise marks on my inner thighs. They looked like carpet burns. Or pole burns, in this case.

"I saw the video. You were workin' it, girl," Delaney laughed as she rounded the corner.

"You filmed me?" I felt all of the color drain from my face. I had done what Mr. Marshall warned us not to do.

Shit!

"Not me." Delaney pointed to Shelby. "Her."

Shelby walked over to the bar. "I'm sorry. I'll delete it, if you want."

"Just please tell me you didn't post it." I suddenly felt the nausea I'd been fighting burn the back of my throat.

She crossed her fingers over her heart. "I promise I didn't."

"I wouldn't let her, baby." Raven approached me from behind and gathered me in his arms. "I told her it would get us in trouble."

"And we sure as hell don't need that," Josh added.

"Why didn't you tell me?" I looked up at Raven. "Or why didn't you stop me?"

"I tried to, but you were determined to show me what you could do." Raven's brows shot up and he gave me a wicked grin. "And Shelby is right. You can work a pole, baby! Where did you learn moves like that?"

"Oh, God." My head hit Raven's chest. "Anything else you guys want to tell me about last night?"

"Lexi," Raven lifted my chin, "don't be embarrassed. We've all had our nights. Last night was yours."

"And Luke's." Delaney sighed. The dark circles around her eyes told me she had probably been up all night with him. I guess she was returning the favor for all the times my brother had taken care of her. Or better yet, he was getting her back for all the times he had to take care of her drunk ass.

"How is Luke?"

"Hung over. Big time." Luke dragged himself into the kitchen, still looking half-drunk. "Do you have any chicken noodle soup?"

"Soup?" I asked, wondering if he was sick or just hung over.

"Yeah, in the pantry." Josh pointed to the door to the right of him.

Delaney opened the pantry door and pulled out two cans. "Want one, Lexi?"

"Why would I want soup? I'm not sick, just hung over."

"Are you serious?" Josh looked at me with confusion.

"It's the best cure for hangovers," Raven said, nodding to Delaney, affirming I would eat it.

"I didn't know that," I openly admitted. Then again, when it came to drinking and partying, I really didn't know much. At least, not like my friends and brother.

"Trust me. It works," Luke slurred as he plopped down on the seat next to me.

"I'm surprised you're alive." I gave him a once over. His beautiful blue-green eyes were bloodshot and his hair was a disheveled mess. His after five shadow was a little thicker than normal and he still reeked of alcohol. "You were downing those Fireball shots like water."

"Don't remind me. I'm never doing that shit again. That cinnamon burns when it comes out of your nose."

"Gross." I shuddered as the reminder suddenly hit my taste buds.

"Oh hell, I was going to ask if you wanted another one," Josh laughed.

"Eff you man." Luke flipped him the bird. "I'll remember that the next time we're in the gym."

"Aww, hell. I should have kept my mouth shut." Josh immediately returned his attention to the ball of dough in front of him. "Since it's raining and everyone feels like shit, I thought we could hang out here tonight and watch some movies on Netflix."

"And eat some of your homemade pizza." Shelby dotted the tip of Josh's nose with some flour.

"Of course, sweets. I can also make one of those cookie desserts, if you want."

"I love those." Shelby stole a pepperoni from one of the pizzas Josh had just set on top of the stove behind him.

"I saw that." He pulled the dishtowel off his shoulder and popped Shelby on the butt. She shrieked and then grabbed his hand, using his palm to rub the pain away. They continued to flirt with each other as Delaney dodged them, carrying a big bowl of soup for Luke.

"Yours is heating up, Lexi."

"Thanks."

When the microwave beeped, Raven brought the soup to me along with some crackers. Luke and I sipped the broth and ate our crackers slowly, but managed to finish it. And they were right. It definitely was a cure for hangovers. Although I didn't feel one-hundred percent better, I did feel functional.

After everyone ate pizza and Josh's cookie dessert, with the exception of me and Luke, we watched a scary movie. Throughout the entire movie, I snuggled up to Raven, hiding behind his shoulder and covering my ears with my hands. Watching horror movies was not my thing. I enjoyed sleeping too much to waste it on being scared all night.

When the movie ended, Shawn walked to the kitchen and returned with a few beers in his hands. He handed one of them to Raven, but before Raven took it, he looked at me. "Do you mind?"

"We're staying here, right?"

"Yeah, we're not going anywhere, Lexi," Shawn said, urging him to take it.

I shrugged. "I don't care, as long as you don't leave or get wasted like I did last night."

"I'm staying right here, baby. And don't worry, I'll only have one or two, tops."

"Want one?" Shawn asked, trying to hand me one.

"No, thanks." I recoiled at the thought.

"Sorry." Shawn patted my shoulder. "Still feeling the effects from last night, huh?"

I pulled my feet onto the couch and tucked them under me. "Unfortunately, yes."

"I'll take one." Delaney held out her hand.

"You want one?" Shawn offered one to Luke.

"Hell no." Luke turned his head quicker than I had. Apparently, he felt worse than I did.

"Anyone up for a little music?" Josh strolled into the living room, strumming his guitar. The strings melded together in beautiful harmony as he moved his head to the beat of the music. I listened intently, trying to place the melody. Finally, I was able to pick out the notes. It was a John Mayer song.

"Yeah, man, bring it on." Raven flipped off the TV and we listened to Josh play a few songs. Shelby sat on the floor directly in front of him as he serenaded her. It was really sweet. Raven held me close and we swayed together, relaxing against each other. I waited for him to sing, but he just hummed along as he drank his beer. Luke and Delaney sat curled up together while Shawn and Kyle relaxed on another sofa, sipping their beer.

"Yay." I clapped when he stopped. "You play really well."

"Thanks. Hey, what can you play on the piano?" Josh motioned with his head to the baby grand in the front sitting area.

A tingle of excitement filtered through me. "Lots of things." I smiled. "Hold on a minute." I ran to our room and retrieved my Kindle. I pulled up a website where I downloaded most of my music. "What can we play together?" I hummed, searching through a few options.

"I can pick up just about anything." Josh hit a few chords, showing me his skills.

"Alright." I walked to the piano and everyone gathered around. I lifted the fallboard and my fingers hovered over the keys. I took a deep breath. "Give me a few minutes to warm up. It's been a few months since I've played."

Delaney mouthed. "Will you be okay?"

I nodded and shot her a quick wink. I allowed my fingers to take over as they glided up and down the keys. It may have been a few months, but my fingers claimed their territory quickly. What I loved most was the way my ring sparkled as my fingers hit all the right notes.

"Damn, you're pretty good," Josh said, trying to pick up on the melody.

I laughed. "I'm not playing anything in particular."

"What are you going to play for me, baby?" Raven slid in next me, twisting the top off another beer. "Relax. It's only my second."

"And your last?" I asked with a raised brow.

"Of course."

I smiled, hoping he was being honest with me. I wasn't trying to tell him what to do, just watching out for him like I had promised. "I can play *Lean On Me*." I nudged him, hoping he'd recall the first time we sang together. I also wanted to ease the tension building between us.

He dipped his chin and a wide smiled spread across his face. "I remember that day."

"I do, too." I inclined my head in his direction.

"I don't know if I can play that song." Josh tried a few notes, sounding a little off key. "Do you know any country?"

"No." I shook my head. "I tend to play more classic rock, top-forties, or oldies — you know, for my parents." I immediately started playing the intro to one of my dad's favorite songs by Journey.

"Oh, yeah." Josh nodded his head to the beat of the music, picking out the chords rather quickly.

"I didn't know you played rock songs." Raven looked at me.

"Do you know the words?"

He shook his head. "No."

"Look it up on my Kindle." I motioned for him to pick it up. "Josh, do you know the words?"

"Not really, just the chorus." He repeated the words, closing his eyes as he sang at the top of his lungs. "Shit, I can't sing like Steve Perry."

"Hell, neither can I," Raven laughed.

Josh and Raven turned to Luke. "Don't look at me. She sucked the all music genes from me."

"Yeah, but you got the sports talent, leaving me with none," I reminded him. Everyone laughed. "What about you, Shawn? Kyle?"

They both shook their heads and lifted their bottles to their mouths. They weren't even going to try.

Raven belted out the words and we cheered him on. With a hand pressed to his chest and the other holding my Kindle so he could see the words, he said, "Lexi, I'm forever yours, faithfully." He sounded nothing like Steve Perry and was seriously off key, but I didn't care. It was the emotion behind his words that made it so special. I started singing, "Whooa, oh-oh-ooh," and everyone joined in. We laughed and continued singing, not caring if we hit the right notes.

"Hey, what about his song?" Josh began to strum the beat of a familiar song.

"Isn't that Jeremy Kay?"

"Yep." Josh closed his eyes as he sang the lyrics.

"Do me a favor and look up that song so I can get the chords," I asked Raven as I tried a few on my own.

He found the song and then set my Kindle in front of me. "Thanks, babe." It took me a minute or so, but I finally got the chords down. Before long, we were all swaying side to side and singing at the top our lungs. It was great playing alongside Josh. We were able to follow each other flawlessly. In the end, I played *Lean On Me*, and everyone joined in, including Luke. It was one of the best times with my friends, brother, and of course, Raven. The memories we made, were ones I'd never forget. Raven had definitely made it the best Spring Break ever.

Just as we wrapped up the song, we heard a bunch of racket. "What is that?

"Are those gun shots?" Shawn turned his head, searching for the direction of the noise.

"It's fireworks." I pointed outside, catching a quick glimpse of a spray of flickering lights.

Raven got up from the piano bench and I followed him. Peering out the window, we saw a group of people on the beach. "Someone's popping fireworks."

"This is private property." Josh removed the strap of his guitar from around his neck and set it against the wall.

"I'll go with you," Raven said, following him to the back door, still carrying his beer in his hand.

"Me, too," Shawn quickly added. Luke and Kyle followed behind them while us girls watched from inside.

"I hope they don't get into a fight." Shelby chewed on the edge of her nail. "Josh has been drinking all day."

"He didn't seem drunk." I crossed my arms, keeping one eye on what was going on outside, while looking at Shelby.

"It usually sneaks up on him. And when it does, he's hot-headed." She lifted to the tips of her toes so she could see over the fence at the edge of the Marshall's property.

"I'm glad Luke is a happy drunk," Delaney said, pressing her hands against the glass. "But tonight, he's not drunk. And that's what worries me."

I laughed. "If I wouldn't have seen it with my own eyes, I would have pegged him for being an angry drunk."

"Really, why?" Shelby asked, pulling a chair to the window and standing on it.

"My brother is more introverted and analytical. Sometimes it can be interpreted as being angry."

"You've got that right," Delaney huffed. "Sometimes, when he's only had a few drinks, he gets pissy, like he did at the bowling alley."

I didn't comment. I knew why Luke reacted the way he had, I just didn't want to bring it up. If Delaney hadn't been sleeping with so many guys, especially one of Luke's teammates, then he wouldn't have got into that fight.

"I couldn't figure him out when we first met." Delaney rolled her eyes. "It took a while. I guess I should have just asked you."

"By the way, you never told me how you two hooked up. I know I introduced you to him, but when did you guys start talking?"

Delaney wrapped her arms around her body, her face bubbling up in elation. "It was at—"

"Oh shit. That guy just hit Josh." Shelby jumped off the chair, knocking it down in the process.

"Damn it!" I screamed as we darted out the door. Something deep inside the pit of my stomach told me this was going to end badly. Why didn't I tell Raven not to drink? I should have taken the beer bottle from his hand before he followed Josh.

We rounded the pool and flew down the stairs to the beach. Three guys stood face to face with Raven, Luke, and Kyle. And by the looks of it, they weren't ready to play ball. Even though it was dark, I could see the tattoos covering their arms and legs. Except, these tattoos weren't attractive. These were the kind a person received while in prison. To the right, another guy hovered over a piece of wood covered with tubes and rockets. There was enough firepower lined up along the beach for a small show. It was scary to see them pointed directly toward the house. "Raven, don't!" I pleaded as I stumbled through the thick sand. "Let's just go back inside."

Raven motioned for me to stay back, but I refused. I had made a promise to keep him out of trouble and I would do just that.

Shawn had his arms laced through Josh's, holding him back as he cussed and yelled, "Get the fuck off my property!"

"Josh, stop!" Shelby jumped in front of him, trying to get him to calm down, but he was too riled up to listen. "Please, sweetie. Not tonight."

"What are you going to do about it? Huh?" A guy a head taller than Luke, and about the same build, took a step closer. He lifted his chin, continuing to goad Luke. "Huh? Whatcha gonna do?" The guy was acting like a total prick — he was begging for them to start something with him.

"Look, man," Luke held up his hands, "we don't want any trouble."

Delaney started toward the guy, but I grabbed her arm, holding her back. "Don't. Just stay put."

"Just get your shit and leave." Raven pointed to the mound of fireworks. "Like my friend said, this is private property. You need to pop that elsewhere."

The guy that was standing over the fireworks started gathering them and I sighed in relief. Before I could relax, a fairly large guy , about the size of Cage, jammed his index finger into the middle of Raven's chest. "Fuck that. You can't make us leave." He looked over his shoulder. "Gabe, leave our shit there. We're not going anywhere." I was sure Raven could hold his own since it looked like fatty did more drinking than working out.

"You need to take your finger off of me before I break it," Raven warned.

The guy smirked and then retrieved his finger. I watched Raven for a second, making sure he wasn't about to jab the guy in the face when Gabe dropped the stuff in his hands.

No. No. Just go. Just leave.

"Yeah, we're not going anywhere. So take your punk asses and go back inside." Gabe crossed his arms over his body, taking a defensive stand. Didn't they realize they were the punk asses? My heart pounded in my ears and my throat thickened with a sickening feeling worse than any hangover.

Kyle darted toward Gabe. "You need to go. Now."

Gabe threw his head back and cackled. "You jocks think you're tough shit with your fancy houses and fancy cars. But you ain't shit without daddy's money."

"Fuck you." Josh twisted and turned, vying to get free from Shawn's grip.

"Screw you, man." Kyle shook his head. "You don't know shit."

"I know enough." Gabe met Kyle's gaze in a challenging stare off. Even though the guy was shorter than Kyle, he didn't back down. His hands curled into tight fists and the muscles in his arms twitched, as if ready to spring into action.

"You need to get the fuck out of my face," Kyle said, pushing the guy.

Gabe responded with a quick blow to Kyle's face. Kyle's head snapped to the side and he stumbled back, trying to catch his footing. Shawn released Josh and they rushed forward. Shelby screamed but Josh didn't pay her any attention.

"No! Stop!" I yelled, reaching for Raven. The last thing he needed was to get in a fight. In one quick movement, Raven pushed me out of the way and I fell to my butt. Sand sprayed across my face and into my mouth as Delaney and Shelby sprung forward. I spat and coughed as I scrambled to my feet. Raven was in an arm to arm battle with the guy. Both of them head to head and nearly knee deep in the sand.

Delaney dove in, fists raised, and punched the guy provoking Luke. I scrambled after, grabbing her arm and trying to pull her away, but took a step back as Luke and her pounded on the guy. I turned to see Shelby, straddled on the back of one of the guys, her arms around his head as Josh punched in the stomach.

Kyle and Shawn had Gabe pinned to the ground as they pounded on his face.

This was bad.

Very bad.

Everyone was fighting except for me. Fists were flying, feet were kicking, people were screaming and cussing — this was one big FUBAR, as my brother would say, and there was nothing I could do to stop it. I looked around for something to use to break them apart, like a piece of wood or stick, but there was nothing. What the hell did I know about fighting? Before I could think of anything, a siren sounded and everyone stopped. It was the cops. Raven was totally screwed.

Σ

Chapter 15

The next morning, Josh told everyone to go home. The party was over. No one talked as they packed their stuff. The mood was sullen and all the magic made was gone. Spring Break had definitely gone to shit. Everyone, including me, received a ticket for disorderly conduct. What made matters worse was that all the guys had received tickets for public intoxication — including Raven.

What the hell were we going to do? The part that sucked the most was that Raven's blood alcohol level was .09, just .01 over the legal limit of intoxication. Why the hell did I let him drink? It was my damn fault for not stopping him. It was also my fault for arguing with the cops and telling them to give him a breathalyzer test.

Never again.

The more I thought about the situation, the angrier I got. It was also Shawn's fault for offering it to him. But most of all, it was Raven's fault for drinking two beers when he knew he shouldn't have been drinking period. I also had to be realistic about the situation. We weren't planning on leaving or going anywhere, so I honestly didn't think it was going to be a problem. He clearly wasn't drunk, but because of the fight, he was going to pay for his mistakes — again.

The first thing Raven did when he got up was call his attorney. But Mr. Marshall was on a flight, returning from Tahiti. Every hour, he checked his phone, making sure he hadn't missed a call. Worry etched deep around Raven's eyes.

He was slowly drifting away, being pulled by the demons he fought so hard to destroy and remove from his life. And it scared the hell out of me.

"Hey, man, we're out of here." Luke shook hands with Josh. "Thanks for letting us stay here."

"Yeah, anytime. Are we still on for next week?"

They chatted for a while about working out, Luke's crazy baseball schedule, and how my parents wanted him to go to a scout camp.

"Text me as soon as you know something." Delaney hugged me.

Giving her a tight squeeze, I said, "Okay. I just don't have a good feeling about this."

"I know, but hopefully Josh's uncle can figure something out." She looked at me with a hopeful smile.

"Thanks, Shelby. It was fun while it lasted," Delaney whispered.

"Of course." Shelby wrapped her arms around her and gave her kiss on the cheek. "We'll do it again. Say, after graduation?"

"That's a great idea." Delaney's eyes widened.

"Sis," Luke called, "be careful."

"You, too." I eyed him. "No drinking and driving."

"Shit, I'm done drinking for a while." He turned to Raven. "Good luck, man. Keep me posted."

"Yeah, thanks." Raven shook his hand. "See you at the gym."

Luke told Shawn and Kyle bye before grabbing their bags and heading out the door.

"Have you heard from my uncle yet?" Josh asked as Raven returned to the living room with our bags.

"No. Not yet." Raven let out a long, drawn out sigh, resting his hands on his waist.

"Don't worry." Josh patted Raven on the back. "I'm sure he'll figure something out."

I started to walk out of the room, but stopped when I saw Raven's body flinch and the muscles in his arms tense.

"Easy for you to say. You're not the one that has their football career on the line." Raven's face hardened and his nostrils flared.

"What?" Josh's jaw jutted out and the expression on his face told me exactly what he wanted to say. "Don't get all pissed off at me."

"If your dumb ass neighbors wouldn't have called the cops, we wouldn't be in this situation!" Raven yelled at Josh.

"What the fuck did you want me to do?" Josh raised his arms and puffed out his chest. This didn't look good. "They were popping off fireworks right over the house. One could have landed on the roof and caught fire."

"Sweetie. Calm down." Shelby rushed into the room and pleaded with Josh, but he shoved her hand off his arm.

Raven didn't say anything, just plopped on the couch and buried his face in the palms of his hands. I sat next to him, rubbing his back to ease the worry that plagued us both. Fighting and arguing wasn't going to solve anything. It only made matters worse.

"Shit. You're the one that started it!" Josh pointed to Kyle. "If you wouldn't have pushed that asshole, the fight wouldn't have started."

"Me? Hell, you're the one that started yelling at them instead of talking to them like a civilized person." Kyle's green eyes darkened. His face reddened and it wasn't from the sunburn he earned on the sunny shores of South Padre Island.

"Get the fuck out of my house!" Josh yelled and Kyle shouldered past him. With the way Kyle balled his hands into fists, the muscles pulsating in his arms, I knew it was taking everything in him not to punch Josh.

I quickly stood up. "Guys. Guys. Look, everyone is to blame. We all screwed up. It is what it is. What we need to do now is figure out what the hell we're going to do."

"No shit, Sherlock," Shawn barked.

"Hey, is that necessary?" Raven eyed Shawn.

"Sorry, Lexi. I'm just pissed about the whole thing."

"I know. So am I, but now isn't the time for us to turn on each other. We need to stick together." Raven needed the support from his friends. He was the one with the most at risk.

"Let's go, Shawn. I'm ready to get outta here." Kyle threw his backpack over his shoulder.

"Kyle," Josh called, "I'm sorry, dude. I'm just pissed over how everything went down."

"Whatever." Kyle wouldn't even look at him, just opened the front door and walked out of the house.

"Josh, Shelby. I appreciate the hospitality." Shawn waved. "Take it easy, man. I'll be in touch," Shawn told Raven and they did their manly handshake.

Josh walked Shawn out the door, whispering something to him about Kyle. From what I could tell, Josh was telling Shawn to talk to Kyle and make sure he wasn't mad at him.

Raven's phone rang and he quickly dug it out of his pocket. "It's Mr. Marshall," he said, darting to the bedroom and shutting the door.

I waited about thirty minutes before I knocked on the door. "Raven, can I come in?"

"Yeah."

Slowly, I opened the door. Raven was sitting on the edge of the bed, his body slummed and his head hanging toward the ground. I shut the door behind me and knelt in front of him. "Raven, what did he say?"

After a few seconds, Raven's eyes met mine. Redness circled the hazel depths, causing them to look more brown than green. Tears streaked his face and he looked like all life had been sucked out of him. A familiar pain struck the center of my chest and my throat tightened. I hated to see him so upset, but I had to stay strong. I knew he was battling the demons eager to convince him of how weak he was and that he was nothing but a loser.

"He said I needed to tell Coach. Be honest."

"I think..." I took a hard swallow, trying to find my non-squeaky voice. "I think that's a good idea. It's better to be upfront about what happened."

"If I do that, I might as well quit." The demons were taking over and they were winning.

"Why would you do that?" I reached for his hands, but he pulled them away. "You have no idea what Coach is going to say."

Raven stood to his feet. "Yeah, I do. He's going to tell me I'm done."

"No, he's not."

He skirted past me and looked out the window, not saying another word. I knew there wasn't anything I could say that would change what was going through his mind, but I at least had to try. I loved Raven too much to see him give up. He deserved to live his dream and I was going to do everything I could to make sure he did. But not only that, we deserved each other, and I wasn't going to let this rip us apart.

I got up and walked over to him, wrapping my arms around his waist. With my cheek resting on his back, I held him tightly. The sound of his heart thudded in a low murmur. His body was tight, and I could tell he was holding it all in — the pain, the stress, the anger. All of it ready to combust upon pressure.

"Babe, I don't know what's going to happen, or what Coach is going to do, but we have to believe that Mr. Marshall is going to be able to make a case for you. But regardless of what happens, I want you to know that I love you. I love you more than anything. And if Coach kicks you off the team, it won't change how I feel about you, or the fact that I still want to marry you."

"Come here, baby." Raven moved me in front of him. He held me close, exhaling a deep breath and relaxing into me. His chin rested on top of my head and his chest moved in slow, languid movements. Only the sound of our beating hearts could be heard in the quietness. We stayed like that for a few minutes, allowing the worries to drift away.

Looking at him, I told him, "We have to have faith, Raven. We have to believe that everything is going to be okay." I stroked the side of his head, running my fingers through his thick, light brown hair, wishing I could turn the hands of time. But I couldn't.

"Pray that it will, baby, because Mr. Marshall didn't sound very hopeful about the situation."

My fingers stopped and I retrieved my hand. "What did he say?"

"That he'd do whatever he could, but since everyone got a ticket, it really didn't help my cause. He's going to work to get the ticket dismissed, but he said I should have never volunteered to submit to a breathalyzer test."

"I'm sorry that I told the cop to give it you. I knew you weren't drunk, so I thought it would work for you, not against you. I had no idea." I shook my head and glanced at the floor. I was such an idiot.

"It's not your fault." Lifting my chin with his finger, he said, "You had no idea."

"Tough way to learn." I pressed my lips together and continued shaking my head.

"I know. I know, baby." With our arms wrapped around each other, we stared out the window, watching the waves roll in one at a time and crash against the shore. On the surface, the ocean seemed so peaceful, so calm. It wasn't until you got in the water that you realized the power behind the water. If you weren't careful, it would pull you under without warning. It felt like that was Raven's life right now. Things had been peaceful and calm, everything going in the right direction, until we let our guard down. Raven was being sucked under again and I had no idea if he would be able make it out this time.

Once we got back to Fort Worth, Raven called Coach. By the way Raven reacted and stormed out of the apartment, I knew it wasn't good. I wanted to tell Josh to go after him, but since they weren't talking much, I knew Raven needed to work things out on his own. He came back a few hours later, drenched in sweat and breathing heavily, as though he'd been running. After he showered and calmed down, he told me that Coach was pissed and that he would have to go through another hearing, just like last time.

I was dreading it, but I had figured it was coming. Even though I knew that he didn't want to hear it, I encouraged him to tell his mom. She had the right to know. He promised me he'd tell her later. It didn't take long for the rumor mill to start, everyone posting comments on every social media site about Raven. I truly hated all the drama and people talking behind our backs, but I dealt with it. Raven had warned me, so I knew what I was getting myself into. But I wasn't willing to walk away from him. I loved him too much.

By the end of the week, the hearing was scheduled for the following Tuesday. I hadn't heard from Trish like I normally did every week. She made it a point to check with me to see if Raven had gone to counseling and how he was doing. I was sure he had told her about the breathalyzer test, and I hoped she wasn't pissed at me. Aside from the test, I knew she wasn't happy about what happened, especially after I had promised to look after Raven. I was just as irresponsible as he was and it pissed me off.

"Time to go, dude." Josh stuck his head in Raven's room. Once Mr. Marshall said that he'd need all of us there to testify on behalf of Raven, they finally resolved their differences. We were in this together.

"Alright." Raven stood in front of the mirror, adjusting his tie. It felt like déjà vu. Only three and half months ago, we were in the same spot. Nothing had changed. No, I take that back. A lot had changed. Raven was improving, working out the demons, learning how to let go of his hurtful past, and we were building a new life together. Until we let our guard down and made a stupid mistake. I just prayed he wouldn't have to pay for it.

"Here's your jacket." I held up his coat and helped him slip it on. Raven pulled on the collar and rolled his shoulders. Damn, my man was hot. "You look really good in a suit."

"Lexi, now is not the time," he remarked, his face serious.

"Sorry, just trying to lighten the load." I waited for him to say something, but he didn't. He grabbed his phone, shoved it inside of his jacket, and walked out of the room. I knew he was stressed, so I held back the ugly words dying to come out of my mouth.

Shelby and I followed the guys out of the apartment and headed toward the car. Parked in front of the apartment complex was Raven's mom, Trish. She rolled down the window when she saw us coming. "Get in. Now."

Shit.

"I'll see you there." Raven told Josh as we got into his mom's car. She didn't greet us like she normally did, and by the way she peeled out of the parking lot, I knew she was pissed.

"Mom, aren't you supposed to be at work? You didn't have to come. I would have called you." Raven held onto the handlebar above the window as Trish sped down the street. I tightened my seatbelt, making sure it held me firmly in place.

"Yes, I am supposed to be at work, but since you decided to be irresponsible, I had to take off. Tell me, Raven, did you and Lexi have a good time in Padre? Was it worth it?"

"Mom—"

"Don't 'Mom' me. This is serious, Raven. What the hell were you two thinking?" The light turned red and she slammed on the breaks. My body flung forward and I gripped the back of Raven's seat.

"Trish, Raven only had two beers that night. Everything was fine until those idiots starting popping off fireworks by the house. You should actually be proud of him. With the exception of that night, he didn't drink the entire week we were there. We even went to a club and he drank soda. He was our designated driver."

She looked over her shoulder. "You want me to be proud?" The light turned green and Trish gunned it, crossing over the busy intersection as she headed toward campus. "Raven might lose his one and only chance of ever being picked up by a national football team. And all for two beers. I hope those beers were damn good."

"I'm sorry. It's all my fault. Raven promised to take me for my birthday. I knew we shouldn't have gone, but I wanted to."

Raven turned around and stared at me. I gave a slight shrug. It was my fault just as much as it was his. "Don't listen to her, Mom. She told me we shouldn't go and I talked her into it."

"That's why I'm pissed at both of you." Trish stopped at the light near the end of the campus. "Where the hell am I going?" She threw her hands up in the air.

"Turn right and then pull into that first parking lot." Raven pointed down the street.

Luckily, Trish found a parking spot right in front of the building where Raven's hearing was being held. I was glad, because Trish continued lecturing us until Mr. Marshall and Steve arrived. No wonder Raven felt down at times. I'd never had anyone make me feel so bad before. It was almost worse than how my mom treated me. Instead of Trish being supportive, like she was last time, she was accusatory. Part of me couldn't blame her, but Raven needed her support.

Josh and Shelby arrived after we did, followed by Shawn and Kyle. Mr. Marshall asked that we all be there to give a testimony about what happened that night and show the academic and athletic board that we had received tickets as well. Luke and Delaney were the last to arrive, and by the looks of it, they had just gotten it on somewhere. Delaney's makeup was smeared and Luke's hair was a disheveled mess. I hope she was remembering to take her pill. If not, she'd surely end up pregnant.

"Y'all wait out here. Steve will come to get you when it's time," Mr. Marshall instructed as he held the door open for Raven.

"Good luck, baby." I reached for his hand before he entered the room.

"Thanks." He leaned forward and gave me a quick kiss on the lips.

The door shut and I sat down on the bench outside. A few minutes later, Trish started crying. Tears gushed from her eyes as she sobbed quietly. I took out a tissue from my purse and handed it to her.

"Trish, are you okay?"

"No." She took the tissue and blew her nose. "I'm a horrible mother."

Everyone looked at me, so I scooted closer and wrapped an arm around her. She leaned against my shoulder, heaving and sobbing. "No, you're not. You're just concerned and worried, like all of us."

"Yes," she sniffed, "but I shouldn't have yelled at Raven. Not like that. He needs my support and yours, too." She sighed in a rapid succession of breaths. "Will you forgive me? Please?"

"Of course." I pulled another tissue from my purse and handed it to her. "I think of you as my mother-in-law. The last thing I want is for us to be mad at one another."

"Oh, Lexi." She threw her arms around my neck and pulled me close to her, crying hard. "I'm so sorry."

"It's okay, Trish." I patted her on the back. "Really, it is." Delaney made a quirky expression and I shot her a *what the hell am I supposed to do* look.

For several minutes, I reassured her that I wasn't mad at her and that I accepted her apology. I explained what happened once again, when she started asking several questions. Josh and Shawn even chimed in, telling her exactly what Raven and I had already told her. I knew she believed us; she just needed to hear that her son wasn't to blame. At least, not completely.

The door opened and I quickly turned to see Raven dart out. "Raven?" I shot out of my seat and ran toward him. "What happened? Tell me. What did they say?" I tried to get him to look at me, but he turned his head and kept walking. He stopped at the end of the hallway and gripped the railing, leaning over it. His body was rigid, but frail at the same time.

He buckled over and I took a step forward, hoping he was thinking of doing anything stupid. "It's over, Lexi." His voice was heavy, filled with pain, guilt, and tears.

"What's over, babe?" I reached my hand toward him, but held it steady, afraid to touch him. "Tell me."

He pushed away from the railing. "Everything," he snapped. His fingers flew to his neck and worked frantically, trying to untie the knot on his tie. Red marks streaked his face as he breathed heavily. I took a step back, not wanting to get in the direct line of fire. "Baby, talk to me. Please?"

"Fucking shit!" he yelled as he struggled with the fabric. He stopped messing with the tie and grabbed the sleeves of his jacket. In one quick tug, he literally ripped his suit jacket off his body. The sleeves separated from the material and he looked like a madman, tearing his clothes in two. My eyes blinked rapidly, unable to process what had just happened.

"Bro, you alright?" Josh stepped up behind me.

"Get the fuck away from me," Raven seethed, introducing a new demon I had never seen or heard before.

"Okay, just calm down," Shawn held out his hands as he neared Raven, "everything is going to be okay, man. It's not the end of the world."

"Easy for you to say!" Raven jabbed his finger in Shawn's face.

"Son, stop, please. You're scaring me," Trish pleaded, latching onto me for support.

"Everyone just get the fuck away from me," he spat, his eyes dark with rage and his incisors baring like he was ready to slash us apart. In one quick yank, he ripped off the tie and threw it to the floor.

"Raven, baby." I pressed my hands together, praying that God would help calm him down. The last thing I wanted was for him to do anything stupid. "Please, tell me. What do you mea by everything?"

"Just...everything." He turned and ran down the stairs. Tears welled in my eyes. In the pit of my stomach, I knew what he was referring to. Not just football — us.

Σ

Chapter 16

"Anything?" Trish asked as we sat on the couch in Raven and Josh's apartment.

Glancing at my phone for the umpteenth time, I said, "No."

We were both worried about Raven. Things were worse than we thought. Not only had Raven been kicked off the team, he had been dismissed from the university — permanently. Coach was apologetic. He said he had given Raven every opportunity to clean up his act, but he couldn't keep forgiving him. He had given him one too many chances and Raven had blown all of them. The board of admissions ruled that Raven didn't possess the conduct appropriate for the type of students they wanted representing their school. They did offer to provide him counseling for one year, however.

The coach encouraged me to make sure Raven attended his counseling sessions. Although he seemed genuinely concerned for him, I was less inclined to agree. I did the honorable thing and told him I would, even though I wanted to tell him to go to hell. In all honesty, I guess I couldn't blame him. He had a football program to run, not a center for troubled individuals.

"What are we going to do?" I wrapped my arms around my legs and rocked back and forth. "I mean, what if he—"

"Don't say it. Don't even think it." Trish let out a long breath. "Nothing's going to happen to him. This isn't like last time."

"No, it's worse!" I cried out, trying to stop the vicious thoughts from running rampant in my mind.

"Shawn is with him. He's not going to—"

The door to the apartment opened and Josh and Shelby walked in. "Hey."

"Did you find him?" I sprang to my feet, shoving my fingers through my hair. I refused to accept any bad news. Raven would be fine. He'd come home and we'd get through this together. We had to. We loved each other too much to let this rip us apart.

"No, we didn't." Josh closed the door behind Shelby. "But I got ahold of Shawn. He's with him."

"Oh, thank God." Trish relaxed against the sofa cushions and her body slumped.

I released the breath I'd been holding since we left the hearing and collapsed onto the couch next to her. I didn't know how much more I could take of this. The stress, the worrying, it was eating me alive. It was also driving Trish into the ground. But I loved Raven, and I was going to stand by his side, no matter what.

"Are you alright?" Shelby sat next to me, taking my hand in hers.

"No. I'm worried sick about him. Did you see the anger in his eyes? The way he tore his jacket off his body?" I took in a few quick breaths. "I've never seen him react that way before. Have you?" I looked at Shelby, Josh, and then Trish.

"It's been a very long time since he's reacted this way. He has me so worried." Trish placed her hand on my leg. "I hate to see him so upset. It scares the shit out of me."

"Just give him a little time." Shelby grabbed both our hands. "I'm sure he's going to be okay. Shawn is with him. He'll watch after him."

"I hope so, Shelby." Trish squeezed her hand, heaving a heavy sigh.

"Shelby is right. Raven is going to get through this." Josh sat on the coffee table in front of us. "Once the shock wears off and he gets his head together, he'll come home."

"What if he doesn't?" I wiped the tears from my face. Just thinking about what he'd said had me ready to claim temporary insanity. Surely, he didn't mean it. Things couldn't be over between us.

"Lexi," Josh gave a lighthearted laugh, trying to calm me, "he might need a day or two, but he's going to come back to you. The boy is in love with you — trust me."

Josh talked to us while Shelby made us some warm chamomile tea, claiming it was the best for nerves. And she was right. The warm tincture soothed my dry, parched throat and calmed my racing pulse, but it did nothing to relieve the pain deep within my soul. A pain that could only be soothed by Raven.

"Oh my, it's almost six." Trish looked at her watch. "I've got to get home to check on the boys." She put her cup on the coffee table.

"Do you need me and Josh to follow you home?" Shelby asked.

Trish fumbled with her jacket, trying to put it on. "No, I'll be fine. Just stay here with Lexi."

"Are you sure, Trish? I don't mind." Josh helped her slip her arms through the sleeves.

"I'm positive. I'll be okay." Her lips parted into a broken smile. The hurt, the stress, all the worrying she had endured over her son, was wrapped up in that one expression. Looking at me, she said, "Please call or text me as soon as you hear from him."

I gave her a tight hug. "I will. And call me if you hear from him first."

"You can count on it." She gave me one last squeeze before letting go.

Josh walked Trish to her car and I checked my phone again. Nothing. What the heck was going through Raven's mind? Why wouldn't he answer me? Was he regretting taking me to Padre for my birthday? Did he regret those two beers? Did he regret proposing to me? Most importantly, did he hate himself? I pulled myself into a ball and rested my chin on my knees. It was going to be a long night.

I woke up a few hours later on the couch with my phone clutched to my chest and a blanket covering me. The TV was turned on, an infomercial about weight loss playing on the screen. Shifting positions to work the tightness out of my back, I noticed I had a text message. I quickly hit the message button and saw that it was Trish. She wanted to know if I'd heard from Raven. The clock flashed 2:06 a.m., so I decided to hold off on texting her until the morning. I scrolled to Raven's name and read back over the last message.

Me: Babe, please call me. Tell me you're okay. I'm worried sick about you. So is your mom.

But there was no response. It was as though Raven wanted nothing to do with me; as though he didn't feel the need to tell me he was okay. But why? This was killing me! I was his fiancée. Why was he shutting me out? We had talked about this two weeks ago on the beach. He promised not to shut me out again. He promised that he was learning how to deal with his demons. He promised that he had changed. But nothing had changed. Raven still refused to let me in. How could I be his wife if he wouldn't turn to me during his times of need?

Wiping the tears from my eyes, I picked up my phone and typed him another message.

Me: I love you, Raven. No matter what. Don't ever forget that.

With the phone clutched tightly in my hand, I prayed he wasn't doing anything stupid. My phone flashed a warning light, telling me it needed to be charged before turning dark. I walked to Raven's bedroom and plugged my phone in.

I took off my clothes and grabbed Raven's white undershirt thrown on top of the chair. I dropped to the edge of the bed and slipped it over my head. With my fingers curled around the collar, I covered my nose and mouth and inhaled deeply, taking in his signature scent. It surrounded me, but it didn't cradle me like it normally did. My soul knew what I refused to believe. I glanced at his empty pillow and another round of tears made their appearance. Damn, I wanted him here with me. Crawling on my stomach, I buried my face in his pillow.

Please, Raven, don't break me again.
Please don't let me fall.
Please don't leave me.
My heart can't handle it.

The words repeated across my lips, over and over, as I sobbed for what seemed liked hours. I cried for us. But most of all, I cried for him. For his hurt. For his disappointment. For everything he was going through. For what life had done to him. It wasn't fair.

Wrapping my arms around me, I reveled in the softness of his cotton shirt as it caressed my skin. I imagined he was here with me, holding me, while I promised him everything would be okay. That he'd get through this with me by his side. That there was still hope for his football career. But all I could do was wish it was him holding me, instead of me holding myself.

"Lexi, you okay?" The door squeaked as Shelby stuck her head in the room.

"No, not really." I wiped my nose with the back of my hand. The tears still hadn't stopped, even though I felt completely dehydrated.

Sitting on the edge of the bed, she brushed my matted hair away from my face. "He never came home, did he?"

"Nope." I laid in Raven's bed, looking at his empty side — a side that didn't have to be empty.

"Did you hear from him or Shawn?" She plucked a few tissues from a box on the nightstand and handed them to me.

I shook my head, fighting back the hard tears. The ones that would send me into another heaving spell. I was so tired of crying. Tired of worrying. Tired of begging. Tired of everything.

Why was Raven making things so difficult for us?

"Did you need a ride back to campus?" Shelby asked.

"No, I'm going to wait here until he comes home." I blew my nose and sighed heavily, making a horrible quivering sound. I was hot a mess once again. Raven's hot mess.

"Okay." She brushed her fingers through my hair one last time before getting up. "Text me if you need anything."

"And definitely text us when he gets here." Josh peeked in the room. "Because he will be back." A big smile covered his tanned face. I knew he was trying to make me feel better, put my restless mind at ease, but nothing was helping. Holding Raven and knowing he was okay was the only thing that would stop this incessant worrying.

"Thanks, guys." I managed to give a small smile and they shut the door.

For another hour or so, I stayed in bed, waiting for Raven to walk through the door. But he never showed. Around eleven, I took a shower and got dressed. Somehow, I had to pull myself together. Raven needed me and I had to be strong for him. I was his only hope. My heart had to hold up. I didn't have time to be weak.

I picked up my phone and sent Shawn another message.

Me: Shawn, please let me know something. I'm freakin' out over here!

I waited and waited, staring at the screen on my phone, but he never responded. Completely resolved to nothing, I turned on the TV, hoping to get my mind off things. ESPN came on, the main station that Raven and Josh watched, and I regretted pushing the button. It was all over the news. The sports newscasters were talking about Raven. About what had happened and what this meant for his football career. Not wanting to hear it, I turned off the TV and went back into Raven's room.

I grabbed my bag and went to the kitchen table. Taking out my laptop, I powered it up. I had to do something before I went crazy. That was when I remembered I had two tutoring sessions this afternoon and edits due for both of them.

Crap.

I quickly sent the two students a text and told them that I couldn't meet, but that I would send them their edits by tonight. Then I called Dr. Phillips and told him that I wasn't coming in today. He said he understood, and I'm sure he knew why. It was no secret that Raven and I were engaged, and if ESPN knew the latest on Raven, then the entire university knew as well.

Just as I opened the first paper to edit, my phone rang. It was Shawn. I fumbled to pick up my phone, my hands shaking in anticipation. Was Raven okay? Where were they?

"Hello?" I answered in a rushed tone.

"Lexi?" Shawn said in a low voice.

"Is Raven okay?" I gripped the edge of the chair and waited with baited breath. "Please tell me he's okay."

"Lexi, calm down. Raven is fine." Shawn tried to put my frazzled nerves at ease by using a calm and steady tone.

"Thank God." I let out a huge sigh as my body slumped on the table. It felt like a ton of bricks released from my chest and I could finally breathe. Barely holding myself up, I took in small inhalations as I tried to focus. "Where is he?"

A door closed and it sounded like Shawn stepped outside. "He's here with me at my parent's house."

"Oh." I relaxed in the chair. "Why aren't you at your apartment?"

"Um, you see, he got kind of drunk last night... I didn't want anyone seeing him, so I brought him to my parents."

"Oh, yeah, I guess that would've been bad. Good thinking."

"He's really hung over and still beside himself," he whispered in a low voice, making it hard to hear him.

"I understand. Is he mad at me? Is that why he won't talk to me?" I had to know. "I mean, you heard him, he said it was over." My heart beat faster as I recalled the scene from yesterday.

"No, Lexi. He doesn't blame you. He blames himself, if anything. Trust me, he loves you, girl."

"Good." My heart let out a soft sigh and my shoulders relaxed. Raven still loved me. He wasn't blaming me. He wasn't mad at me. I just hoped he still wanted to be with me. "When are you bringing him home?"

The line was quite for a moment and I heard a lady talking in the background. I listened for a moment to see if I could hear Raven, but the sound was muffled. "Lexi, I gotta go. Just give him a day or two. Let him work through this on his own. He'll be back."

"Alright." I might have agreed verbally, but physically, I needed to see him. I needed to know he was okay. Most of all, I needed to hear directly from Raven's mouth that it wasn't over between us.

"Okay, talk to you later."

"Shawn, wait."

"Yeah?"

In a desperate plea, I said, "Promise me you won't let anything happen to him."

"I promise."

"Thanks." I hung up the phone and then sent everyone a message, telling them that Raven was with Shawn and he was okay. After texting back and forth with everyone, I finally decided to try to get some work done.

With a renewed purpose, I was able to finish the edits for the two students. Diving nose deep into something I enjoyed seemed to help the time pass. How I concentrated, I don't know. Maybe it was because I was going on Shawn's words, in true faith, that Raven would be home soon. Maybe it was because the two papers were by students taking a creative writing class and their stories really sucked me in.

I stayed at Raven and Josh's apartment one more night, hoping that I'd awaken to Raven standing over the bed. But that was wishful thinking. Instead, I woke up to the alarm on my phone. I really didn't want to go to class, but I'd already missed Tuesday because of the hearing and I had a test next week in two classes. If I didn't go today, I'd be screwed.

A knock came at the door and for a second, I got excited. But then I realized if it were Raven, he would've walked in. "Are you up, Lexi?" Shelby's voice filtered through the door.

"Yeah, come in." I tied the laces on my black Chucks and stood up.

"Need a ride to class?" Shelby stood in the doorway, a smile touching her lips. I guess she was glad to see me up and moving around, instead of crying in bed.

"Yeah, if Josh doesn't mind." I shoved my laptop into my book bag and grabbed my purse.

"I don't mind." Josh slipped by Shelby and walked in the room. "I'm watching out for Raven's girl." He wrapped his arm around me and gave me a slight squeeze until I finally smiled. Hearing those words struck a chord within me. A lighthearted chord that only Raven could make sound beautiful. More beautiful than my fingers hitting the keys on the piano. "Quit worrying, Lexi. He's going to come back. Just give him some time."

"I know."

I went to class, but it was pointless. All I did was think about Raven. Whether he was okay. When he was coming home. Why he wouldn't text or call, despite what Shawn had told me. After class, I met Josh, Shelby, and Delaney at the student union dining area. I hadn't been in there since Raven proposed to me. It brought back all the good memories until I noticed that all eyes were on me — once again. Word spread fast about Raven and everyone was talking about him. He was the main topic of conversation and I was the second.

"Are you okay?" Delaney asked. "You haven't even touched your salad."

"I guess I'm not hungry." I shrugged, twiddling with the diamond on my engagement ring. Every time I turned it a certain way, the light would hit it just right, causing it to sparkle. Just like Raven's eyes when he asked me to marry him. "I guess I hate all of this gossip going around." I looked over my shoulder and immediately caught Abby, the brunette Silicone Triplet, whispering to one of her friends. It was obvious whom they were talking about.

Delaney pivoted in her chair and rolled her eyes. "Forget about those bitches." Delaney stood up and shot them the finger. "That's right. Mind your own fuckin' business."

"Laney." I pulled on her scarf until she dropped to her seat.

"Oh my God, those girls are going to come over here and want to start something." Shelby glared at Delaney. "I already got one ticket, I don't need another. And I surely don't need to get kicked out of school."

My eyes closed. It was so easy for people to joke about that, but it was something else entirely when it impacted you or someone you loved.

"Lexi, I'm sorry. I—"

"It's okay." I held up a hand, telling her to stop before she said more damaging words.

"Seriously, girl, calm down," Josh told Delaney. "We're all walking a fine line here."

And he was right. We didn't need any more drama.

"Sorry. I'm just trying to watch out for my girl." Delaney leaned her head on my shoulder. It seemed like everyone was watching out for me, except for the one person I wanted to most — Raven.

"Sorry, Lexi. I guess we should have eaten off campus." Josh gave me a heartfelt smile. "We can go, if you want." He started to grab his backpack.

"No, it's okay. Let's just eat and go back to the apartment. I want to see if Raven is back."

Everyone finished their food, except for me. The voices, everyone staring at me, the whispering behind my back — it was too much. All I could think about was Raven. I had to talk to him. I had to see him. I couldn't wait any longer. It had been nearly two full days.

It seemed like it took forever to get back to the apartment. I held onto the back of Shelby's seat, my leg bouncing with anticipation as we pulled into the parking lot of the apartment. Immediately, I noticed Raven's car was gone.

"Stop the truck. Stop the truck." I unfastened my seatbelt and flung the door open before Josh even had a chance to fully stop.

"Lexi. Wait!" Josh demanded, but I ignored him.

I jumped out of the truck, scanning the parking lot for Raven's Charger, but it was nowhere in sight. I fumbled for the keys in my backpack as I stumbled across the gravel and onto the sidewalk. My pulse raced, feeding my blood with the adrenaline it needed to get me up the stairs. I took them two at a time, slipping at the very top. My chin clipped the edge of the metal step and I let out a yelp.

"Lexi. Let me help you!" Shelby called.

I didn't wait for her. I pulled myself up, holding onto the railing. Leaving my backpack behind, I stumbled to the front door. My hand shook as I tried to get the key in the hole. After several attempts, I finally shoved the key in the opening and unlocked the door. I turned the knob and pushed the door open.

"Raven?" I hobbled in the front door, holding onto my leg. "Are you here?"

My eyes darted around the living room and then the dining room, but there was no sight of him. I limped my way into his bedroom and pushed the door open. The room was stripped bare. The pictures of us on the nightstand were missing. The alarm clock and lamp were taken, too. Everything was gone, except for the furniture. The closet door was left open, revealing only my clothes. All of his belongings were gone. My body heaved forward and I fell on top of the barren mattress. Tears gushed from my eyes as everything I had feared came true. Everything was over, just like he'd said. Raven had left me again.

$$\Sigma$$

Chapter 17

"Lexi?" Dr. Phillips called to get my attention.

"Yes, sir?" I shut the book I had been staring at for the last ten minutes. For the past four weeks, I had managed to get by without Raven, devoting all my efforts to studying. Graduating from college was all I had left. I was hanging from the gallows of heartache with a heart that was barely holding together. But life went on, and I was doing my best to try to get my life going again. Finals were in two weeks and graduation in three. I was getting the hell out of PHU with my degree.

"Do you have a minute? I'd like to talk to you about a few things." He stood in his doorway, chewing on the tip of his eyeglasses.

"Yes." I gathered my stuff and walked into his office. I shut the door and sat on the worn pleather chair. It was like déjà vu and I immediately felt sick. For his sake, I hope he didn't have another athlete for me to tutor. If so, I'd lose it.

"How's everything going?" He reclined in his chair and it squeaked as he rocked back and forth.

I shrugged. "Okay, I guess." Dare I tell him that I had actually gone a full five days without crying? That this was the first week I had actually felt a little stronger? That I was going to make it without Raven? I was definitely making progress in removing myself from The Raven's trap. "I mean, as good as I can be."

I caught him glancing at my ring finger. Using my thumb, I casually slipped the diamond under my palm. Even though I had come to terms with the fact that Raven left me, without even as much as a text, phone call, or a letter to say why, I still couldn't take my ring off.

"Do you have a job lined up? You haven't asked for any referrals or spoken with me about working this summer. I know you're graduating in a few weeks."

"No." I sighed. "I haven't had time to look." Truthfully, I had no idea what I wanted to do. I was barely making it through school. I needed to get my shit my straight, because I really didn't want to go back home. As of now, that was my only option.

"Have you thought about grad school?" He folded his glasses, set them down, and leaned against the desk. "Because I could sure use a part-time Senior Writing Consultant and it would be perfect for a grad student." He winked.

"Seriously?" The world immediately seemed brighter and so did his offer. I hadn't even considered grad school. I had just wanted out of PHU, but the more I thought about it, the more it made sense. If I was going to take my editing career seriously, a master's degree would definitely make it possible. Not only that, but it would give me time to get my grounding. I was used to school, studying, and editing papers. Keeping up with that pace wouldn't be a problem. Going out into the world, working for some corporation, scared me a little. Maybe it was because I didn't feel like I was ready for that big of a change yet. Thanks to Raven.

"Yes, and as long as you're accepted for the fall semester, you can work here during the summer."

My throat tightened and without warning, my eyes watered. I was crying again.

Shit.

"I'm sorry. It's just that—" With the pads of my thumb, I wiped under my eyes, completely overcome by the fact that I wouldn't have to move back home as long as I could find a roommate and somewhere to live.

"It's okay. I know you've been through a lot lately." He handed me a few tissues. "I also have something else for you to consider." Stalling, he gauged my reaction, as though trying to determine whether he should tell me, probably fearing I'd break down sobbing.

"Okay," I sniffed, "what is it?"

He shifted in his chair and then said, "I got a call from an alumna that graduated about five years back. She's working on self-publishing a young adult book and is looking for an editor. I immediately thought of you."

"Wow." A new emotion surfaced, transforming my sadness into tears of joy. "Really?" I had been thinking about doing some freelance editing for writers, but hadn't taken the time to look into it. Recently, there had been a huge explosion of indie writers, and I saw posts occasionally on Facebook and Twitter asking for editors.

"If you're interested, I'll let her know."

"Yes." I wiped my nose and straightened in my chair. "I'd like that."

"Great." Dr. Phillips smiled. "Think about grad school and the part-time job offer and let me know what you decide." He scribbled her name and email on a sticky note and handed it to me.

"Okay. I will." I stuck the note in my backpack and headed for the door. "Thanks, Dr. Phillips. You don't know how much I needed this."

"My pleasure, Lexi."

I laid in bed that night, thinking about what Dr. Philips had presented to me. It seemed logical and like a good move for me. The only thing to consider was how the hell I was going to pay for grad school. My parents had paid for the past four years, I wasn't about to ask them to send me to grad school, too. I was also tired of being at PHU. The rumors, the snickering, the memories, both good and bad — it was all here, every freakin' day. It was as though Raven was staring me in the face. Everywhere I turned, I saw images of him — of us. Everything reminded me of him. The library, the stadium, and especially the damn piano I had to pass every day in my dorm. There was no escaping it. PHU lived and reeked of The Raven's trap. But I had choices. I could finish school and get as far away from the memories of Raven and me as possible or learn to deal with them.

One thing was certain. I didn't run. No, Lexi Thompson wasn't afraid to face her fears. If I wanted this, I would have to learn to overcome them. Then I could start living life for me. Raven had made his decision, and it didn't include me.

A renewed purpose filtered through me and by the end of the week, I had made my decision. I had officially applied for grad school and a personal loan to cover the cost. The part-time job at the writing center would cover my living expenses. If I landed a contract with the indie writer, it would only sweeten the deal. Only thing left was finding a place to live. Everything was falling into place, I just had to wait and see what happened.

The best part was I had never felt so strong in my entire life. There was a new Lexi Thompson and I liked her even better than the one that was with Raven. I had officially broken free of The Raven's trap and it felt so damn good.

"It's official!" I smiled, unable to hide the gleam radiating from within me. "You're looking at the newest PHU grad student."

"Are you serious?" Delaney jumped off the couch, taking down the curtains. "I can't believe it!"

I held up my official acceptance letter. "It just came in the mail today." I shut the door to our dorm and weaved my way through the boxes of stuff. We had four days to pack everything and get out. It was amazing how much stuff two girls could accumulate over the years.

"So, does that mean you're moving in with me?" Delaney grasped the curtains tightly as she waited for my answer.

"Yes. I mean, where else would I go?" I dropped the envelopes on the coffee table cluttered with pictures she'd taken down. After informing Delaney that I'd applied to graduate school, she told me that she was getting an apartment fairly close to campus. Luckily for me, she got a killer deal on a one year lease for a two bedroom. Her parents were giving her one year to get her photography business going, agreeing to support her financially. I had a roommate and a place to live.

Delaney jumped off the couch, nearly tripping on the scattered boxes as she grabbed my hands. "We're going to have our own apartment. We're getting our own place." She danced around with me in the narrow space.

I laughed. "Delaney, we've had our own place for the past two years."

"The dorm doesn't count." She released my hands. "I don't know how you feel about going back to school, but if that's what makes you happy, go for it. In fact, I haven't seen you this happy in a very long time."

I caught her looking at my ring finger. My bare ring finger. Last night, after I took a shower, I decided I didn't want to wear it any longer, so I put it in a safe place. It was part of breaking free from Raven. Even though, deep down, I still loved him. He would always own a part of my soul. Despite my efforts to eradicate him from my life, I cared about him and found myself thinking about him constantly, but not enough to call him. I knew where he was, or at least, I had an idea.

Trish called me after he'd showed up at her house and told her that he was leaving town and moving to New Orleans with his grandmother. She begged me to call him and I told her I would think about it, but I never did. He was the one that walked out on me. I had done everything to stay by his side. I had deposited all my trust in Raven's bank and he drained it.

Spent it.

Every single bit of it.

Regardless, I didn't hate him. I hated the demons that had successfully won the battle in ripping him from my life. They were the true enemy, not Raven.

"I am happy, actually." I giggled. "I'm going to be going to grad school, working part time in the writing lab and..." I paused.

"And?"

"Editing for J.S. Christensen."

"Who's that?" she gave me a dumbfounded look.

"Not that you'd know of her, but she's an alumna from five years back who's self-publishing young adult books. I did a sample edit for her and she hired me to edit her next three books!" I jumped up and down. "Can you believe it?"

"That's great!"

A pain hit my side and I stopped. "Oww." I limped to the couch and sat down.

"Are you okay?"

"Yeah." I took a drink of my water. "A weird pain, that's all. Anyhow, I can't believe it." I propped my feet up on a box. "Now I'll have plenty of money to save for a car. But not only that, my loan was approved." I picked up one of the envelopes from the coffee table and waved it at her.

"Sweet."

When I told Dad my plans, he was excited for me and offered to pay my tuition, but I refused. I had to do this on my own. The best thing was we'd been keeping in touch weekly, ever since the breakup. I guess he was worried about me. Without fail, he continued to urge me to call my mom, but the last thing I wanted was to hear her nagging voice, especially after everything that happened. And I definitely didn't want her to try to hook me back up with Collin. Those days were over.

"I know." I smiled.

"Then that means one thing."

"What's that?"

"We're going shopping!" Delaney scrambled to slip on her flip-flops.

"Shopping?" I yawned as the sudden urge to take a nap settled over me. "I don't know, Laney. I'm not up for shopping today. I think I want to catch up on my sleep."

"What? Are you crazy?" She reached in her back pocket. "My dad gave me a budget to go shopping for stuff for the apartment."

"That's great. We can go tomorrow or something." I yawned.

"What?" She grabbed her keys and dangled them in the air. "We only have a few days to get out of here and I already got the key to the apartment."

"But we have plenty of time." I unbuttoned my jean shorts, wondering what the heck I ate to make me so bloated.

"Please, Lex. I'm eager to get some new things. Besides, we need furniture."

"Oh, yeah, forgot about that." I lowered my feet to the ground. On a tight budget, my only option was to ask my dad if I could use my bed and dresser from the house.

"Come on." She waved the card in front of me. "I'll get you a new comforter for your room with matching curtains, pillows... whatever you want."

"You mean your dad will." I pushed her hand away. "And that's not right. I'll just use what I have until I can save up for a new one."

"You're so boring."

"Whatever," I laughed. "It's called being practical and living within your means."

"Yeah, those words aren't in my vocabulary." She snickered and pulled me off the couch.

Delaney managed to talk me into going shopping and our first stop was a furniture store. We perused the rows of sofas and sectionals, along with dining tables. It didn't take long to find something we both liked. If it weren't for Delaney's parents, we wouldn't have any furniture. We really were fortunate.

Delaney paid for the furniture and scheduled a delivery for the next day.

"Let's go to Target." She smiled as she pulled onto the road.

"I'm too tired." I rubbed my back and adjusted the seat belt. Sitting in the library for the past few days had really done a number on my muscles. I needed to get to the gym and stretch, or get in a good workout with Luke. Thinking of it made me cringe. All I wanted to do was crawl in bed and sleep for a few days.

"Seriously? You sound like an old woman. What's wrong with you?"

"Nothing. I'm just tired from finals."

"That was two days ago."

"So. I need my beauty sleep." I propped my elbow against the ledge of the window and rested my head in my hand, closing my eyes. My stomach let out a loud rumble and I opened my eyes. I had eaten lunch, why was I already hungry?

"Was that your stomach?"

"Yes, I'm starving. Can we please get something to eat?"

"I guess, do you want to—"

"There's a Pizza Hut inside of Target." I sat up, my mouth salivating. "Oh, and I'm dying for some of their popcorn and an Icee."

"Oh. My. God. Are you serious?" Delaney cast me a dumbfounded stare. "Since when does rabbit-food eating girl want junk like that?"

"I don't know. Just sounds good." I resumed my resting position and closed my eyes, catching a ten minute nap.

Within ten minutes, I devoured a personal pan pizza with extra cheese and pepperoni. It was as if I hadn't eaten in days. After that, I got a large bag of popcorn and a cherry Icee.

"I can't believe you're eating all of that." Delaney's face twisted in disgust when I shoved a handful of popcorn into my mouth.

"You want some?" I mumbled, dropping a few pieces on the floor.

"No thanks. I'm working out with Luke later. I'll be puking if I eat all of that. You should come with us."

"I'll think about it." I pointed to a blender on the shelf. "Hey, was this the one you saw on that infomercial the other night?"

"Yeah, how much is it?"

"Shit. Ninety-nine dollars." I started to push the basket down the aisle when she stopped me.

"I need it. Luke wants me to start drinking these workout shakes."

"Whatever," I belted out in laughter. "You want it so he has something to make *his* shakes with when he spends the night. Admit it."

"Yeah, yeah." She grabbed the box from the shelf and set it in the buggy. We picked out everything we needed for the apartment and, against my wishes, I chose a new comforter set with matching curtains and shaggy toss pillows. It would look fab in our new place.

"Oh crap, I forgot something." Delaney turned the buggy around and I followed her, pushing another buggy.

"Holy crap. This thing is heavy. We've probably got over a thousand dollars' worth of stuff."

"I know. Don't remind me." She raced toward the beauty and health section of the store.

"What budget did your parents give you?" I stopped, feeling winded. That pizza and junk food had done a number on me.

"Umm." She shuffled through the boxes of tampons and that was when it hit me.

My period. When was the last time I had my period?

I closed my eyes, trying to remember. March, April... I scanned my memory. I couldn't remember. It was the fifteen of May and typically, I had my period the first week of every month. It should have come already.

Shit.

I grabbed my phone and quickly went to the calendar. I scrolled through April and nothing. I scrolled through March and sighed when I saw the fifth marked. I had only missed April and May.

No!

Was I pregnant? Not possible. I had an IUD. Besides, the doctor had warned me that my periods might stop. I was fine. There was no way I was pregnant.

"Come on, let's go." She took off down the aisle and I stopped as we passed the pregnancy tests.

"Hold on." I motioned for her to wait.

"What?" She turned around and followed my line of sight. Stepping close to me, she said, "Why are you looking at PTs?"

I covered my face and started to cry, the emotions pouring out of me like a baby. It was like I already knew the answer before taking the test. Something in the center of me stirred and it wasn't my intuition — it was something else.

"Lexi?" Delaney shook me. "Why are you crying?"

"I..." I heaved a big sigh and then used the napkin from my Icee to blow my nose. "I'm late."

She narrowed her eyes. "How late?"

"April late."

"Fu—Okay. Um. Shit." She ran her fingers through her hair.

The room began to tilt and I broke out in a cold sweat. If I was pregnant, Raven was definitely the father. "Oh God, I feel sick." The pizza, popcorn, and cherry Icee were threatening to make an appearance all over the floor at Target. I darted toward the bathroom near the pharmacy and made it just in time.

Ten minutes later, I dragged myself over to where Lexi was waiting for me, sitting on a bench outside the bathroom. "Are you okay?"

"Not really." I wiped my forehead with a wet paper towel. "And I don't think it's a stomach bug."

"Here, sit down." She got up and helped me to the bench. "Do you need some water?"

"Yeah."

She bent down, took a water bottle from the case we were going to buy, and handed it to me. Normally, I would have protested, but I didn't give a shit. I felt like crap. I took a few sips and let my head hit the wall.

She slid next to me. "I thought you had an IUD."

"I do."

"Damn. Hopefully you're not, but I think you should take a test just to be sure."

I lifted my head. "I think you're right."

After a few minutes, I felt well enough to walk, so we checked out. She got the car while I waited with the buggies. I was thankful for the cool breeze since I was sweaty and clammy all over.

She pulled up to the curb and we loaded up the car. "I think we should go to the apartment. It's closer than the dorm and we need to take this stuff there anyway."

"Yeah, that's fine." I closed my eyes, praying what I already knew wasn't true.

We left everything in the car, except for the toilet paper and pregnancy tests. "Why did you buy so many?" I fumbled with the three different brands, stuffing them in a bag.

"Just to make sure. You never know." She opened the door and I headed straight for the bathroom with Delaney in tow.

"All you have to do is hold the stick in your urine stream for like five seconds."

I turned around. "How do you know?"

Her eyes widened. "Just trust me, I know. And you'll need this." She handed me the empty Icee cup. "Just rinse it out and pee in it, otherwise you're going to have to pee like three times."

"Oh, yeah, good thinking." Obviously, this wasn't Delaney's first rodeo.

With shaky hands, I struggled to unwrap the plastic from the first box. "Here, I can't do it."

I grabbed another box and managed to open it. The instructions were a mile long. "What the hell?"

"I know, like you want to read all that shit." Delaney rolled her eyes and tore open the package with her teeth.

Scanning the change-my-life-forever booklet, I found the instructions quickly. "Okay, you're right. Hold the stick for five seconds in your urine stream and then place the cover on the tip. Results in three minutes." It sounded easy enough.

I quickly unzipped my shorts and sat on the toilet.

"Wait. The cup." Delaney quickly rinsed it with water before handing it to me.

With her back turned, I stuck the cup between my legs and peed, filling it halfway.

"Is this enough." I carefully set the cup on the counter and then tore open the package of toilet paper.

"Um, yeah, that's plenty." She scrunched her nose and then picked up one of the sticks.

"Sorry, I can do it, if you want." I flushed and then pulled up my pants.

She shook her head. "It's just pee. Not vomit."

"Oh, please don't mention that word right now." My stomach tensed just thinking about the bathroom at Target. I felt sorry for the next person who used it.

"Sorry." She gave me a heartfelt smile.

I washed my hands and watched with an unnerving patience as she dipped three different sticks into the cup of urine. She handed them to me and I replaced the caps on all of them, lining them up side by side.

"That's it." She washed her hands and then dried them on her shorts. "Now, we wait."

I set the timer on my phone and sighed. "I need to sit down." Walking into the hall, I slid to the floor.

She sat next to me and I leaned my head against her shoulder. "I like the apartment."

"Yeah, I do, too." She laced her arm through mine. "It's going to be great." It was clear that all the excitement was gone. If I were pregnant, she wouldn't want me living with her. A crying baby, dirty diapers, and empty bottles all over the place — yeah, didn't sound so fun.

"What time are they delivering the furniture?"

"Around three." She tapped her feet together, wiggling her toes. "Man, I need a pedi."

"Yeah, me, too. I noted my chipped nail polish. "Since they're coming at three, that gives us time to move our stuff." I glanced at my phone — two minutes, fifteen seconds.

"Yeah, it does."

"I really like the colors we picked out. It's going to look great." Whatever came to mind, I said. Anything to keep my mind off the clock counting down to predict my fate.

"I've always wanted to decorate in brown and turquoise," Delaney said with little oomph in her voice.

"Those are really great colors."

The buzzer sounded and we both jumped. I turned the alarm off and Delaney stood up. Extending her hand, she pulled me to my feet. "It's now or never." I nodded and took a deep breath. My knees wobbled as I walked back into the bathroom. This time, it seemed ten times smaller as the walls narrowed around me.

Slowly, I leaned over the counter, looking at the three sticks with Delaney peering over my shoulder. All three tests showed small crosses.

"Oh no." Delaney covered her mouth.

"Where are the instructions." I tossed the Target sack behind me and grabbed one of the inserts.

Reading through it frantically, I found the results section. "Cross means positive, dash means negative." I read it again and looked at the sticks. "No. No." I fumbled through the mess on the counter and reached for another instruction booklet. "Plus means positive, minus means negative." I shook my head.

"They're all positive, Lexi," Delaney said in a hushed voice.

"But I have an IUD. It's not possible." My hands fell to my side as the instructions slipped to the floor. I didn't feel so strong any more. In fact, I felt completely weak and vulnerable. This was horrible. What the hell was I going to do? I had just been accepted into grad school and got an apartment with Delaney.

"Come on. Let's go back to the dorm." She wrapped an arm around me. "We'll figure everything out. No need to panic."

"Wait. What time is it?" I grabbed her wrist, looking at her watch. "It's three-thirty. They're still open. Let's go." I grabbed her hand, pulling her out of the bathroom.

"What? Who's open? Where are we going?" Delaney stumbled behind me.

"The health center. I want them to test me."

"But the results are going to be the same."

"You never know." I opened the front door. "Let's go."

Delaney drove us back to the university and straight to the health center. Neither of us said anything, aside from my occasional, "Hurry!" I think we were both in shock. On the way there, I checked the PHU website and verified the hours. I knew that student services were open until Tuesday and since I was still technically a student, they had to see me. We found a nearby parking spot and entered the facility.

I approached the window, thankful there wasn't a line. "I need to see a doctor or nurse practitioner," I told the girl behind the counter.

"Do you have an appointment?" She glanced at her computer.

"No, but it's an emergency." Confirming a pregnancy was an emergency, right? At least, from my viewpoint it was — screw them if they didn't agree.

"Okay. Just scan your student ID at the kiosk to your right and complete the questionnaire. It will let you know your wait time. We'll call you when a room is available."

"Thanks." I removed my student ID and scanned it as she'd instructed. I scrolled through the options and stalled when it asked for the reason. *STD Testing, AIDS Testing, Birth Control, Pregnancy Testing.* The list was damaging to the ego. I selected *Pregnancy Testing* and sat down next to Delaney. By four thirty, I had peed in a cup and was in a room, waiting to be seen.

"What the hell am I going to do if I'm pregnant?" I asked Delaney, feeling the perspiration form on my forehead. My stomach felt like an ocean, crashing with waves, making me dizzy to the point of severe nausea, but I wasn't sure I had anything left to throw up.

"Hmm, I think you know your options," Delaney said with a tight lip. She knew I didn't want to hear the truth.

I always felt that women should have a choice when it came to their bodies. Abortion for the right reasons seemed logical. Except when you're faced with making that decision. "Oh God, how the hell did I end up in this mess?" I covered my face with my hands, praying I could move the hands of time.

"It's called sex."

I removed my hands and bit out the words, "I know that, Delaney."

The door opened and we both plastered on fake smiles.

"Hi, I'm Dr. Sheri Adams." She extended her hand and I shook it.

"Hi, I'm Lexi and this is my friend, Delaney."

"Hello, ladies." She glanced at her tablet, as though referencing who had the appointment. "So, Lexi, we ran a pregnancy test at your request."

"And..." I waited, holding the air in my lungs.

"And the results are positive."

I felt like someone had dropped a ton of bricks on my lap without warning. Even though it shouldn't have been a surprise after doing three home pregnancy tests, I guess I was hoping for some kind of miracle, like their test could reverse the effects of enjoying sexual ecstasy in South Padre Island.

"I don't understand. I have an IUD. I shouldn't have been able to get pregnant." I paced the room back and forth, processing my options, because now it was definitely reality.

Dr. Adams took a seat and said, "Why don't you sit down for a moment, so we can talk?"

I sat on the table and faced her. She scanned through her tablet. "I see that you had the IUD inserted on January tenth, correct?"

"Yes, that sounds correct." I quickly checked my phone, making sure.

"And did you a have a menstrual cycle that month?"

"Yes, I had just finished my period when I had it inserted."

She typed in the information on her tablet as I spoke. "Okay, what about February. Did you have a period then?"

"Yes, and it was regular... well, maybe a little heavier than normal. And I had a period on March fifth," I sighed. This couldn't be happening. Not to me. What had I done to deserve this? "I don't understand. Why didn't it work? I was told that it was effective immediately."

"They are, but sometimes periods can stop. They can also alter your hormones, though you didn't have the one with hormones."

"Yes, I was informed of that. That's why I wasn't concerned when I missed my period the last two months."

"The IUD can also shift and if that happens, an egg can slip through."

"What do you mean it can shift?" I narrowed my eyes at her.

The doctor set the tablet on the counter behind her. "Well, when it is first inserted, it's not firmly imbedded. So, during a heavy period or vigorous activities, such as sex, it can shift."

"Yeah, Raven is pretty big." Delaney nudged me.

My head spun around. "How the hell do you know?"

She held up her hands. "No, I didn't mean his junk — I wouldn't know about that. I'm just referring to him being a muscular guy and..." she shook her head, "never mind."

"Laney, you're not helping."

The doctor tried to conceal the smirk on her face. I had to admit, it did sound funny hearing Delaney plead her innocence to me, but it didn't change the fact that I was supposedly pregnant, or that Raven *was* really big. Like deliciously big.

Why do I keep thinking about him?

"If the first day of your last period was March fifth, then you would have been ovulating from March seventeenth through the twenty-second, based on a twenty-eight day cycle," she said, pointing to a calendar she retrieved from the counter.

No wonder I was so horny.

"Were you sexually active during those days?"

Was I? That was an understatement. That's all Raven and I did — have sex during Spring Break. I recalled how happy we were. We had just gotten engaged the week before. We had definitely celebrated. "Yes, I was. My fiancée and I had sex several times," I said with a heavy voice.

"Then I think it's safe to say that the test is correct."

Shit.

"So, I would like to do a sonogram. By my calculations, you should be about eight weeks pregnant." She smiled and I wanted to cry.

"Great."

She opened a drawer and pulled out a hospital gown. "If you'll please put this on, with it open to the front, we can take a look." Before she walked out of the room, she turned around. "And don't forget to get undressed from the waist down."

"I need to take off my panties so you can see my belly?" I glanced at Delaney out the corner of my eye. Did this lady doctor have something else in mind?

"Yes. I will do a sonogram across your stomach first, but if I can't see anything, I'll need to do a vaginal sonogram. I'll also need to remove the IUD. We can't leave it in there if you're pregnant."

"Oh, yeah, forgot about that."

She shut the door and I felt the color drain from my face. I hoped I wasn't pregnant. It could just be the IUD preventing my periods and showing a false positive — if there was such a thing.

"I'll just wait outside." Delaney walked toward the door and gripped the doorknob.

"No. I need you in here," I said, unzipping my shorts. "Unless you'd prefer not to be."

She dropped her hand and turned around. "Of course I do. I'm here to support you, Lexi."

I gave her a lopsided smile. Hearing her say that made me want to cry. Why the hell was I feeling so emotional?

Oh God. Maybe four tests hadn't lied after all...

Come to think of it, I had been very emotional the past few weeks, but I had good reason to be. My fiancée left me. I finally decided what I wanted to do with my life. I had been accepted to grad school, received a promotion at the writing center...

Shit! This is all going south quickly.

I got undressed and slipped on the nightgown. I wanted to get this over with and be on my way. As I sat on the cold table with my arms supporting my body, I tried to avoid the footrests staring at me. I mean, who in the hell likes to sit spread eagle while someone sticks a cold instrument inside of you? Had to be a man that invented that technique; I doubted it was a woman.

"Damn, I should have opted for the pill instead. Maybe I wouldn't be going through any of this"

"I told you." Delaney looked up from the magazine she was thumbing through. "Damn, how old is this magazine? I didn't know Christina Aguilera was pregnant."

"I think she already gave birth." A knock sounded at the door. "You can come in," I said, laying against the paper cover beneath me.

The doctor shut the door and sat on a stool to the side of me. "Move up, just a little." She took out a clear bottle from a drawer and shook it a few times. "We'll start with your stomach first. It might be a little cold."

She opened my nightgown and squirted a jelly like substance all over my slightly protruding belly. When did my stomach start looking like that? It had always been very flat and lean. Something was definitely wrong. She flipped on the computer monitor and pressed the mouse- like instrument to my stomach. Flesh bumps dotted my skin and I took a deep breath.

"Laney." I reached my hand out toward her and she quickly came to my side.

"Okay, let's take a look." She moved the wand around my belly as I stared intently at the screen. It was hard to make out the images since everything was in black and white. It looked like a scrambled TV station to me. She pressed a few buttons and zoomed in on my uterus. At least, that's what I assumed she was looking at. "Ah ha. There you are."

"What? There's what?" I lifted my head, trying to get a better view.

"Just looks like a bunch of circles to me," Delaney said, squinting her eyes.

"See that wishbone looking thing that's a little crooked?"

"Yes."

"That's your IUD."

"Oh," Delaney and I said simultaneously.

Then she pressed the instrument firmly against my stomach and moved upward. She hit another button on the keyboard and the screen zoomed in again. "And see that?" Using a mouse on the keyboard, she circled two areas on the screen. "Those would be your babies."

"Babies?"

"What the fu..." Delaney started and stopped.

"Wh-what do you mean 'babies'?"

"Just a minute." The doctor continued to move the instrument around my stomach with one hand, capturing different angles by pressing a few buttons on the computer. "Here's a better position."

Delaney and I both leaned forward as she positioned the computer screen so we had a better view.

"Here's one embryo sack," she placed a circle around it, "and here's another one."

"Oh God." I thought I was going to pass out. She couldn't be serious. Not one baby... but two? Twins. Go figure. How the hell would I manage taking care of two babies? I wasn't even prepared to handle one. What was I going to do?

Cry.

Scream.

Tell Raven?

I closed my eyes. The last thing I wanted was for him to be with me because I was pregnant. It wasn't right. I wanted him to be with me because he loved me, not because we were having *babies*. He left me because he didn't want to be with me. This didn't change anything.

"I'm so screwed," I muttered under a heavy breath.

Delaney must have been thinking the same thing because she took a few steps back, hitting the wall. "You're pre-pregnant with tw-twins?"

"Yes, she is and my calculations are correct. You're measuring right at eight weeks and three days." She typed some information into the computer. "Which means you probably got pregnant on March seventeenth."

"That was my birthday."

"Must have been some birthday." The doctor raised a brow.

"Oh no."

"Is something wrong?"

I took a hard swallow, trying to calm my racing heart. Even though I had never thought much about being pregnant, I'd seen the warning signs about drinking while pregnant. What if all the alcohol I'd consumed the night of my birthday caused the babies to have birth defects?

"Yes, I got really drunk the night of my birthday. I mean, *really* drunk. Will that will affect the babies?"

The doctor cleaned the jelly from my stomach. "No, it was too soon. I don't think you have anything to worry about. Unless you've continued to drink for the past eight weeks."

"No, I haven't had any alcohol since then."

"Can you tell what they are?" Delaney eyed the screen.

"No, it's too soon. The sex will be recognizable around week eighteen." She pressed another button and a printer spat out a few pictures. With a quick wrist, she tore them from the feeder. Folding them up neatly, she handed them to me. "Here are the pictures of your babies."

I took them from her and looked at the top picture. *Hi, Mom! Hi, Dad!* She'd typed the message on the front, one for each embryo. Tears streamed from my eyes and my throat thickened.

I was pregnant.

With twins.

And they were Raven's.

There was no way I was aborting my babies. With or without Raven, I was going to do this. I was having these babies.

"Okay, Lexi. I need to remove the IUD next. But I have to warn you, there is a risk of miscarrying."

"Miscarrying?" I quickly wiped the tears from my face. "What if we leave it in?"

"That would be worse. Especially with twins." She opened another drawer and took out a pair of needle nose plyers and a metal insert. My stomach tensed. "Since you're only eight weeks, you're at a twenty-five percent risk, so I think you'll be fine. I do have to warn you though, because when I remove the

IUD, I'm disturbing the uterus, which is where the embryos are. The body could naturally abort them. I want you to take it easy for the next few days, okay? I'll give you my card. Call me if you have any problems."

"I'm supposed to move in the next few days. I'm graduating on Saturday."

"You should be fine for Saturday, unless you miscarry. No heavy lifting or overexerting yourself." She smiled and patted my hand. "It's not worth the risk."

"Okay."

"Let's get that thing out." She motioned for me to put my feet in the stirrups. I guess I would have to get used to it since I was officially pregnant. With twins. Lord help me.

Σ

Chapter 18

"Get up! It's moving time." A rapid succession of knocks startled me and I bolted upright.

I gasped for air and blinked several times. "Shit. You scared me."

"Why aren't you up already?" Luke stood in my doorway, wearing shorts and a PHU ball cap backwards. The ends of his hair curled up and it looked sweaty and hot. "I texted Delaney this morning."

"What?" I yawned and reached for my phone. It showed fifteen minutes to noon. I'd been asleep since nine o'clock — completely spent from yesterday's events and shocking news. I think I deserved to sleep late.

"Shit. Did she not tell you?" My brother huffed. "Laney, I thought—"

"Yeah, I thought you said you'd be here after twelve." She hopped around on one leg, trying to tie her tennis shoe. "I was just about to wake her up."

"You should've already been up and ready to go. Josh is on his way with the truck, so if you're shit isn't ready, you're SOL." Luke stormed out of the room past Delaney, bumping into her. "What's ready to go?"

"Just a minute!" she hollered back. "Hey, I'm sorry. He text me around nine and said that he was helping Josh move and once they were done, they'd come over here and help us." She sat on the edge of my bed. "I told him to come because we could use their help." Glancing at my midsection, she asked, "How are you feeling?"

I stretched. "Okay. Just a little sore."

"Take it easy and let everyone do the carrying. Just act like your moving stuff so no one will think anything." She got up as Luke called for her again.

"Laney?" I motioned for her to wait.

"Yeah?"

"Let me tell Luke, okay?"

She nodded. "Sure. I won't say anything."

I'd just found out a few days ago that Josh and Shelby were moving into a new condo on Seventh Street. It made me a little sad. There were so many good memories at that apartment, but without Raven there, it made sense why Josh wanted to move. Especially since Shelby got a job in downtown Fort Worth and he was getting ready for the draft.

Throwing back the covers, I crawled out of bed and quickly dressed. Thankfully, I had almost everything packed except for my bedding and stuff I was using daily. I stripped my bed and shoved the sheets, blanket, and pillows into a large trash bag. It didn't take me long to pack my bathroom and have everything ready just as Josh and Shelby walked in the door.

"Hey, Lexi." Shelby gave me a kiss on the cheek. "You look different."

"Um," I shifted my weight, making sure my tiny pooch wasn't showing. Wearing workout shorts and a loose tank top, I made sure it hid my mid-section well. "I got my hair cut last week." I ran my fingers through the strands.

"It does look a little shorter, but no, that's not it." Using her finger, she traced a circle in the air, as though marking me. "You're glowing."

"Oh." My mouth hit the floor. I was glowing? Really? That wasn't good for masking my pregnancy from my friends.

"Hey, Lex." Josh approached me from behind and placed me in a bear hug.

"Josh!" I squealed.

"We sure miss hanging out with you."

"I know, I do, too." I smiled, wiggling out of his arms wrapped just above my stomach. It's weird how in one day I went from not knowing I was pregnant with twins, to being extra cautious. But I had to be, at least for the next few days. "Did you already move into your new place?"

"Sure did."

"You'll have to come by and visit." Shelby fingers were working through her hair as she made a braid.

"I will."

"Everything ready to go?" Josh asked, surveying the dorm.

"Yep." I pointed to all the boxes in the hall.

"Then let's get it, girl." Josh popped Shelby on the butt and she jumped.

"Sweetie." She grabbed his arm and planted a kiss on his lips. They looked so happy — excited about moving in together, starting their life together. I hated to admit it, but I missed that so much. Envy was never a problem for me, but I really wanted what they had for Raven and me. Too bad that chance was over.

Everyone shuffled around the dorm, grabbing boxes and bags as they helped us gather our belongings. I followed Josh and Shelby outside, only carrying my bedding since it wasn't that heavy. I did what Delaney recommended so no one would think I wasn't helping.

"Wow." I stared at a large U-Haul truck parked at the curbside. "Luke didn't say you were bringing this big thing."

Josh unlocked the back gate and lifted it. "He said you gals needed help moving and since I don't have to return this truck until tomorrow, I thought we could do it in one trip."

"Thanks, I appreciate it. Sure makes it easier for us."

A bare mattress and brown furniture immediately caught my attention. Josh cleared his throat a few times. "So, um, these are Raven's. I tried to call him, but his phone isn't working. I talked to Trish, but she said she didn't have room for them. She told me to ask you if you wanted them."

How ironic that I needed furniture for my room and it happened to be Raven's. "Oh." I sighed and crossed my arms. Did I really want to be sleeping on the mattress that we'd shared so many times? Where I'd lost my virginity? That mattress was full of our memories.

Shit.

"If you don't want it, I'll just drop it off at the Goodwill."

"No." I raised a hand. "I mean, yes, I'll take it. I was going to get my furniture at my parents, but this works out better."

"Alright." He smiled and took the bags from my hands, sliding them into the truck.

I trudged back upstairs and gathered a few more things as everyone picked up boxes and took them to the truck. It was evident that Raven would be a permanent part of me, even if we weren't together. And if I were able to give birth to his babies, I would see him in them. There was no escaping it. Raven would be a part of me forever.

"I think that's it," Delaney said, holding a box with odds and ends.

Luke took the last box from my hand and I relaxed my arms. "Say your goodbyes, girls."

My lips twitched to the side. A lot had happened in the last two years. Part of me was glad to be moving on, while another part of me felt sad.

"Lots of memories were made in that room." Luke nudged Delaney as she slipped into her bedroom, doing a double check.

"Yeah, but we've got a new one to start on." She winked at him and he grinned.

I walked into my bedroom and did one last glance. Sitting on my bed was a vision of Raven, his hands folded as he leaned against his thighs, the soft glow of my nightlight making him appear Godlike. The night he'd brought me home from the frat party was so vivid. Almost like it was yesterday. It was the night that he confessed he wanted to have sex with me. I had thought that *would be the night.*

I laughed under my breath as a tear escaped. If only I wouldn't have fallen into his trap. But it was too late for that. I ran my hand over my little bump. His trap was right there in the center of me. Two of them. I sighed and turned around, leaving those good times behind me. I turned off the light and shut the door. They would remain there forever.

We locked up the dorm and went downstairs. "I'll turn in our keys," Delaney said, taking my copy as we exited the elevator.

"Okay, I'll be outside."

Luke followed her to the residence desk and I headed for the door. As I entered the foyer, I stopped for a second, glancing at the baby grand piano that held a lifetime of musical memories. I hadn't played since Spring Break, but the last time I had played this one was with Raven. The tears reappeared, streaming down my cheeks and spilling into my hair.

Approaching it, I glided my hand over the sleek black wood. Nothing would ever take away the love I had for playing — not my mom and especially not Raven. Regardless of the pain it brought or the happiness it spread, the piano would forever be my favorite pastime.

I dropped my purse to the floor and slid onto the bench. Running my fingers along the keyboard, I collected the dust and wiped my hands. I'd never forget the first day Raven showed up as I was playing *All of Me.* I couldn't believe he was watching me play. A tiny smile escaped from my lips. The best part was when we sang *Lean On Me* to each other. I had promised to be there for him, no matter what. Why didn't he let me do that? Why did he have to walk out on me?

I shook my head and rested my fingers along the ivory. Pressing my fingers in unison, I began playing a familiar melody. It was like the notes were dying to be released. I played with all of my soul, not missing one. I had given all of myself to Raven, yet he had chosen not to accept it.

All of me honestly loved all of him.

Loved every bit of him.

Everything about him.

And I had thought he loved me equally. One thing was certain, I wouldn't trade the time I had with him. It was magical while it lasted. For as long as I lived, despite what happened with my pregnancy, I was still willing to give all of me to him.

Forever.

A warm hand touched my shoulder and I stopped playing. "Come on, we gotta go," Luke said with a caring voice. I smiled at him and sniffed repeatedly as another round of tears released. How I wished it would've been Raven's hand instead of my brother's.

I got up and placed Luke's arm around me. He gave me tight squeeze. We didn't say anything, but we didn't have to. My brother knew what tormented me and what pain I was in because of Raven. He held me, giving me the comfort only a brother could instill. After a few minutes, we released our embrace and headed outside, leaving all of the memories behind us.

"I can't believe this is it," Delaney said, pulling out of the loading zone. "We're graduating and moving on with our lives."

"I know, it makes me sad. But it's not like I won't be up here every day in a few weeks."

"So, are you still planning on going to grad school?"

"I don't know." I shrugged. "I really haven't had time to think about it."

"You've got time." She grabbed my hand. "Don't worry about it right now."

"I'm sure it'll all work out in the end."

I leaned my head against the window, watching students walk in and out of buildings as Delaney drove through the campus to our new apartment. Purple and white banners attached to light poles flapped in the wind, advertising PHU's baseball and football team. No doubt, PHU didn't seem the same without their star quarterback, but as the saying goes, nothing good lasts forever.

We pulled up to the complex and the urge for a nap hit hard. The short drive had definitely relaxed me; I was ready to lay down for a late snooze. I struggled to get out of the car, feeling ten times heavier than normal. I couldn't imagine what I'd feel like in six months. Thankfully, our apartment was on the first floor and stairs wouldn't be an issue.

"Home sweet home." Delaney opened the door and we walked in. I immediately slumped to the floor in the living room as everyone took a self-tour.

"It's nice." Josh stood with his hands on hips, scanning the living room.

"It's so cute." Shelby went from room to room.

"Thanks, I got one helluva a deal." Delaney huffed, then dumped a bag in the middle of the hallway.

Luke dropped a few Target sacks from yesterday's shopping excursion onto the floor and I immediately grabbed one of the pillows Delaney had bought for me. Unable to hold my head up, I clutched the pillow in my hands and remained on the floor.

"What the fuck?" Luke kicked my leg, but I was too tired to protest.

"Hey, don't kick her." Delaney slammed her fist into his side.

"We don't have time for a nap. We've got a truck to unload." He pointed toward the parking lot.

"In a minute." The incessant need to close my eyes took over. It was as though my head felt like a nine pound bowling ball, ready to topple off my body. "I just need a five minute catnap."

"Are you serious?" Josh huffed.

"Are you okay?" Shelby knelt next to me, stroking my hair. "You look a little pale."

I nodded, unable to open my mouth. Sleep was all my body wanted, everything else would have to wait.

"I'm not going to unload all your shit while your lazy ass sleeps." Luke's voice rose louder and I knew he was mad. "That's not cool, Lexi. You can't expect us to do all the work while you take a break. It's not right and you know it."

Through half parted eyes, I looked at him, trying to think of a good excuse. "I'm sorry, I just..."

"Man, screw this." Luke headed for the door and Delaney grabbed his arm.

"Luke, please. I need your help," Delaney pleaded, but he shoved her hand away. He wasn't buying it. "Just leave her alone. We can do it without her."

"Fuck that." He shoved past her and flung the door open.

"Wait!" I bolted upright and the room spun around me.

"Whoa." Shelby braced me with her arm as I leaned against the wall and closed my eyes, trying to steady the awful sensation. "I don't think she's okay."

I held up my hand as my stomach did a somersault. Swallowing a few times, I managed to keep my lunch down. This pregnancy thing wasn't going so well. "I can explain. Just... please, don't go. We need your help. I need your help."

"Then explain." Luke slammed the door. "Because I'm always doing everything for you."

My head spun around. "Seriously? Is that how you feel? Because I've never asked you to do anything for me." My eyes welled up, turning me into an emotional rollercoaster again.

This sucks.

"You might not have asked, but Mom and Dad sure expected it." Luke's face turned red and his jaw hardened as he pressed his lips together.

I straightened, feeling a surge of adrenaline. The dizziness subsided and I was ready to get to the bottom of his shitty attitude once and for all. I was tired of it. "That's what this is all about?" I shoved my finger in his face. "I never expected you to do anything for me, other than giving me a ride here or there, but that's it."

"Maybe so, but my whole life I've had to watch after you. Go where you go. Follow all your steps. Make sure you didn't do anything stupid." He slapped my finger, knocking my hand to the side. "Well, I'm not doing it anymore. I'm done."

"Good. I don't need you to watch after me. I'm a grown woman. I can make my own decisions."

"And how's that working out for you?" Luke crossed his arms. "Huh?"

I eyed Delaney. Had she told him? She made a cross over her heart, as if swearing to the secret only we shared.

"You walked away from a guy who really loved you and gave yourself to someone who tossed you aside. Just like I warned you."

"You're still pissed about Collin?" I knew it. Even though he would never admit it to me, he'd been upset all along. I guess I couldn't blame him. Collin had been his best friend since middle school.

"No, I'm not pissed about Collin. I told you it was between you and him. It just hate seeing you upset all the time and

knowing that he didn't give a shit about you infuriates me."
Luke balled his hands into fists.

Josh shifted his weight and I prayed this wasn't about to
turn into a big fight.

"You don't even know what you're talking about." Tears
poured from my eyes as I battled my emotions for Raven —
knowing exactly what tormented him daily. But it wasn't my
place to tell. "You have no idea what he's been through."

Luke rolled his eyes. "Lexi, everybody knows Raven's story."

"Luke, stop." Delaney urged him to tone it down, but he
ignored her.

"You might know his public story, but I know his *real*
story." I clutched my hand to my chest, feeling that familiar tug
that gripped my heart. "And I know that he probably still loves
me, but he just can't get over what happened."

With a laugh, Luke said, "You've got to be kiddin' me. If he
walked through that door, you'd take him back, wouldn't you?"

I stared at Luke, unable to answer him. Wrapping my arms
around my midsection, I embraced our creations. Even though
I loved Raven, I wasn't sure I would take him back, despite
being pregnant. He hurt me and walked out on me too many
times. It wasn't like I just could brush it under the rug and give
it another whirl.

"You would." His face turned stoic.

"And if I did, that's my decision." I pointed to myself with
two fingers. "Not yours, not Dad's, and surely not Mom's. In
fact, what I decide to do is in my control." I dropped my hands
to my belly. "And if I want to have these babies then I will. And
no one is going to tell me differently."

"What?" Luke's eyes widened and his mouth fell open.

Delaney covered her mouth and shook her head.

"Oh shit." Josh looked stunned and his head jerked back.

"Oh my God, you're pregnant!" Shelby through her hands
up in the air. "Does Raven know?"

A sudden knock on the door startled us. Delaney opened the door. "Deliver for Delaney Dukahkis." A middle-aged guy wearing a T-shirt with Furniture World over the pocket smiled as he held up a clipboard. Great timing.

"Oh, yes. That's me." Delaney turned toward the guy.

"You're pregnant?" Luke said in a low voice.

With my hands, I covered my face. I had ratted on myself. *Shit.*

"What's going on?" Shawn's voice echoed to the right of me. "Is this where the party is at?"

I dropped my hands. Could this get any worse?

Everyone looked at Shawn and he hesitated to step into the apartment.

"Hey, man." Josh shook his hand. "Thanks for coming."

"Yeah, were you guys waiting on me?" He looked at Luke, Delaney, and then me. "Are you okay, Lex?"

I wiped my tears and took a deep breath. "Yeah, pregnant."

"Oh, that's go—you're what?" Shawn did a double take, the whites of his eyes popping out.

Now that the secret was out, I decided to tell him, too.

"Where do you want this?" The delivery guy reappeared as two guys followed behind, carrying our sofa.

"Oh, um," Delaney scanned the living room, "how about right here, in the center."

We shifted out of the way as the movers came toward us.

"Let's go to your room so we can talk." Luke pointed down the hall.

I walked to my empty bedroom and turned around to see everyone, except Delaney, file in behind me. My personal business had just became everyone's interest.

"How long have you known?" Luke's voice had transformed from anger to concern.

"I found out yesterday."

"Do Mom and Dad know?"

I shook my head. "No."

"Are you going to tell them?"

I dropped my chin and peered at him through my lashes. "I'm going to have to eventually. I'm on their insurance."

"How far along are you?" Shelby sounded the most enthusiastic about my situation.

"Eight weeks, but..." I shifted, unsure I should give them more details than they needed.

"But what?"

I straightened and took a deep breath. We were all adults and we'd all had sex. We knew about birth control. Or at least, knew something about it.

"There's a twenty-five percent chance I could miscarry."

Shelby sighed, "Oh no, why?"

I swallowed the lump in my throat. "They had to remove the IUD and it could cause the fetuses to abort."

Luke took a step back. "Did you just say fetuses?"

"Uh, yes. I'm pregnant with twins."

"Aw, hell." Shawn rolled his shoulders, his body quivering.

"I guess I missed that part." Luke took off his ball cap and ran his fingers through his hair. "How the hell are you going to manage two kids?"

"You got pregnant with an IUD?" Shelby glanced at me, then at Josh.

"Good thing you're on the pill, sweets." Josh told her and then looked at me with apologetic eyes. "Sorry, Lexi. Didn't mean to throw one at ya."

I blew off his comment. "Word to the wise, never opt for an IUD. They obviously don't work." I smirked.

"Damn, Lexi, I don't know what to say." Shelby gave me deep, sympathetic look. "I'm here for you." She glanced at Josh. "We're here for you. Whatever you need." She immediately wrapped her arms around me and I hugged her tightly.

"Thank you. I appreciate it."

"Are you going to tell Raven?" Josh asked, bringing my situation to head.

"Eventually." I knew Raven had a right to know, but I hadn't decided on when I was going to tell him. I needed some time to think things through. The last thing I wanted was for him to take me back because I was pregnant.

"Lexi, I think he has a right to know." Shawn wrapped an arm around me. "If he's the dad, I know he'd want to know."

I looked up at Shawn. "Of course he's the dad. And I know it's only right to tell him, just give me some time to process a few things. What I need to do first is rest for a few days, like the doctor ordered, and then make it to graduation."

"Okay. If you need help getting in touch with him, let me know." Shawn pulled me closer. "I care about both of you."

"I know you do." I patted him on the chest. "I'll let you know."

"Then I guess we better get your bed set up first." Josh turned to Luke, urging him to follow.

"Yeah, just a moment." Luke motioned with his head. "Lexi, can I talk to you for a moment in private?"

"I'll help you." Shawn followed Josh and Shelby out of the room.

Luke shut the door and I took a deep breath. I'd never liked confrontation and I felt bad about what had just happened. But a part of me was glad we finally got it out in the open, exposed our true feelings — they had been repressed for too long.

Luke immediately gathered me into his arms. "I'm sorry, Sis. I didn't mean to unleash on you like that. I had no idea you were pregnant. And I'm sorry that Raven left you. I'm here for you, you know that."

I squeezed my eyes shut, resting my chin on his shoulder. My nose stung and my throat tightened. No matter how hard I tried to hold back the waterworks, they made their reappearance. "It's okay. I'm sorry that you've been feeling that way toward me," I mumbled against his shirt. "I hate that Mom and Dad put that burden on you. It's not right."

"It was more Mom than anything. You know how she is..."

I shook my head and sniffed. He increased the space between us and lifted my chin with his finger, bringing our eyes level. "I know you don't want to hear this, but you need to tell Mom and Dad. Or at least Dad."

"I know. I will." I pressed a hand to my temple. "Everything has happened so fast. I need a day or two to clear my head."

"I understand, but graduation is in six days and..."

My head jerked up. "And what?"

Luke sighed and gritted his teeth together. "Mom is planning this big barbecue afterwards. She's sent invitations to the entire family."

I let my head fall back as my shoulders fell forward. "Are you serious?"

"Yep. I'm surprised Dad hasn't told you."

"He's been texting me since yesterday, telling me he needs to talk to me. I told him I was busy packing and I'd call him later. That's probably what he wants to tell me."

"Probably." Luke wiped a tear from my check. "Don't worry, Sis. I know you'll be alright." He kissed me on the forehead and released me from his embrace.

"I know I will," I sighed. "I'm going to have two babies to take care of. Can you believe that?"

"No." He smiled. "I guess what happens in Padre, doesn't stay in Padre," Luke snickered.

I punched him in the arm. "That's so not funny."

"Sorry, Sis." He walked toward the door and opened it. "You know I'm here for you."

"Thanks. I'll make sure to take you up on that offer once they're born."

Later that night, I lay on Raven's mattress, cuddled in my new bedding, thinking about what Luke told me. I knew that I needed to tell my parents. Graduation was on Saturday and I hadn't spoken to my mom since New Year's Eve. I thought about what my friends said, and yes, they were right. I needed to tell Raven, too. He had a right to know. I just wasn't ready. Not yet.

Σ

Chapter 19

"Luke's outside!" Delaney hollered across the apartment. "He said to hurry. He wants to miss rush hour traffic."

"Okay, I'm coming." I grabbed my purse and headed for the door. I told Luke I was ready to tell Mom and Dad and asked him to take me. With graduation four days away, I figured I'd better get it over with.

We locked up the apartment and headed to the parking lot, where Luke was waiting.

Delaney opened the door and I got in the backseat. "Thanks, Luke, for taking me."

"Yeah, no problem." He lowered the radio and kept his eyes firmly planted on Delaney's butt as she got in the car.

"Hey, sexy." Delaney shot him one of her seductive looks as she slid into the front seat.

"Hey there, yourself." Luke leaned over and kissed her on the lips.

Her hands cupped his face and then spread into his hair. She tangled her fingers through his thick waves as they stayed lip-locked. Luke moaned and I immediately felt uncomfortable..

I hit the back of the seat, stopping them before things got out of control. "Are you two going to kiss all day or what?"

After three long seconds, they finally stopped. "So, Sis, how you doing?" Luke adjusted the rearview mirror.

"Totally disgusted."

"Sorry." Delaney glanced back at me, her eyes pleading for me to forgive her.

"Take a nap, you'll feel better."

I yawned and settled against the seat. A nap did sound really good.

Luke shook his head. "What are you going to do when you go back to work and classes start? I'm sure grad school is more demanding than undergrad."

I shrugged. "I don't know. I'll see how things go." I checked the messages on my phone. Nothing new showed up. Now that Shawn and Josh knew, I wondered if they'd told Raven. A tiny part of me wished they would so I didn't have to. But I didn't have time to think about Raven. I had to get my thoughts together on how I was going to break the news to my parents. I typed a text message to my dad, telling him I was on the way to see him and Mom. Closing my eyes, I thought about my options. What I should say first and what I needed from them.

"Lexi. Wake up." Luke slapped the back of his seat. "Damn, I thought she said she took a nap." I heard everything he said, I just couldn't open my eyes.

"She did," Delaney answered. "Lex. Hey, girl, you okay?" She shook my arm and I shifted.

"Hey, Lex, here comes Mom."

I pried my eyes open and bolted upright. "Where?"

Luke laughed. "I knew that'd get you up."

I hit the back of his seat with my palm, pushing him forward. He was back to his old tricks like when we were young. It made me smile. "Shithead."

Delaney opened the door and I slid out first. I turned around when I heard the car door shut. "Hey," I motioned for her to roll down the window, "aren't you coming inside?"

She gave me a meek shrug and nodded toward Luke, as if trying to tell me he was the one making the decisions.

"Sorry, Sis. You have to do this one alone." Luke peered through Delaney's window, giving me a thumbs up. "You'll be alright."

"Uh." I crossed my arms and pursed my lips together. "But I ne..." I stopped, realizing what I was about to say. I really didn't need Luke or Delaney. He was right; I needed to tell my parents on my own. I was a grown woman that had been dying to express her independence and had done so defiantly for the past year. The result of everything I had done wasn't anyone else's problem. It was mine and I was taking responsibility for the decisions I'd made. "You're right. Thanks." I smiled and stepped away from the car.

"Text me when you're ready to leave and we'll come pick you up."

I nodded and waved as he backed out of the driveway. I turned around and took a deep breath. It was now or never. Taking one step at a time, I approached the front door, rehearsing exactly what I'd say to them. Just as I reached into my purse to grab my keys, the front door opened.

"Hey, princess."

"Hi, Dad." I smiled.

"I hurried home as soon as you said you were on the way." Dad loosened the tie around his neck as he held the door open for me. "Where's Luke?"

"He and Delaney went to the mall. They'll be back in a little while."

"Who's at the door, hon?" Mom's voice echoed through the foyer. "I don't want to be late for—" Mom stopped dead in her tracks with her mouth ajar. Her eyes darted to my dad and then back to me.

"Hi." I gave a short wave, waiting to see if her reaction would soften.

"Lexi. Wh-what are you doing here? I mean, it's about time you came home. Your sister and I have been doing all the

planning for this graduation party. I hope you appreciate it."
She tucked her short hair behind her ear and pushed her
shoulders back. Her new hairstyle definitely made her look
more sophisticated and more her age. She still hadn't given up
on coloring it to cover the grey, though.

"Thanks. I, um, I need to talk to you and Dad." I shut the
door behind me and walked past them toward the living room,
keeping a straight face. If I didn't keep my focus, I knew I'd lose
it and start crying. My hormones continued to wreak havoc on
my emotions — I found myself crying at almost anything,
including commercials. I was pathetic.

"Well, we were just about to leave for dinner." She held up
her arm and checked her watch. She fumbled with the bangles
on her wrist and let out a small sigh. "Where's Luke? I guess we
can all go eat and then—"

"Olivia, I think dinner can wait." Dad ushered her toward
the living room.

"Travis, we told the Stanley's we'd be there at six." Mom
sounded perturbed that her dinner plans had been postponed
rather than happy to see me. Nothing had changed, that was
for sure.

"Sit." Dad placed a hand on her shoulder and forced her
down to the couch. With his other hand, he whipped his
phone out of his pocket and typed a text.

"What are you doing?" she questioned, but dad remained
silent as his fingers worked quickly.

"Now they know we aren't coming." He smiled and sat next
to her.

Way to go, Dad!

I wish I could've recorded the entire incident, because I
knew Luke wasn't going to believe me. Apparently, some things
had changed. I hated to say it, but Dad had finally grown a pair.

"What is it that'd you like to talk to us about, princess?" Dad smiled as he leaned forward with his hands folded in his lap.

Mom didn't say anything, just flapped her long, faux lashes at me, as if telling me, "This better be good". Oh boy, would it be.

My legs shook as adrenaline coursed through my body. Inside my chest, the gun had just sounded and the horses had been released, galloping at full speed, as if eager to get away from the nerve-wracking scene. Easing onto a chair, I took a deep breath and positioned myself to face them.

I can do this.

"I just..." I took a few deep breaths, trying to get the horses to slow down, but they refused. "I, um, wanted to let..." No matter how many times I'd repeated the words in my head, I couldn't say them.

"I think what Lexi is trying to tell us is that she's decided to go to graduate school." He winked at me and I whimpered.

"Oh, sweetie," Mom sighed as her hand flew to her chest. "I'm so happy for you. That's the best news ever." She scampered toward me and embraced me in a tight hug. Slowly, I wrapped my arms around her, unsure whether her reaction was genuine. "You'll definitely earn more money with a master's degree. You can work your way up to administration." She released me, keeping her hands on my arms. "Who knows, maybe you can become a vice principal."

Oh God.

"Yeah, um, I'm not going to grad school for education."

"You're not?" Mom stood upright, her bubble completely burst. "Then what are you going to do?"

I shifted in my chair. "I've decided to get a master's degree in English and creative writing instead."

Her hands flew to her hips. "And what do you hope to do with that?"

"What I've been doing, editing." I smiled.

She shook her head and returned to the couch. "And what exactly are you *editing*?" She pursed her lips together and folded her arms against her body.

"Does it really matter?" I challenged her stare, not ready to back down. "I'll continue editing student papers like I have been. I was also promoted to a Senior Consultant in the writing lab with Dr. Phillips. I'll be working there while I go to grad school. That's why I moved in with Delaney." I decided to leave the whole part about editing for J.S. Christensen out of the conversation. She'd never understand and I didn't feel like explaining it to her.

"That's great news, Lexi. Congratulations." Dad got up and gathered me in a hug.

"Thanks, Dad." I loved how he pretended he didn't know. It was our little secret.

"I thought you were moving back home this weekend. Don't the dorms close on Friday?" She looked at my dad and then back to me. "I thought that's why you showed up...to tell me you were sorry about everything and ask if you could live here."

"Um, I think it's you that owes me the apology." I gritted my teeth. "Your words caused a lot of heartache for me and Raven."

"Me?" Mom's voice raised three octaves. "I had nothing to do with that boy's behavior. And what does it matter now? He got kicked out of school and off the football team, right? And Dad told me he left you — *again.*"

Thanks, Dad.

"Lexi, Olivia," Dad spoke up, "let's not go down that path. Let bygones be bygones. I want both of you to apologize and put all of this in the past."

He looked at me and then at Mom. "Olivia, you go first."

Mom rolled her eyes and tilted her head to the right. "I'm sorry, Lexi. I'll learn how to keep my opinions to myself and let you decide how you want to live your life." Her words were more sarcastic than honest. "There, you happy?" She glanced at Dad out of the corner of her eye.

I knew he'd been talking to her, which was good, but it did nothing for me unless she was sincere. I didn't need her to save face. Tears welled up in my eyes again. It really sucked that I couldn't have a better relationship with my mother. Especially with everything I was facing. I had no idea how I was going to raise two babies on my own.

"I'm sorry, too, Mom. I'm sorry that I don't meet your standards or do everything that you want me to do. I'm sorry that you don't approve of my choices." I pointed to myself and the tears released. "I'm sorry that you couldn't accept Raven, like you accepted Collin. But most of all, I'm sorry that you don't treat me like you treat Ashley, because I could really use a friend right now."

"Lexi, a mother is not supposed to be a friend." Her eyes glossed over, but she didn't cry. "My role is to make sure I raise you to do the right thing and put you back on track when you rear off. And that's all I've ever done. I've only wanted the best for you, Luke, and Ashley. Can't see you that?"

"Then that explains it." I wiped my cheeks with the back of my hands. "I appreciate all of your hard ass advice, but in the end, it really didn't help me because I'm pregnant. And I'm having twins," I blurted without even a second thought. "And Raven is the father."

My mom's face turned to stone, like I had just knocked the life out of her. Dad did a double take. "Lexi, you didn't tell me...how long have you known?" He sounded like he was betrayed or hurt that I hadn't told him.

"You're what?" Mom breathed heavily, as if still trying to process the words. "Why weren't you being more responsible? What about all those condoms. How did..."

"I found out this past Saturday." I exhaled, releasing all the tension and calming the racehorses inside of my chest. It was over. They knew. "I would've told you sooner, but it's been quite traumatic."

"Traumatic. This is devastating. How far along are you?" Mom ran her fingers through her hair repeatedly, turning into a ball of frazzled nerves.

"I'm eight weeks."

"Give me your phone." Mom motioned to Dad.

"Why?" Dad eyed her suspiciously.

She swallowed a few times. "I, um, need to look up the cut off for abortions."

"Abortion? And you call yourself a Christian?" I shot up, rage hitting my blood stream. "I'm not aborting my babies!" I cradled my stomach. "Not after all I've been through."

"Relax, Lexi." Dad rushed to my side. "No one is telling you to get an abortion." He eased me back onto the chair, keeping an arm wrapped around me.

I sat, gripping the handles of the chair, when I really wanted to be ripping out her hair. The nerve she had. This was woman was un-freakin-believable. She was never going to give up until she got what she wanted for me.

"What have you been through?" Mom questioned, as if I didn't know what I was talking about. "You have no idea what it's like to be pregnant with twins, deliver them, and raise them."

"Not yet, but if I haven't lost them by now, then it's meant to be."

Mom and Dad looked confused and I knew I'd said too much. Why couldn't I just keep it simple? I knew there wasn't an easy way out of this one.

"Let me explain." My shoulders dropped as all my energy drained from me. Arguing with my mom sucked the life out of me. "I had an IUD and got pregnant with it, so they had to remove it. The doctor said there was a twenty-five percent chance I could lose the babies."

"Oh, Lexi." Dad placed his hand on my back, giving me a gentle rub. "I'm sorry."

"So, yes, I was being responsible, but it didn't work. So there you have it. I'm pregnant with twins, so I could really use your support. I need to see a doctor and, if possible, stay on your insurance until I figure out what the hell I'm going to do."

"How are you going to go to grad school?" Mom still wasn't getting it.

"I don't know. I have the summer to think about it."

Mom fell back against the couch. With her hand on her forehead, she looked just as spent as me. "My God, Lexi. You graduate on Saturday and you're just telling us."

"I found out a few days ago. What did you want me to do? Call you the second I left the health center?"

Mom rubbed her head. "I need an aspirin. Travis, will you please—"

"Yeah, yeah. I've got it." Dad went to the kitchen to fetch mom her copout, like always.

Dad returned with her aspirin and a glass of water. "Thank you, hon."

"I think you should seriously consider moving back home. Having two babies at once is a lot of work." He handed me a glass of water.

"Thanks, Dad." After taking a few gulps, I said, "I know and I probably will, but give me some time to get my head straight, please."

"Does Raven know?" Mom pressed the cold glass of water to her forehead, as if she were the one pregnant and facing a life changing event.

"Not yet."

"Are you going to tell him? Because I think he has a right to know," Dad chimed in.

"I know. It just that..." I closed my eyes, trying to fight the emotions tugging at my heart and stirring the babies in my belly. Would I ever be okay without Raven? I wanted him to be a part of the babies' lives. It was only right.

Dad kneeled next to me. Taking my hands in his, he said, "It's okay, Lexi. You've got plenty of time to decide what you want to do. And whatever you decide, we will be here to help you. You can count on that."

Tears dripped from my eyes. "Thanks, Dad. You don't know how much I needed to hear that."

"I love you, princess" He rose up and kissed me on the forehead.

"And I love you, too, sweetie." Mom joined us, wrapping an arm around me. "This won't be easy, but I'll help you, if you want."

"Thanks, Mom."

We hugged and cried. It was the best family hug I'd ever had in the whole twenty-one years I'd been alive. Why did it take something so drastic to bring us together?

"Thank God," Luke muttered as the last row of graduates approached the stage.

"Tell me about it. I'm dying over here." I shifted and stretched in my chair. The Texas sun was directly overhead and being outside in the middle of May on the football field wasn't exactly fun. I had no idea how Raven played in the heat while wearing so much equipment. My cheeks flushed just thinking about it. "You have to stop somewhere before we head to Ashley's. I'm starving to death."

Luke shook his head. "Why am I not surprised?"

Saturday had arrived before I knew it and we were at the end of our three hour graduation ceremony. Excitement was definitely in the air and I struggled with my emotions once again. Luckily, Luke and I were sitting side by side, since we shared a last name, and I had him for support. The pangs of pregnancy hunger and sleep called to me. I had no idea how I'd made it this far. Maybe it was because I knew I was closing one chapter in my life and getting ready for the next.

"Graduates, please stand," the dean of admissions announced.

We stood, donning our purple robes and square graduation caps, proud of our accomplishments. Whistles echoed throughout the crowd and a few whoops followed. Laughter spread throughout and I smiled, even though part of me was a little sad. It was supposed to be a joyous day and it was, but something was missing. And that something was Raven. Being on the field he'd played on for three years didn't seem right. Especially since I was carrying his babies. Without warning, the waterworks released and I blotted my eyes for the umpteenth time.

"Graduates, if you will take your tassels and flip them to the left." The dean demonstrated on his own tassel and we followed. Silly string sprayed through the air, covering us in a web of purple and white. More tears fell and I couldn't help but feel excited. I had finally earned my degree. "Parents and friends, I'm happy to introduce the graduates of Park Hill University!" The dean of admissions spread his arms and the crowd erupted into a loud cheer. Confetti shot out, covering us in a rainbow of colors. Luke took out a bullhorn and squeezed it several times.

"Hey, you're not supposed to have that." I pushed his arm down, hoping no one saw, but he didn't care, doing it three more times.

"We did it, Sis! We did it!" Luke threw his arms around me, picking me up.

I squealed. "Yes, we did!"

After we hugged some of our friends and wished them well, the field filled with families and friends. Everyone darted in different directions as they searched for their loved ones. Luke held my hand as we searched through the crowd, hearing a familiar voice.

"Luke! Lexi!" Delaney jumped up and down, waving at us.

"Laney!" Luke ran to her and picked her up, spinning her around as he kissed her repeatedly. Never had I seen my brother display that much emotion. Delaney had definitely changed him. Maybe for the better.

"We did it!" they said in unison as they hugged.

"Lexi, come here." Delaney waved for me to join them. "We graduated!" She threw her arms around my neck and my brother encased his arms around both of us. No doubt, it was a great day, but I just couldn't seem to get as excited as they were. Something was wrong with me.

"Selfie, selfie." Delaney held up her phone and snapped a pic of us. "Damn, I wish I had my camera."

"Make sure you bring it tonight," Luke told her.

"I will." Delaney's head darted to the side. "Look, there's Jordan and Forbes." She waved at them and they shuffled toward us.

"Oh my God, we're graduates!" Jordan jumped up and down, screaming at the top of her lungs. Forbes looked equally excited as he yelled and hooted. Everyone had their special someone to celebrate with, except for me. Out of the corner of my eye, huddled with a few other baseball players, was Collin. I ducked my head in the crowd and hoped he hadn't seen me. He was the last person I wanted to see. As I turned and headed in the opposite direction, I slammed right into someone.

"Lexi?"

I looked up, my eyes traveling along a large frame. "Shawn? Hey."

"Congrats, girl!" He pulled me into a tight bear hug, nearly squeezing the air out of my lungs. "We're PHU grads!"

A painful smile emerged as I begged for release. "Can't... breathe."

"Oh, shit." His arms loosened and I took a deep breath. "Sorry. You alright?" He glanced at my stomach.

I nodded and straightened my graduation cap. "Yeah, I'm okay." I gave him a smile and patted my belly. "They're fine, too."

"Good." He grinned and shot me a wink. "I didn't mean to hurt you, it's just that," he let out a roar, "it's such a freakin' awesome day." He pumped a fist in the air and Josh jumped him from behind. I took several steps back, keeping a safe distance as I laughed outwardly. Inwardly, I wanted to cry. I was going to miss seeing these guys have fun. What hurt the most was not seeing Raven here to celebrate his friend's accomplishments, but even more, mine.

"Lexi, we finished." Shelby locked hands with mine and raised our arms high above our heads as she danced around. "We're graduates!"

"Yes, we did." I followed her lead, trying to keep up with her. The girl was a bundle of energy — energy I was dying to have.

"I can't believe it." Tears streamed down her face and I struggled to keep my emotions in check.

"Lex, come here, girl." Josh hugged Shelby and me at the same time. "I'm so proud of you."

Shawn slipped under our tight huddle. "I'm going to miss you guys."

"We'll still see each other," I said, trying to keep the mood high, because I was quickly falling into the pits of sadness once again.

"You're coming over to my parent's house tonight, right?" Josh asked, while a few of the other football players high fived him.

"I wish I could, but my sister is having a barbecue at her house for us."

"Oh, damn," Josh said, his head bobbing between me and his other friends.

Shelby pouted. "You and Luke should come by later, if you can."

"We'll try." I spotted Luke and Delaney with my parents. "I better go. I'll message you."

"Yes, don't forget." Shelby gave me a quick kiss on the cheek.

"See ya, Shawn, Josh," I told them bye and they waved back.

I pushed my way through the crowd, darting bursts of silly string along the way.

"There you are, sweetie." Mom placed an arm around my waist and gave me a gentle kiss. "Sorry." She rubbed her lipstick off my cheek. "I'm so happy for you and Luke." Her eyes watered and she quickly swiped them away. "Luke, baby." She motioned for him to join us.

Luke threw his arm around my mom and let out a "Woo hoo!"

"I'm so proud of my twins." Mom smiled as we both kissed her on the cheek. Delaney snapped a picture of us and we laughed. "Travis, get in the picture," she said, motioning for my dad. Delaney took a few pictures of us with our parents and all of us together.

"There are my parents." Delaney stood on the tips of her toes, flapping her arms in the air.

"Luke, we're going to head to your sister's. We'll see you there shortly," Dad said, holding my mom's hand.

"Okay. See ya there," Luke replied as Delaney dragged him with her.

"Do you want to come with us or go with Luke?" Mom continued to rub my lipstick stained cheek.

"I'll wait. Delaney is coming with us." I wasn't sure if my parents knew about them, but I figured they knew something.

"Okay." She smiled. "See you in a little while."

I walked to where Delaney's parents were standing. "Hi, Mr. and Mrs. Dukahkis."

"Lexi, it's so good to see you." Delaney's mom squeezed my hand. "Are you doing okay?"

Delaney told me she'd told her mom, asking for advice since she had suffered multiple miscarriages in her life, which brought them to adopt her. "Good." I nodded as my lips started to quiver. Would the tears ever stop?

"Congratulations, Lexi. Thanks for keeping our daughter in check." Mr. Dukahkis winked as he rubbed my arm.

"Sure." I sniffed and swallowed a few times. "We've kept each other in check." I winked as I cast a side glare to Delaney. I had met her parents over a year ago when I went to the farm with Delaney. They were really nice country folk, as most Texans would say. After a brief conversation, I stepped away, allowing Luke to talk to them — it was his first time meeting them.

I looked up and down the field. It brought back so many memories. No matter how hard I tried, I couldn't stop thinking of Raven. When he snuck me into the stadium and took me to the Marshall's suite to have my first beer — not to mention, tried to kiss me — and when I sat in the bleachers, wearing his jersey as he played one hell of a game. I cradled my body and closed my eyes, allowing the sweet memories to take over me. My life would never be the same without him.

Σ

Chapter 20

"Lexi, we're here." Delaney shook me and I blinked a few times.

"Damn, I fell asleep." I yawned and tried to focus. Unmarked white vans and luxury cars parked along the large circular drive told me we were at my sister's house.

"Girl, that's all you do," Luke teased as he helped me out of the car.

"I'm sorry. I can't help it." I straightened the maxi dress Mom had bought me, hoping it hid my baby bump. The last thing I needed was Aunt May or Uncle Fred rubbing on me. Mom promised that she wasn't going to tell a soul — not until I told her it was okay to spread the word. Hopefully, she kept to her promise.

We entered my sister and brother-in-law's stately house and I immediately felt out of place. Wait staff shuffled around, bringing in folded white chairs and round tables. The dining room, where we had most of our family Thanksgivings on the twenty-foot wood table, was set up with a buffet fit for a king. Flowers in purple and white decorated the table with tiny steel dragons embedded in the vases.

"What the hell?" Luke twisted his mouth to the side. "Looks like a freakin' wedding. Not a backyard barbecue."

I rolled my eyes. "That's Ashley for you."

"Speaking of the devil, here she comes."

"Yes, and put that over there. No, I didn't want cubed ice." She shoved a glass in a guy's hand. "I asked for soft ice pellets. You've got one hour to get thirty pounds here. Now get to it."

"You're shittin' me." Delaney looked at both us. "I don't think I'm dressed right for this party." She kicked out her leg from under her purple, off-the-shoulder dress, showing her brown cowboy boots that had PHU on the side.

"Relax. You're fine." Luke showed us his square-toed boots under the pant leg of his jeans.

"Luke, Lexi. Everyone, the graduates are here!" Ashley held out her arms and motioned for everyone to clap.

A few of our distant cousins, aunts, uncles, and people I didn't know, cheered for us.

"Your sister is a freak," Delaney whispered and I laughed.

"Tell me about it." I plastered a smile on my face as I nodded in thanks.

"Play nice." Luke nudged me and then threw an arm around Ashley's neck. "Great set up. Who's getting married?"

Ashely shot him one of her big, fake smiles as she wrapped her claws around his hand, pulling his arm away from her. "Stop it, you ungrateful S.O.B.," she gritted through her teeth.

"Thank you for the party." I leaned over and hugged her.

"It was nothing." She waved her hand in the air, showing off her sparkling diamonds.

"You really didn't have to do all of this for us." I did a quick sweep of the room and stopped at the dragon ice sculpture. "It's really too much."

"Nonsense." My brother-in-law, Ryan, walked up. "You only graduate from undergrad once." He shrugged. "Why not go all out?"

"Thanks, man." Luke shook his hand. "We appreciate it."

"Yes, thanks, Ryan," I added before they turned and walked away.

"She didn't do it for us. It's all about them. Showing off everything they have," Luke whispered in my ear as he shuffled us through the house and out toward the back. "Let's get some air. It's too stuffy in here."

"Tell me about it," Delaney sighed.

Outside was a huge white tent with tables lining a makeshift dance floor overlooking a lagoon-type swimming pool. Interspersed along the lawn were more round tables and long buffet style tables on each side, allowing guests an easy access to food, including me.

On the other side of the pool, there was a band setting up. "Shit. I hope she hired someone decent." Luke lifted his chin, scoping out the scene.

"Knowing her, it's probably someone famous."

"That would be awesome." Delaney took a few steps closer, as though trying to see who was in the band.

"You're right. This does look like a wedding." I opened a shiny stainless steel covered pan and stole a couple of appetizers.

"A little too pretentious for me, but shit, I'm going to party it up with buddies." He spotted a bar and headed straight for it.

Delaney and I followed him, trekking through the thick, carpet-like grass. "What buddies?" I pulled Luke by the arm.

"My baseball buddies, who else? Besides, I've got some celebrating to do."

I eyed him. Last night, Luke found out he got the job as a trainer for the PHU baseball team. He was sitting on cloud nine. I was happy for him, but he just made life a little more difficult for me. I didn't need complicated. I needed easy — especially tonight.

"What did you want me to do? Not invite him? I've known him my entire life."

"I know. It's just that..." I stopped. Luke was right. He and Collin had been friends since middle school. Things were over between us. There was no reason for me to avoid him. "Nevermind. It's fine."

"Look, I'm sorry, Sis." Luke placed a hand on my shoulder. "If you don't want him here, I'll tell him."

I shook my head. "It's okay, really."

"Thanks." Luke smiled. "I also invited several guys from the team."

"Like who?" Delaney's eyes widened.

"Don't worry, I didn't invite Winston or Riley," he huffed and then turned toward the bartender. "What type of beer do you have?"

Delaney sighed in relief. After what happened that night at the bowling alley, they were still at odds with each other, and I was sure it had to do with Delaney.

"Here are your choices, sir." The guy pointed to a neatly printed menu on the bar.

"Hell, what's not on this list?" Luke scanned through the menu. "Um...give me a Blue Nun."

"Right away." The bartender popped the top off the bottle and handed it to Luke. "We also have Fireball shots this evening, if any of—"

"Oh, hell no." Luke shuddered.

"No, thanks." I took a step back.

The bartender laughed. "Too many bad memories with it?" He wiped the countertop with a neatly folded white cloth.

"No, too many good ones." Luke lifted his beer and took a drink.

The bartender looked in my direction. "It was our twenty-first birthday."

"Oh." The bartender smiled. "Anything for you ladies?"

"A bottle of water, please."

"And you?" His eyes darted to Delaney.

"Um, I'll take..." she started and then paused, "I guess I better wait. Your parents are walking this way."

"Oh, great." I hid behind Luke. "Here's comes Aunt May and Uncle Fred with them."

"Nope," he laughed. "You have to tell them hi." He urged me toward them and I cringed. "If I have to play *For He's a Jolly Good Fellow* one more time, I'm going to scream."

"Ashley and Ryan's piano will be waiting." Luke held up his beer. "Uncle Fred, Aunt May. We were just talking about what a great time we had on New Year's Eve and how—" I sucker punched Luke in the back. "Ow."

Luke introduced Delaney to our aunt and uncle and we talked with them for a while. In turn, they introduced us to some of our cousins that Dad had mentioned over time. It was nice to meet our extended family, but I was glad when Luke saw Forbes and Jordan walk in with a few of his friends. It gave us a great excuse to part ways.

"Excuse me, but I see some of our friends," I informed my cousins and they nodded. "Hey, Jordan." I waved to her and a couple of people in the crowd turned to see who I was flagging.

"Lexi, Delaney." Jordan flapped her hands in the air, indicating she had spotted us.

"Glad you could make it." I gave her a hug.

Delaney placed her drink in Shelby's hand. "Taste this."

"Okay." She took a quick sip. "Hey, that's good." She lifted the cup and continued drinking until Delaney motioned for her to hand it back. "Sorry, we're late," she licked her lips, "but we got some great news!" She bounced on the balls of her feet, elation pouring out of her body. "Forbes got picked up by a minor league team in Cincinnati!"

"Oh my God! That's freakin' awesome!" Delaney screamed and they embraced, jumping up and down.

Forbes walked up with Luke, wearing a huge smile. Luke had a smile, equally as big.

"Congratulations, Forbes. You must be very excited." I gave him a pat on the back.

"Thanks, Lexi." He squeezed me in a hug. "It's a start. I'll see how it goes."

"I'm sure you'll do well." I looked up at him, realizing for the first time how tall he was, then again I was wearing flats so maybe I was just really short.

"What about you?" His look turned serious. "You doin' alright?"

"Yeah, sorry to hear about... well, ya know." Jordan lips turned into a lopsided smile.

"It's okay." I blinked the tears away, hating that every time someone mentioned what had happened between Raven and me sent me into a tailspin of overflowing emotions.

"I love this song! Let's go dance." Jordan grabbed my hand and Delaney's, pulling us to the dance floor. I started to protest, but figured I'd try to make the best of the night.

I moved slowly; nothing like the way I had on Spring Break or at frat parties. I didn't want to take the chance, but at the same time, I didn't want to seem like something was wrong with me. Even though Ashely hadn't hired a famous singer, the band played everything. After two songs, I sat down and watched everyone dance. And all it did was remind me of Raven. In fact, every song practically reminded me of him. And it sucked. Especially since I loved music so much.

For the next few hours, I chatted with family and friends, trying to convince myself that I just needed to shake it off, like the song said, and move on. I could do this without him. I had a degree. I would be able to provide from my children and myself. As long as my parents were helping, I could handle it. I'd be just fine without him.

Delaney pulled me to the dance floor and after a short dance, I headed into the house for the tenth time to use the restroom. *Another lovely inconvenience of pregnancy.* Would it ever get better? After spotting a small line for the bathroom near the front entrance, I remembered there was one in the study. I entered the lightly dimmed room, surrounded by books from floor to ceiling, and ran right into the last person I wanted to see.

"Collin." My palms pressed against his firm chest and I stumbled back. "I-I didn't see you."

"Lexi." His expression seemed equally as surprised as mine. "H-how are you?" His warm hands wrapped around my arms, keeping me from losing my balance while holding me inches from his face. I froze, completely taken by surprise with the way his sparkling green eyes appraised me.

I took a step back and managed to speak. "Fine." I hated when my voice sounded like a mouse.

He released his gentle grip and slid one hand into the pocket of his twill shorts. The muscles in his chest flexed underneath the smooth cotton of his polo-style shirt and I caught myself staring more than I should've been. "Sorry, I wasn't watching where I was going." His eyes darted around the room. "I was taking in this beautiful library."

I waved off his comment and brought my eyes back under my control. "It's okay. I wasn't paying attention either."

With a partial smile, he said, "Good to see you." He stepped to the side and headed for the door.

Without much thought, I reached for his hand. "Collin?"

"Yes?" He turned around, keeping his fingers wrapped around mine. I wanted to pull away, but it felt too good, even though I didn't want it to.

"Congratulations." I released the air lodged in my lungs and took a steady breath. There was no reason for me to freak out or panic. I was an adult, I would handle this as such. "Luke told me you signed with St. Louis to be their pitcher."

A huge grin spread from ear to ear and he rubbed his beard, which was a little thicker than normal. "Yes, I did."

"That's wonderful. You deserve it!" I smiled at him. "You've worked so hard for this and never gave up." Casually, I slipped my hand from his before he got the wrong impression.

He ran a hand through his sandy blond hair and it fell perfectly to the side. With that simple movement, all the memories rushed in without warning. This wasn't good. "I guess all my hard work paid off."

"It did, and you should be proud." His gaze fell to my midsection and I crossed my arms over my body. "So, when do you leave?" I asked in an attempt to distract his attention away from my pooch.

"Monday morning."

"So soon?" My breath hitched in my throat and I cleared it a few times.

"Yeah, I have to report to practice on Tuesday. My first game is on Friday."

"Will you be pitching?"

His shoulders lifted and he tilted his head to the side. "We'll see."

"I'm happy for you, Collin. Really, I am." The sensation of tears threatened and I had no idea why I wanted to cry— again. I wasn't regretting my decisions or wishing I had another chance with him. I couldn't explain the sadness and happiness that filtered through me. "I wish you the best." I quickly swiped the tears that rolled down my cheek. "I really do."

Damn it.

"Lexi." Collin gathered me in his arms and I willingly allowed him to embrace me. "Are you okay?"

"Yes." I nodded and sniffed. "I'm a bit of a hormonal mess right now. That's it. Really, I'm good."

"I'm sorry." His hand cradled the back of my head and I rested my cheek against his the fullness of his chest. His upper body moved in a fast rhythm and I could feel his pulse pounding loudly in my ear. I just prayed it wasn't beating wildly for me. I wouldn't know how to handle it, especially not now. "I know you've had it rough these past few months."

The waterworks released at full speed and I cried hard.

Letting out every feeling.

Every thought.

Every memory I had of us. I guess I hadn't truly let go of my feelings for him, or maybe pregnancy was bringing it all out again. Whatever it was, it felt good and sucked at the same time. I was certain I'd moved past him.

"It's not your fault. It was my choice." I wiped under my eyes with the tips of my fingers, smearing my mascara. "It's the path I chose."

"Regardless, I'm sorry that he left you." With his index finger, he lifted my chin, aligning our eyes. For the first time ever, I felt a real connection. A deep, intimate one that never existed when we were together. Something in him had changed and his eyes said everything he could never tell me. How much he cared about me. How much he loved me. And how I broke his heart. For the first time, I felt responsible for everything.

"You warned me, but I didn't listen." I reminded him, feeling the need to blame myself for any heartache I caused either of us.

"Still, I hate that you're facing this alone." His gaze dropped to my stomach and his finger left my chin, wavering in front of me before landing at his side.

I looked down at my belly and then back at him. "You know."

A look of disappointment etched deep into the corners of his eyes before transitioning into an envious green. It was color that never existed for him, but apparently I had caused it. "Yeah, Luke told me." He pulled me a little closer and I studied the way he held me — the proximity of my body to his and the distance of our lips. Never had he held me this way. *Damn him.* I searched his face closely, wondering what else was going through his mind.

I shifted, increasing the space between us. Things were starting to get a little too comfortable. A tiny part of me wanted to curse Luke, but the other part was kind of glad he told him. I wanted him to know, even if it hurt him.

"I want you to know that I admire your decision to go through with this. You could've chosen the easy way out, but didn't."

"Thank you." An insurmountable amount of love filled me, all of me, for my unborn children. I knew I had made the right choice, regardless of whether Raven knew or not. I was having these babies, with or without him.

"I just wish that the circumstances would've been different." He stroked my hair and I let out a soft sigh. "Because you wouldn't be standing here crying. We'd be rejoicing."

I pressed my lips together, feeling the sting in my nose and the burning in my eyes. "I know." I closed my eyes, my heart dropping into my stomach. As painful as it was to hear, I knew he was right. I had chosen the difficult path and I was paying for it. Regardless, it was a decision I'd never regret. I loved Raven.

"More than anything, I wish I could tell you I'd be here for you, but I can't." His voice faltered and his eyes glazed over as they filled with tears. In all the years I'd know him, I'd never seen him cry. Collin wasn't one that wore or showed his emotions. But tonight, he was definitely opening himself up to me.

Without even saying it, I knew why he couldn't. "You found someone, right?"

"Yes." He closed his eyes and lowered his head. With a deep breath, he said, "And I'm in love with her."

An unexplainable happiness surrounded my heart, but also tugged at it. He deserved to find someone that would love him and honor him — be patient, because I couldn't. "That's great, Collin. I knew you would."

He raised his hand, and with his thumb, he traced my lips. My body quivered, but I told myself to stay strong.

Not to fall for his touch.

For his sweet affection.

It would be my worst decision — ever.

His hand cupped my face and he stared directly into my eyes. "I would've given anything for it to be you instead."

For one full minute, my heart stopped. It was more than I could handle. More than I could take in. Collin was professing that he still loved me. But it wasn't what I wanted. There was only one man for me. He was the one that kept my heart beating, even though he refused to keep a hold of it. I took a hard swallow and mustered up the courage to set things straight between us. "I know. I wish things would've work out between us, but they didn't."

The pain behind his eyes told me this was hurting him more than it was me. "Know this, Lexi, you'll always have a special place in my heart." He pressed his lips to mine and I felt his tears drip to my face.

"And so will you."

"Thanks for coming with me." I pulled into the parking lot of my new OB/GYN's office and turned off the car.

"I don't mind." Delaney opened the passenger door. "It's kind of nice not to drive."

My parents wanted to buy me a new car, but I refused. After much deliberation, my dad decided to buy my mom a new Lexus and gave me her old one, which was only six years old.

"This ride is sweet. You can drive me around anytime." Delaney shut the door carefully.

"As long as you don't mind sitting in the back and keeping an eye on the twins."

"Sure. Aunt Delaney would be more than happy to help." My eyebrows shot up. It was the first time I'd ever heard her call herself "Aunt". Were things moving that fast that she was ready to marry Luke? I guess time would tell.

I signed in and filled out the necessary stack of papers, grateful that my parents were allowing me to stay on their health insurance. It definitely removed unneeded stress. Once the twins were born, I'd have to consider other options, since my dad wouldn't be able to cover them. After twenty minutes, they called my name and Delaney followed me into the exam room. The nurse took my vitals, drew some blood, and told me to put on a gown and wait for the doctor. The same as last time, except this time, I already knew I was pregnant. It was still nerve wracking because the doctor was going to make sure everything was okay after having the IUD removed.

I flipped through a pregnancy magazine, trying to keep occupied as I waited. Pictures of newborn babies cradled in their mom's arms made me smile. It was hard to imagine that in twenty-nine weeks, I'd be doing the same. "Delaney, I want you to take some picture of me once I get a little bigger, and after the babies are born."

"Okay. Sure."

I turned the page and a picture of a famous football player with his newborn son laying against his bare chest, stared at me. The ripples of his muscles secured the small infant within his arms, and I couldn't help but picture Raven holding his babies. My throat tightened, but I pushed the lump down. Closing the magazine, I promised not to cry — not anymore. I had done enough crying over the past twelve weeks. This week was a turning point, not having cried one day. Maybe I was finally getting over the hormonal riot going on in my body, or maybe I had finally accepted that Raven was out of the picture for good.

"Oh, hell no." Delaney held up a brochure that talked about vaginal delivery. "When the time comes, I'm not letting my baby's head stretch my vajayjay. I'll just opt for a C-section instead."

A laughed escaped me. "Yeah, I guess Luke wouldn't like that." I motioned for her to hand me the brochure. "I'll probably need a C-section regardless. I'm not sure I could push out two babies."

"I don't know about that." She eyed me, as if trying to peek under my gown. "Your vayjayjay might be big enough."

I slapped her arm in a playful manner. "Oh, whatever. I've only had sex with one guy, not ten or twenty."

She shook her head. "Now that's just low."

The door opened and I mouthed, "I'm sorry".

"Lexi?" A short, heavy-set woman with light blonde hair greying around the temples entered the room. "I'm Dr. Williams." She extended her hand and I shook it.

"Hi, nice to meet you."

Glancing at my chart, she said, "Thanks for having your records from the university health center transferred to us. I reviewed your history and want to do another sonogram, just to make sure the babies are doing okay since removing the IUD."

"Okay, sounds good."

"Based on your last period, your chart indicated that your due date is around December seventeenth. What a wonderful Christmas present." She smiled.

"Yes, two babies," I sighed, with a grin.

I could do this on my own. For the past two weeks, I'd been working in the writing lab and editing for J.S. Christensen. It was working out perfectly. But what about grad school? I wasn't sure I could handle that, too. And with my growing belly, I knew I had to tell Dr. Phillips soon and decide whether to withdraw from fall classes.

The doctor did a quick examination, listening to my heart and lungs. "Everything sounds good." She pushed a button on the wall and a buzzing noise sounded. Shoving her thick hands into plastic gloves, she said, "I need you to lie down so we can take a look at the babies."

"Okay." I brought my legs up and reclined against the examination table. The door opened and the nurse returned. Taking my chart, she positioned herself behind the doctor, preparing to take notes.

"I'm going to squirt a jelly-like substance over your stomach. It might be warm."

"Warm?" I lifted my head, trying to catch a glimpse of where she kept it. "The one at the health center was cold."

She winked. "We keep ours nice and warm for our future mommies."

"Oh." *Mommies.* I hadn't really considered myself a mom yet, but I guess that's what I would become.

"Just relax and keep your eyes right here on the screen." She pointed to a monitor that was a little larger than the one at the health center.

"Oh, wow. This looks totally different." The screen illuminated in an antique brown color, not the typical black and white that most sonograms showed. The image was in 3-D; nothing like the last one I'd had. "Delaney, are you seeing this?"

Two babies, in separate sacks, moved and turned, giving us a clear view of their faces.

"Oh my God!" Delaney squeaked as she scurried to my side. "You can actually tell they are babies." She looked at my growing belly and then back to the screen. I was just as amazed. "That one totally has your lips."

"And forehead." I rolled my eyes, hating that my baby had already inherited the part of me that I didn't like.

"This baby is measuring a little smaller than twelve weeks." The doctor pushed a few buttons as she moved the wand around my stomach.

"Is that a bad thing?" I studied the image that looked a little alien-like. But I didn't care. I knew the baby would be perfect once it was born. Besides, didn't all developing babies look weird?

"No. It's perfectly normally for one twin to be larger than the other."

"My brother was a pound heavier than me."

"So, you're a twin?" The doctor continued to study the monitor as her hand moved over my stomach.

"Yes. Fraternal."

The doctor's eyes lifted. "That probably explains your pregnancy. Fraternal twins tend to be hereditary."

Great. I was the lucky candidate.

"My grandmother had a twin brother, but he died at birth," I sighed, trying to push out any bad thoughts. "Back then, they couldn't do C-sections. My mom said the chord was wrapped around the baby's neck."

She patted my arm. "Science has come a long way since then. You don't have to worry about that, okay?"

I nodded and refocused on the wondrous sight on the screen before me. I was still awestruck at the site of them. It was amazing watching them move and turn inside of me. It made everything seem that much more real.

"Oh, no! Does that mean I could have twins?" A look of worry washed across Delaney's face. "I'm dating her brother."

"Typically, it passes through the female," the doctor informed her.

"Whew." Delaney leaned against the counter behind her. "I don't think my body could handle carrying twins."

I nudged her. "You never know."

"I'm not getting pregnant any time soon." She crossed her arms. "If ever."

"I said the same thing," I pointed to the screen, "and look what happened. Not one, but two."

"I'd die." Delaney shook her head.

The doctor moved the instrument to the other side of my stomach, examining the other baby. She pressed a few buttons, capturing different positions and talking to the nurse in a code that made no sense to me.

"This baby is measuring larger than the other one, but everything looks good."

"Maybe it's a boy!" Delaney voice escalated in excitement.

The doctor laughed. "It's a little early to tell. When Lexi comes come back in six weeks, we should be able to tell the babies' gender. As long as they are cooperating, that is."

"Hopefully, they will be." I kept my eyes on the screen, part of me hoping I was having a girl and a boy.

"Oh, wow." Delaney leaned forward. "That one has Raven's profile."

The baby was turned to the side, giving us a perfect glimpse of a tiny straight nose and square jaw. It was a mini version of Raven. I reached toward the screen, eager to touch my unborn child. To let him know how much I loved and needed him. My eyes stung and I blinked rapidly, trying to prevent any more crying, but it was no use. Tears streamed from my eyes, spilling into my hair. The baby looked exactly like its daddy. Too bad Raven wasn't here to see it.

"Can I please get a few pictures?" I wiped my eyes.

"Yes, of course. I've been capturing several different angles for you." The nurse handed me a tissue.

"Thank you." I wiped my nose. "I've been so emotional lately."

"That's perfectly normal. You're hormones are in flux, hopefully they'll start settling down a bit."

"I hope so." I honestly didn't know how much more I could take.

Delaney reached for my hand and I latched onto it. At least I had my friend to help support me, along with my parents. But could I really do this without him? Did I really want our babies to grow up not knowing their father? Raven didn't know his father, and look what that did to him. I didn't want that for my children...our children. My selfishness wasn't fair to them.

"Are you ready to hear the heartbeats?" The doctor asked, her finger hovering over a button.

"Yes." I cleared my throat.

A loud whishing sound, ten times louder than the first time I'd heard it, filled the room.

"Why is it so fast?" My ears followed the waves, taking in the incredible sound that gave even more confirmation of the lives growing inside of me.

"Babies' heartbeats are naturally fast. Usually one-hundred and forty to one-hundred and sixty beats per minute."

Delaney's mouth dropped open. "That's amazing."

"It's unbelievable."

The doctor switched off the volume after a minute or so. I wished I could have recorded it, just so I could listen to it every night. Hearing the strength behind those beats gave me the willpower to go on. My heart would survive for them, but I wasn't sure I wanted to go on without Raven.

Would I ever feel right without him?

What if he never said goodnight to his babies?

Could I live with myself knowing that I had kept this from him? It wasn't right and I knew it. He needed to know and I had to tell him. Regardless of what that meant for us. For our babies' sake, he had to know.

Σ

Chapter 21

The next morning, I got up and packed my bags. I'd stayed up most of the night thinking about Raven and me. The time we had spent together. The loved we shared. Most of all, the lives we created that were growing inside of me. Maybe it took a while for my heart to align with my head, but when it finally did, a huge spark ignited. Whatever it was, I knew I had to tell him.

Not only that, I had to see if I could pull him out of the pits. It wasn't over for his football career. When I called Shawn to tell him I was telling Raven, he was glad. He also told me about the supplemental draft that was nearing. Even though Raven had missed the filing date for the regular draft, he still had a shot at getting picked up. The least I could do was encourage him to consider it.

"You're up early." Luke stood in the kitchen, wearing only his boxer briefs as he made a bowl of cereal. His hair was sticking up in all directions, appearing as if Delaney had her hands splayed through it the entire night.

"Will you carry this to the car for me?" I set my duffle bag on the floor.

He did a double take, still pouring his milk. "Shit." He quickly lifted the carton, spilling some in the process. Eyeing my bag, he said, "You're going to go tell him, aren't you?"

I nodded. "Yes. It's only right."

Walking over to me, he placed his hand on my shoulder. "Do you want me to take you? I will."

"Are we going somewhere?" Delaney shuffled out of her bedroom, her hair a matted mess and black smeared around her eyes. I didn't say anything, taking in my options. It took a few seconds for it to register with her. "You decided to tell him." A huge smile morphed. "It's about damn time."

"He needs to know." I held onto the straps of my purse and fished out my keys. "And I need to go alone."

"Do you know where he is?" Luke leaned against the counter, crossing his arms.

"Yes. I talked to Trish and confirmed that he's still staying with his grandmother in New Orleans."

Luke's eyes widened. "You're driving to New Orleans...by yourself?"

"Yes." I shifted my weight. "I can make the drive."

"It's like eight hours, or ten, if you consider how many times you're going to stop to pee. Why not just call and tell him?" Leave it to Luke to remind me of the inconveniences I endured on a daily basis.

"His phone doesn't work and I didn't ask for her mother's number." Even if reaching him over the phone was an option, I didn't want to do that. I had to tell him in person. He had to see me, so that he would know that I was telling the truth.

"It's a little over an hour if you fly." Delaney's fingers worked furious, typing information into to her phone. "And you can catch a flight in two hours from DFW Airport."

"And what do I do once I get there? Take a taxi or rent a car?"

"Yes. It's safer," Luke tried to reason with me, "not to mention, quicker. If you leave right now," Luke counted on his fingers, "you won't get there until seven or eight o'clock tonight. And that's if you don't stop to take a nap." He winked.

He had a point. It was a long drive and going alone was sort of dangerous. I turned to Delaney. "How much is that flight?"

An hour later, Luke and Delaney dropped me off in front of American Airlines gate 23D. The security line was short and since I only had two bags, it made it easy for me to get through. I grabbed a sandwich and chips at the Chili's To Go stand along with a bottle of water and sat down in the waiting area. I ate my sandwich as I waited for my flight to board. After I finished, I took out my phone and dialed my mom's number. I needed to tell my parents where I was going. Worrying about me was the last thing I wanted.

"Hello?"

"Hi, Mom."

"Lexi." Her voice sounded a little winded. I hoped I hadn't interrupted anything. "Just a second." I heard some female voices in the background and noises that confirmed that she was probably outside. "Sorry, sweetie. I was playing tennis with my friends. We were just wrapping up because it's getting hot. Is everything okay?"

June was already promising to be a scorcher. I was glad that my last months of pregnancy would be in the winter.

"Yes, I just wanted to let you and Dad know that I'm about to catch a plane to New Orleans." I had told my parents that Raven had moved there to stay with his grandmother. Reflecting on the situation, it made sense why he left, but I still needed to hear it from him.

Silence filled the other side of the line. "I respect your decision and hope it goes well. I'm not going to tell what to do, but if you need anything, just give us a call."

"Thanks, Mom. I'm not sure what's going to happen. I...I just want to tell him. I'll start from there and see how it goes." I quickly swiped an escaping tear. I had to be strong. I couldn't let Raven see me cry.

"How long will you be there?" she pressed, as if ready to tell me not to go. But nothing was going to stop me. I had to do this. Besides, this wasn't about her. It was about me, Raven, and our babies.

"I don't know. Maybe a few hours, maybe a day. I really don't know."

A heavy sigh filtered through and the disappointment was evident. "Just promise me you'll call or send us a text to let us know you're okay."

"I promise."

"Look, Lexi, I may —"

"Flight 302 to New Orleans is now boarding. Advantage and Platinum members, you may start boarding," the flight attendant announced.

"Mom, I have to go. They're boarding."

"I love you, Lexi." Mom's voice squeaked.

"I love you, too. Talk to you soon." I hung up, grabbed my bags, and got in line.

Within fifteen minutes, I was onboard and buckled up, ready to test my fate once again. I pulled out my laptop and decided to finish editing the last few chapters of Christensen's book. I never realized how much I enjoyed editing fiction stories. It was definitely more interesting than essay and non-fiction papers.

The flight was short. Before I knew it, the flight attendant had ordered for all electronics to be stored away. As the plane cleared the clouds and approached the outskirts of New Orleans, my heart raced. I was scared. What the heck was I going to tell Raven? How would I break it to him?

Hi. Shawn told me to tell you that you should try out for the supplemental draft. Oh, and by the way, thought you should know you're going to be a daddy. Not of one child, but two. So, take care. Bye.

No. That wouldn't work. I had to break it to him gently. I also had to encourage him to give his football career one more chance. The last thing I wanted was for him to freak over my pregnancy, or be mad because I was telling him what to do with his life. I had faith in his football abilities and I had to help him see that, but on the flipside, my heart couldn't forget what he had said.

Me, pregnant, would be a bad thing.

The nick he carved in my heart by his debilitating words was enough pain to last a lifetime, especially since it had come true. I had no idea how he would react.

All these thoughts had kept me from him — kept me from telling him that I was pregnant. A voice inside told me that it was just as easy to keep it that way. That he wouldn't want to be a part of the babies' lives. That he wouldn't care about the supplement draft or even try. That he wouldn't fight for me. It hurt. I had been here one too many times. I was tired of it. Yet, I was going back to it.

The plane landed on the runway of Louis Armstrong International Airport and I thought about staying onboard and flying back to Fort Worth, but I couldn't do that. Despite the nick he caused and the pain I had endured, I still loved him. Not only did I need him, but he needed me — our children needed him.

A man helped me grab my duffle bag from the overhead storage unit and I headed down the narrow aisle, leaving all negative thoughts behind me. I walked through the jet bridge and the mugginess of the Louisiana swampland hit me. It was worse than Texas. I was glad I had decided to wear shorts and a loose tank top. I walked through the airport, keeping my thoughts focused on the task at hand.

I could do this.

I wanted to do this.

There was no turning back.

Exiting the airport, I headed toward the taxi line. I didn't feel like going through the painstaking process of renting a car and trying to find my way around the city. Besides, according to Google Maps, Raven's grandmother's house was only fifteen minutes away. I just hoped he was there.

I got in the taxi and shut the door. "Where to, Miss?"

Glancing at my phone, I read the address Trish had given me.

"You've got it." He nodded at me through the rearview mirror and headed down the street. "You don't sound like you're from around here." He smiled, his chubby cheeks spreading across his face.

"I'm not. I'm from Texas," I said, trying to be cordial. All I wanted to do was get my conversation straight in my head. The words kept jumbling and this guy wasn't making it any easier.

"I should've known. Pretty girls like you are always from Texas."

"Thanks."

"Sure." He pulled on his Fedora and I turned my attention to the street, hoping he wouldn't ask me any more questions or make any comments.

As the taxi drove through an old neighborhood, I imagined what it had been like for Raven when Hurricane Katrina hit. I tried to imagine what he endured at twelve years of age as he watched his house get washed away. Framed houses, stacked neatly on top of each other, lined the streets and I couldn't help but wonder just how many people had lost their homes. Not to mention, loved ones.

Holding my phone, I watched the icon move along the streets, inching closer to Raven. With each block we passed, I felt water rushing over me, just like a hurricane, sweeping away the demons that told me I didn't need to give him another chance. That I had no business being there. That he wouldn't want to see me. That he wouldn't care whether I was pregnant.

In reality, I wasn't ready to take him back. But as the car turned from left to right, that familiar tug in the center of my chest awoke inside of me. The flame that burned inside of me still existed. It hadn't gone out. It had been turned on low, ready to ignite at a moment's notice.

The fire we had created was like no other. A wildfire that burned hot and crazy, ready to tear down everything in its path. And just like that, I was willing to do whatever it took. If only I could turn back the hands of time and make everything right. If I could have him hold me like he used to. Kiss me and make love to me without ever ceasing.

Damn, there was no getting away from The Raven's trap.

"4517 45th Street," the driver announced as he pulled up to a neatly manicured lawn. Standing with his back facing the street was Raven. He was trimming the hedges in front of the house. The muscle shirt he wore was drenched in sweat and his head was neatly shaved — his beautiful brown hair gone.

The driver told me the balance and I handed him my credit card, my hand shaking as reality hit.

I was there.

"Could you wait here? What will it cost?" I gathered my purse, but decided to leave my bag in the taxi.

The driver looked at his watch. "You're in luck. I need to take my lunch and I brought my food." He held up a metal box with characters on the front, like the ones Luke used to have in elementary school.

"Awesome." Maybe being from Texas was working in my favor. "Hopefully it won't be too long."

"I can wait thirty minutes. After that, I have to charge." He handed me back my card.

"Okay. Can you honk, so I'll know?"

He shrugged. "Yeah, sure."

I opened the door and got out of the vehicle. As soon as I shut it, Raven turned around. He did a double take and his body stiffened. I stood there for a moment, unsure of what to say.

The draft. I need to mention the supplemental draft. Get him on board with saving his career before telling him I'm pregnant.

I took a step forward but stopped when the wind pressed against my clothes, causing my protruding belly to stick out. I wasn't sure if I could hide twelve weeks of pregnancy from him. Surely, he'd notice.

He dropped the hedge trimmers in his hand and darted toward me, but his stride wasn't one that indicated he was dying to see me. It was quite the opposite. "What are you doing here?" He leveled me with a harsh stare and I reached for the taxi door handle, but stopped.

I'm a strong woman. I can do this.

I let go and turned around to face him. "I need to tell you something."

He eyed me suspiciously and I quickly shifted my purse over my stomach. "Why didn't you just call?"

"I would have, but your phone isn't working."

"That's because I turned it off." He scowled and I couldn't help but wonder what happened to the man that would smile from ear to ear when he saw me. That could light up any street with the glow beaming from him whenever I got close. Why was he acting so bitter toward me? Did he know? Had Shawn told him I was coming to see him? Or had Shawn told him I was pregnant? I had to know.

With one hand on my hip, I held his gaze. "Why did you leave me?"

His jaw tightened as he bit out the words, "That's what you came here for?"

I ignored his comment and stuck to my plan. "Were you that chicken shit that you couldn't tell me in person?"

"Lexi, just go back home." He waved me off like I wasn't even worth his time and turned around. It was like a slap in the face and for a moment, I felt like one of his hoes that he so easily tossed to the side after he got what he wanted.

I followed him to where he was working in the yard, watching him scalp a shrub to the near root. "Why do you keep thinking you're not good enough for me? I don't get it."

"Because I'm not, Lexi." He huffed a few times and then stopped cutting. "Can't you see that? Why do you want to be with a loser like me?" He flung around and faced me, jabbing a finger in the center of his chest so hard, I thought he'd poked a hole. "I can barely support myself, much less you. And I sure as hell don't expect for you to support my ass."

Oh no. I couldn't possible tell him I was pregnant now.

I threw my hands up in the air, defeat quickly setting in. "Do you really think I'm that shallow? Do you think I'm that money hungry or something? Because if I gave you that impression, I'm sorry. I don't care what profession you choose, Raven, as long as it's legit. There are plenty of other occupations aside from football."

"Like what?"

"I don't know, how about landscaping? Looks like you've been doing a great job on your grandmother's house." I did a quick glance of the perfectly manicured lawn. "Why not start a business?"

His face twisted in disgust. "I don't want to do this shit for a living." He tossed the trimmers to the ground and I sighed in relief. The last thing I needed was to accidently get stabbed by a pair of razors sharp knives. Not that he would, but the demon inside of him was making a grand appearance and it scared me a bit. "I'm only doing this to help my grandmother, not because I enjoy it."

"Fine. I'm just giving you an example. But if you love football that much, you should consider the supplemental draft."

There, I said it.

"Wh-what?" His voice was on the verge of a condescending laugh. "No one is going to pick me up. No team wants a player with off-field issues, especially not mine." He laughed hard and rolled his eyes.

"You don't know that, Raven."

"Trust me, Lexi. It's over for me. My football days are long gone. The dream is gone. Just like that." He snapped his fingers. "I'm nothing but a washed out, ex-druggy, ex-drunk, who will never amount to nothing." He sighed heavily, picked up his shirt, and wiped the sweat from his face. His stomach tensed and I caught a glimpse of a heavy set of abs that had definitely vamped from a six pack to an eight pack. The indentations on either side of his waist formed a deeper V and he looked leaner than ever. He had seriously been working out.

My approach wasn't working so I had to try something different. Not to mention, he was really pissing me off. "Alright. Fine. I can't force you do anything. You have to want to make something out of your life. The only thing I can do is encourage you. In fact, that's all I've ever done. I had hoped I was going to be a part of your life, but I see that being away from me hasn't changed anything."

"Lexi, I'm not good for you. Just go back to—"

"Don't." Anger boiled my blood. "Don't even say his name." I jammed my finger into his chest, my eyes on the verge of tears. "My life has been turned upside down because of you. I gave you everything, Raven. All of me." Tears gushed from my eyes and there was no stopping them. "I gave myself to you freely and you just turned your back on me. Like everything we had meant nothing to you. We were engaged to be married! Did that not mean anything to you?" I grabbed a fistful of his shirt and then pushed him away. My heart pounded, ready to explode into a thousand pieces. Pieces I had been holding onto by a thread.

His eyes narrowed and glazed over, as if ready to release all the hurt that had been tormenting him. "I'm sorry, Lexi. I never meant to hurt you."

"Well you did more than that, Raven." I started to turn around and then stopped. I had come there for another reason. A more important reason than telling him about the supplemental draft — his babies. "Before I go, there's something else you need to know."

"Save it, Lexi. Nothing will change how I am."

My body heaved forward and I swayed back. The sandwich threatened to make a reappearance, but I willed it stay. I refused to break down in front of him. I was telling him no matter what it did to me.

"You're impossible." I took a few deep breaths. "I just traveled five hundred and thirty five miles hoping that maybe you still wanted to be with me."

"Why?"

"Because I haven't given up on us. And most of all, I haven't given up on this." I reached into my purse and pulled out the first sonogram that said *Hi Mom, Hi Dad* and shoved it into his hand.

"What's this?" He stared at it for a moment, his eyes narrowing as he studied the images. The paper wavered in the wind and he grabbed the edge with his free hand. His face shifted from surprise to realization. "Yo-you're having a baby?"

"Two, actually."

"Wh-what?" His face paled and he swayed to the side. I reached out to keep him steady.

"Are you okay?"

"I...I don't believe this." His mouth hung open as he continued to stare at the picture. I waited for him to say something, *anything*, but he didn't. He remained silent, looking at me, then at the paper in his hand, his eyes blinking repeatedly. "But you said you had an IUD."

"I did. It didn't work."

"Fu—ck."

At that moment, I knew. He didn't want any part of this. Coming here was the biggest mistake ever. The unspoken words of my mother were right — just like always. Raven wasn't ready to accept the responsibility. I'd be raising our children on my own.

"Don't worry." I snatched the slick paper from his hand. "I don't want anything from you. I just wanted the kids to know who their dad is. I had also kind of hoped you wanted to be a part of their lives. Ya know, since you didn't know your dad."

His nostrils flared to life and his chest rose, like a dragon getting ready to blow fire. He took in a deep breath and unleased on me. "Fuck you, Lexi. That's not fair." He shoved his finger in my face, keeping it several inches from my cheek.

I blinked twice, not believing what I had just heard. No way in hell was I going to stand there and take his shit. I had done everything for him and he had proved to me, once again, that he was still the same old Raven. "You know what? Life isn't fair, so fuck you, Raven." I darted to the taxi, tears streaming down my face. "Go, just go!" I yelled as I slammed the door behind me.

"Okay, okay." The driver peeled out and I didn't bother to turn around to see if Raven had come after me. "Where to?"

I sighed heavily, unable to stop the tears. "The airport." We'd never talked to each other that way before. Raven held no regard for the news I shared with him. How could he be so cold? So heartless? I had hoped time alone would have helped him clear his head, but it hadn't. We were done. Over. Why did life have to suck so hard?

I heaved forward as the string that was holding the pieces of my heart together snapped, scattering them into a million pieces. The pain traveled throughout my body, creating new holes that I knew could never be repaired. I was permanently damaged. The Raven's trap had turned deadly.

After several long minutes, I managed to stop crying. I fell against the back of the seat and stared out the window, watching everything pass by me in a blur. No matter how much it hurt, I had done what I needed to do. I had told Raven. Now I could get on with my life. I was stupid for thinking that he'd want to be a part of our babies' lives. I'd just have to do it without him. I had done my part, but he refused to own up to his.

As the taxi drove through the neighborhood, we passed a local high school. A big sign in front read *Summer Football Camp pre-season game tonight. The Dragons vs The Bears this Saturday at 6 p.m.* I closed my eyes. I had to be seeing things. I relaxed against the seat and took a deep breath. I would be okay. I was a strong, independent woman. I didn't need Raven. I could make it on my own.

As I opened my eyes, the light turned green, and the driver turned onto the onramp for the freeway. I glanced out the front windshield, making sure we were headed in the right direction when a huge billboard caught my attention. *South Padre Island - Where the fun begins.* A whimper escaped my lips and my shoulders slumped. It was where it ended, not where it began.

"Are you okay, Miss?" the driver asked, a look of concern covering his face.

"Yes. Pregnant and very emotional, that's all."

"Oh. Sorry. I mean, congratulations. That's if you want it to be." He stumbled through the words and I turned away, not wanting to hear his pathetic excuses.

The taxi came to a halt and I cringed. "What's wrong?"

"Sorry, looks like construction traffic. Tell you what, I'll flip off the meter for now."

That was honestly the least of my worries. I kept my eyes on the side of the road, hoping to avoid anything else when I saw a church with a huge sign on the front. *First Christian Church - Where families come first.*

"Oh, God, why?" I held the sonogram to my chest, cradling my unborn children.

I promise to take care you guys no matter what. Mommy loves you both.

I covered my face and continued to cry. Why had Raven reacted that way? Did he not love me anymore? What had I done to deserve this? Nothing had gone the way I had planned. Life really did suck.

"I know a shortcut," the driver announced. I was sure he was tired of hearing me cry. "I'll have to do some back tracking, but I'll get you to the airport. What time is your flight?"

"I don't know." I shrugged. "I don't have a ticket yet."

His eyes narrowed. "I'll still get you there on time."

The driver sped past cars, driving on the shoulder until he reached the next exit. He raced down the service road and made a U-turn, heading back in the direction of Raven's grandmother's house. The taxi came to a sudden halt as cars lined the service road. Apparently, everyone headed to the airport had the same idea. The driver inched his way forward, switching lanes at every opportunity, and then cut through a parking lot. Conveniently, I caught a glimpse of another sign. *At Lincoln Memorial Hospital, we not only specialize in birthing babies, but birthing multiple babies. Tours daily at our new women's center.*

"Stop! Stop!" I pounded on the back of the driver's seat, unable to handle the pain tugging at my heart.

"Okay. Okay." The driver stopped the car and put it in park. "What is it?"

I motioned for him to give me a minute and I cried.

Cried for Raven.

Cried for everything we had been through.

Cried for our unborn children.

Cried because my heart only belonged to him.

What the hell was I doing? Why was I allowing my stubbornness to get in the way? He needed to know how I felt, what I wanted.

Him.

Only him.

Only Raven could feel the void in my heart.

Only Raven could make me feel like no one else in the world mattered.

Only he could hear the sound of my soul.

I needed him.

I was the only one who belonged in The Raven's trap. Period. And it was my job to make him see that.

"Take me back," I heaved, trying to stop the tears.

"Take you back?" His voice lilted and he must have thought I was some kind of crazy pregnant woman. And I was — nothing but a hot mess. Raven's pregnant hot mess.

"Yes, take me back to..." I searched for my phone to get the address when I realized I didn't have my purse. I must have dropped it when I was arguing with Raven. "Shit, I don't have my phone."

"It's okay. I have the address." He pressed a button on his GPS and the addressed popped up.

I wiped the tears away and blew my nose as he flung the car into drive. I had to tell him, plead my love for him one more time. If he still turned me down, then at least I could tell our children that I did everything I could to earn their father's love. That I had done everything I could to help him turn his life around. I owed it not only to them, but to myself. I owed it to us. I was willing to put my pride aside and find out if there was any hope for our love.

The taxi driver drove like a bat out of hell and had me in front of Raven's grandmother's house in less than five minutes. "Thank you, just a minute and I'll get my wallet."

"It's okay," he waved for me to get out of his vehicle, "it's on the house. I'll just say you were in labor. No charge." He smiled.

"Thank you." I grabbed my other bags and got out of the car.

As soon as I shut the door, the taxi hauled ass, tires spinning and smoke curling as he raced out of sight. I looked for Raven, but he was nowhere to be seen. Dropping my bag, I hurried to the front door as fast as I could with my little belly before I changed my mind. As I raised my hand to bang on the door, it swung open and I plunged forward.

"Lexi! Thank, God." Raven caught me in his arms. "Why did you leave? I was so worried about you." He smothered me in kisses, catching me totally off guard.

My hands flew to his clean shaven face as I tried to capture his lips. But they were all over me. I could barely catch my breath, let alone his lips. "I thought you didn't care." I held him steady until he pressed his forehead to mine.

"No, baby. I was in shock, that's all. I'm so sorry." Raven's eyes connected with mine and that familiar gaze in his beautiful green eyes reemerged, capturing my heart once more and pulling the pieces back together until they formed that perfect shape.

"I'm sorry, too." I didn't think twice about accepting his apology.

"I love you. I love you so damn much it hurts." The pain behind his voice broke me quickly, sucking me right back into that familiar trap. But I didn't care. I needed to be in his trap forever.

"I love you, too, Raven." I pressed my lips to his, savoring every bit of his taste. I missed it so damn much. I didn't ever want to be without it again. "Not one day has passed that I didn't think of you. Of us. Of our babies. I never stopped loving you."

"Oh, baby, I was wrong. So wrong to leave you." His hands traveled up and down my arms, caressing me and filling the void that had plagued me for the past twelve weeks. Not only did I need his magnetic touch, I needed to feel that warmth more than he knew. "I feel terrible that you've been facing this on your own. When did you find out?"

"Four weeks ago," I said in a hushed voice.

"And you had no way of telling me." His eyes closed for a moment as he pressed his forehead to mine. "I'm such an idiot."

I cupped his cheek and held his face tenderly in the palm of my hand. "Well, you're my idiot." I sniffed, relieved that his love had truly come back to me. His hand covered mine, warmth wrapping around me, causing every tense muscle to finally relax.

"Will you ever forgive me?" he asked against my lips. His words peeled away the hurt, the torment, the pain, until they found their way to the center of my chest. They implanted themselves, ready to seal all the pieces that had just come together. All I had to do was accept it.

"It's not that easy, Raven. I don't want you to take me back just because I'm pregnant. I need to know that you love me, regardless. That you want to be with me, no matter what." I lifted his chin, reconnecting our gazes. "I can't keep going through this. You're breaking my heart and I'm not sure how much more I can take."

"I promise I won't hurt you again," he pleaded with so much emotion, my heart was ready to be sealed. "I'll do whatever it takes, baby. Please, just say you'll take me back."

"I want to, Raven, but—"

"But what?"

I hesitated for a moment before deciding that I needed to tell him. Today was all about being open and honest. I had nothing to lose. "I'm scared that the next time something bad happens, you'll walk out that door and not only leave me, but our children."

He shook his head. "No, Lexi. I could never do that to you — to them." His hand dropped to my stomach and his eyes closed. Tears rolled off his cheeks and onto my stomach. My throat tightened and my own tears released, but I pressed forward, being totally transparent with him.

"But you have, Raven. That's just it."

"Then I'm going to have to prove you wrong." With the pads of his thumbs, he wiped my sorrow away. "These past few months have been hell. And I've realized how much I need you... how much I love you."

"And I need you just as much. Our children need you. But you'll have to work really hard to prove that to me. Twenty minutes ago, you didn't want to hear about other kinds of work and now you're ready to do whatever it takes." I searched his eyes deeply and they were just as transparent as I had been. Had Raven learned to finally let me in? Bring down the walls and allow me to truly see him?

"I know it sounds crazy, but when I saw you get in that taxi and leave, I never thought I'd see you again. See my children." His hand rested on my stomach. "I could never live with myself knowing that I abandoned you and them. So, yes, I'll do whatever you want me to do. As long as I can be with you and the babies, I'll do it." Raven seemed eager to prove his love for me, but I knew words were just words. I needed to see action behind those words in order to believe him.

With a firm voice, I said, "I want you to continue the counseling sessions." He let out a soft sigh, but I didn't stop. "When you were seeing Dr. Galen, you were doing so much better. You were healing, recovering."

"I know." His chin dipped.

"You need that, Raven." I lowered my head, trying to see his face. "Our relationship needs it. But most of all, our children are going to need a daddy that can show them what it takes to be strong, to fight back, to persevere through the darkest times." Silence filled the space between us. His forehead tightened as his eyebrows drew together. "Do you think you can do that, Raven?"

Slowly, he lifted his head. "As long as I'm with you, I can do anything, Lexi." He laced his fingers through mine and dropped to his knees. His green eyes filled with guilt, apologies, and most of all, remorse. "Please tell me you'll still be my wife. There's no one else in the world that I'd rather be a husband to." He placed our hands on my stomach and smoothed my shirt over my round belly. "Hi. It's your long lost dad. But I'm here now and I'm going to take care of you and your mom. I promise to always be there for you, no matter what." He rested his face against my stomach, keeping our hands steady on my bump. Tears flowed down my cheeks and I felt the wetness from his eyes seep through my shirt.

My stomach quivered and the babies turned. "Oh, they heard you," I giggled, ecstatic that he had that effect on them.

Raven's lips turned upward in a big smile as tears dripped from his eyes. "That's because they know who their dad is."

"I love you, Raven." I wrapped my arms around him and held him close.

"I promise to love you forever, Lexi. Just give me one more chance. Please."

"Only if you really want my heart. I'm done letting you borrow it. If you really want it, you're going to have work for it and once you have it, you're going to be stuck with it for the rest of your life."

"Good, because it's the only heart I want, aside for our children." His eyes widened as he stood up. "Damn, we're having twins."

I laughed. "Yes, in twenty-eight weeks."

"Do we know what they are?" He continued to caress my stomach, as if he couldn't wait to hold them.

"Not yet. But at the next appointment, we should know."

He grinned. "This is going to be fun."

I snorted. "Uh, we'll see. Luke and I were terrible when we were little."

"I guess that means one thing." His expression turned serious.

"What's that?" I sniffed.

"You'll be the one disciplining them."

I shook my head. "Oh, no, we're doing it together."

"And that's what I love about you." His hand spread under my jaw and he cupped my cheek. "I can honestly tell you that there wasn't a single day that passed where I didn't think of you. I never stopped loving you."

"I never stopped loving you, Raven."

"So, you'll still marry me?" He wasn't giving up.

"Let's just take this slow, okay? Like I said, you have a lot of proving to do."

He nodded. "I know. And I will. It was wrong of me to walk out on you like that. I feel terrible. I was so selfish. Not being there for you." He caressed my stomach. "For our babies." "Please, Lexi. Just tell me you'll marry me." His eyes glazed over once more. "I promise you won't be disappointed. I'll be everything you need and more. I'll do whatever it takes to earn your trust and show that I can support us. Just, please, don't leave me. I need to know you're on my side."

I wiped the tears from his checks. "Raven, there's only side I want to be on."

With hopeful eyes, he asked, "What side is that?"

"The winning side," I said with a huge smile.

The End

Epilogue

One Year Later

"You look gorgeous, Lexi." Mom kissed my cheek. "Radiant as ever." Tears stained her bright pink cheeks.

"Stop crying, Mom. You're messing up your makeup." I handed her a tissue. I was glad we had started getting along and that she had finally accepted that I was marrying Raven.

"I know, I'm sorry." She blotted the area under her eyes.

"And if you don't stop, you're going to make me cry." I blinked a few times, warding off the impending threat.

She shook her head. "No, crying. Its bad luck."

I waved off her comment. "No, it's not. That's just some stupid old wives tale." My phone chimed and I glanced at the reminder. My mother was right; caring for two babies wasn't easy and I used my phone to keep me on track with everything. "Who has the babies? Where's Mimi?"

"Relax," Delaney said, shutting the door. "I just checked on them. Mimi and Trish have them and they're doing fine." Raven's grandmother, Mimi, had been a life saver; practically moving in with us to help care for the twins. I didn't protest. I needed all the help I could get.

"Okay." I took a breath and tried to relax. I was a little nervous. Raven and I were headed to the Caribbean for a week without them. Jonah and Nevara had barely turned six months old and I knew Mimi and Trish would have their hands full. My mom and dad had offered to stay at our house in New Orleans, but I didn't want to inconvenience them.

"Yes, everything is going to be fine," Delaney assured me, pinning a strand of hair that kept falling in front of my face with a bobby pin. "You and Raven are going to have a wonderful honeymoon. Time alone, which you both need." She squeezed me in a hug and I smiled.

"I know. It's just hard not to think about the twins. They're still so little." I adjusted the bobby pin one more time. Jordan had twisted my hair into a fishbone braid on top and swept it to the side, giving it a slightly messy, but sexy look. After graduation, she decided to get her cosmetology license and open her own salon in Dallas. I hired her to do our hair and makeup and she had done a spectacular job. Tiny rhinestones sparkled as I checked the back of my hair with a mirror.

"Don't mess with it." Delaney pulled my hand away. "It looks great."

"Do you think Raven will like it?" I set the mirror down on the counter.

Delaney laced her fingers through mine and took a step back, taking in my strapless, beaded ball gown with chiffon ruffling along the full skirt. It was fairytale-like and everything I had wanted in a wedding dress. And I got it because Raven bought it for me. "He's going to freak when he sees you walking down the aisle."

"Good. I want him to be totally in awe."

She nodded. "Believe me, he will."

"And what about Luke?" I eyed her long, purple, strapless dress that made her boobs pop out more than intended. "Did he like the dress?"

She rolled her eyes. "You brother loves me in anything." Then she leaned forward, and whispered, "But mainly he likes me wearing nothing."

I playfully slapped her arm. "TMI, Delaney."

My mom eyed us suspiciously and we both laughed.

A knock came at the door. "Lexi, it's time."

My heart rate kicked up a notch and I took a deep breath. "I'm ready."

My dad opened the door and butterflies swirled inside of me.

"You truly are a princess, Lexi." Dad gathered me in his arms and I hugged him tightly. "Raven is one lucky man." Dad's eyes misted and he gave me a quick kiss. Clearing his throat, he said, "And I couldn't be happier to walk you down that aisle and give you away."

"Awe, Dad." I cupped his cheek. "I love you. Thank you for everything."

"I just want you to be happy, Princess. That's all." I turned to Mom and motioned for her to join us. She wrapped an arm around me and Dad, embracing us both. "I'm happy that we're a family again."

"And what about me?" Ashely quickly interjected. My sister had apologized to me for everything — for her behavior and for being jealous of me for so many years. I wasn't sure what she was jealous about because she was Mom's favorite, but I accepted her apology, eager to put the past behind us. Part of me wondered if she still had an ulterior motive, but only time would tell. For now, I would do my part and love her since she was my sister.

I looked over Dad's arm. "Yes, that means you, too, Ashley." I waved for her to join us.

"I better not be left out." She rolled her eyes and strutted toward us, pulling Mom and Dad's arms apart so she could join our circle.

"All we're missing is Luke," Mom said, tears filling her eyes.

"Did someone say my name?" Luke burst through the door.

"Shut it! Before someone sees," we all shouted.

"Relax." He closed the door with a flick of his wrist. "Everyone is seated." He twisted his lips to the side and shook his head. "Are y'all done hugging and crying? Raven is already at the front waiting for you."

"Oh, we better go." I started to break free, but stopped. "Come here, Luke." I reached for his hand and pulled him into our family hug.

"Seriously?" His shoulders slumped forward as he resisted for a second. Then he jumped in, wrapping his arms around us in a tight bear hug.

"Careful, you're going to mess up my dress."

"Ugh. Stop complaining," he taunted. "You wanted me in, now you have to take it."

We laughed and smiled as Delaney snapped a few picture of us. It was a great family hug.

I straightened my dress and did one last check in the mirror. I was ready to walk down the aisle and become Mrs. Raven Davenport.

Dad laced my arm around his. "You ready?"

"Yes." My cheeks hurt from smiling so much. Raven had captured my heart for good.

Lifting the layers of my dress, we walked out of the Marshall's guest bedroom and down the hallway. When Raven and I announced we were getting married, they offered their house and we agreed. Twice the size of my sister's house, sitting on a few acres, and overlooking a beautiful lake, it was the perfect venue. Raven spared no expense, giving us the wedding of my dreams. But in all honestly, there was only one thing I wanted.

Him.

The fine crystal and china didn't matter.

The thousands of white roses and purple hydrangeas didn't matter.

The white tent cloaked in thousands of tiny white lights that made the ambiance fairytale-like didn't matter.

All that mattered was that I had him in my trap. And my trap was one without a revolving door — it was where he belonged.

The back door opened and the music started. Delaney, Shelby, Ashely, and my cousin, Kenzie, who had recently returned home after graduating from college in California, proceeded before me. My niece tossed the petals along the white strip that lead directly to where my heart belonged.

Raven's arms.

"Easy now. Don't trip." Dad helped me down the steps that led to the backyard transformed into the most breathtaking place for a ceremony. Fragrant flowers were interspersed along the patio area, hanging elegantly from posts wrapped in white and purple organza material. Our family and friends filled the white wooden chairs and my heart raced with an excitement that only Raven could create.

I immediately spotted Trish and Mimi with the twins. I nearly broke out in tears when they lifted them in the air for me to see. Even though things had been tough, I absolutely had no regrets. I'd stuck by Raven's side, did what I had to do for our children, and in the end, I was rewarded with a man that loved me unconditionally.

Cameras flashed and people awed as I walked down the aisle, one step at a time. Standing underneath a massive arch of roses and trailing flowers, was Raven. Dressed in a sleek black tuxedo, he looked like he was ready for a photo shoot with GQ magazine.

Damn, my man is freakin' hot.

And I'm marrying him!

Josh stood behind him, along with Shawn, Luke, and his brother, Trey. Our gazes connected as I marched to the beat of the music directly toward him. I was so happy. I was finally going to be his wife and I couldn't wait. It had been an eventful year, but Raven had proven himself to me by doing exactly what he said he was going to do. Seeing the counselor on a regular basis, learning to let go of all of his demons, and providing for us, just like he promised. The best part was that he had earned my trust, which allowed me to love him unconditionally in return.

Two weeks after we had returned to Fort Worth, Raven had announced that he would be a free agent. A few days later, he got a call from the coach in New Orleans. They invited him to a private practice session and he willingly obliged. By the end of the week, Raven had signed a contract with them, earning him a hefty salary and bypassing the supplemental draft altogether. Because of that, I decided to put grad school on hold, devoting my time to editing for indie writers and preparing for the twins to arrive instead.

Raven started practice the following week and we moved in with his grandmother until we could find a house. Right before the first game of the season, Raven purchased our first home, strengthening our relationship even more. Everything had happened so fast, but I knew it was meant to be. A true blessing from God.

"Take good care of my princess." Dad smiled and winked his left eye before placing my hand in Raven's.

"Always," he said, with a firm nod.

Dad gave him an approving smile and then slipped away. Raven stared at me for a few seconds, his eyes sweeping over me in a full and deliberate notion. "Damn, Lexi, you look exceptionally beautiful."

"Thank you." I eyed him for a moment. "And you look damn sexy in that tuxedo."

"Wait to see what's underneath." He winked.

I giggled and then we turned to face to the preacher.

"Family and friends, we are gathered here today to celebrate the union of Lexi Ann Thompson and Raven Renee Davenport." Tiny awes filtered through the crowd and the twins babbled. Everyone laughed and we turned around to admire our wondrous creations. Nevara had her daddy's personality, but looked exactly like me, where Jonah was definitely more calm and subtle like me, but favored his dad. I knew I'd have my hands full with him.

The preacher continued, reciting the traditional marriage ceremony. Raven and I agreed that it would be too nerve wracking to come up with our own vows; keeping it simple was exactly what we wanted. We exchanged vows, pledging our love to one another in sickness and in health for all eternity. Raven slipped the ring on my finger and I placed a band on his. With our hands interlocked, we turned to face the crowd.

"Family and friends, I'm happy to introduce to you, Mr. and Mrs. Davenport." Everyone clapped and I heard Nevara start crying. Raven and I both shook our heads. Our little girl was definitely a drama queen. "You may now kiss your bride."

"I never thought this day would come." Raven gathered me in his arms and dipped me, planting a deliciously enticing kiss on my lips. More yells and whistles flooded the air and I laughed.

After we took pictures with our family and friends, we entered the large tent located behind the swimming pool. The tent was absolutely exquisite, like the kind you see in movies or magazines for the rich and famous. But we were far from that. Round tables decorated with tall vases over flowing with white and purple flowers, took my breath away. Thousands of twinkling lights shimmered underneath the purple organza draped from floor to ceiling. Hanging in the center of the tent was a huge crystal chandelier that cast a myriad of colorful prisms all over the room. The bride and groom's cakes were divine; I dreaded cutting into them.

"It's beautiful, Raven." I kissed him on the cheek. "Thank you."

"Anything for you, baby."

The music lowered and the DJ said, "The bride and groom have arrived. If they can please take the dance floor."

"May I have this dance?" Raven held out his hand in true gentlemanly fashion.

"Of course." I placed my hand in his and he led me to the center of the room. Raven slid his arm around my waist and pulled me close, wearing a dashing grin. "Are you happy?"

"More than you'll ever know." His eyes lit up. "The most beautiful woman in the world is now my wife, I have a son and a daughter, and I'm living my dream, playing football for a living. What more could I ask for?"

"I love seeing you happy." I stared deep into his eyes. "It shows me how much you've healed."

"You're right, baby. I've come a long way." His gaze traveled past mine, recounting the dark moments in his life. His neck tensed and he took a hard swallow. "Thank you for standing by my side. I know it wasn't easy."

My eyes filled with tears, but I swallowed them back. "When you love someone, you're willing to do whatever it takes to help them, and that's exactly what I did."

"And for that, I'll always be grateful." His eyes closed and he kissed me, softly, passionately, instilling so much love within me that it shook me to my core. In that one kiss, he showed me how thankful he was that I had stayed with him, through the heartache and all the pain. His gazed stayed fixed on mine. "You look radiant, Lexi. Happy."

"That's because I am." I laced my finger around his neck, resting in the warmth of his embrace and feeling completely secure. We swayed to the beat of the music, my dress rustling against his tuxedo pants as the lights danced around us. Today was one of the best days of my life. No questions asked.

"Good. I want to keep you that way forever." He nuzzled by neck and that familiar rush warmed my belly. The fire that only Raven could light.

"That's easy. All you need to do is love me, stay loyal to me, and be there for me and the twins."

"Then it's a done deal," he said with a voice more confident than ever.

I narrowed my eyes. "So just like that, you figured it all out?"

He turned me and then drew me close again. "Yep. I finally figured out what it will take to keep you trapped forever."

I tilted my head to the side. "I hate to break it to you, but I was caught in your trap a long time ago."

"Really?" His head jutted back. "How long?"

I pressed my lips together, thinking back to the first time I knew he had me. "Since the day I met you outside the library to help you with that Stephen Crane paper."

His lips spread into a wide grin. "That far back?" He rubbed the slight scruff on his chin. I had clearly struck his ego. And tonight, I'd be stroking something else. "Damn, that was like the third time we got together."

"I know." I ran my fingers through the sides of his hair, glad that I had convinced him to let it grow back. "You're quite the charmer, in case you haven't noticed."

"There's only one woman I want to charm, and that's you." With his lips a fraction away from mine, he said, "Lexi, you're my end and my beginning."

A new nest of butterflies came to life and I reveled in their reappearance. He knew how to make my heart take flight. "Raven, as long as you are with me, there's no place I'd rather be."

He twirled me around and then dipped me. With his eyes appraising all of me, he said, "And where's that?"

My smiled emerged from the depths of my heart and I handed it to him without any doubt. "Right here, in The Raven's trap."

Need more of Lexi and Raven?

Read the story from Raven's point of view in
A Different Side
Coming March 2015

About the Author

Born and raised in the United States of America in the great state of Texas, CM Doporto resides there with her husband and son, enjoying life with their extensive family along with their Chihuahua and several fish. She is a member of Romance Writers of America, where she is associated with the Young Adult Special Interest Chapter. To learn more about her upcoming books, visit www.cmdoporto.com and sign up to receive email notifications. You can also like CM Doporto's fan page on Facebook and follow her on Instagram, Twitter and Pinterest.

Other Books by
<u>CM Doporto</u>

YOUNG ADULT

The Eslite Chronicles

The Eslites (short story prequel)

The Eslites, The Arrival

The Eslites, Out of This World (Summer 2015)

NEW ADULT

The Natalie Vega Saga

Element, Part 1

Element, Part 2

The University Park Series

Opposing Sides

The Same Side

The Winning Side

A Different Side (March 2015)

My Lucky Catch (June 2015) - Luke and Delaney's Story